Palgrave Gothic

Series Editor
Clive Bloom
Middlesex University
London, UK

Dating back to the eighteenth century, the term 'gothic' began as a designation for an artistic movement when British antiquarians became dissatisfied with the taste for all things Italianate. By the twentieth century, the Gothic was a worldwide phenomenon influencing global cinema and the emergent film industries of Japan and Korea. Gothic influences are evident throughout contemporary culture: in detective fiction, television programmes, Cosplay events, fashion catwalks, music styles, musical theatre, ghostly tourism and video games, as well as being constantly reinvented online. It is no longer an antiquarian pursuit but the longest lasting influence in popular culture, reworked and re-experienced by each new generation. This series offers readers the very best in new international research and scholarship on the historical development, cultural meaning and diversity of gothic culture. While covering Gothic origins dating back to the eighteenth century, the *Palgrave Gothic* series also drives exciting new discussions on dystopian, urban and Anthropocene gothic sensibilities emerging in the twenty-first century. The Gothic shows no sign of obsolescence.

Elana Gomel • Simon Bacon
Editors

Lunar Gothic

The Influence of the Moon on the Gothic Imagination

palgrave
macmillan

Editors
Elana Gomel
Tel-Aviv University
Tel-Aviv, Israel

Simon Bacon
Poznań, Poland

ISSN 2634-6214 ISSN 2634-6222 (electronic)
Palgrave Gothic
ISBN 978-3-031-92620-4 ISBN 978-3-031-92621-1 (eBook)
https://doi.org/10.1007/978-3-031-92621-1

This Palgrave Macmillan imprint is published by the registered company Springer Nature Switzerland AG.
The registered company address is: Gewerbestrasse 11, 6330 Cham, Switzerland

Elana Gomel • Simon Bacon
Editors

Lunar Gothic

The Influence of the Moon on the Gothic Imagination

palgrave
macmillan

Editors
Elana Gomel
Tel-Aviv University
Tel-Aviv, Israel

Simon Bacon
Poznań, Poland

ISSN 2634-6214 ISSN 2634-6222 (electronic)
Palgrave Gothic
ISBN 978-3-031-92620-4 ISBN 978-3-031-92621-1 (eBook)
https://doi.org/10.1007/978-3-031-92621-1

This Palgrave Macmillan imprint is published by the registered company Springer Nature Switzerland AG.
The registered company address is: Gewerbestrasse 11, 6330 Cham, Switzerland

Acknowledgements

Books are strangely collective efforts and not just of those that are in the final stages, but all those that were part of it at the various stages, as well as those that listened to thoughts, that gave advice, or even just patiently listened to grumps and complaints. Without any of those people, all those tiny pushes, shoves and reasons, books just wouldn't get over the line. So to all of you, many, many thanks. Of course, there are those who more obviously helped get the book completed and so huge thanks to everyone who managed to get their chapters written, the contributor forms filled, and then send it all in. Thanks too to Clive Bloom who runs this terrific Gothic series at Palgrave, and of course, Lina, who helped to keep everything moving forward.

With this, co-edited collections are pretty reliant on the "team" working together and so a big pat on the back to each other for sorting out another book with incredibly little stress and the enthusiasm to do another one. And last, but never least, our respective other-halves, Jim and Kasia, for their encouragement and support throughout the process.

ACKNOWLEDGMENTS

Contents

Notes on Contributors

Simon Bacon is an independent scholar based in Poznań, Poland. He has written and edited over thirty books on various subjects including *The Gothic: A Reader* (Peter Lang Ltd., 2018), *Horror: A Companion* (Peter Lang Ltd., 2019), *Eco-Vampires* (McFarland, 2020), *The Anthropocene and the Undead* (Lexington Books, 2022), *The Evolution of Horror in the Twenty-First Century* (Lexington Books, 2023), *1000 Vampires on Screen Vols 1 & 2* (BearManor Media, 2023), *Gothic Nostalgia* (Palgrave Macmillan, 2024), *The Palgrave Handbook of the Vampire* (Palgrave Macmillan, 2024), and *The Palgrave Handbook of the Zombie* (Palgrave Macmillan, 2025).

Octavia Cade is a speculative fiction writer from New Zealand. She has a PhD in Science Communication, and her academic work has appeared in a number of journals, including *Horror Studies* and *Supernatural Studies*. She has had approximately seventy short stories published in magazines such as *Clarkesworld*, *Asimov's*, and *Fantasy & Science Fiction*. She was the 2023 Ursula Bethell writer in residence at Canterbury University, and has recently received an Arts Grant from Creative New Zealand for her latest novel.

Jasdeep Kaur Chandi is a researcher who received her PhD from the University School of Mass Communication, Guru Gobind Singh Indraprastha University, Govt. of NCT of Delhi, India. Her research interests include popular culture, digital cultures, fandom studies and new media. Her published works include research articles and a book chapter on East Asian popular culture, their fandoms and practices. She presented her research in several international annual conferences organized by International Communication Association, International Academic Forum, Academy of Korean Studies, Southwest Association of American/ Popular Culture and International Association of Mass Communication Research.

Lauren Christie earned her PhD in English Literature from the University of Dundee and is now the academic staff developer for the University of St. Andrews. Her doctoral thesis examined the function of monsters in children's literature through the lens of bibliotherapy. She has designed and delivered modules on topics from children's literature to literary monsters. Lauren is currently working on her monograph, and her publication record spans Stephen King studies, fictional psychopaths and serial killers, and children's literature.

Cathleen Allyn Conway is a poet and PhD graduate of Goldsmiths, University of London, where she examined intersections of Sylvia Plath, the vampire, and the Gothic in experimental poetics. She has published on Plath in the *Guardian* and elsewhere. She also the author of the poetry collection *Bloofer* (Broken Sleep Books, 2023) and the pamphlets *Nocturnes* (Cherry Dress Chapbooks, 2024), *American Ingénue* (Broken Sleep Books, 2021), *All the Twists of the Tongue* (Grey Book Press, 2018), and *Static Cling* (Dancing Girl Press, 2012), as well as academic articles on *Dracula*, *Star Wars*, *Ghostbusters*, and vampirism and race.

Nicole C. Dittmer PhD, is a lecturer in Victorian Gothic Studies at The College of New Jersey, proofreader and editorial board member at *Studies in Gothic Fiction*, and advisory board member of *ETAP* for Lexington Books. Her works include "Malignancy of Goneril: Nature's Powerful Warrior" (2020), *Monstrous Women and Ecofeminism in the Victorian Gothic, 1837-1871* (Lexington Books/Fortress Academic, 2022); *Penny Dreadfuls and the Gothic: Investigations of Pernicious Tales of Terror* (University of Wales Press, 2023); *Penny Bloods: Gothic Tales of Dangerous Women* (British Library Publishing, 2023); "Victorianism and Ecofeminist Literature" (2022); and "From Becoming to Being: The Material-Semiotic Abhumanity of Peri-to-Post-Menopausal Women in the Victorian Gothic" (2024).

Phil Fitzsimmons is currently an independent researcher and consultant in education and organisational learning. Prior to this, he was head of education (Alphacrucis University College Sydney, Australia), assistant dean-research (Faculty of Education, Business and Science—Avondale University, Australia), director of research (San Roque Research Institute, California), and senior lecturer (University of Wollongong, Australia). His current research interests include Australian Gothic literature, popular culture, and adolescent spirituality.

Sharon M. Gallagher has been teaching a variety of writing and literature courses to a diverse group of students in higher education since 1993. Two of these regularly taught courses are Mythology and Occult Literature. While teaching, she earned her PhD and wrote her first book, *The Irish Vampire From Folklore to the Imaginations of Charles Robert Maturin, Joseph Sheridan Le Fanu, and Bram Stoker* (McFarland & Co Inc., 2017), which reflects her ongoing interest in nineteenth-century Irish literature, the Gothic, and folklore.

Elana Gomel is Associate Professor in the Department of English and American Studies at Tel- Aviv University. She has taught and researched at Princeton, Stanford, University of Hong Kong, and Venice International University. She has authored many academic books, including *Bloodscripts: Writing the Violent Subject* (Ohio State University Press, 2003), *Narrative Space and Time: Representing Impossible Topologies in Literature* (Routledge, 2014), and *Science Fiction, Alien Encounters, and the Ethics of Posthumanism: Beyond the Golden Rule* (Palgrave Macmillan, 2014). She is also a fiction writer who has published more than a hundred short stories, several novellas, and four novels.

Suzanne FitzGerald Heskin is a PhD candidate in History of Art at the University of York. Her research interests include medieval art, early Christian art, illuminated manuscripts, narrative tapestries, devotional imagery, female spirituality, and medieval literature. Focusing on literary and visual language interaction, her work questions how complex identities are constructed and communicated through art. With a graphic design and illustration background, Suzanne explores pictorial communication strategies, centring on the dialogue between text and image.

Marta Miquel-Baldellou PhD, is a member of the research group Dedal-Lit at the University of Lleida, and she is currently taking part in a research project on the matrix of ageing, gender, and creativity. She has recently been granted a postdoctoral research scholarship to work on a project on the Gothic fiction of Stephen King from the perspective of myth criticism. Her areas of research are comparative literature, gothic fiction, gender, and ageing studies. Her work has been published in different international academic journals, such as *The ESSE Messenger*, *Nineteenth-Century Gender Studies*, *The Edgar Allan Poe Review*, and *Age, Culture, Humanities*, and in books edited by international publishing houses, such as Peter Lang, Transcript Verlag, Brill/Rodopi, Cambridge Scholars Publishing, and Fairleigh Dickinson.

Fernando Gabriel Pagnoni Berns PhD, is a professor at the Universidad de Buenos Aires. He teaches courses on international horror film. He is Director of the research group on horror cinema "Grite" and has authored a book about Spanish horror TV series *Historias para no Dormir*, and has edited books on film directors James Wan and Wes Craven, and on the Italian *giallo* film and horror comics. He is currently editing a book on Dario Argento and another one on Baltic horror. He is Director of "Terror: Estudios Críticos" (Universidad de Cádiz), the first-ever horror studies series in Spain.

Patrycja Pichnicka-Trivedi is a PhD candidate at the University of Warsaw. She has been published in *Kultura popularna*, *Praktyka teoretyczna*, *Polish Journal of Political Science*, and monographs. She has participated in national and international conferences and was chosen as finalist in the Professor Jerzy Buzek competition for Scientific Debut 2019. Scholarship of Bassi Foundation and PROM grants. She is a member of WEIRD Fictions Research Group i Nonanthropocentric cultural subjectivity and is writing a comparative thesis on the representations of Otherness in popular culture. Besides popular culture she is interested in intersectional studies, biomedical anthropology, posthuman studies, and postcolonial studies.

Nahid Shahbazi Moghadam is an assistant professor of English Literature in the English Department of Semnan University (Iran). Her areas of interest are the grotesque, twentieth-century British fiction, Modern Persian fiction, comparative literature, and literary translation. She has published articles in these areas and translated fiction (Mervyn Peake's *Boy in Darkness and Other Stories* and William Golding's *Lord of the Flies*) and non-fiction (*Introducing Criticism in the 21th century* and *The Grotesque* from Routledge New Critical Idiom Series).

J. Simpson is a researcher, academic writer, journalist, and critic, specialising in the Gothic, "dark", experimental, and avant-garde with a focus on horror/SF, folklore, and paganism. He has published essays with *Little*

White Lies, *Suspira Magazine*, *PopMatters*, and *Lost Futures* and has numerous forthcoming essays on the Gothic scheduled with Palgrave. He has also delivered presentations on Lynchian music for the Manchester Centre for Gothic Studies and Gothic Afrofuturist music for Sheffield Gothic. He also makes music and DJs as dessicant.

Jacqueline Weal completed a BA in English Literature at Simon Fraser University, earning a Master's degree in literature and film at the University of British Columbia. She is currently an instructor at Langara College in Vancouver, British Columbia, where she has taught since 2004. Jacqueline teaches poetry, film, and novels, including in literary surveys and specialty courses, such as Biographies, Romantic Comedies, and Shape-Shifters. She also co-instructed a UK Gothic Field School exploring all aspects of the Gothic, from fashion and music to film and literature.

Kevin J. Wetmore Jr. is the author of over a dozen books, including Eaters of the Dead: Myths and Realities of Cannibal Monsters (Reaktion Books, 2021) and The Theology of Battlestar Galactica (McFarland, 2012), as well as over a hundred book chapters, journal articles, and essays, on topics from ghosts on the Japanese stage to African Adaptation of Greek tragedy to Shakespeare in graphic novels. He is also the twice-Bram Stoker Award-nominated editor of books such as Uncovering Stranger Things (McFarland, 2018) and The Streaming of Hill House (McFarland, 2020). He is an actor, director, and fight choreographer who lives and works in Los Angeles.

List of Figures

CHAPTER 1

Introduction

Elana Gomel and Simon Bacon

The Moon exerts a powerful influence on Earth. Seasons and tides are shaped by its gravitational pull. Some scientists believe that without our satellite, life itself would be impossible. But even greater than its geophysical role is the Moon's cultural impact. It has been a significant presence in all human cultures since they began. Lunar deities, such as Greek Artemis or Chinese Changxi, preside over the night. Ghosts and werewolves emerge when the Moon is full. Despite scientific denials, the supposed synchronicity between lunar cycles and menstrual periods is firmly established in folk beliefs. The Moon is a constant element in fairy tales and pagan rituals, the dark twin to the Sun and the ruler of occult and malevolent forces. "The importance of the moon has less to do with its proximity to Earth than with its centrality in the human imagination" (Brunner 2011). Unsurprisingly then, the Moon has played an important role within the Gothic imaginary as well, from gazing upon the "midnight labours" of Victor Frankenstein (Hunter 2012, 33) to resurrecting vampires on the hilltops in Greece and from Méliès' anthropomorphised orb in the

E. Gomel (✉)
Tel-Aviv University, Tel-Aviv, Israel

S. Bacon
Poznań, Poland

E. Gomel, S. Bacon (eds.), *Lunar Gothic*, Palgrave Gothic,
https://doi.org/10.1007/978-3-031-92621-1_1

movie *Trip to the Moon* (1902) to the steampunk-Moon-Nazis of the *Iron Sky* franchise (Various: 2012–2019). Not forgetting, of course, the generations and multicultural hordes of werewolves and shapeshifters that have howled at the lunar tumescence in derision, pain, and ecstasy. In many senses, just as the Moon has fuelled lycanthropic transformations, it has powered the creatures of the night to turn dreams into nightmares and darkness into a terrain of shadows ghosts, and mystery, the very life blood of the Gothic.

Darkness and the night, both literal and metaphorical, are essential to the Gothic, which is, in the words of Anne Williams, the "art of darkness" (1995). Williams, not unlike Fred Botting in *The Gothic: Essays and Studies* (2001), goes on to read the Gothic as a return of the repressed, and a revealing of what is hidden by the rules and codes of acceptable behaviour of society. This is taken further by Williams who, compressing the Romantic and the Gothic into one, sees the turn in the late eighteenth century to the reason and rationality of the Enlightenment as symbolising daytime to the night of Romanticism—from which grew the "darkness" of the Gothic. While this leads to the obvious correlation of light with the conscious mind and dark with the subconscious, Williams extends her analogy so that reality becomes the realm of patriarchal control, and night one of the feminine imagination and sensual freedom. Within this the Moon is "archetypally female" (Williams 1995: 123), or even "maternal" (Williams 1995: 193), which follows on from the "softer" view of the night afforded by the Romantic mind as opposed to the sharper configuration seen in the Gothic proper. If Romanticism saw the night in general and the Moon in particular as representing the imagination and dreams, the Gothic mind conceived of it as the source of nightmares. Here, the night is the dark doppelgänger of the day, full of howling wolves, glowing eyes, and stars that mark the fate of those looking upon them. Within this, the Moon is as much a source of anxiety as it is mystery, and rather than being a point of illumination is an evil influence empowering and resurrecting werewolves, vampires, and other creatures of the night, becoming a trope of transformation, dark potential, and repressed desires unleashed. In this sense it is less maternal and more monstrous mother.

This more active and transformative nature of the Moon further sees it as a means of gothicising other genres and modes as it brings its dark influence into the intersections it makes with them. Science fiction is one genre where the intrusion of the lunar inevitably turns scientific romance into scientific mystery and even horror. With the rise of astronomy in the nineteenth century the Moon became a subject of speculations about alien life. The first, and so far only, extraterrestrial body where human beings have physically set foot, the Moon occupies an oversized place in dreams of exploration and nightmares of conspiracy. There is a tradition of lunar voyages in speculative fiction, going back to the Roman writer Lucian, and since then Moon-based narratives have become a significant part of contemporary popular culture, as source of life and mystery, but also death and destruction: if the waxing and waning "face" of the Moon fuels Earth-based Gothic, the dark-side, forever turned to the depths of space, is its doppelgänger double that hides the horror of its true intentions for humanity.

Astonishingly, there have been few academic volumes dedicated to the representation of the Moon in literature, cinema, and other media and even less so in relation to the Gothic. Indeed, just as the Moon is often part of the setting for Gothic and horror texts while never the focus, so too it seems to appear in many books and articles addressing the Gothic without being the main topic under discussion. Of the very few books where the Moon is centre stage is *Moon: A Brief History* (2011) by Bernd Brunner which, as its title indicates, looks at the general cultural significance of the Moon. *Horror in Space: Critical Essays on a Film Subgenre* (2017), edited by Michele Brittany, contains some discussions of films set on the Moon such as *Apollo 18* and *Moon* but does not differentiate between lunar and other extraterrestrial settings. And while there have been many academic articles analysing specific Moon-related texts, such as Jules Verne's *From the Earth to the Moon* and H. G. Wells' *The First Men in the Moon*, few of those have attempted to theorise what makes Moon-based or lunar-focused speculative fictions Gothic.

This is exactly what we attempt to do in this volume. Our goal is to define the genre of Lunar Gothic as it is expressed in different forms of media; to chart its boundaries in relation to science fiction (SF), fantasy, and horror; and to explore its articulations in global cultural contexts with particular attention given to non-Western texts and traditions. No other comprehensive study of this scope exists.

Historical Background

Contemporary Lunar Gothic can be seen to have two main sources. The first is loosely based around Moon-based folklore. Every human culture affords an important role to our satellite. In many traditions, the Moon is gendered feminine. Hekate, the Greek goddess of night and witchcraft; Diana, the Roman goddess of the Moon; and syncretic pagan deities, such as Isis, demonstrate the imaginary connection between phases of the Moon and the female body. While male lunar deities also exist, the common folkloric imagery of the Moon in many European and some Asian cultures is that of mysterious and dangerous femininity. Within the Gothic imagination the Moon is also linked to animalistic monsters, such as werewolves, that blur the boundary between beast and human. The legend of lycanthropy is closely tied to the phases of the Moon (Otten 1986). Alongside this are tales of the regenerative powers of moonbeams affecting both flora and fauna, and of course the undead, a full Moon in particular signifying a weakening of the borders between the natural and supernatural worlds, the living and the dead. Unsurprisingly then, ghosts and spectres often seem to find form and energy in moonlight, as do magical rituals, sabbaths, and demonic summonings.

The other source of Lunar Gothic is the history of astronomy. As the closest celestial body to Earth, the Moon has always attracted scientific inquiry. Galileo Galilei drew the first observational map of the lunar surface in 1609, and more astronomers followed suit. As the power of telescopes grew, these maps became increasingly accurate. The Moon was the primary goal of the space race during the Cold War, as the USSR and the US competed in reaching our satellite. The USSR sent automatic probes (the Lunokhod), while the US launched the Apollo programme that culminated in the first Moon landing in 1969. The scientific progress in exploring the lunar surface created an impetus for the development of SF focused on the Moon.

The tradition of fictional lunar voyages goes back to the Roman writer Lucian of Samosata whose *True Story* depicts the protagonist blown to the Moon by a whirlwind. There he encounters a variety of strange and frightening creatures and is drawn into a war between the King of the Moon and the King of the Sun. Edgar Allan Poe's "The Unparalleled Adventure of One Hans Pfaal" (1835) follows Lucian's lead in mixing satire, burlesque, and outright fantasy. But later nineteenth-century lunar voyages became more science-oriented. Jules Verne's *From the Earth to the Moon* (1867) envisions using a giant canon to propel a Moon-bound vessel, and endeavours to depict the space travel with some degree of scientific accuracy. H. G. Wells' seminal *The First Men in the Moon* (1900) combines evolutionary speculations with vividly realistic depictions of the lunar surface. Yet, these varying descriptions of an alien world, and occasionally those that live there, always contain something of the uncanny, an environment and peoples described in direct comparison to our own, making the "homely" Earth not as safe, familiar, or isolated as we once thought: in making the lunar world seem real and vital, the complacent Earth becomes less so and more porous to the expanse of outer space around us.

However, Wells' "scientific" novel also foreshadows the subsequent development of Lunar Gothic. While devoid of any supernatural elements, it is very dark in its representation of the ant-like society of Selenites inhabiting shadowy caverns under the surface of the Moon. Its imagery of darkness and light, of misshapen monstrosities infesting our satellites and eventually threatening Earth itself, has strong Gothic overtones, despite the overall framing of the novel being scientific and rationalistic. It is as if the pagan and folkloric associations of the Moon penetrated the discourse of science, contaminating it with echoes of fear.

The subsequent development of Lunar Gothic epitomises the coming-together of these seemingly disparate trends: pagan mythology and scientific aspirations; horror and rationality; echoes of the past and visions of the future. In the Polish writer Jerzy Żuławski's *The Lunar Trilogy* (1901–1911), for example, the Moon is a vision of both Edenic splendour and nightmarish degeneration as the descendants of stranded astronauts struggle to survive and populate the planet. The closer to the time of the Lunar Landing, the more "scientific" Moon-based SF gets, but it never loses that Gothic edge. Robert Heinlein's "hard" SF novel *The Moon is a Harsh Mistress* (1966), for example, realistically depicts a lunar colony struggling for independence but its vivid representation of the Moon's deadly environment gives it a decidedly dark and claustrophobic ambiance. In many ways such narratives become a concentration of the Earth, an exiled excess that expresses the darkness at the heart of humanity.

Lunar Gothic as a contemporary cross-media genre arises precisely from this blending of SF and Gothic. Because of its duality, it straddles the dividing line between natural and supernatural. The Moon is far more than a neutral setting in these narratives; it becomes an active plot participant, a character in its own right whose influence often exceeds that of actual human beings who fall under the spell of its malevolent influence.

Defining the Genre

Lunar Gothic, as mentioned previously, intersects with and subsequently gothicises many other genres, seeing its influence spread across narratives featuring the effects of the celestial orb on the Earth, through to those that are set on the planet itself.

Movies such as *Moon* (2009) and *Apollo 13* (1995) and the recent South Korean TV series *The Silent Sea* (2021) epitomise the unique features of Lunar Gothic that incorporate aspects such as the techno-Gothic—the presence of the Moon suddenly making technology a source of anxiety and existential threat. Along with this are the visual claustrophobia of the settings; the plot centred on a violent mystery; intimations of the supernatural that never quite coalesce into a full-fledged ghostly explanation of the events; and haunted, solitary protagonists. The space technology in these movies is depicted as a hostile and dehumanising force that fails to ward off the dangers of the lunar environment, or even seemingly collaborates with them in killing off human intruders. While the Moon is lifeless, there are often hints of secret and malevolent lifeforms lurking in the nooks and crannies under the lunar surface: the Moon as monstrous mother sees it is an environment that is immanent with Gothic expectation that will instantly change into the unfamiliar and overtly hostile.

These features are even more prominently displayed in literary fictions of Lunar Gothic. Many of them start as conventional SF, set on a lunar station or a spaceship, only to devolve into haunted-house ghost stories or zombie apocalypses. In such novels as Sharman DiVono's *Blood Moon* (1999), Johan Harstad's *172 Hours on the Moon* (2012), Rick Chesler's *Luna* (2015), and Peter Clines' *Dead Moon* (2019), the Moon becomes a stage for the familiar Gothic tropes—ghosts, zombies, doppelgängers, and dark labyrinths.

Lunar Gothic intersects with space horror (sometimes called dark SF), a subgenre of SF epitomised by the *Alien* franchise, which is "horror set in space", and distinguished by specific formal and thematic tropes: a claustrophobic location (a spaceship or space station), "a high body count, and an alien antagonist" (Brittany 2017, 1–7). But Lunar Gothic is far more extensive than space horror. Following in the footsteps of Verne and Wells, it often engages with the issues of national competition, geopolitics, colonisation, and space travel (Kim Stanley Robinson's *Red Moon*, 2018). But even where the focus seems exclusively on technological or political issues, the Gothic ambiance of the Moon is evident in the darkness of the setting and the emphasis on violence in the plot.

The other side of Lunar Gothic is constituted by the texts in which the Moon is not the setting but rather a remote influence that affects events on Earth or becomes a source of a supernatural contagion. Examples include Ramsay Campbell's *The Hungry Moon* (1987) and Al Sarrantonio's *Moonbane* (1989). Such texts, whether cinematic, literary, game, or other, are often framed as supernatural. But they also involve elements that are specific to the genre, such as references to the lunar landing or attempts to rationalise the folkloric tradition of lycanthropy via some sort of a pseudo-scientific explanation.

Situated at the intersection of horror, SF, the Romantic, and folk horror, Lunar Gothic is a unique cross-cultural and cross-media hybrid genre whose influence will only grow as the possibility of another Moon landing draws closer. And yet despite its importance and topicality, no single book addresses its history, conventions, and articulations in different media. This volume will fill this lacuna. We offer a broad perspective on the importance and scope of Lunar Gothic in different media, while also articulating a general theoretical framework for understanding this unique genre.

Structure and Content

Lunar Gothic is divided into five parts. Part I: "The Evolution of Lunar Gothicity" contains chapters that address the historical roots of Lunar Gothic in the development of science, the rise of modernity, and the cultural cauldron of the long nineteenth century. The chapters in this part show how Lunar Gothic intersected with the literary tradition of Gothic, borrowing some of its conventions while developing a narrative vocabulary of its own. In "'He looks not like the People of the lower Orb': Behn's *The Emperor of the Moon* as Proto-Lunar Gothic", Kevin J. Wetmore, Jr. discusses the first science fiction play in the world written in 1687 by Aphra Behn, the first professional female playwright. Inspired by Galileo's invention of the telescope, *The Emperor of the Moon* is a farce about the dangers of scientific obsession. "Phases of the Moon in *Varney the Vampire*; or, the *Feast of Blood*" by Sharon M. Gallagher uncovers the hidden strain of Lunar Gothic in the famous Victorian penny dreadful and postulates the connection between the Moon and the cultural icon of the vampire. Suzanne FitzGerald Heskin's "Satire, Science, and Scepticism: Viewing the Lunar Hoaxes of Edgar Allen Poe and Richard Adams Locke as

Discourse on Uncertainty in the Antebellum Period" discusses the lunar hoaxes of the Victorian age, in which the obviously fanciful "reports" of voyages to the Moon were published as true accounts, and considers how they reflected the distrust of science, directly leading to the Moon-landing conspiracy theories of our own age. The last chapter in this part, "When the Full Moon Rises: Masculinities, Aging, and Updating the Lycanthropic Myth in Stephen King's *Cycle of the Werewolf*" by Marta Miquel-Baldellou, advances into the twentieth century, discussing Stephen King's Gothic novella as an intersection of the folkloric lunar traditions and the contemporary discourse of biological science. It also leads up to the next part, which deals with issues of gender.

Part II: "The Moon and Gender Poetics" focuses on the long-standing connection between the Moon and femininity and its articulation in modernity and postmodernity. In "the terror of the rustics"; or, Witches and Werewolves: Lunar and ecoGothic Monstrosities in Catherine Crowe's "A Story of a Weir-Wolf" (1846) and *The Nightside of Nature* (1847), Nicole C. Dittmer analyses the writing of the notable Victorian spiritualist Catherine Crowe and shows how it reflects the cultural conflation between wild nature and untamed femininity. "Children of the Night's Light: The Moon as a Structuring Element of Vampire Fiction from Polidori's *The Vampyre* to *The Twilight Saga*" by Patrycja Pichnicka takes up the connection between the Moon and the figure of the vampire analysed in Gallagher's chapter in Part I and considers its historical context in the transition of the vampire from Eastern European folklore to Western European literature. It also shows how the lunar elements in the literary depictions of the vampire evolve to embrace and eventually embody its solar opposite. In "Crackle and Drag: Sylvia Plath's Lunar Gothic in 'The Moon and the Yew Tree', 'The Rival', and 'Edge'", Cathleen Allyn Conway argues that lunar elements in Plath's late poems are used to channel her own suffering as an abused and mentally ill woman in a patriarchal society. It also makes a case for Plath as a Gothic writer.

Part III: "Lunacy and Transformation" examines the deeply embedded connection between the Moon and instability of identity. The very word "lunacy" as a synonym of mental illness indicates how the folkloric motif of the waxing and waning Moon inducing lycanthropy has been absorbed by the scientific and political discourses of identity formation. The chapters in this part also expand into non-Anglo-American traditions, showing the universal reach of Lunar Gothic, and analyse literary, cinematic, and digital texts, demonstrating how Lunar Horror operates as a transmedial genre. In "Illuminating the Darkness: Lunar Representation in Children's Literature", Lauren Christie focuses on two examples of books meant for children, Chae Strathie's *The Loon on the Moon* and J. K. Rowling's *Harry Potter and the Prisoner of Azkaban*, to show how representations of the Moon change in relation to the age of the intended readership. Following this is "The Lunar Poetics of Transformation in 'The Yellow Wallpaper'", by Jacqueline Weal, which addresses one of the feminist classics, "The Yellow Wallpaper" by Charlotte Perkins Gilman, and shows the submerged narrative of lycanthropic transformation in this much-analysed story. "Lunacy: Anxieties of Modernity in Luigi Bazzoni's *Footprints on the Moon*" by Fernando Gabriel Pagnoni Berns makes a case for the conflation of *giallo* and Lunar Gothic to articulate the anxieties about identity dissolution haunting modernity.

Part IV: "Lunar Cultures and Identity" continues the transnational and global momentum of the previous part, focusing on folk horror lunar traditions across the globe as vehicles for political aspirations and identity formations. "Be Afraid of the Dark: The Moon in Folk Horror" by J. Simpson discusses the persistence of pagan elements in British horror by Ramsay Campbell, Elizabeth Hand, and the TV series *The Moondial*. The next chapter in this part, "Lunar Gothic and the Grotesque in Hūshang Golshiri's 'The Wolf'" by Nahid Moghadam focuses on a novel by an Iranian modernist writer that brings Lunar Gothic into the global arena and further highlights the destabilisation of modernity. This is followed by "The Moon in *Requiem for a Beast*: An Apophasis of Colonial Transgression and Indigenous Suppression" by Phil Fitzsimmons, which focuses on the use of the Moon, both in Western and Indigenous Australian contexts, to express historical traumas. In "Moon, Music, and Melancholia: Gothic Aesthetics in Kuroshitisuji's *Lacrimosa*" by Jasdeep Kaur Chandi shifts the perspective to Japan and how regional representations of the Moon are combined with classical Western ones to produce a uniquely transcultural vision of Lunar Gothic.

Part V: "Lunar Futurities" returns to the techno-scientific roots of Lunar Gothic and probes the intersection of rationality and fear in Moon-oriented SF. Elana Gomel's "Blood Moon': Lunar Monstrous Spaces in Gothic Science Fiction" argues for the narratological distinctiveness of Lunar Horror as a unique genre at the intersection of scientific rationality and Gothic sublimity, focusing on its poetics of space. In "Sterility Across Chasms: Dead Worlds and Technological Imaginations in Meredith Ann Pierce's *Darkangel* Series", Octavia Cade discusses the concept of sterility in both its ecological and personal meanings and shows how the lifeless surface of the Moon in Pierce's novels becomes a symbolic stage for the interaction between folk horror and technological sublime.

References

Botting, Fred. 2001. *The Gothic: Essays and Studies.* Cambridge: D.S. Brewer.

Brittany, Michele. 2017. *Horror in Space: Critical Essays on a Film Subgenre.* Jefferson: McFarland.

Brunner, Bernd. 2011. *Moon: A Brief History.* New Haven: Yale University Press.

Hunter, J. P. 2012. *Mary Shelley Frankenstein: The 1818 Text, Contexts, Criticism.* New York: W.W. Norton.

Otten, Charlotte. 1986. *A Lycanthropy Reader: Werewolves in Western Culture.* Syracuse: Syracuse University Press.

Williams, Anne. 1995. *Art of Darkness: A Poetics of Gothic.* Chicago: University of Chicago Press.

Further Reading

Novels and Stories

Baxter, Stephen. 1998. *Moonseed.* London: Voyager.

Bova, Ben. 1998. *Moonwar.* London: Harper Voyager.

Budrys, Algis. 1960. *Rogue Moon.* New York: Mass Market Paperback.

Burroughs, Edgar Rice. 2002. *The Moon Maid* [1923]. Bison Books.

Christopher, John. 1969. *The Lotus Caves.* London: Hamish Hamilton.

Clarke, Arthur C. 1955. *Earthlight.* New York: Mass Market Paperbacks.

Clarke, Arthur C. 2002. *A Fall of Moondust* [1961]. London: Gollanz.

Campbell, Ramsay. 1987. *The Hungry Moon.* London: Arrow Books.

Chesler, Rick. 2015. *Luna.* N.L.: Severed Press.

Clines, Peter. 2019. *Dead Moon.* N.L.: Amazon Publishing.

DiVono, Sharman. 1999. *Blood Moon.* New York: DAW.

Harstad, Johan. 2012. *172 Hours on the Moon* [2008 in Norwegian]. London: Hatchette.

Hautala, Rick. 1989. *Moonwalker.* New York: Kensington Publishing.

Heinlein, Robert A. 1966. *The Moon is a Harsh Mistress.* New York: G. P. Putnam's Sons.

Herbert, James. 1985. *Moon.* New York: New American Library.

Kane, Paul. 2016. *Lunar.* London: Crossroad Press.

Kessel, John. 2017. *The Moon and the Other.* Simon and Schuster.

Kepler, Johannes. 2017. *The Dream, or The Posthumous Work on Lunar Astronomy* [1634]. Independently Published.
Lem, Stanislaw. 1982. The Hunt [1965]. In *More Tales of Pirx the Pilot.* San Diego: Harcourt Brace Jovanovich.
Lucian of Samosata. n.d. A True Story [2nd Century AD]. https://www.gutenberg.org/ebooks/45858. Accessed 28 Oct 2024.
MacDonald, Ian. 2015. *Luna: New Moon.* Tor Books.
McDevitt, Jack. 2000. *Moonfall* [1998]. New York: Eos.
Pierce, Meredith Ann. 1990. *The Darkangel Trilogy.* New York: Guild America Books.
Poe, Edgar Allen. 1835. The Unparallelled Adventure of One Hans Pfaal [1835]. In *The Collected Writings of Edgar Allan Poe, vol. 1.: The Imaginary Voyages,* 1981. ed. B. R. Pollin. Boston: Twayne Publishers.
Robinson, Kim Stanley. 2018. *Red Moon.* London: Orbit.
Rollins, James. 2021. *The Starless Crown (Moonfall Book 1).* New York: Tom Doherty.
Sarrantonio, Al. 1989. *Moonbane.* London: Bantam Books.
St. John Mandel, Emily. 2022. *Sea of Tranquility.* Pan Macmillan.
Verne, Jules. 1867 *From the Earth to the Moon* [1865] and *Around the Moon* [1869]. https://www.gutenberg.org/ebooks/12901. Accessed 28 Oct 2024.
Weir, Andy. 2017. *Artemis.* New York: Crown Publishers.
Varley, John. 1993. *Steel Beach.* New York: Ace.
Wells, Herbert George. 1900 *The First Men in the Moon* [1901]. https://www.gutenberg.org/files/52501/52501-h/52501-h.htm. Accessed 28 Oct 2024.
Żuławski, Jerzy. 2020. *Trylogia Księżycowa [Moon Trilogy]* [1901–1911]. N.L.: Zmok Books.

Story Collections

Ashley, Allen, ed. 2019. *The Once and Future Moon.* London: EibonVale Press.
Gauvreau, James, ed. 2023. *Moon: The Book of Lunar Horror and Dark Fiction.* N.L: Draft2Digital.

Non-fiction Studies

Boyle, Rebecca. 2024. *Our Moon: How Earth's Celestial Companion Transformed the Planet, Guided Evolution, and Made Us Who We Are.* London: Random House.
Brunner, Bernd. 2010. *Moon: A Brief History.* New Haven: Yale University Press.
Chaikin, Andrew. 2007. *A Man on the Moon: The Voyages of the Apollo Astronauts.* London: Penguin Books.

Hutton, Ronald. 2001. *The Triumph of the Moon: A History of Modern Pagan Witchcraft*. Oxford: Oxford University Press.
Reichl, Eugene. 2019. *The Soviet Space Program: The Lunar Mission Years, 1959–1976*. Atglen: Schiffer Military History.
Shepard, Alan, and Deke Slayton. 2011. *Moon Shot: The Inside Story of America's Moon Landings*. New York: Open Road Media.
Stone, Robert, and Alan Andres. 2019. *Chasing the Moon: The People, the Politics, and the Promise That Launched America into the Space Age*. New York: Ballantine Books.

PART I

The Evolution of Lunar Gothicity

CHAPTER 2

"He Looks Not Like the People of the Lower Orb": Behn's *The Emperor of the Moon* (1687) as Proto-Lunar Gothic

Kevin J. Wetmore Jr.

It may surprise some to learn that the first science fiction play in the world was written in London in 1687 by Aphra Behn, the first professional female playwright. Almost a century and a half before Mary Shelley wrote *Frankenstein*, Behn, inspired by Galileo's invention of the telescope, crafted her 1687 drama *The Emperor of the Moon* as a Restoration farce about the dangers of scientific obsession and the challenge of spectacles. Although appearing a century before the Gothic properly began, Behn's play contains forerunners of the genre, albeit in a farce, reducing their threat to comedic menace. Although not the first to posit the idea that there is a complex civilisation with its own culture on the lunar surface, Behn is the first to use the idea to "gaslight" a citizen scientist for a spectacular play (literally—based as much on spectacle as text) that presents aliens as monstrous (and also ultimately not real).

K. J. Wetmore Jr. (✉)
Loyola Marymount University, Los Angeles, CA, USA
e-mail: Kevin.Wetmore@lmu.edu

E. Gomel, S. Bacon (eds.), *Lunar Gothic*, Palgrave Gothic,
https://doi.org/10.1007/978-3-031-92621-1_2

At play's start, Dr Baliardo of Naples, Italy, obsesses over his new telescope, believing the moon is not only inhabited but organised as a constitutional monarchy, and plans to spy on the ruler of the moon. His daughter Elaria and his niece and ward Bellemante feel neglected, not least because Baliardo is so obsessed with the moon he will not entertain offers of marriage to the young women. Their respective preferred paramours, Don Cinthio and Don Charmante, form a plan to gain permission to marry Elaria and Bellemante, as well as to cure Baliardo's obsession by disguising themselves as aliens and claiming to be the Emperor of the Moon and his brother, the Prince of Thunderland. Baliardo, delighted that the aliens from the moon wish to marry his daughter and ward, agrees to a masque-like pageant that the lovers perform in an abandoned building. There, Baliardo is greeted by the Emperor of the Moon's court and the entire zodiac, narrated by Galileo and Kepler—actually all servants paid to play aliens and the famous scientists. Once unmasked, the gathered company forces Baliardo to admit his obsession and he consents to the marriages.

What is fascinating, however, is the play's dramatisation of the belief that there is a complex civilisation with its own culture on the lunar surface, the first ever presentation on stage of a lunar (or indeed any alien) civilisation. In carrying out their ruse, the young lovers plan an elaborate ancient history of the moon to be shared with Baliardo by the Emperor, for which they craft convincing costumes and props, and use the lunar story to gaslight Baliardo into agreeing to the marriages. In an inverse of the Gothic, it is not the ruins of the Earth but the newly found ancient structures on the moon that hold mystery and horror, eventually revealed to be an intrigue to ensure the respective family lines continue. The plot elements of the Gothic are all present, but pressed into the service of a comedic farce. *The Emperor of the Moon* (hereafter *Emperor*) is one of the earliest examples of a proto-lunar Gothic, and a forerunner to later Gothic narratives. It anticipates Gothic themes such as madness, deception, and supernatural events later revealed to have natural explanations, delving into forbidden literature, and, of course, the moon as a significant presence in the narrative. The Gothic loves the moon. So does Dr Baliardo.

To argue that *Emperor* is proto-Gothic requires us to consider the presence of Gothic elements in the theatre before the Gothic even existed. Gothic drama's origins are late eighteenth-century Anglo-European, but the theatre has had Gothic elements since its inception. Evina Sistakou observes that "Greek tragedy abounds with gothic elements, manifest in the gory details of murder descriptions, in the ghostly apparitions of the dead, in the terrifying appearance of gods and demons. Messengers vividly recounting scenes of horror which take place offstage" (2012: 39). These elements continue in the Roman theatre as well. Within the British tradition, the influence of Elizabethan and especially Jacobean tragedy profoundly shaped the Gothic tradition. Nick Groom observes that the drama of the English Renaissance, especially revenge tragedies, "led directly to the Gothic fictions of the next century" (2012: 38). Plays such as Kyd's *The Spanish Tragedy*, Marlowe's *The Massacre at Paris*, Webster's *The Duchess of Malfi* and *The White Devil*, and Shakespeare's *Titus Andronicus*, *Hamlet*, *Macbeth*, *King Lear*, and even *A Midsummer Night's Dream* provided models for later Gothic authors for revenge plots, "the cult of the macabre", sexual violence (threatened, implied, and actual), gory violence, and a world of lingering supernatural possibility, haunted by witches, ghosts, and fairies, both imagined and real (Groom 2012: 32–42).

Before the advent of the Gothic, however, the Restoration (1660–1700) also contributed to the development of an eventual Gothic theatre and perpetuated the theatre of the English Renaissance. After the restoration of the monarchy following the interregnum and the reign of Lord Protector Oliver Cromwell, a new theatre began to flourish, shaped by memories and adaptations of the drama of the English Renaissance. Restoration authors rewrote Shakespeare for contemporary tastes, and comedy, heroic tragedy, and excess were all at the centre. The Restoration also developed a horrific drama, a sort of proto-Gothic of its own. In *The Horror Plays of the English Restoration* Anne Hermanson argues that a century before Gothic drama actually appeared there were a group of plays in the 1670s and 1680s that "are characterized by a cynical and unrelenting depiction of evil, violence, an insatiable human drive for power, and an explicit absence of providential justice or moral absolutes" (2014: 1). Like the English Renaissance dramas before them, these plays are filled with horrors, and would be considered horror dramas by today's standards, but neither the term "horror" nor "Gothic" was available to them then. These proto-Gothic plays feature scenes of madness, incest, monstrosity, evil atheists, vengeful monstrous women, and the destruction and ruin of weak, flawed men. Aphra Behn herself contributed at least one play to this genre: *Abdelazer; or, The Moor's Revenge* (1676).

Gothic Horror

In the wake of the advent of Gothic literature at the end of the eighteenth century—*The Castle of Otranto* by Horace Walpole (1764), Ann Radcliffe's *The Mysteries of Udolpho* (1794) and *The Italian* (1797), and *The Monk* by Matthew Lewis (1796), etc.—Gothic drama rapidly followed. The most likely first Gothic play was Walpole's *The Mysterious Mother* (1764), which was circulated as a manuscript but never performed (Cox 2002: 126). A number of early Gothic dramas were in fact adaptations of novels: *The Castle of Otranto* became *The Count of Narbonne* (1781), and *The Monk* saw the light of the stage as *Aurelio and Miranda* (1798). Gothic novelists also contributed directly to the stage, such as Matthew "Monk" Lewis's *The Castle Specter* (1797).

Emperor, however, does not follow the path of the dark "cult of the macabre" of the later Gothic or the contemporary Restoration horror play. Instead, it blends *commedia dell'arte* with romantic farce using some of the tropes of the Restoration horror (in a comedic setting) to tell what we might term a proto-Gothic romantic farce. Behn's main source was a French play, *Arlequin, empereur dans la lune* (1684), performed by Italian *commedia dell'arte* (Spencer 1995: xviii). Being commedia, *Arlequin* was mostly unscripted, improvised by the performers. Behn took the basic plot and wove it into a tightly scripted comedy that follows the dictates of Restoration romantic farce. The Italian commedia origins are immediately apparent in Behn's play, with characters named Scaramouch and Harlequin, both clever servants in competition with one another. By his very name, Dr Baliardo is a *dottore*, a caricature of pedantic learning who is often an obstacle to young lovers, of which *Emperor* has two pairs: Eliara and Don Cinthio and Bellemente and Don Charmante form the *inamorata*.

Emperor also marks the next in a series of plays that followed roughly the same scenario, with only the details differing. Behn's play before Emperor was *The Lucky Chance, or an Alderman's Bargain*, a five-act comedy first staged in the Spring of 1686. In that romantic farce, two clever young women, Leticia and Julia, are betrothed against their will to older, pedantic but wealthy gentlemen, Sir Feeble Fainwou'd and Sir Cautious Fulbank, their ridiculous names as evidence of their unfitness to marry young, bright, beautiful women. The women together and separately manipulate the situation with the assistance of clever servants until the men admit they are too old to marry and Leticia and Julia are then betrothed to more age- and temperament-appropriate partners (see Behn

1995: 183–270). This is, of course, standard Restoration fare—machinations and comic plots in order to get the young lovers properly married to the correct person. Behn's plays follow this plot, albeit both from a female perspective and with a great deal of wit and satire.

The Emperor of the Moon itself is perhaps the quintessential version of this plot, proving popular and influential. Lowenthal reports that, "Behn's *Rover; or, The Banish'd Cavaliers* and *The Emperor of the Moon* were her most popular plays, and productions of each continued consistently throughout both the Restoration and the eighteenth century" (2003: 226). Less well known now, *The Emperor of the Moon* was a profoundly popular play in the United Kingdom for a century. As with Shelley over a century and a half later, Behn's literature explores gender roles and examines the place of women within society, not accepting the status quo but pushing for a sense of equality and a perception of woman as intelligent and rational.

The original context of the play was a London undergoing radical social, political, and cultural transformation amidst scientific advancement. In 1660 the monarchy was restored after eighteen years as a Puritan-governed nation. Merely five years later in 1665, the plague hit London hard. The following year, 1666, the Great Fire destroyed much of the city. The so-called "Popish Plot" and the Exclusion crisis followed in the 1670s, driving disaffection with the monarchy again and a realisation that the social and political stability the restoration of the monarchy was expected to bring was short-lived at best and non-existent at worst. Society was again driven by fear, paranoia, and social scheming. In that sense, the context of Behn's plays provides an awareness of both ruins and rebuilds (the fire), of bodies as fragile and abject things (the plague), of the world as driven by intrigue and plotting to achieve one's desired goals (political crises)—a proto-Gothic awareness of the past intruding on the present and nearby, lurking in ruins and attics, haunting us.

Further driving the drama of both the Restoration and the Gothic is the advent and use of new technology, both for the stage and in the world. While the actual inventor of the refracting telescope is unknown, in 1609 Galileo Galilee developed his own refracting lens which he called a *perspicillum* in Latin (meaning lens) or occhiale in Italian (meaning eyeglass) (Rosen 1947: 23). In 1611, Giovanni Demisiani coined the term "telescope" and it has been called thus ever since, sparking a pan-European fascination with the device. Its advent plays a key role in the play.

Behn was also interested in science and in astronomical theory. She translated Bernard le Bovier de Fontenelle's *Entretiens sur la pluralité des mondes* (1686) under the title *A Discovery of New Worlds* in 1688. The book popularised Copernican theory and posited the possibility of cosmic pluralism, or that people might exist on other planets. The third chapter offers an analysis of the possibility of life on the moon and what it might look like (see de Fontenelle 1990: 37–47). Most interestingly, de Fontenelle postulates that moon people would closely resemble Earth people: "whoever saw an inhabitant of the Moon and an inhabitant of Earth would note clearly that they were from closer-together worlds than an inhabitant of Earth and an inhabitant of Saturn" (de Fontenelle 1990: 46). He further notes that, given the proximity to the moon, "we should see blessed souls from the Moon arriving here at some point in the not-too-distant future" (de Fontenelle 1990: 43). It is these suppositions from de Fontenelle that drive Dr Baliardo's obsession and not only convince him that he can observe a civilisation on the moon through his ridiculously giant telescope, but also to believe Don Cinthio and Don Charmante when they claim to be from there.

It is not merely the advent of technology in the realm of science that drives Restoration and Gothic drama (and *Emperor*), but also the development of stage technology. Hermanson reports an explosion of new inventions, devices, and special effects for Restoration drama that powered both the spectacle demanded by audiences at the time and the elaborate effects of plays such as *Emperor* (2014: 13). Al Coppola notes that the place where *Emperor* premiered, the Dorset Garden Playhouse, had "state-of-the-art machinery and stage tricks", all of which were put in the service of the spectacle of the final act, which Coppola calls a "tour de force of farce" (2008: 483). The entire show displays "all the delicious excesses of the theatre" (2008: 483). Likewise, the Gothic drama was a theatre of elaborate effect and spectacle, relying on new technologies. Jeffrey N. Cox relates that "The Gothic theatre of shock and wonder was arguably the first form to capitalize fully on evolving lighting techniques, new stage effects, and the increasing presence of music behind the action" (2002: 127). It was, in short, a theatre that relied upon "spectacle, music and special effects" (2002: 127). Spectacle and technology drove both the Gothic theatre and the performance of Restoration drama. *Emperor*, with its many songs, spectacular ending, and plot, presaged the Gothic drama's approach to theatre. Judith Milhous observes that *Emperor* belongs to a type of play called "Dorset Garden Spectaculars" and part of the "machine-farce boom" (1984: 43). The play relies on huge spectacle, achieved through special effects, stage machines, and elaborate costumes designed to overwhelm and impress the viewer. Following Milhous, Katherine Mannheimer observes, "In its embrace of the supernatural, the trend pushed theatrical spectacle to phantasmagorical, cataclysmic extremes" (2011: 40).

Emperor thus delivers a Gothic science fiction spectacle before either genre existed. The play posits the perceived existence of aliens: strange beings, not human but intruding on human realms. Although revealed to be humans in disguise, the aliens are believed to be real moon beings by Dr Baliardo. Done for comic effect, yes, but Behn has clearly absorbed the writings of de Fontenelle (as have Don Cinthio and Don Charmante), as Baliardo questions the moon people, and they answer his anthropological questions to share about their culture and society. Thus, even though an elaborate ruse to gain the doctor's permission for marriage, the aliens are presented as "extraterrestrial creatures" (as Cynthia Lowenthal terms the disguised lovers and servants of *Emperor*) that are representations of "monstrous identity", beings "excluded from the human community" because of their race or non-human characteristics (2003: 144).

Men pretending to be aliens from the moon as part of a larger ruse to win fortune and the hands of the women they love carries a very Gothic connotation, similar to the discovery in more than one Gothic novel that the spirit haunting the ruins is actually a human being. The ghost is actually a long-lost family member or spurred lover, not a supernatural being. The revelation of a lack of an inexplicable presence does not mean that the Gothic narrative is not Gothic. *Emperor* substitutes aliens from the moon for ghosts in the ruins, but the effect is the same: haunting contact from beyond, followed by prosaic revelation.

The Emperor of the Moon, named after the alleged character Baliardo observes and Don Cinthio performs in the masquerade, is thus the leader of the aliens and the representative of the moon and simultaneously a ruse, a fraud, a prank, and a spectacular joke. The moon becomes both Baliardo's obsession and recurring motif throughout the play as both thing obsessed upon and thing not real. Dr Baliardo is referred to in the first scene of the play as a "lunatic" in the true meaning of the word: someone driven mad by the moon (1.1.87). His obsession with the moon is played humorously, for laughs, although it clearly exasperates everyone else in the household. Read seriously, his obsession is a madness; he is a lunatic, and a potentially dangerous one at that. He neglects his duties and his family. He spends his money on an enormous telescope, one over twenty feet long (which the servants complain about having to carry around and move), and books on the moon. “He is always travelling to the moon”, complains Scaramouch, one of his servants, referring for the doctor’s proclivity to stare at the moon through his telescope when it is visible and to otherwise obsess over and endlessly reflect upon the moon when it is not (1.1.89). This is a repeated theme throughout the play. However, Scaramouch acknowledges the good doctor is a truly wise and knowledgeable man, a profound scholar, and “as grave and wise a man in all argument and discourse, as can be met with”, except when someone mentions the moon, in which case “he runs into ridicule, and grows as mad as the wind” (2.1.247–249). These motifs are also reflected in Gothic themes: madness, “lunatics”, obsession, the quest for forbidden or hidden knowledge, and even the moon itself are constant presences in Gothic literature and drama.

Baliardo’s daughter Elaria likewise illuminates his obsession: “And so religiously [he] believes there is a world there, that he discourses as gravely of the people, their government, institutions, laws, manners, religion and constitution” (1.1.90–92). The audience is informed that his obsession began with the reading of strange and forbidden books about the moon: Lucian’s *Dialogue of Icaromenippus*, *A Discourse of the World in the Moon*, and “an heroic business called *The Man in the Moon*, if you’ll believe a Spaniard who was carried thither, upon an engine drawn by wild geese” (1.1.96–98). Behn does not mention de Fontenelle’s *Entretiens sur la pluralité des mondes* in this list, but it is both an obvious text to be included and a clear influence on the play and Dr Baliardo and all who have read de Fontenelle. Dr Baliardo dwells upon curious tomes of forgotten lore, to steal a line from Poe, and also the latest scientific texts to formulate his own theory of moon culture, moon people, moon politics, and moon society. He studies both texts from antiquity and contemporary travel narratives (albeit questionable ones). It is the last volume, *The Man in the Moon* by “a Spaniard”, that shows the play’s targets of satire—those who are so educated and obsessed with subject mastery they ignore common sense and their own experience in favour of crackpot accounts.

Mopsophil, another servant, refers to the astronomical and mathematical instruments Baliardo wears around his waist as “all his little devils with horrid names, his microscope, his horoscope, his telescope, and all his scopes”, referring to the use of these instruments as “my master’s conjuring” (1.1.124–126). Her comic line also demonstrates a key theme of the play: the confusion of the scientific for the pseudoscientific, the blending of the rational with the irrational. He has both "microscope" and "horoscope", which to Mopsophil (and perhaps even Baliardo) are both within the same category of means by which the world might be studied, interpreted, and understood.

The play begins in media res, with the young lovers plotting "a farce, which shall be called *The World in the Moon*" to be presented to Baliardo as if it were a real alien invasion (1.1.106–107). Initially, Don Charmante disguises himself as "one of the cabalists of the Rosicrucian order" (1.1.113). This designation also carries with it a hint of Gothic themes: mystic orders, conspiracies, and secret societies which involve the clergy. He enters "dressed in a strange fantastical habit", suggestive of the later Gothic "evil clergyman" trope (1.2.SD24). In his appearance, he resembles a human, but is also slightly different, per de Fontenelle's supposition that moon people will look like, but not exactly match, Earth people. "He looks not like the people of the lower orb", pronounces Scaramouch (1.2.22). He enters as a harbinger, a warning figure common to Gothic narratives. From his arrival, Baliardo begins to discourse and question about the moon, and Don Charmante fills his ear with supernatural declarations. When Baliardo asks how the Emperor of the Moon has heard of him, he is told, "Our intelligence is by ways more secret and sublime: the stars, and little demons of the air, inform us all things, past, present and to come" (1.2.32–34). He further informs Baliardo that the world, indeed all worlds, is populated with divine species and supernatural beings, and humans should be encouraged to mate with them. He explains how Alexander the Great was "begot by a salamander, that visited his mother in the form of a serpent" and Merlin, "that famous philosopher", was the product of a nun being seduced by a salamander (1.2.95–98). The Emperor of the Moon, he tells Baliardo, has also fallen in love with a mortal, and wishes to marry her. This announcement, of course, is designed to inspire Baliardo to allow his daughter and niece to marry the Emperor of the Moon and his brother. As with the Gothic, marriage and relationships are at the centre of the narrative and the plot within the plot to fool Baliardo.

Don Charmonte also places pictures on the lens of the telescope while Dr Baliardo is distracted, so the doctor looks through the telescope and sees a moon maid, leaning on a cloud, and later the Emperor himself looking back at Baliardo, who now believes with all his heart not only that there is a civilisation on the moon, but that through their telescopes the Emperor and his brother have fallen in love with Baliardo's niece and daughter. Since he himself has now seen a beautiful moon maiden, he knows the moon can spy on his family, too.

In the next scene, when Don Cinthio is discovered with Elaria, she cries out, "Oh, heavens! A madman", and Don Cinthio feigns madness to escape (1.3.154). Playing at insanity is what allows a young man caught in flagrante delicto to escape unrecognised. Again, Behn hints at what is to come with the Gothic, a theme inherited from Shakespeare and the Renaissance: feigning insanity as part of a larger scheme to achieve one's objectives.

There follows in act two a bit of commedia-style silliness in which the servants repeatedly strike Baliardo while insisting he has not been hit at all. Growing more desperate at his situation, in which he can no longer trust his own senses or experiences (also a Gothic theme), Baliardo draws a pistol and points it at Scaramouche's chest, determined to find out if Scaramouche is real or some sort of trickster spirit. Scaramouche then calms him down by explaining he is indeed Scaramouche and the doctor has woken him from a dream which was actually a message from the moon. The Emperor wishes to marry his daughter, Baliardo is told, and the Prince of Thunderland wishes to marry his niece. "May I credit this?" a stunned Baliardo asks (2.3.162). He then recalls that the "famous Rosicrucian", who was actually a moon alien, told him the Emperor loved a mortal, and is delighted to learn it is his own daughter (2.3.165). He consents to the union and after some discussion is told the moon people will come to Earth and bring them all into space for the great wedding event.

The servants, daughter and ward, and young suitors finally stage a massive theatrical mechanical pageant for the lunatic: floating zodiac signs fly through the air, a giant moon appears and waxes, a voice issues through a "stentraphon" announcing the imminent arrival of the Emperor. Kepler and Galileo, played by servants in disguise, are presented as translators and cultural ambassadors for the Emperor of the Moon. Baliardo experiences a variety of physical sensations. He falls to his knees, he is thrown to the floor on his face, he experiences flight himself. Then the Emperor and the Prince of Thunderland arrive, descending down in "a chariot…made like a half moon", to meet the human who has been observing them, and whose women they wish to marry (3.3.SD135). Part of the Emperor's entourage includes a real priest, who then, with Baliardo's blessing, marries the two couples while a song is sung and various moon creatures dance and celebrate.

It is all a glorious spectacle, made more ironic by the fact that the audience is watching the on-stage audience experience the spectacle very differently. Baliardo believes he is actually seeing an alien arrival, accompanied by glorious effects and spectacle. The theatrical audience is aware that what they are watching is artifice within artifice. There is no "willing suspension of disbelief" as the play has indicated up front that this is not real, only a spectacle. It calls attention to itself as a ruse to entertain the audience while convincing and astounding Baliardo.

As part of the subplot, Scaramouche and Harlequin have been competing for the hand of Mopsophil, and, disguised as Kepler, Scaramouche sees an opportunity. He asks Baliardo (as Kepler) for her hand in marriage and Baliardo, delighted, accepts. Scaramouche, perhaps forgetting himself, removes his disguise to kiss his betrothed and Baliardo realises he is not Kepler. Very quickly the entire affair is unmasked, and Baliardo sees that he has been duped:

> Doctor Baliardo: Are not you then the Emperor of the Moon?
> And you the Prince of Thunderland?
> Cinthio: There's no such person, Sir.
> These stories are the phantoms of mad brains,
> To puzzle fools withal—the wise laugh at 'em,—
> —Come sir, you shall no longer be imposed upon.
> Doctor Baliardo: No emperor of the moon; and no moon world!
> Charmante: Ridiculous inventions.
> If we'd not loved you, you'd been still imposed on;
> We had brought a scandal on your learned name,
> And all succeeding ages had despised it.
> [Baliardo leaps up].
> Doctor Baliardo: Burn all my books, and let my study blaze,
> Burn all to ashes, and be sure the wind
> Scatter the vile contagious monstrous lies. (3.3.211–224)

He is assured, however, that these will be good marriages and his daughter and niece are well matched. The entire need for the moon-ruse was due to his own obsession. He closes the play by citing Socrates, noting the only thing one can really know is that one knows nothing.

As Jane Spenser notes in her introduction to the play, "If the foolish doctor is deceived by appearances, those same illusions are what delight the audiences" (1995: xix). This, too, could be applied to the later Gothic on multiple levels: the machinations of Ambrosio the Monk, Count

Manfred from *The Castle of Otranto*, or Montoni of *The Mysteries of Udolpho* (all of which also examine women being forced to marry—or not marry—against their will) are designed to terrify and traumatise the characters, even as they delight and move the reader/audience. In the end, Restoration horror plays, Restoration romantic farces, and Gothic drama are all designed for the same purpose: to have an emotional impact on the audience through manipulation and spectacle. Behn, through her own translation work and a group of Italian performers in France, found inspiration to make the moon a place of mystery and manipulation, presenting perhaps the ultimate deception: an alien invasion from the moon being the ruse used to allow two young women to marry the men of their choice. Dr Baliardo is tricked, but so is the audience, albeit with their knowledge and consent. We are here to see spectacles, even if we know they are not real. Lunatics are those who have been driven mad by the moon, but Behn reminds us that they can be cured by convincing them first that they are encountering moon people, by placing them within an elaborate masquerade, and then revealing the reality behind what they thought was real. Perhaps that is the most Gothic element of the play: that for Dr Baliardo, the play shows how easily one's illusions can be ripped away, one's reality can be revealed to be unstable at best and a complete illusion at worst, one will realise that one's previous reality was "the phantoms of mad brains", and one must continue to live in this new mad world, albeit one without moon-madness, only the madness of the normal.

References

Behn, Aphra. 1995. *The Rover and Other Plays.* Oxford: Oxford University Press.

Coppola, Al. 2008. Retraining the Virtuoso's Gaze: Behn's *Emperor of the Moon*, the Royal Society, and the Spectacles of Science and Politics. *Eighteenth-Century Studies* 41 (4): 481–506.

Cox, Jeffrey N. 2002. English Gothic Theatre. In *The Cambridge Companion to Gothic Fiction*, ed. Jerrold E. Hogle, 125–144. Cambridge: Cambridge University Press.

de Fontenelle, Bernard le Bovier. 1990. *Conversations on the Plurality of Worlds.* Translated by H.A. Hargreaves. Berkeley: University of California Press.

Groom, Nick. 2012. *The Gothic: A Very Brief Introduction.* Oxford: Oxford University Press.

Hermanson, Anne. 2014. *The Horror Plays of the English Renaissance.* London: Routledge.

Lowenthal, Cynthia. 2003. *Performing Identities on the Restoration Stage*. Carbondale: Southern Illinois University Press.

Mannheimer, Katherine. 2011. Celestial Bodies: Readerly Rapture as Theatrical Spectacle in Aphra Behn's *The Emperor of the Moon* Restoration Studies in English Literary Culture, 1660–1700. Vol. 3, 1 (Spring): 39–60.

Milhous, Judith. 1984. The Multimedia Spectacular on the Restoration Stage. In *British Theatre and the Other Arts, 1660–1800*, ed. Shirley Strum Kenny, 41–66. Washington, DC: Folger Library.

Rosen, Edward. 1947. *The Naming of the Telescope*. New York: Henry Schuman.

Sistakou, Evina. 2012. *The Aesthetics of Darkness: A Study of Hellenistic Romanticism in Apollonius, Lycophron and Nicander*. Leuven: Peeters.

Spencer, Jane. 1995. Introduction. In *The Rover and Other Plays by Aphra Behn*. Oxford: Oxford University Press.

CHAPTER 3

The Moon and Vampire Mythology and Folklore: Or, Lunar Influences in *Varney the Vampire*'s Bannerworth Storyline

Sharon M. Gallagher

The First Phase: Why *Varney*?

James Malcolm Rymer's[1] *Varney the Vampire* (1845–1847) may not be the first text considered when thinking about the moon in nineteenth-century vampire Gothic literature. John Polidori's *Vampyre* (1819), Joseph Sheridan Le Fanu's *Carmilla* (1872), and Bram Stoker's *Dracula* (1897) are often the ones that come to mind when discussing vampire literature, and the *Vampyre* is not only considered the first long fictional work in English featuring a vampire, but it also introduced the moon as

[1] There is an ongoing debate about the authorship of *Varney* which centres around two writers: Thomas Peckett Prest (1810–1859) and James Malcolm Rymer (1814–1884); either or both receive author attribution in the currently available reprints of *Varney*. For the sake of simplicity, consistency, and the printed version of *Varney* cited here, Rymer appears as the author.

S. M. Gallagher (✉)
Penn State University, The Behrend College, Erie, PA, USA
e-mail: smg16@psu.edu

E. Gomel, S. Bacon (eds.), *Lunar Gothic*, Palgrave Gothic,
https://doi.org/10.1007/978-3-031-92621-1_3

essential in resurrecting the vampire after death (Polidori 1997: 15–16). This moon-vampire association is recognised as a literary addition to vampire folklore because the characteristics of the eighteenth-century Eastern European vampire's influence on English literature did not contain any stories which indicated that vampires were resurrected by moonlight. The 1732 English articles which are credited with initiating the literary use of the vampire in England were "Foreign Advices for March, 1732" in *The Gentlemen's Magazine* (1732, 681) and "Foreign News, Friday, March 10, Medrevga in Hungary, Jan. 7, 1732" in *The Grub Street Journal* (16 Mar. 1732: [303]). Both summarised the investigation into the case of Arnold Paul who was suspected of causing illness among his community after his death. He was disinterred, diagnosed as possessing signs of being a vampire, staked, burned to ash, and returned to his grave. The articles also indicated that "those who have been tormented or killed by the *Vampyres* become Vampyres when they are dead", so the remains of Paul's deceased victims also experienced the same treatment ("Foreign Advices…" 1732: 681). Nowhere was it indicated in either article that the moon played a part in bringing vampires back to life. These reports intrigued many scholars in the eighteenth century who conducted their own investigations. One of the best-known and widely translated of these works was Augustin Calmet's exhaustively researched *Dissertations Upon the Apparitions of Angels, Dæmons, and Ghosts, and Concerning the Vampires of Hungary, Bohemia, Moravia, and Silesia* (1759), and it did not report any connections between the moon and vampires within the extensive information collected from the countries listed in its title.

More recent research does note a connection between the moon and reanimation in folklore. Matthew Beresford's *From Demons to Dracula: The Creation of the Modern Vampire Myth* observed: "objects such as agricultural tools or other inanimate objects can turn into vampires if left outside on the eve of a full moon" (2011: 9). While not an outdoor agricultural instrument, the portrait of a Bannerworth ancestor, which bears a remarkable resemblance to Varney, is exposed to the light of the full moon: "from the effect of the moonlight which was streaming over it, the portrait on the panel looked exceedingly life like" (Rymer 2008: 54). One may be tempted to argue that the portrait's likeness came to life in the form of Varney, but Varney is seen by several of the characters the night before this scene, so it is an imaginative leap to connect the belief described by Beresford. It is also unclear if nineteenth-century English fictional writers using the vampire in their works were aware of this and extended the moon's powers to reanimating humans. Still, the moon does play an important role in *Varney* and offers many opportunities for lunar analysis,[2] but there is space to explore only one here: the moon and its literary folklore/actual folklore representation when examining the appearance of the moon in the Bannerworth storyline[3] within *Varney*.

The serial nature of Rymer's tale and his eclectic use of inspirational materials results in a story which presents the moon in a variety of ways and allows for analysis that could use a range of mythological, folkloric, literary, travel, psychological, and scientific sources, which could easily lead to a discussion of the moon that is as difficult to reconcile and organise coherently as Varney's story, especially in a short chapter. A search through *Varney* reveals that the word "moon", singly or as part of another related word like "moonlight", is used 333 times; 144 of these usages occur during the tale of the Bannerworths (Rymer and Prest 2021). The presence of the moon throughout this storyline often appears as part of vampire folklore, rather than as part of a Gothic setting. It reinforces and adds to the vampire folklore that was created within literature by English authors, while also suggesting connections to global vampire folklore and mythology such as that from Scandinavia which may not have been previously considered as part of nineteenth-century English vampire literature.

The Second Phase: The Moon, Myth, and *Varney*

Within the first few pages of Chapter 1, Rymer demonstrates his familiarity with the eighteenth-century Eastern European vampire outbreak reports with his detailed description of Varney's long fingernails and tall and gaunt stature (Rymer 2008: 37), but Varney also possesses the notably pale skin and mesmerising gaze of Polidori's Ruthven (1997: 3), though Varney's face is never described as "beautiful", drawing women[4] to actively seek out his company as they do Ruthven's (Polidori 1997: 3). Details like these have prompted many scholars to note how the eighteenth-

[2] Other usages of the moon which will not be examined here but offer opportunities for further research include the connection between the moon and madness, moon and water, moon as a divine character in Varney's hero journey, and the moon within descriptive passages which are reminiscent of nineteenth-century published travel journals.

[3] Chapters 1–92, 95, 97–98, 102–103, 108, and 110 are identified by Curt Herr as the Bannerworth Saga (Rymer 2008: 31).

[4] Women who are drawn to Varney are attracted to his title and the belief that he has the wealth associated with it, so they scheme to marry him or have their daughters marry him.

century Eastern European vampire stories that were popularised by the 1732 vampire reports published in English periodicals ("Foreign Advices for March, 1732" 1732: 681; "Foreign News…" 1732: [303]) and works like Calmet's directly influenced the English literary vampire. Carol A. Senf summarises these conclusions in *The Vampire in 19th Century English Literature*: "What the reader sees in the vampire in nineteenth-century literature is the result of writers combining at least three broad strands: folkloric treatments of posthumous magic, earlier literary characters—such as the rake and the villains and temptresses of the Gothic novel, and (later in the century…) responses to genuine changes in social roles for men and women" (1988: 20). Evidence of the first two criteria regularly appears in the Bannerworth tale. One instance is when Varney shares his history[5] with the Bannerworths: "…I came across a man who said that he was a Hungarian, and who was full of strange stories of vampyres. Among other things, he told me that a vampire could not be drowned, for that the waters would cast him upon its banks, and, if the moonbeams fell upon him, he would be restored to life" (Rymer 2008: 359). This is one of many occurrences where *Varney* alludes to Eastern European vampire folklore and prior literary influences like the moonlight restoring a vampire to life. However, Curt Herr notes in his thoroughly annotated edition of *Varney* that Rymer included new additions to nineteenth-century vampire literature, like Varney's "fang-like" teeth (Rymer 2008: 37),[6] so a closer analysis of other instances of literary and/or actual vampire folklore involving the moon may show more originality and complexity than Rymer has been previously credited with in *Varney*. One of these areas is the lunar literary folklore surrounding the repeated resurrections in the Bannerworth story, inspired by Polidori's Ruthven, but the moon's role in the vampire folklore presented in *Varney* extends beyond mere repetition of these influences.

The vampire and its connection to the moon presents an argument for originality in adding to the literary vampire folklore and extending the folklore influence beyond eighteenth-century Eastern Europe. After Varney's assault upon Flora Bannerworth in the first chapter, houseguest and family friend Mr. Marchdale was the first to say that Flora was attacked

[5] One of many histories that Varney will claim throughout the serial.

[6] Footnote 6 by Curt Herr (Rymer 2008: 37).

by a vampire (Rymer 2008: 45). Flora independently concluded that she had been the victim of a vampire attack and told her brother Henry that she knew this because she had read about the vampire "in the book of travels in Norway, which Mr. Marchdale lent us all" (Rymer 2008: 48). The first connection made among the characters to the vampire is a Norwegian one, not Eastern European, despite the eighteenth-century English setting of the tale. This is repeated during the exchange between Henry and Mr. Chillingworth where more folklore sources for the vampire are added and the first connection between the vampire and the moon is made:

> "... I understand that in some countries, particularly Norway and Sweden, the superstition is a very common one." [Mr. Chillingworth]
>
> "And in the Levant." [Henry Bannerworth]
>
> "Yes. The ghouls of the Mahometans are of the same description of beings. All that I have heard of the European vampyre has made it a being which can be killed, but is restored to life again by the rays of a full moon falling on the body". (Rymer 2008: 51)

Here the European vampire is connected to the moon. After Mr. Chillingworth departed, Henry reflected that the attack on Flora the previous evening occurred the night before the full moon.

> He [Henry] took from the shelves of a book case the work which Flora had mentioned, entitled, 'Travels in Norway,' in which work he found some account of the popular belief in vampyres.
>
> He opened the work at random, and then some of the leaves turned over of themselves to a particular place.... There was a note at the bottom of one of the pages at this part of the book, and Henry read as follows:—
>
> "With regard to these vampyres, it is believed by those who are inclined to give credence to so dreadful a superstition, that they always endeavour to make their feast of blood, for the revival of their bodily powers, on some evening immediately preceding a full moon, because if any accident befall them, such as being shot, or otherwise killed or wounded, they can recover by lying down somewhere where the full moon's rays will fall upon them". (Rymer 2008: 51)

The specificity within these paragraphs extends beyond Polidori's use of the moon:

> ...a robber met him [Aubrey], and informed him that it [Ruthven's body] was no longer there, having been conveyed by himself and comrades, upon his [Aubrey's] retiring, to the pinnacle of a neighboring mount, according to a promise they had given his lordship [Ruthven], that it should be exposed to the first cold ray of the moon that rose after his death. Aubrey was astonished, and taking several of the men, determined to go and bury it upon the spot where it lay. But, when he had mounted to the summit he found no trace of either the corpse or the clothes..... (Polidori 1997: 15–16)

Polidori's brief passage leaves the reader to conclude that the moonlight has resurrected Ruthven, which is why there is no trace of him where the robbers left the body. Rymer adopts this literary folklore tradition of moon resurrection and firmly establishes the moon's importance by the specificity of timing a vampire's feeding cycle to occur the day before the moon is at its brightest just in case the vampire requires the moon's resurrecting powers. Rymer adds something new to the literary vampire folklore. Rymer also includes at least five different instances in the Bannerworth storyline of the moon resurrecting a vampire, which leaves no doubt for the reader that the moon is directly responsible for continuing the vampire's existence in the event of its unexpected disruption. One of the more detailed descriptions of the moon returning Varney back to life occurs as the result of Mr. Marchdale[7] and Varney manipulating Tom Eccles into shooting Varney so he may witness the resurrection and frighten Tom into spreading the horrific story among the townspeople to keep them away:

> ... there was Sir Francis Varney, raising slowly one arm with the hand outstretched towards the moon, as if invoking that luminary to shed more of its beams upon him. Then the body moved slowly, like some one writhing in pain, and yet unable to move from the spot on which it lay. From the head to the foot, the whole frame seemed to be convulsed, and now and then as the ghastly object seemed to be gathering more strength, the limbs were thrown out with a rapid and a frightful looking violence....
>
> This was a state of things which continued for many minutes, and then the body showed evident symptoms of so much returning animation, that it was about to rise from his gory bed and mingle once again with the living....
>
> Sir Francis Varney now, as if with a great struggle, rose to his feet, and looked up at the bright moon for some moments with such an air and man-

[7] As *Varney* progresses, Rymer reveals that Marchdale is Varney's partner who proves to be a greater villain than Varney.

ner that it would not have required any very great amount of imagination to conceive that he was returning to it some sort of thanksgiving for the good that it had done to him. (Rymer 2008: 268)

The moon had brought Varney back to life, adding actual scenes of such an event to the literary vampire tradition and establishing the moon's role in its folklore.

Rymer does not limit Varney's story to reinforcing previous literary vampire folklore. Specifically citing Norway as the source of this lunar information in the initial chapters of *Varney* warrants some closer scrutiny to determine whether it is an addition of more literary folklore, a part of existing (but perhaps previously unexplored) vampire folklore, or a possible blending of both. The 1847 preface to *Varney* by its unnamed author claims:

> A belief in the existence of Vampyres first took its rise in Norway and Sweden, from whence it rapidly spread to more southern regions, taking a firm hold of the imaginations of the more credulous portion of mankind.
>
> The following romance is collected from seemingly the most authentic sources, and the Author must leave the question of credibility entirely to his readers, not even thinking that he is peculiarly called upon to express his own opinion upon the subject.
>
> Nothing has been omitted in the life of the unhappy Varney, which could tend to throw a light upon his most extraordinary career, and the fact of his death just as it is here related, made a great noise at the time through Europe and is to be found in the public prints for the year 1713....London Sep. 1847 (Rymer 2008: 34)

The preface reflects the Gothic tradition of over 80 years before *Varney* when Horace Walpole first published *The Castle of Otranto, A Story Translated by William Marshall, Gent. From the Original Italian of Onuphrio Muralto, Canon of the Church of St. Nicholas at Otranto* in 1764 (1990), which set the soon to be familiar precedent that claimed that their audience was reading a true story, translated from an actual text from another era. Walpole's preface to the first edition elaborates on the title page's claim (Walpole 1990: 3–6), and despite Walpole's retraction of the claim in the second preface for the second edition four months later (Walpole 1990: 7–12; Lewis 1990: viii), it would become part of Gothic literature.

In addition to again specifying a significant Scandinavian influence on vampire folklore in general, Rymer provides a year for Varney's death which precedes the vampire reports which appeared in the previously noted English news accounts[8] by almost 20 years and Calmet's dissertation by over 30 years, and none indicated the moon in any way ("Foreign Advices for March, 1732" 1732, 681; "Foreign News…" 1732, [303]; Calmet 1759). In typical *Varney* fashion, the date of Varney's death as well as the Scandinavian origins of vampire folklore are later contradicted. As Herr noted, the Bannerworth storyline shifts from taking place in the early to mid-eighteenth century to the late eighteenth century[9] (Rymer 2008: 67), so the 1847 preface claiming 1713 as the date of Varney's death is problematic. Chapter 40 also contradicts the Preface while adding something else to the Scandinavian vampire folklore claims:

> That dim and uncertain condition concerning vampyres, originating probably as it had done in Germany, had spread itself slowly, but insidiously, throughout the whole of the civilized world.
>
> In no country and in no clime is there not something which bears a kind of family relationship to the veritable vampyre of which Sir Francis Varney appeared to be so choice a specimen.
>
> The *ghoul* of eastern nations is but the same being, altered to suit habits and localities; and the *sema* of the Scandinavians is but the vampyre of a more primitive race, and a personification of that morbid imagination which has once fancied the probability of the dead walking again among the living, with all the frightful insignia of corruption and the grave about them.
>
> Although not popular in England, still there had been tales told of such midnight visitants…. (Rymer 2008: 196–197)

This excerpt notes three significant items about vampire folklore: (1) It originated in Germany (not in Norway and Sweden as the preface claims); (2) The Scandinavian *sema* has origins in "a more primitive race"; and (3) Vampires are not popular in England. The German connection and the

[8] The 1732 accounts are regularly cited as sparking "the vampire craze" which manifested itself as a subject in English literature. This does not mean that there were not any mentions of vampires in English publications prior to 1732; cited pre-1732 publications include Henry More's *An Antidote Against Atheism; or, An Appeal to the Naturall Faculties of the Minde of Man, Whether There Be Not a God* (1655) and William of Newburgh's *The History of English Affairs* (2001) originally published 1196–1198. See References for complete citations.

[9] Footnote 23 (Rymer 2008: 67).

lack of popularity of native vampire folklore in England is supported by the research of many scholars and expressed by Senf that "nineteenth-century English writers learned about the vampire from at least three distinct sources: folklore, eighteenth-century German literature, and scientific discussions of primitive beliefs" (1988: 23), while also not forgetting the influence and popularity of early Gothic literature. Grenville Pigott's 1839 London publication of Scandinavian mythology also stated that while a subject of research and translation, it was not popularly known among the English:

> The Mythology of the ancient Scandinavians, respecting which so much curious information has been brought to light, of late years, by the researches of many distinguished writers, in Germany, Denmark, and Sweden, has hitherto excited but little attention in this country [England], although the subject is well calculated to awaken our interest, *not only as the source of most of our popular superstitions* [emphasis mine],[10] from when the favourite authors of our early childhood and of our maturer age have drawn their witches, their fairies, their dwarfs, their giants, and their ghosts; but in an historical point of view also, for a short retrospect will suffice to shew, that *the religion of Odin must have exercised a great and lasting influence on the character and institutions of the inhabitants of Great Britain.* (Pigott 1839: vii–viii, emphasis mine)

Pigott argues that despite little popular interest in Scandinavian mythology, existing English folklore and fiction have utilised it to such an extent that he will show its tremendous influence on Great Britain. This raises a question about the possibility of the moon's power of resurrection tracing back to an older, non-Eastern European source which may have directly influenced English folklore and nineteenth-century vampire fiction. Pigott's claims of his English contemporaries' limited knowledge of Scandinavian mythology appear to be reinforced by published travel journals from the time. A search through *HathiTrust* for books published before 1845 in English with "Norway"[11] in their titles yielded five travel

[10] Andrew Joynes' *Medieval Ghost Stories: An Anthology of Miracles, Marvels, and Prodigies* (2001) is one twenty-first-century source which provides support for this claim among its many translated stories.

[11] Norway was used because of the "Travels in Norway" title referred to by both Flora and Henry in Chapter 4 of *Varney* which connected the moon, the vampire, and Norway.

journals.[12] Searching "moon" in each of these texts yielded results, but all were descriptive in nature (usually about travelling by night) and not related to any retellings by the travellers of local mythology or folktales. Additional searches through the texts for "vampyr", "vampire", and "*sema*" yielded no results. Rymer's Scandinavian vampire inspiration and its possible connection to the moon seemed to end here.

However, Pigott did note a vampire connection later in his work: "...they [old Scandinavians] believed that these spirits, called by them Draugr, remained with the bodies which they had once inhabited, and at times wandered about the earth. Hence the general prevalence of the belief in spectres in the north of Europe, a belief not yet eradicated" (1839: 355–356). Matthias Teichert in his essay "'Draugula': The *Draugr* in Old Norse-Icelandic Saga Literature and His Relationship to the Post-Medieval Vampire Myth" provides a thorough analysis of the *draugr* found in Icelandic sagas which were "based on events and persons from the early history of the Icelandic Free State (ca. 900–1050 AD)" (2013: 3). Teichert's work presents a "code of the *draugr* myth" as a list of shared characteristics among the stories (2013: 11). Several are familiar to those well versed in vampire mythology and/or literature, but there is no mention of the moon or Rymer's "*sema*" (Teichert 2013: 11–12). The closest characteristic to any resurrection ability is: "The *draugr* is able to recover from a temporary enfeeblement" (Teichert 2013: 12). Teichert also notes that these characteristics may be older and/or influenced by "non-Nordic traditions, especially Celtic lore...and undead stories circulating in Northern England and recorded in the Latin language in *Historia rerum Anglicarum* by William of Newburgh (written ca. 1198)" (2013: 12). So, the *draugr*[13] may have a possible connection to England's written records and/or older oral tradition from the Celts.

Among Teichert's primary sources was the *Eyrbyggia Saga*. Sir Walter Scott (1771–1832), one of the most popular authors of his time, published a collection of his prose works in 1827 which included "Abstract of the Eyrbiggia-Saga", and Scott's preface to it reported:

[12] Edward Daniel Clarke's (1838) *Travels in Various Countries of Scandinavia...*, Charles B. Elliott's (1833) *Letters from the North of Europe...*, George Matthew Jones's (1827) *Travels in Norway, Sweden, Finland, Russia and Turkey...*, *Travels in Sweden, Denmark, and Norway* (1926), and William Rae Wilson's (1826) *Travels in Norway, Sweden, Denmark, Hanover, Germany, Netherlands*; see References for complete publication information.

[13] The five previously referenced English travel journals were also searched for "*draugr*" but yielded no results.

> This article first appeared in a work entitled Illustrations of the Northern Antiquities [1814], published under the charge of two distinguished Antiquaries, Robert Jamieson, Esquire, of Edinburgh, and the late Henry Weber. The extremely curious information, on the subject of Scandinavian Antiquities, which the volume contains, (it will be easily supposed the author is not speaking of his own slight share in it,) deserved a better reception than it met with, as the public gave no encouragement to continue the work. (1827: 443)

Scott's observation of the lack of public interest in the subject when the work was initially published, even with the famous author's name attached to it, supports Pigott's claim 12 years later that while excellent work was being done in the field, there was not much popular interest among the English. A search of "moon" within Scott's 1827[14] text revealed a connection between the moon and the dead in the saga:

> On the night when the conductors of Thorgunna's funeral returned to Froda, there appeared, visible to all who were present, a meteor, or spectral appearance, resembling a half-moon, which glided around the boarded walls of the mansion in an opposite direction to the course of the sun,* and continued to perform its revolutions until the domestics retired to rest. This apparition was renewed every night during a whole week, and was pronounced by Thorer with the wooden leg, to presage pestilence or mortality. (Scott 1827: 492)

Scott's asterisk (*) directs the reader to a footnote which makes connections to the sun and moon and Celtic, Egyptian, Greek, and Roman influences:

> Whatever revolved with the sun was reckoned a fortunate movement. Thus, the Highlanders in making the *deasil*, a sort of benediction which they bestow in walking round the party to be propitiated, always observe the course of the sun. And witches... made their circles, *widdershins*, as the Scottish dialect expresses it, (*wider-sins* Germ) or in opposition to the course of the orb of light. The apparition of the half-moon reminds us of Hecate, of the mysteries of Isis in Apuleius, and of a passage in Lucian's 'Lears,' where the moon is forced down by magical invocation. (1827: 492)

[14] A great number of Scott's works were republished after his death and among them was *The Miscellaneous Prose Works*. *HathiTrust* indicates that this text was also published in 1836 and 1844, which may have made them accessible to Rymer while he was writing *Varney*.

It is not specified whether this meteor, spectral "half-moon" object occurs during the waxing or waning of the moon, but the waning of the moon is usually associated in mythology with "sickness and death" (Cashford 2003: 310). This agrees with Thorer's foretelling of sickness or death at the object's appearance, much like the eighteenth-century Eastern European vampire's association with inexplicable epidemics in communities. Scott also refers to "the Hungarian vampire" (1827: 502) when telling the story of how the problematic activities of the deceased Thorolf Baegifot were decisively ended with his disinterment, cremation, and scattering of his ashes (1827: 501–502), a very familiar and effective method of dealing with vampires in both folklore and literature. What does not appear in a search of *The Miscellaneous Prose Works* is *draugr* or *sema*.

The Next Phase: *Varney* and Further Lunar Research

While the preceding information supports Rymer reinforcing and adding to the literary vampire folklore of lunar reanimation, *Varney* also presents a new line of inquiry into literary vampire folklore and actual global vampire mythology by including multiple (and contradictory) Scandinavian references in the Bannerworth tale where the moon often appears. Further research is required to determine if there is a direct connection between the moon, the vampire, and actual Scandinavian mythology in *Varney* since the research into Scandinavian mythology's vampire-like creatures in this chapter has not pursued every possibility and, to date, the source for Rymer's *sema* has not been found in any of the consulted works.[15] Teichert's mention of Celtic sources and Scott specifying Scottish words also present the possibility that Rymer's *sema* may have originated from a yet to be located oral and/or written tale.[16]

The initial proposal for this chapter was quite different from the final submission because a closer analysis of *Varney* and the moon revealed that there was not one definitive statement which would account for all the

[15] Rymer's use of *sema* continues to intrigue me, but the need to meet deadlines temporarily paused further investigation into this line of inquiry; however, I will continue the search.

[16] The research surrounding Augustus Hare's "The Vampire of Croglin Grange" being inspired by the initial *Varney* chapters led to the argument that the Croglin Grange tale was significantly older than Rymer's (Ross 1963: 103–109; Fanthorpe and Fanthorpe 2010: 260–267), which presents the possibility that Rymer was also inspired by oral stories.

moon's appearances in the tale. Herr expressed a broader hope for scholarly research in the conclusion to his introduction of *Varney*: "a few moonbeams have poked through the murky clouds and a thin resurrecting moonbeam has illuminated his limp body. Varney never really died; he was simply hidden from view patiently waiting for the perfect charismatic entrance: a spotlight of moonbeams welcoming him to the twenty-first century" (2008: 25).

There has been an increase in scholarly attention to *Varney* in the twenty-first century, but like the story itself, the further one progresses, the more possibilities emerge for research. The moon is one of these intriguing subjects, and Chapter 88 presents several options for further investigation. Though it is not the last chapter of the Bannerworth storyline, it is the last chapter in which Varney appears. The moon appears at least 13 times in a range of scenes: assisting Varney in eluding both a determined mob (Rymer 2008: 352) and the Bow Street Runners sent to arrest him (Rymer 2008: 363–364); appearing in Varney's history where he recalls the first time the moon brought him back to life, his first encounter with the informative Hungarian (Rymer 2008: 359); explaining lunar science to Flora (Rymer 2008: 362); and conveying the vital information that the Bannerworths need to reclaim their rightful property (Rymer 2008: 365–369). It also significantly reveals that despite the humanising influence of the Bannerworths, Varney is still separate from their world: "the moon fell across his [Varney's] face, and gave it a ghastly hue, that, added to his natural paleness and wounds, gave him an almost unearthly aspect" (Rymer 2008: 355). Varney is like the flawed heroes of mythology who have a fate to fulfil under the guidance of a protective deity, but this is the subject for a different chapter.

References

Beresford, Matthew. 2011. *From Demons to Dracula: The Creation of the Modern Vampire Myth*. London: Reaktion Books.

Calmet, Augustin. 1759. *Dissertations Upon the Apparitions of Angels, Dæmons, and Ghosts, and Concerning the Vampires of Hungary, Bohemia, Moravia, and Silesia. By the Reverend Father Dom Augustin Calmet, A Benedictine Monk, and Abbot of Senoners in Lorraine. Translated from the French* [1746]. London: M. Cooper, at the Globe in Pater-Noster-Row. Eighteenth Century Collections Online, Gale Primary Sources.

Cashford, Jules. 2003. *The Moon Myth and Image*. New York: Four Walls Eight Windows.

Clarke, Edward Daniel. 1838. *Travels in Various Countries of Scandinavia: Including Denmark, Sweden, Norway, Lapland and Finland.* 3 vols. London: T. Cadell and W. Davies. HathiTrust.

Elliott, Charles B. 1833. *Letters from the North of Europe: Or A Journal of Travels in Holland, Denmark, Norway, Sweden, Finland, Russia, Prussia and Saxony.* London: Key and Biddle. HathiTrust.

Fanthorpe, Lionel, and Patricia Fanthorpe. 2010. *The Big Book of Mysteries.* Toronto: Dundurn Press.

Foreign Advices for March, 1732. Mar. 1732. *The Gentlemen's Magazine; or, Monthly Intelligencer*, 2 (15): 681. British Periodicals, ProQuest.

Foreign News, Friday, March 10, Medrevga in Hungary, Jan. 7, 1732. 16 Mar. 1732. *The Grub Street Journal* no. 115: [303]. British Periodicals, ProQuest.

Herr, Curt. 2008. Introduction. In *Varney the Vampire; or, The Feast of Blood.* 1847, ed. Curt Herr, 8–25. Concord: Zittaw Press.

Jones, George Matthew. 1827. *Travels in Norway, Sweden, Finland, Russia and Turkey; also on the Coasts of the Sea of Azof and of the Black Sea; with a Review of the Trade in Those Seas, and of the Systems.* Vol. 1 & 2. London: John Murray. HathiTrust.

Joynes, Andrew, comp. and ed. 2001. *Medieval Ghost Stories: An Anthology of Miracles, Marvels, and Prodigies.* Martlesham: Boydell Press.

Lewis, W. S. 1990. Introduction. In *The Castle of Otranto: A Gothic Story*, Horace Walpole, 1764. Oxford: Oxford University Press, vii–xvi.

More, Henry. 1655. *An Antidote Against Atheism; or, An Appeal to the Naturall Faculties of the Minde of Man, Whether There Be Not a God.* 2nd ed. London: J. Flesher. HathiTrust.

Newburgh, William 2001. The 'History of the Events of England' of William of Newburgh. In *Medieval Ghost Stories*, edited and translated by Andrew Joynes. Martlesham: Boydell Press, 134–142.

Pigott, Grenville. 1839. *A Manual of Scandinavian Mythology Containing a Popular Account of the Two Eddas and of the Religion of Odin.* London: William Pickering. HathiTrust.

Polidori, John. 1997. The Vampyre. In *The Vampyre and Other Tales of the Macabre*, ed. Robert Morrison and Chris Baldick, 3–23. Oxford: Oxford University Press.

Ross, F. Clive. 1963. The Croglin Vampire. *Tomorrow: World Digest of Psychical Research and Occult Studies.* Spring: 103–109.

Rymer, James Malcolm. 2008. *Varney the Vampire; or, The Feast of Blood* [1847], ed. Curt Herr. Concord: Zittaw Press.

Rymer, James Malcolm and Thomas Peckett Prest. 14 Jun. 2021. *Varney the Vampyre (or: The Feast of Blood)* [1847], 3 vols. E-book edition: Roy Glashan's Library. https://freeread.com.au/@RGLibrary/Collective/VarneyTheVampyre.html.

Scott, Sir Walter. 1827. Abstract of the Eyrbiggia-Saga. In *The Miscellaneous Prose Works of Sir Walter Scott, Bart. In Six Volumes*, vol. 5, 441–512. Edinburgh: Whittaker & Co. HathiTrust.

Senf, Carol A. 1988. *The Vampire in the Nineteenth-Century*. University of Wisconsin Press.

Teichert, Matthias. 2013. 'Draugula': The *Draugr* in Old Norse-Icelandic Saga Literature and His Relationship to the Post-Medieval Vampire Myth. In *The Universal Vampire: Origins and Evolution of a Legend*, ed. Barbara Brodman and James E. Doran, 3–16. Vancouver: Farleigh Dickinson.

Travels in Sweden, Denmark, and Norway. 1926. London: Bentham and Hardy. HathiTrust.

Walpole, Horace. 1990. *The Castle of Otranto: A Gothic Story* [1764], ed. W. S. Lewis. Oxford: Oxford University Press.

Wilson, William Rae. 1826. *Travels in Norway, Sweden, Denmark, Hanover, Germany, Netherlands, etc.* Oxford: Longman, Rees, Orme, and Green. HathiTrust.

CHAPTER 4

Satire, Science, and Scepticism: Viewing the Lunar Hoaxes of Edgar Allen Poe and Richard Adams Locke as Discourse on Uncertainty in the Antebellum Period

Suzanne FitzGerald Heskin

During the Antebellum era in America, there was a prevailing air of disbelief as many scientific discoveries challenged previously held ideas of subjects believed to be unknowable. Advancements in astronomy, such as the first sightings of the return of Halley's Comet, captured the public's imagination, drawing their attention skyward. Moreover, this scientific revolution corresponded with the print revolution, which gave the masses unprecedented information.

For the first time, readers were exposed to mass media through the proliferation of printed materials. Within many of these tomes, articles describing scientific discoveries ran alongside fictional stories, blurring the lines of discernment between fact and fiction for the emerging middle-class reading public. In addition, public displays of legitimate scientific demonstrations coincided with spectacular exhibitions designed to

S. F. Heskin (✉)
University of York, York, UK

E. Gomel, S. Bacon (eds.), *Lunar Gothic*, Palgrave Gothic,
https://doi.org/10.1007/978-3-031-92621-1_4

entertain the public with elaborate hoaxes advertised as scientific discoveries. These cultural phenomena contributed to indoctrinating a sceptical worldview into Antebellum society.

By 1827, technological advancements, namely the new steam-driven, two-cylinder press, increased newspaper production to roughly 7000 copies per hour. As the cost of paper plummeted, newspaper production doubled, further driving the price down from approximately six cents a copy to one cent in the following decade (Fang 1997: 48–52). As such, affordability expanded readership to include classes outside of the elite.

Drawing the attention of this emerging audience of the working class was mass information ranging from pertinent news stories to works borne from prominent Antebellum writers' imaginations. It was not uncommon to read an astronomy article detailing the spectacular occurrence of a meteor shower, side by side with an extraordinary story detailing a man's voyage to Antarctica on a mysterious galleon ("MS. Found in a Bottle" by Edgar Allan Poe 1833). Further blurring the lines between factual accounts and fictitious entertainment was the complexity of literary language employed by the authors of these editorials. Men of science constructed their narratives with poetic prose to capture their readers' imaginations, while fiction authors utilised scientific discourse to shape their compositions with an air of academic authority. The result left the general public in a state of unbalanced thought, questioning the potential validity of authoritative voices portrayed in the media. On this stage, Edgar Allen Poe and Richard Adams Locke found an audience primed for information and entertainment.

In 1835, two separate series of articles appeared in prominent periodicals claiming to be factual accounts detailing explorations of the Moon. The first, written by Edgar Allen Poe, appeared in the June issue of the *Southern Literary Messenger*. The second series of articles, written by Richard Adams Locke, followed a few months later in the August edition of *The Sun*. Both narratives fluctuate between verisimilitude and fatuity, creating sensational accounts and leaving their audiences struggling to decipher between fact and fiction.

Poe begins his story, "The Unparalleled Adventure of One Hans Pfaall", with the public account of an unusual manuscript detailing a man named Hans Pfaall's journey to the Moon. The document, presented to the Burgomasters of Rotterdam, entails the extraordinary adventure of how Pfaall successfully navigated himself to the Moon with the fabrication of a hot air balloon equipped with an ingenious device that compresses the vacuum of space into breathable air. Poe constructs the first half of his story by describing the construction of the balloon in extreme scientific detail. The second part of the journey describes the harrowing events Hans experienced in his ascent to the Moon in the novelistic style of an adventure tale. However, the descriptive language becomes vague once the protagonist reaches his destination, and the narrative jumps forward again to the present. Poe leaves us in the end with an overtly comical scene of incompetent authorities vying to validate the absurd tale.

Similarly, Richard Locke's "The Great Moon Hoax" narrative seeks to describe astronomical discoveries made by Sir John Herschel, the famous astronomer, at the Cape of Good Hope through a great telescope he both designed and built. The text begins by describing the telescope's construction with intricate scientific detail. The narrative's latter parts chronicle the incredible discoveries of the landscape and inhabitants of the Moon, concluding with the destruction of the observatory in an immense fire. Many readers in 1835 believed *The Sun*'s serial articles were factual accounts. This reception was partly due to its presentation as a reprint from the *Edinburgh Journal of Science*, a small-press scientific journal that had ceased publication in 1832.

When reading these articles through the lens of a modern worldview, it is difficult to understand how these hoaxes could have been understood as anything other than fiction. Although the claims of these articles as successfully duping the public have been overstated, it is still true that some readers accepted these works as factual accounts at the time of their publication. To understand the reception of these articles by Antebellum readers, we need to examine the constructs of the media and the dissemination of information particular to mid-nineteenth-century society. With this in mind, this chapter examines the Lunar Hoaxes of Edgar Allen Poe and Richard Adams Locke through the lens of the contrasting ideologies of the Antebellum period in an age of prolific scientific and technological advances. By examining the intertextuality of "The Unparalleled Adventure of One Hans Pfaall" and "The Great Moon Hoax", this chapter illustrates how these satiric articles reveal the opposing creeds of optimism and doubt in a rapidly changing world. It will also demonstrate the works' engagement with society's widespread curiosity for the unknown while revealing the concurrent contrast of awe and scepticism towards scientific advancement and authorial authority.

Historically, scholarship on the moon hoaxes generally follows lines of inquiry that either examine the articles as the first examples of science fiction or as commentary on the Antebellum print revolution. For instance, in the Introduction to *Voyage to the Moon and Other Imaginary Lunar Flights of Fancy in Antebellum America*, Paul Gutjahr claims that "Poe's 'Hans Pfaall' set the course for what would later come to be called 'hard science fiction' writing" (Gutjahr 2018: Intro xx). Alternatively, in his article "Poor Poe: On the Literature of Revulsion", Gavin Jones argues that more than being a pioneering work of science fiction, "Hans Pfaall" questions the system of authoritative credibility. According to Jones, the narrative's emphasis "lies not in establishing the scientific validity of fictional events, but rather in establishing the fictionality of the authoritative discourse that claims credit for 'news,' 'science,' and 'fact'" (Jones 2011: 8).

In the case of Locke's "The Great Moon Hoax", many scholars believe that Locke intended to create a satire aimed at the "plurality of worlds" theory and its proponents. In this vein, Doug Dunlop, for instance, argues that Locke believed science should be separate from religion and not utilised as support for "questionable religious theories" like the debate over the plurality of worlds (Dunlop 2013), and was directly placing Reverend Thomas Dick in his crosshairs.

Recent scholarship, such as Maurice S. Lee's "Genre, Science, and 'Hans Pfaall'" and Lara Langer Cohen's *The Fabrication of American Literature*, discusses the construct of narrative under conditions of uncertainty prevalent in the Antebellum age. In his article, Lee suggests that Poe's intentions were less an attempt at fabricating a hoax and instead functioned as "a test of verisimilitude during the scientific and print revolutions of the Antebellum period", thus performing as "a daring experiment and exhibition" (Lee 2018: 17). This chapter builds on these ideas by exploring the composition of storytelling in both tales, which utilise a combination of factual scientific knowledge with fictitious flights of fancy. In essence, although entertainment may have been the intention of these works, they are historical commentary giving insight into some of the core tenets of Antebellum society while giving birth to the new literary genre of science fiction.

Fraud in Antebellum America took many forms. Rapid technological advances coupled with the proliferation of mass media made the social soil ripe for scam artists, hoaxsters, and "confidence" men. Additionally, as commerce shifted from agricultural to industrial, moving large portions of the population from rural to urban settings, opportunities arose in all trade areas to capitalise on the curiosity and ambitions of the emerging working classes. Promises of miraculous cures, affordable utopian real estate, inflated currency, and proof of the existence of mythical creatures and men on the Moon abounded in a landscape void of any regulatory system to debunk false claims. As a result, early nineteenth-century Americans were both captivated and confused while navigating the murky waters of truth and untruth. It was these very issues that Poe and Locke were commenting on in their satires, cleverly using the vehicle of the hoax as an additional metaphor for critiquing the Gothic machinations of their society.

From 1834 through 1836, rapid economic expansion exploded throughout the nation. Fuelling this fire was a massive real estate boom coinciding with America's westward expansion, made possible by the transportation revolution connecting the country from East to West. Gold and silver began to pour into the United States from foreign countries, prompting the banks to print more paper money, driving the supply rate up to 30% (1834–1836) from a mere 2.7% in the early 1830s (Campbell 2020). Financial institutions, known as "property banks", began to spring up to accommodate loans to enslavers in the South and speculators purchasing large quantities of land in the West. The acquisition of these lands derived primarily from the expansion of slavery and the forced removal of Native Americans from their ancestral lands, which provided enormous funding for the government (Campbell 2020).

Some of the most prolific purchasers of these Government lands were capitalists from the eastern states. Termed "speculators", these investors were seduced by the promise of fast and furious investment returns. Speculative returns were to arise from resale at an exorbitant price or by charging inflated interest on loans to legitimate settlers to purchase their lands. In one account, a prominent speculator named Cyrus Woodman received letters claiming "700 per cent appreciation in western land investments in eighteen months and that one could make 100 per cent a year in such purchases" (Gates 1969: 307). Nevertheless, these speculations proved to be exaggerations, and numerous stories began to appear in newspapers telling tales of shady speculators desperate to sell their land. One such complaint appeared in *The Union*, a newspaper circulating in Nashville, Tennessee, from 1835 to 1837. The complaint read, "those who have been to the West, where towns are made in the night (on paper) sold in an hour and built up in a week have seen the arts of speculators who purchase a quarter section of land, lay it out in town lots, make a map of the surrounding country, laying down railroads and canals, all centring in their towns, which is thus demonstrated to be the future 'Emporium of the west'" (Walters 2010: 16). The language of this complaint reveals the scepticism that Antebellum society was experiencing in response to what Aaron Skaolski termed the "Great American Land Bubble" that swept up both capitalists and the ordinary man in its wake.

Thus, it is not surprising that both Poe and Locke satirically turned their attention to the Moon as the new frontier, ripe with real estate prime for the taking. In fact, the September 5, 1835, edition of Philadelphia's *Atkinson's Saturday Evening Post* printed a land auction advertisement from the *Commercial Advertiser* that read:

> GREAT CHANCE FOR SPECULATION—Will be sold on the first day of April next, at 11 o'clock, P.M.,... nine thousand building lots situated in the territory recently discovered by Sir John Herschel. The tract composed of three lots is that in which the vegetable gold is found. It has hitherto been sold as pasture land, giving nourishment to large flocks of sheep with one horn and a flap over their eyes, which will be sold with the lots if desired.

Of course, this ad ran after Locke's story was revealed as a hoax; nonetheless, it also mocked the Antebellum fervour for real estate opportunities.

In both Poe's and Locke's narratives, each author describes the potential merits of the lunar landscape in vastly different ways. In Poe's story, Hans Pfaall tumbles "headlong into the very heart of a 'fantastical-looking city,' finding himself amid a 'parcel of idiots'" (Poe 1850: 43). Perhaps here, Poe is commenting on the fantastical speculations that consumed investors during the real estate boom of the 1830s, along with the exaggerated promises of speculators plotting cities on meagre parcels of land.

In contrast, Locke's narrative describes dazzling jewel-encrusted landscapes of quartz crystals resembling precious gemstones rising from the hilltops "like church steeples in the vales of Westmoreland" (Locke 1859: 32). So vast are these fields of jewels that the narrator declares, "In fact we could not conjecture where this gorgeous land of enchantment terminated; for as the rotary motion of the planet bore these mountain summits from our view, we became further remote from their western boundary" (Locke 1859: 34). It is interesting to note the language that Locke uses in his descriptions of the crystal landscapes. By choosing the countryside of Westmoreland as a comparison, he is perhaps creating a pun that refers to the accumulation of "*more land*" in the *West* that was driving the real estate frenzy in 1835. Furthermore, this "land of enchantment" appeared boundless, much like the speculations of wealth promulgated by the eager Antebellum investors.

Another analogy that Locke could be asserting is the connection between land value and natural resources, which prompted some investors to acquire copious acres of reserved land in the western United States. In one account, a group of capitalists from New England ventured "to buy 77,220 acres of reserved land believed to contain lead ore [becoming] the first scheme to establish a monopoly over a natural resource in the territory" (Gates 1969: 309). In this scenario, Locke's crystals represent the valuable minerals in the western lands, which attracted investors seeking to establish mining rights for an enormous profit.

By the 1830s, the public's fascination with mechanical, technological, and scientific wonders accelerated. Driven by the wealth of knowledge now widely accessible to the masses via the thriving newspaper industry, scientific discoveries became a popular source of entertainment. As Maurice Lee points out, "empirical experiments required witnesses to verify their outcomes, and as a result, they were often performed not only in the controlled environments of laboratories but also in venues that mixed education and entertainment, scientific method, and spectacle" (Lee 2018: 343). Such scientific lectures, known as the Lyceum movement, attracted large public gatherings to witness incredible scientific demonstrations, becoming one of the most popular forms of adult entertainment during the Antebellum period. This pageantry is demonstrated in "Hans Pfaall" as Poe begins his story with "a vast crowd of people,... assembled in the great square of the Exchange in the well-conditioned city of Rotterdam" (Poe 1850: 1). The gathering crowd witnesses a phenomenon "not to be in any manner comprehended" as the onlookers "stood open-mouthed below". Poe is recreating the atmosphere of the Lyceum movement, setting the stage for his unparalleled astronomical adventure.

Much like the whimsical balloon in "Hans Pfaall", scientific lecturers recognised the need for a visual demonstration to captivate their audience using various apparatuses to amaze and entertain the public. These scientific displays rapidly increased in popularity during the Antebellum period and were increasingly tailored to the interests of the masses. According to author Sally Gregory Kohlstedt, "Expository science, or popularised science, reached unprecedented and perhaps unsustainable levels in the first half of the nineteenth century. Audiences heard prominent lecturers speak in terms relevant to their situation, transposing themes of industry and technology with those of science without self-consciousness" (Kohlstedt 1990: 439). A large part of this tailoring process involved using unself-conscious language designed to engage the non-scientific public, simultaneously educating and entertaining. However, just as the scientific community was utilising the popular vernacular, Locke carefully constructed his language to emulate the high-brow discourse of academia. As stated by author William N. Griggs, the hoax's success was due to Locke's ability to maintain "a pretty firm grasp upon the credulity of nearly all but thoroughly taught minds, by its plausible display of scientific erudition" (Griggs 1852: 17).

Many popular scientific displays began in the parlour rooms of affluent society's armchair enthusiasts. This population segment included the upper classes of society with the means to attend university, travel, and acquire collections of curiosities. However, members of the population outside of genteel society began to resent the implications that scientific knowledge belonged exclusively within the aristocratic domain, viewing these private social gatherings with antagonism and scepticism (Kohlstedt 1990: 433). As a result, parodies of these pretentious lectures for the privileged began to arise in print and public forums, criticising the practice of obtaining knowledge solely to appear cultured in high society. One example was a humorous frontispiece designed by Charles Jameson Grant for the *Penny Magazine of the Society for the Diffusion of Useful Knowledge* in 1832 (https://wellcomecollection.org/works/hdawwp83/items). Grant illustrates a parody of the "March of Intellect". In the centre are caricatures of Lord Brougham, one of the founders of the *Edinburgh Review*. Brougham was known for his unfounded attacks on the findings of famed astronomer Sir William Herschel, the father of the astronomer John Herschel from Locke's Moon hoax.

One of the most recognisable figures of the Lyceum movement is P.T. Barnum. Barnum's American Museum marked a vital intersection between science and popular culture. The professional, scientific community members genuinely valued the specimens exhibited in the natural history collections, which included a menagerie of live animals featuring the first exhibition of a hippopotamus in the United States (Betts 1959: 355). Ever the greatest showman, Barnum marketed his exhibitions through "the potent power of the printer's ink" (Barnum 1888: 61), placing a series of sensational advertisements emphasising the alleged scientific validity of his specimens. Such claims were verified in some cases by prominent scientists, including Professor Louis Agassiz of Harvard University, who testified to the authenticity and importance of Barnum's whales in 1861 (Betts 1959: 356). Although Agassiz's testimony was legitimate, Barnum revelled in confusing the lines between fact and fiction to a gullible public. For example, to promote his famous "Feejee Mermaid", in 1842, Barnum invented a British scientist named "Dr J. Griffin", citing him as the procurer of the astonishing creature (Cook 2001: 82). Of course, the scientist and the mermaid proved an elaborate hoax, but not before thousands of patrons parted with their twenty-five-cent pieces into Barnum's pocket.

The art of the con in Antebellum America capitalised on the public's scepticism as much as it contributed to it. At some point, the public felt compelled to dispel disbelief for curiosity and the draw of potentially outsmarting the conman. As Jonathan Elmer suggests, the dynamics between the con and its subject "depends upon transforming the sceptical witness into the willing participant" (Elmer 1996: 181). Poe and Locke were, to a degree, operating within the principles of this dynamic. Nevertheless, their ultimate purpose was to expose the cultural propensity of the hoax by using satire to comment on the absurdity of society's willingness to entertain the ridiculous. As Griggs argues, "Locke was precisely the writer to check so mischievous an epidemic of imaginative and spurious philosophy, by a well-timed satire, 'out-heroding Herod' in its imaginative creations, supplying to satiety the morbid appetite for scientific wonders then universally raging" (Griggs 1852: 17).

Since the Ancient Greeks, humanity has contemplated the universe and humankind's place in it. One theory that developed in antiquity was the concept of a plurality of worlds existing in the vast universe. The principle of this theory is that if we believe the number of atoms and the universe to be infinite, then philosophically, the existence of other worlds containing the same properties and laws as our world is theoretically probable. This concept spurned the belief that these other worlds could potentially be inhabitable. Beginning in the Renaissance and prevailing through the nineteenth century, the theory adapted a religious subtext that asserted the belief that God, in His infinite wisdom, would have created other worlds as perfect as our own (Dunlop 2013). Many prominent astronomers embraced aspects of this theory. Even William Herschel contemplated the potentiality of life on the Moon and the Sun. However, one of the leading advocates of this theory in the Antebellum period was the admired author and amateur astronomer Reverend Thomas Dick. Reverend Dick published several texts claiming that over 21 trillion inhabitants exist within the solar system, of which over 4 billion reside on the Moon (Dick 1838: 305). Reverend Dick was not alone in his belief in the potential existence of Lunarians. For example, an article published in 1824 by German astronomer Baron Franz von Paula Gruithuisen cited his observations evidencing roads and monumental architecture on the Moon's surface (Dunlop 2013).

The core ambition of Reverend Dick was to reconcile religion with empirical science, which was the antithesis of Locke's viewpoint. Locke supported the separation of science and religion, believing that the adulteration of empirical science should not form a basis supporting dubious religious theories such as the plurality of worlds (Higgitt 2015). Based on the evidence of Locke's opinion, many historians believe that his "Great Moon Hoax" was a direct attack on Thomas Dick and his theories of cosmic pluralism. Griggs, for example, credits an article Dr. Thomas Dick allegedly wrote in the 1826 edition of the *Edinburgh New Philosophical Journal* as the inspiration for Locke's narrative (Griggs 1852: 4–5). However, although an article by Dr Dick appears in that volume (Dick 1826: 41–51), he is not the author of the passage to which Griggs is referring (Jameson 1826: 389–390).

Nevertheless, the passage describes the "discoveries" of Gruithuisen and, therefore, could have inspired some of the imagery described in Locke's story. Undoubtedly, his outlandish descriptions of humanoids with batwings, creatures resembling unicorns, and gem-laden landscapes mock the ideas central to the plurality of worlds theory. Furthermore, his narrative includes a passage describing a temple, potentially addressing Gruithisen's claims of Lunarian structures while positing a satiric commentary on the "religio-scientific rhapsodies" of Reverend Dick (Griggs 1852: 8):

> It was a temple—a fane of devotion, or of science, which, when consecrated to the Creator, *is* devotion of the loftiest order; for it exhibits his attributes purely free from the masquerade, attire, and blasphemous caricature of controversial creeds, and has the seal and signature of his own hand to sanction its aspirations. (Locke 1859: 43)

Locke's phrasing with the use of terms like "blasphemous caricature" and "controversial creeds" seems to be sardonically addressing the issues surrounding the intersection of science and religion that was at the core of Reverend Dick's philosophies.

Poe, too, seems to devote a few lines of his story to an even more astonishing belief held by some proponents of the plurality of worlds theory, known as counterpart theory. Beginning with Democritus, this belief hypothesised that multiple versions of every human exist in other worlds analogous to our own (Warren 2004: 358). At the end of "Hans Pfaall", Poe illustrates this "doppelgänger" theory by recounting:

> ...the incomprehensible connection between each particular individual in the moon, with some particular individual on earth—a connection analogous with and depending upon that of the orbs of the planet and the satellite, and by means of which the lives and destinies of the inhabitants of one are interwoven with the lives and destinies of the inhabitants of the other (Poe 1850: 44).

The synchronic relationship between the citizens of both worlds in Poe's narrative echoes the ancient Greek philosophies on the atomic arrangement of the cosmos.

Much of the scholarship on "Hans Pfaall" addresses Poe's allegorical use of the balloon and bellows imagery, proposing these images as metaphors parodying the literary nationalist system of the mid-nineteenth century known as the puffing system. Editors and reviewers established the American puffing system to promote or "puff up" American literature as a unique and valuable expression of national literary culture. However, these critical acclaims were bestowed upon texts regardless of their artistic virtue. The widespread application of puffery in Antebellum America became the *de rigueur* of literary criticism, developing into the less-than-sincere practices of self-reviews, paid reviews, and exchanges of favours (Cohen 2012: 33). The anonymity of literary reviews facilitated these practices and legitimised their authors under pretences. Akin to Barnum's sensational advertisements, sceptical readers argued that puffery exaggerated the merits of particular works, adding another layer of duplicity to a society already plagued by deception.

As a literary critic, Poe was an outspoken detractor of the puffing system, declaring American literati as "one vast perambulating humbug" (Poe 1841: 90). His criticism of puffery permeates the narrative of "Hans Pfaall". One can easily read the metaphors of the inflated balloon, "manufactured entirely of dirty newspapers", in the shape of a "fools-cap" (perhaps referring to foolscap folio, a traditional paper size used in printing), to the assembly of burghers who "puffed" on their pipes while observing the "curiosity, and the cause of so much smoke" (Poe 1850: 4).

While Poe's language constitutes his thinly veiled criticism of puffery, Locke's "Great Moon Hoax" utilises language in a verisimilitude of the language used by literary reviewers. In the introductory paragraph of his narrative, the author promises "the whole civilised world, recent discoveries in Astronomy which will build an imperishable monument to the age in which we live, and confer upon the present generation of the human race a proud distinction through all future time" (Locke 1859: 1). Such a grandiose statement is precisely the type of verbiage employed by proponents of puffery.

In an 1835 lecture, "American Criticism on American Literature", Edward S. Gould claims that the biggest obstacle to advancing American literature was "an unfortunate propensity, on the part of the public, to admire indiscriminately, and with little qualification, every thing American" (Gould 1836: 7). Gould continues by pointing out that the lack of censorship in literary reviews of the time posed an additional obstacle to the advancement of a nationalistic literary culture. However, not all reviewers were engaging in the dubious practice of puffery.

Reviewers often published their critiques in periodicals boasting widespread circulations with acknowledged reputations. This exposure granted the authors a level of influence bolstered by the public's trust in the press's authority. Many of these reviewers were not professional critics but community leaders such as educators and high-standing members of the religious communities. Such reviewers deciphered texts through the lens of Antebellum morality and social tenets, basing the value of fictional stories on the moral content of their characters and plots. An author must, for example, dispense appropriate punishment upon his villainous characters and recompense to his heroes to be considered to have produced a "good" novel (Machor 2011: 54).

Discernible distinctions between genres were also crucial to reviewers, especially in drawing a hard line between fiction and nonfiction. For instance, stories fusing natural science, politics, and philosophies with the imaginative narrative were deemed crude, inharmonious, and, therefore, "bad" novels (Machor 2011: 55). These opinion pieces were important for shaping how the fiction-reading public received and interpreted fictional texts.

Publication of literary critiques and reviews inevitably influenced the public's reception of novels. In an essay discussing the critic's duties, Poe asserts that the literati were unduly enforcing their opinions upon the reading public based on their preference for specific authors. According to Poe:

> In a criticism on Bryant published in the last number of this magazine, I was at some pains in pointing out the distinction between the popular 'opinion' of the merits of contemporary authors and that held and expressed of them in private literary society. The former species of 'opinion' can be called 'opinion' only by courtesy. It is the public's own, just as we consider a book our own when we have bought it. In general, this opinion is adopted from the journals of the day, and I have endeavored to show that the cases are rare indeed in which these journals express any other sentiment about books than such as may be attributed directly or indirectly to the authors of the books. (Poe 1984: 1118)

Perhaps Poe was right. How accurate were these interpretations of fictional literature regarding the author's intent? Following the revelation of Locke's moon story as a hoax, many figures in the press applauded his ingenuity and accomplished literary prowess. Nevertheless, others "denounced him, with equal vehemence, as a charlatan in science, and imposter in principle, deserving unmitigated execration" (Griggs 1852: 31). Locke himself expressed disappointment in the public's reception of his narrative. Conveying his dismay to his friends, Locke made the following statement: "If the story be either received as a veritable account, or rejected as a hoax, it is quite evident that it is an abortive satire; and, in either case, I am the best self-hoaxed man in the whole community" (Griggs 1852: 30). The satirical intention was not "quite evident" to at least some of the public as the debates continued between sceptics and believers.

It is interesting to contemplate if critics and reviewers played a role in the public's reception of the Moon hoaxes. Both Poe and Locke expressed dissatisfaction with the misinterpreted responses to their tales, with both authors denying the intention to deceive their audiences deliberately. Ten years after the publication of "Hans Pfaall", Poe made the following admission: "I gave up the idea of imparting very close verisimilitude to what I should write—that is to say, so close as really to deceive" (Poe 1984: 1215). Nonetheless, at least initially, the audience eagerly embarked on his unparalleled adventure into the unknown.

By approaching these texts through the lens of Antebellum society, we can gain insight into the ethos of a mid-nineteenth-century culture. The documented fact that a certain percentage of the population readily believed in the plausibility of the veracity of the Moon stories speaks to the tenets of the era surrounding conviction versus scepticism. Moreover, beginning with the prolific dissemination of public information, the rapid advancements in science and technology set the stage for fraudsters to capitalise on the public's curiosity, obscuring the lines between fact and fiction, with minstrel shows touting dubious discoveries running alongside legitimate scientific exhibitions during the Lyceum movement.

Furthermore, America's enthusiastic westward expansion led to duplicitous practices by speculators, which had ruinous consequences for some of the most vulnerable segments of the population. Finally, controversial religious theories expounding the existence of life on other planets led to debates over the separation of empirical science and religion. All these simultaneous events contributed to an age of uncertainty. In response, Poe and Locke provided commentary on these issues while experimenting with the boundaries of credibility within this cultural state of perplexity.

In many ways, today's America is akin to Antebellum society. For example, the explosion of the Internet and cable television networks brought global information to the masses on an unprecedented scale. Further, rapid technological advances have delivered that capability into the palms of our hands. Recent litigation involving social media corporations proves that fake news, hoaxes, and false advertising are as prevalent and indiscernible today as in 1835.

As our world grows smaller through modern modes of communication, our gaze returns to the heavens and their infinite possibilities as the final frontier. In 2025, almost two centuries after the publication of the historic Moon hoaxes, NASA will launch Artemis III, which will endeavour to land two astronauts on the Moon. This mission comes just over half a century since the 1969 lunar landing of Apollo 11, which conspiracy theorists still postulate was a hoax. Despite numerous efforts to debunk the hoax theory, NASA's chief historian Roger Launius reports that approximately 5% (almost 16 million people) of the American population still believe the Apollo moon landing is humbug (Howell 2022). One wonders what Poe would make of that, knowing that his imaginary space odyssey became a reality only to meet with enduring scepticism. Perhaps, in this new age of uncertainty, our fictional narratives will give birth to new possibilities which will undoubtedly encounter a healthy dose of scepticism.

References

Barnum, Phineas Taylor. 1888. *Life of P.T. Barnum, Written by Himself, Including His Golden Rules for Moneymaking: Brought Up to 1888.* Buffalo: The Courier Company.

Betts, John Rickards. 1959. P. T. Barnum and the Popularization of Natural History. *Journal of the History of Ideas* 20 (3): 353–368.

Campbell, Steven. 2020. Panic of 1837. *The Economic Historian.* https://economic-historian.com/2020/11/panic-of-1837/. Accessed 28 Oct 2024.

Cohen, Lara Langer. 2012. *The Fabrication of American Literature: Fraudulence and Antebellum Print Culture.* Philadelphia: University of Pennsylvania Press.

Cook, James W. 2001. *The Arts of Deception: Playing with Fraud in the Age of Barnum.* Cambridge, MA: Harvard University Press.

Dick, Thomas. 1826. Description of a New Reflecting Telescope, Denominated the Aerial Reflector. *The Edinburgh New Philosophical Journal* 1:41–51.

Dick, Thomas. 1838. *Celestial Scenery: Or The Wonders of the Planetary System Displayed Illustrating the Perfections of Deity and a Plurality of Worlds.* New York: Harpers and Brothers.

Dunlop, Doug. 2013. The Great Moon Hoax or Was It—The Joke's on Who? *Smithsonian Libraries/Unbound.* Smithsonian Institution. https://blog.library.si.edu/blog/2013/09/04/the-great-moon-hoax-or-was-it-the-jokes-on-who/. Accessed 28 Oct 2024.

Elmer, Jonathan. 1996. *Reading at the Social Limit: Affect, Mass Culture, and Edgar Allan Poe.* Stanford: Stanford University Press.

Fang, Irving E. 1997. *A History of Mass Communication: Six Information Revolutions.* Boston: Focal Press.

Gates, Paul W. 1969. Frontier Land Business in Wisconsin. *The Wisconsin Magazine of History* 52 (4): 306–327.

Gould, E. Sherman. 1836. *American Criticism on American Literature.* New York: Mercantile Library Association.

Griggs, William N. 1852. The Celebrated "Moon Story": Its Origin and Incidents: With a Memoir of the Author, and an Appendix, Containing I. In *An Authentic Description of the Moon, II. A New Theory of the Lunar Surface in Relation to That of the Earth.* New York: Bunnell and Price.

Gutjahr, Paul. 2018. *Voyage to the Moon and Other Imaginary Lunar Flights of Fancy in Antebellum America.* New York: Anthem Press.

Higgitt, Rebekah. 2015. The Great Moon Hoax and the Christian Philosopher. The Guardian.com. https://www.theguardian.com/science/the-h-word/2015/feb/05/great-moon-hoax-christian-philosopher-history-science/. Accessed 28 Oct 2024.

Howell, Elizabeth. 2022. Moon-Landing Hoax Still Lives On. But Why? Space.com. https://www.space.com/apollo-11-moon-landing-hoax-believers.html. Accessed 28 Oct 2024.

Jameson, Robert. 1826. The Moon and Its Inhabitants. *The Edinburgh New Philosophical Journal* 22:389–390.

Jones, Gavin. 2011. Poor Poe: On the Literature of Revulsion. *American Literary History* 23 (1): 1–18.

Kohlstedt, Sally Gregory. 1990. Parlors, Primers, and Public Schooling: Education for Science in Nineteenth-Century America. *Isis* 81 (3): 424–445.

Lee, Maurice S. 2018. Genre, Science, and 'Hans Pfaall'. In *The Oxford Handbook of Edgar Allan Poe*, ed. J. Gerald Kennedy and Scott Peeples, 337–350. Oxford: Oxford University Press.

Locke, Richard Adams. 1859. Great Astronomical Discoveries Lately Made by Sir John Herschel, L.L., D.F.R.S., etc., at the Cape of Good Hope. In *The Moon Hoax; or A Discovery That the Moon Has a Vast Population of Human Beings*, ed. William Gowans, 7–63. New York: William Gowans.

Machor, James L. 2011. *Reading Fiction in Antebellum America: Informed Response and Reception Histories, 1820–1865.* Baltimore: Johns Hopkins University Press.

Poe, Edgar Allan. 1833. M.S. Found in a Bottle. *Baltimore Saturday Visiter 3* (38): 1.

Poe, Edgar Allan. 1841. Review of The Quacks of Helicon, A Satire by L.A. Wilmer. *Graham's Magazine* 19 (2): 90–93.

Poe, Edgar Allan. 1850. The Unparalleled Adventure of One Hans Pfaall. In *The Works of the Late Edgar Allan Poe, With Notices of His Life and Genius*, ed. Nathaniel Parker Willis, James Russell Lowell, and Rufus W. Griswold, 1–52. New York: J.S. Redfield.

Poe, Edgar Allan. 1984. The Literati of New York City. In *Edgar Allan Poe: Essays and Reviews*, ed. G. R. Thompson, 1118–1222. New York: Library of America.

Walters, William D. 2010. Selling Location: Illinois Town Advertisements 1835–1837. Paper published by the Department of Geography-Geology, Illinois State University. https://geo.illinoisstate.edu/downloads/walters_towns.pdf. Accessed 28 Oct 2024.

Warren, James. 2004. Ancient Atomists on the Plurality of Worlds. *The Classical Quarterly New Series* 54 (2): 354–365.

CHAPTER 5

When the Full Moon Rises: Updating the Lycanthropic Myth Through the Double, Masculinities, and the Coming of Age in Stephen King's *Cycle of the Werewolf*

Marta Miquel-Baldellou

Introduction

As a contemporary master of the horror genre, Stephen King has been heralded for renovating and updating the Gothic tradition, thus giving rise to modern horror narratives grounded in the fiction of classic predecessors. As Ben Indick points out, in his fiction, King has mirrored the main variants in horror that he has inherited, but in so doing, he has also added his own distinctive style (2007: 5). In his major early novels, King devised characters, motifs, and plot lines on the basis of prominent archetypes in the horror genre, as is the case with the vampire in *Salem's Lot* (1977), the house haunted by ghosts in *The Shining* (1975), and the monstrous living dead in *Pet Sematary* (1983), which lay their roots in the Gothic tradition.

M. Miquel-Baldellou (✉)
University of Lleida, Lleida, Spain
e-mail: marta.miquel@udl.cat

E. Gomel, S. Bacon (eds.), *Lunar Gothic*, Palgrave Gothic,
https://doi.org/10.1007/978-3-031-92621-1_5

As Tony Magistrale claims, King's fiction is grounded in the nineteenth-century Gothic romance, particularly with regard to tropes like the pervasiveness of evil, the local region as a backdrop for puritan allegories, and the moral search for selfhood through the journey motif (2002: 100–103). In relation to these themes involving particular Gothic ambiences—like night in the woods—the presence of the moon becomes pervasive given its connotations of romantic legacy which evoke the dark side of nature, the prevalence of the irrational, and the role of dreams. If the moon illuminates the fall of the family manor in Edgar Allan Poe's tale and the walk into the woods in Nathaniel Hawthorne's short stories, in King's fiction, the vampire's pallid face is compared with the moon in *Salem's Lot*, Jack Torrance is warned to beware of the hotel boiler unless he wants to get to the moon in *The Shining*, and Louis Creed first lays eyes on Victor Pascow as a living dead creature once the moon sails out from behind a cloud in *Pet Sematary.* As a contemporary horror writer who pays tribute to the classic tradition, King resorts to the recurrent presence of the moon in historical Gothic literature to invoke the presence of the fantastic in his novels about vampires, ghosts, and monsters. Nevertheless, no other horror archetype has been so intrinsically linked with the moon as the lycanthrope, which King also revisits and renovates in his short novel *Cycle of the Werewolf*, published in 1983.

Over forty years after its publication, *Cycle of the Werewolf* remains the first and only graphic novella that King has published up to date. In an interview, Bernie Wrightson, who illustrated King's text, explains that editor Christopher Zavisa wanted him to work on the illustrations of King's writings, eventually coming up with the idea of a calendar and agreeing that it had to be "a werewolf story because the only thing [that] *all* months have in common is a full moon" (1993: 276). While Wrightson was in charge of the vignettes, King wrote each chapter with the events taking place on each month's night of the full moon, thus ending up with twelve chapters, in an attempt to portray the customary number of yearly full moons, even though, in his afterword, King admitted having taken liberties with the lunar cycle (2019: 128). Although the archetype of the werewolf in horror fiction is intrinsically related to the moon, as Bob Curran notes, the trope of the lycanthrope's transformation as a result of the effects of the moon only became widespread in modern books (2009: 14), particularly in the nineteenth century, when the metamorphosis of a man into a wolf entirely depended on the lunar phases and the presence of a full moon (2009: 170). As a result of early cinematic representations, Gothic narratives featuring the werewolf acquired further popularity in the twentieth century, thus consolidating werewolf lore with recurrent features, such as the cause of the transformation—which range from a curse or sin to disease and affliction, the portrayal of the lycanthrope as a hybrid creature that is partly human and partly beast, the full moon as the activating force which brings about the change, and the shooting of silver bullets as the only way to destroy the creature, which ultimately turns back to its former human form when its tormented existence finally comes to an end.

In *Cycle of the Werewolf*, King draws on the conventional tropes that configure the archetype of the lycanthrope, and hence, as Gary Hoppenstand and Ray Browne note, King does not change the fundamental motifs or recognisable elements of the original myth, but rather adapts them to suit the emotional needs of a contemporary audience (1987). Accordingly, the narrative focuses on Marty Coslaw, a ten-year-old boy in a wheelchair, who lives in the town of Tarker's Mills, in Maine, where a series of local murders begin to take place monthly at each full moon. Marty suspects and finally ascertains that a werewolf is responsible for the deaths, hence implying that one of his fellow citizens, as a member of their local community, transforms into a beast when the full moon rises. Along with his Uncle Al, Marty manages to discover the identity of the werewolf in order to destroy him and bring back the town and its people to its former peace. Hence, apart from adapting the werewolf myth to the everyday life of a local town, King's novella highlights certain aspects which contribute to revitalising werewolf lore and are intrinsically related to the pervasive and recurrent presence of the lunar cycle, which not only gives structural cohesion to the narrative, but also underscores particular discourses that have been associated with the horror archetype of the werewolf.

Along with the vampire and the monster, in *Danse Macabre*, King refers to the werewolf as one of the most influential archetypes in horror fiction, particularly insofar as he associates the lycanthrope with the Gothic character of the double, whereby the individual displays two opposing personalities, correspondingly embodying a reputable self, as an embodiment of the Jungian persona, which contrasts with an infamous self, which personifies the Jungian shadow. From classical times, as the etymological origins of the word reveal, the effects of the lunar or moon beams were believed to unleash the uncontrollable, "lunatic", self of the individual's psyche. In his novella, King draws on this premise, thus establishing a connection between the werewolf, given its intrinsically hybrid nature, and the split psyche of the archetype of the double. Besides, given its fragmented identity, the characterisation of the lycanthrope in King's novella also underscores gender anxieties, insofar as, with the advent of second-wave feminism in the decade of the 1980s, the archetype of the werewolf becomes an embodiment of repressed hegemonic masculinities, while it also hails the prevalence of conventional, and outdated, gender discourses in the wake of emerging alternative masculinities. Finally, as a coming-of-age narrative, King's novella also portrays its young protagonist's ageing process, as Marty Coslaw struggles to defeat the werewolf, thus engaging in a symbolic journey from childhood to adulthood, which enacts the clash between generations, since Marty must fight a member from the older generation to leave his childhood behind and gain entrance into the world of adults. In his novella, King thus revisits and updates the archetype of the werewolf, while engaging in discourses of masculinities and symbolic rites of passage in a coming-of-age narrative. Given the entanglement of the werewolf with the archetype of the double, the contrast between hegemonic and alternative masculinities, and the process of coming of age, the recurrent references to the moon that pervade the novella contribute to interpreting the archetype of the contemporary werewolf as an embodiment of the double, the clash between dominant and alternative masculinities, and the transition from childhood into adulthood.

"The Beast Is Supposed to Walk When the Moon Is Full": Werewolves and Doubles

In King's novella *Cycle of the Werewolf*, references to the moon, particularly when it is in its full phase, revert back to ancestral beliefs and superstitions that regard the full moon as a bad omen and associate it with the termination of a prosperous period. As is stated in the novella, "nights in Tarker's Mills as the moon grows fat for the third time that year are uncomfortable times" (2019: 37). The full moon is thus alleged to anticipate misfortune as a result of succumbing to forbidden acts or contravening some established laws which unleash the anger of primitive deities, thus revealing the latent prevalence of folklore and ancient creeds even in contemporary times. In some passages of the narrative, allusions are made to "those older gods that men worshipped from the safety of stone circles on moonlight nights" (2019: 113), thus establishing a connection between archaic cults and the ancestral influence of the moon. Legends in local folklore underscore the primitive worship of nature and the magic effects of the moon, thus giving rise to mythical creatures like the werewolf, which is intrinsically associated with the mesmerising effect that the moon may have on humans, thus underscoring the lunar capacity to pull humans back to their animal descent. From primitive myths and folklore, the archaic figure of the werewolf has evolved into an archetype in popular fiction, thus prevailing in the collective unconscious by means of its dissemination in horror narratives.

The recurrent portrayal of the werewolf in the Gothic tradition, both in literature and cinema, has contributed significantly to the configuration of its lore by virtue of a series of recognisable features, among them the trope of the full moon, which becomes one of the most distinctive constitutional elements of the myth. As Max Fincher notes, "werewolves transform themselves from human to beast by the light of the full moon, and they can only be killed by a silver bullet" (2016: 733). In King's novella, from Marty Coslaw's perspective as a young boy, the werewolf is described as an imposing beast, stating that it "stood about seven feet tall, was naked, was covered with dark hair all over his body", and it had "big teeth and green eyes", along with "claws [that] looked like hands" and "a tail" (2019: 78). Besides, as Fincher further claims, the archetype of the werewolf has conventionally been associated, on the one hand, with the theme of reversibility, insofar as its transformation blurs the lines between human and animal as well as civilised and savage, and on the other hand, with the theme of cannibalism, since werewolves usually devour their victims, thus displaying their animalistic condition, despite their ulterior transmutation back into their original human shape. Henceforth, the werewolf in King's novella is portrayed as an animal with human traits, thus noting that, "the beast is hunched over, but it is clearly walking on its two rear legs—walking the way a man would walk" (2019: 70). Besides, graphic depictions of the werewolf's attacks on one of its victims display how "the creature's jaws sink into the deltoid muscles of his back and rip upward with terrifying force" (2019: 56), hence reinforcing its cannibalistic instincts to consume human flesh, and in so doing, anticipating its conversion into a human body. Accordingly, the portrayal of the werewolf in King's novella amalgamates most of the conventional qualities attributed to the lycanthrope in horror fiction. Nevertheless, as a writer who revisits and reinterprets the Gothic tradition to adapt it to the anxieties and worries of contemporary audiences, King also introduces some innovations in the lycanthrope's portrayal which revise and renew the main tenets of werewolf lore.

As a result of its representation in early horror films, the werewolf is alleged to be the victim of some fatal curse, often derived from sorcery or black magic, which compels the beast to kill as soon as the full moon rises, and it is often considered an outsider that, in its hybrid condition, blurs established social boundaries. In contrast, though, in King's novella, the werewolf declares, "I wasn't bitten by a wolf or cursed by a gypsy [...] I picked some flowers for the vases in the church vestry one day last November [...] I never saw such flowers before [...] and they were dead before I could get back to town—they turned black, everyone—perhaps that was when it started to happen" (2019: 111). Accordingly, the cause of the werewolf's condition in King's novella does not respond to witchcraft or magic, but rather to the more down-to-earth circumstance of handling a poisonous plant. In fact, scholars like Curran put forward that the "inhaling of a plant such as wolfsbane" may lead a human creature to turn into a werewolf (2009: 184). Besides, since they often frequent moors and woods as suggestive of their existence on the fringes of communities, according to Fincher, werewolves metaphorically personify social outcasts who threaten to destabilise the established social order (2016: 733). Conversely, in King's novella, the werewolf not only happens to be a respectable citizen in the community, but a representative member of the established order, even to the extent that the local constable admits, "it was simply impossible to think of *that* person, of all persons, being the killer" (2019: 80). Correspondingly, even if the characterisation of the werewolf in King's novella comprises many of the traits pertaining to classic werewolf lore, King basically associates it with the archetype of the double, thus emphasising its latent psychological insight, which is precisely brought to the fore symbolically by effect of the moonlight.

According to King, the werewolf, together with the monster and the vampire, is an embodiment of the double and one of the three basic archetypes in horror fiction, which have their roots in the Victorian past (2000: 87). In fact, as King claims, his characterisation of the werewolf is grounded in Robert Louis Stevenson's classic novella featuring the double, in which Jekyll represents the side that is accessible to the public eye, whereas Hyde, as the concealed part of his personality, is only let loose occasionally, hence illustrating the pulse between the conscious and the subconscious selves, which are respectively and mythically endorsed through Apollonian and Dionysian impulses (2000: 90). In the novella, the description of the werewolf highlights its association with an embodiment of the double, as it represents "the sense of being an animal inside and looking perfectly normal outside", and it is described as "like two people [...] like split personalities", thus noting that the werewolf is unaware of "what he is doing when the moon gets full and he goes out and kills somebody" (2019: 77). Hence, in King's novella, the werewolf turns into a variant of the double, but, in contrast with Stevenson's novella, in King's text, the moon acquires particular relevance in order to trigger the appearance of the individual's repressed self.

King's portrayal of the werewolf as a personification of the double is rooted in the approach to lycanthropy as a psychological disorder, and particularly, as scholar Charlotte Otten notes, in a psychiatric condition which may range from schizophrenia to a dissociative typology (1990: 14). And yet, despite involving a case of psychic depersonalisation, in King's novella, the transformation from human into wolf only takes place explicitly by virtue of the full moon, which, in fact, reverts back to classical physiology. As Curran explains, "noting the way in which the weak gravitational pull of the moon affected the tides of oceans, Greek physicians assumed that it had a similar effect upon the moisture that the brain contained", thus causing "the civilised man [...] to be transformed by the pull of the moon into a raging, irrational creature", that is to say, "a lunatic", as a result of the effects of the moon (2009: 171). From classical times, the influence of the moon has been alleged to release an individual's basest instincts, which involved prioritising the subconscious to the detriment of the more rational and judicious self from a psychoanalytic perspective.

As a personification of the horror archetype of the double, for King, the werewolf narrative ultimately turns into a moral tale, and even a religious parable, of Victorian legacy (2000: 92). Nevertheless, as King further argues, if the clergy praised Stevenson's classic novella about the double insofar as it showed the negative results of releasing the individual's vilest instincts (2000: 82), King introduces a twist in this discourse by means of identifying the werewolf with Lester Lowe, who is not only a decent and upright citizen, but also the community's priest. Accordingly, King goes even further than Stevenson, not only turning the werewolf into a respectable member of the community, but also into the man who preaches about the need to repress the natural inclinations of the self. Besides, being an individual whose high sense of moral responsibility allows him to oversee the sinful proclivities of his congregation, Lester Lowe is still liable to succumb to the haunting effects of the moon, which unleash not only his parishioners' evil tendencies, but also his own repressed instincts. Likewise, along with the priest's subconscious propensities, the influence of the moon also releases his latent gender anxieties, particularly as regards the intrinsic association of the werewolf's physical strength, violent outbursts, and feral instincts with the conventional features of dominant masculinities.

"The Moon Disappears… Yet It Is There": Hegemonic and Alternative Masculinities

Owing to its conventional characterisation, as its hair grows exponentially, its muscles hyperextend, and its acts of brutality compel the man to revert back to his animal origins, the werewolf personifies the vicious and violent quality often attached to rough manhood. As Magistrale asserts, in King's novella, as a creature that has conventionally been associated with the male gender, the werewolf metaphorically embodies the kind of dominant masculinity that remains latent in the suburban communities which are often depicted in King's novels (1988: 98). More so, the werewolf makes its appearance once a month, when the full moon rises and, as Magistrale further claims, as a counterpart to the menstruation cycle, during which the female biological rhythms attain more prominence, the werewolf's monthly bestial transformation brings more attention to its coarse manners suggestive of dominant masculinities (1988: 98). Moreover, if the werewolf has conventionally been categorised as male, conversely, even if it is responsible for releasing the basest male instincts in man, in terms of gender, the moon has traditionally been regarded as female. In particular, as Curran explains, in classical mythology, the moon was associated with a triple moon goddess, who comprised Selene as the divine embodiment of the moon often associated with unpredictable behaviour, Artemis as the personification of the nocturnal hunting frenzy given the fact that some animals chased their prey at night, and Luna as the incarnation of the folly characterising lunatics under the influence of the moon (2009: 171–179). In narratives that feature the archetype of the werewolf, it is precisely owing to the female influence of the full moon, which has an effect on tides and women's cycle, that a man releases his vicious instincts and literally turns into a beast. In werewolf lore, the female lunar influence—which has conventionally been related to magic and intuition as eminently feminine as opposed to logic and reason that have traditionally been categorised as masculine—is to be blamed for intoxicating men and urging them to regress to their ancestral origins as beasts.

In King's novella, given his role as priest, Laurence Lowe feels particularly concerned about keeping the intrinsic sinful inclinations of his congregation under check. In terms of gender, it seems relevant that the priest turns into a werewolf when he becomes infected by means of picking up flowers, thus suggesting that any display of rough masculinity on his behalf has been harshly repressed in the public eye. Likewise, Lowe's physical appearance is hardly associated with prominent masculine features, since "he can get away with only shaving once every three days", inasmuch as his hair is often remarkably scant (2019: 112). With this he is portrayed as a timid and sensitive individual who is troubled by bad dreams "from which he awakes, trembling" and "bathed in sweat" (2019: 45). Nevertheless, even if during the daytime the priest manages to repress his rough masculinity, under the influence of the full moon, he unleashes his subjugated desire for violence and wrath. The priest is often haunted by a recurring nightmare in which he is preaching in church when each of the members of his congregation turns into a wolf, until he discovers that his "hands protruding from the sleeves of his good black suitcoat have [also] become snaggled paws" (2019: 46), hence showing not only his fear that each of the figurative lambs in his flock might be a sinful wolf, but that he may also conceal a beast inside. This animalistic portrayal underscores that the precepts of dominant masculinities, which have been repressed for the benefit of the social order, may no longer remain under restraint. As sociologists Judy Chu, Michelle Porche, and Deborah Tolman argue, masculinity has conventionally been associated with features like "physical toughness, emotional stoicism, projected self-sufficiency, and heterosexual dominance over women" (2005: 94), which give way to the discourse of hegemonic masculinity, as coined by Raewyn Connell in 1987, which responds to "the configuration of gender practice" as endorsing "the legitimacy of patriarchy" (2005: 77). In King's novella, haunted by the influence of the full moon, which compels the individual to release his repressed inhibitions, the character of Lester Lowe displays his allegiance to hegemonic masculinity as he literally transforms into a beast, which contrasts with his quiet and conciliatory ways in daylight.

As a werewolf, Lowe displays his repressed brutal instincts and his turn for hegemonic masculinity upon choosing his victims, who either respond to other exponents of dominant masculinities—thus trying to repress in others what he is unable to subdue in himself, but also engaging in a sort of male competition—or to individuals who appear to subvert the established gender discourses—hence arising as a safeguarding embodiment of reactionary politics of gender. As cases in point, one of the werewolf's victims, Alfie Knopfler, is described as "neither scared nor worried; not scared because he weighs two-twenty and most of it is still good old Navy muscle" (2019: 53), thus highlighting his bravery and physical strength, whereas another of the werewolf's victims, Milt Sturmfuller, is a male abuser who "has kept his pretty, silent wife in a bondage of terror for twelve years now" (2019: 29). Conversely, the werewolf also slays a young woman, Stella Randolph, who opens the window of her bedroom willingly, on a night of the full moon, mistaking the werewolf for an ardent lover, thus depicting her as a woman who subverts the conventional prescriptions of gender, which are further challenged in Dan Attias's film adaptation of King's novella *Silver Bullet* (1985), since, in the film, Stella is pregnant and forsaken by her lover.

As an antagonist to Lowe, Marty Coslaw is a young paraplegic teenager who represents the advent of new masculinities. In contrast, Marty's father, Herman Coslaw, who has been indebted to the precepts of dominant patriarchal hegemonies, feels uneasy owing to the alternative sort of masculinity that Marty epitomises. As is stated in King's novella, as a physical education teacher, "Herman lives in a world of violently active children, kids who run races, bash baseballs, swim rally sprints", and "in the midst of directing all this he would sometimes look up and see Marty", which "made Herman nervous" (2019: 61), since he perceives that his son does not comply with the established precepts of dominant masculinity. As opposed to identifiers like action, dominance, and violence, which are conventionally associated with hegemonic male identity, Marty defines his manhood through values such as affection, considerate emotions, and interdependence, which Karla Elliott associates with "caring masculinities" (2016: 240), while he rejects gender violence and establishes respectful relationships with girls of his age, like his sister Kate. In addition, as he is coming of age, Marty discards the tenets of hegemonic masculinity represented by most of his male elders, and instead, he looks up to the kind of alternative masculinity that his Uncle Al—his mother's younger brother—represents. Rather than feeling subjected to established discourses of maleness which compel him to settle down and raise a family of his own, Uncle Al shows preference for indulging in some sort of sempiternal adolescence, and developing a close comradeship with his nephew Marty.

Accordingly, if the full moon urges Lowe to release his repressed instincts, the same influence on Marty involves his display of a new model of masculinity, which unites bravery with kindness. On a night of the full moon, Marty runs away from home to burst the fireworks that his Uncle

Al has given him as a present and, when the boy encounters the werewolf, he manages to save his life by throwing one of the fireworks at the beast. Despite his apparently weaker position regarding the beast's ferocity and strength, not only do Marty's deftness and ability to throw fireworks, which are suggestive of his young age, allow him to defeat the werewolf, if only temporarily, but his actions also suggest that the model of alternative masculinity that he epitomises may destroy the hegemonic masculinity that the werewolf typifies as a ferocious relic from the past. As a result of this, Marty injures the werewolf in the eye, which has metaphorical implications, as Niall Patton argues that the eye has conventionally been associated with male genitalia, thus implying that injuring the eye has often been interpreted psychoanalytically as an act of castration (2004: 868). Drawing on this psychoanalytic explanation, Marty thus disempowers the werewolf by means of a symbolic act of castration that deprives it of its phallic nature, thus threatening its adherence to dominant masculinities. If the rise of the full moon unleashes the werewolf's commitment to hegemonic masculinities characterised by violence and brutality, the influence of the full moon leads Marty to balance his caring nature with an unusual outburst of bravery that enables him to fight and defeat the beast. More so, as Marty struggles against his lycanthropic opponent, he manages to defeat his own fears that see Marty coming of age through a series of rites of initiation in the company of Uncle Al, who acts as his mentor.

"He's Waiting for the Full Moon": Rites of Passage and the Coming of Age

The narrative structure of King's novella is circular, insofar as it comprises a whole year, and the events are happening monthly, when there is a full moon, hence establishing this moment of the lunar cycle as the structuring event that gives unity and cohesion to the text. The changing of the seasons and the passage of time thus acquire particular significance in a narrative that revolves around the coming of age of its protagonist, Marty Coslaw, a ten-year-old paraplegic adolescent who is literally and metaphorically challenged to face his fears and anxieties, as he fights and defeats the werewolf that is threatening his hometown. As Magistrale claims, children in King's novels often go through traumatic experiences that urge them to act older and more sensibly than their young age would allow them, while they feel detached from their relatives and establish bonds with people away from the nuclear family in search of emotional stability

(2006: 82). Jonathan Davis adds to this by saying that in King's novels children are eventually compelled to cross the threshold onto adulthood by means of experiencing challenging events that allow them to gain insight into the imperfections of the world (1994: 48). He further notes that, having left behind the realm of imagination, adults often find it harder to accept the world of the irrational, whereas children carry the wisdom that elders often lack owing to the shortcomings of their adult reasoning (Davis 1994: 49). In King's novella, Marty comes of age as he realises that he must take responsibility for his own safety, but also for his family and town, thus finding himself in the position to rise to the occasion and react like an adult. Hence, as the lunar cycle progresses, and Marty accepts the challenge of defeating the werewolf, allegorically, he also engages in the process of becoming a man.

In King's fiction, there is usually a clash between older and younger generations, as elders have repressed their capacity to appreciate magic, which used to prevail in their childhood, whereas children are too close to the realm of imagination for adults to understand them or take their ideas seriously. Accordingly, in King's novella, Constable Neary does not believe Marty's testimony about how the werewolf looks and tries to find a rational explanation instead, thus arguing that the criminal must have a split personality. He thus dismisses Marty's assumption that a werewolf is to blame for the murders, arguing that the boy's account is nothing more than a child's explanation for these terrible events. As Davis explains, in King's novels, there must be a synthesis between childhood and adulthood experiences so that difficulties are surmounted and resolved successfully (1994: 64). As Marty plans to apprehend the criminal and determine the identity of the werewolf, Uncle Al acts as his mentor, enacting a similar circularity as the periodic cycles of the moon, since, in addition to marking the appearance of the werewolf, the lunar phases also underscore Marty's ageing process.

In contrast with Marty's parents, who are too concerned about their son and want to overprotect him, Uncle Al, who is Marty's mother's younger brother, establishes a closer bond with his nephew. Although Marty's mother believes that Al exerts a negative influence on her son, Marty realises that Al treats him as an equal and allows him to take part in some risk-taking activities that initiate him into the world of adults. As Magistrale claims, Marty feels more attached to his uncle Al because he also perceives him as an outsider who does not quite fit in the established social order, being "an eccentric, single, middle-aged man with no intention of conforming to adult mores" (1988: 99). Insofar as Al is an adult who often acts like a child, whereas Marty is an adolescent whose situation urges him to act like an adult, they feel mutual affection and a special bond between each other. Besides, Al is the only adult that believes Marty's assertion that the criminal is a werewolf who commits the murders on nights with a full moon. In their respective roles as mentor and disciple, Al and Marty are able to fight and defeat the werewolf, as an embodiment of the repressed evil that lurks beneath the world of adults, and it is assumed that they are successful in their endeavour because, as Magistrale claims, unlike the rest of the adults, "they are not rendered helpless by a recognition of their own evil in the werewolf's" (1988: 100). In King's novella, the werewolf thus turns into the antagonist that threatens Marty's integrity, but in so doing, it also urges Marty, as the hero of the narrative, to leave behind his childhood and enter adulthood.

Throughout his coming-of-age process, Marty must undergo a series of metaphorical rites of initiation in conjunction with his investigations about the periodic appearances of the werewolf when the full moon rises. Marty resents the cancellation of the 4th of July celebrations because of the recent murders, causing Uncle Al to buy a packet of firecrackers for his nephew. When Marty is alone in the woods under the radiance of the full moon, he first lays eyes on the beast from which he can defend himself by throwing the firecrackers in its face. Having been able to save his life on his own, Marty feels "a deep exultation in him", since "he has looked into the terrible face of the Beast and lived" (2019: 71). In resemblance to an ancestral rite of separation, whereby the young leave their home to metaphorically die and be reborn as adults, Marty identifies his first encounter with the werewolf under the moonlight as a turning point in his process of coming of age.

Moreover, insofar as Marty manages to injure the werewolf in one of its eyes, he realises that when the creature reverts back into its human shape this injury will become the "mark of the beast" which will allow him to recognise the murderer. After symbolically undergoing a series of transitional rites, Marty is able to unmask the werewolf and identify it as Lester Lowe, thus stating that "he's the werewolf, he's the Beast, it's *him*, and he's waiting for the full moon" (2019: 121). Before fulfilling a final rite of reintegration, Marty asks Uncle Al to provide him with "two silver bullets, and a gun to shoot them with" on the night of the full moon at the end of the year (2019: 122). Well aware of the intricacies concerning werewolf lore, Marty asserts that the only way to destroy the beast involves shooting a gun with a silver bullet, whereby he manages to slay the werewolf and prove to the community and to himself that, despite his troubles and obstacles, he has gained recognition and is allowed to join the world of adults. The rites of separation, transition, and reintegration that Marty symbolically undergoes, during his fight against the werewolf, find their counterpart in the periodic waxing and waning phases of the lunar cycle, which signify the passage of time, together with the eventual disempowerment of the werewolf and the rise of Marty's self-confidence to reach adulthood.

Given the cyclical structure of King's novella, which reflects the phases of the moon and the rites of passage that initiate Marty into adulthood, the struggle that he undergoes in order to fight and defeat the werewolf is also illustrative of the diverse characters and archetypal stages typified in structuralist analyses of folk narratives. Drawing on Christopher Vogler's notion of the mythic structure (1998), King's novella comprises the main archetypes that gain prominence along a symbolic journey. Marty arises as the hero who comes of age in the narrative and must face a series of different challenges. As a mentor, Uncle Al initiates Marty and provides him with the necessary tools and gifts to fulfil his adventure, such as the fireworks which allow him to defeat the werewolf. The series of murders taking place in Tarker's Mills, and particularly the death of Marty's friend Brady, arise as the herald in the narrative, which symbolises the call for adventure that urges Marty to solve the puzzle regarding such mysterious murders. The werewolf, and its human counterpart, Lester Lowe, arises as the shadow which threatens the lives of all the citizens in town. Constable Neary personifies the guardian, insofar as he somewhat hampers the hero's progress owing to his scepticism, whereas Marty's sister, Kate, turns into his ally. In addition to fulfilling the role of the mentor, Uncle Al also embodies the trickster, inasmuch as he triggers change and provides comic relief, whereas, apart from personifying the shadow, the werewolf literally represents the archetype of the shapeshifter, since, given its double role as human and beast, its character changes constantly from the hero's perspective.

Alongside this, King's novella also exemplifies the different stages of the hero's journey whereby, despite his initial fears, Marty accepts the call to adventure, which positions him on his symbolic journey into adulthood according to Vogler's mythic structure. After meeting with his mentor, Marty is ready to accept the challenge and face the werewolf for the first time. Once Marty advances in his investigations and discovers the werewolf's identity, he must defeat it in a final fight, in which the boy is rewarded with the completion of his adventure and his newly gained status as an adult. Finally, Marty goes back to his everyday life, but joins the community with the knowledge and experience that he has gained along his symbolic journey, which have not only benefited himself but also the whole of his hometown. Accordingly, King's novella, which revisits and updates werewolf lore, complies with the mythic structure and archetypes of folk narratives, thus relapsing into ancestral myths and ancient traditions. In these myths, the lunar cycle and the different phases of the moon exert a deep influence on individuals who engage in the different rites of passage, which symbolically enact their transition from childhood to adulthood and their ensuing inclusion within the community as recognised members.

Conclusion

Cycle of the Werewolf was overshadowed by the success of King's early novels *Salem's Lot*, *The Shining*, and *Pet Sematary*, in which the author revisited and updated archetypes of the horror genre, like the vampire, the ghost, and the living dead, all of them creatures of the night that make their appearance when the moon rises in the dark. Nonetheless, among his early novels focusing on archetypes in the Gothic tradition, King also drew attention to the werewolf, which he considered an embodiment of the double, given its intrinsic split personality, its metamorphosis, and its hybrid form as human and animal. In comparison with other horror archetypes, the werewolf arises as the creature of the night which is most influenced by the effects of the moon, insofar as its transformation from human to beast depends exclusively on the lunar cycle and the presence of a full moon. In addition to one of the defining traits associated with the werewolf, the moon also acquires other functions in King's novella. Since the twelve chapters are organised around the annual calendar, the lunar cycle provides the basic narrative structure in the narrative, each chapter portraying the events taking place once a month, on a night with a full moon. Besides, being a graphic novella, the paratextual content, in terms of illustrations, draws attention to the moon as a latent presence which precipitates the action and the development of the plot. Given the symbolic connotations attached to the moon, as a result of its cyclical nature and its connection with dreams and the imaginary, the moon, as a pervasive trope in King's novella, paves the way for critical interpretations that underscore the awakening of the irrational self through the horror archetype of the double, anxieties regarding repressed dominant masculinities in the wake of second-wave feminism, and the transitional passage from childhood towards adulthood.

Although King had already addressed the latent danger underlying domestic animals in his novel *Cujo*, published in 1981, in which a pet dog transforms into a deadly beast capable of attacking a child, it is in *Cycle of the Werewolf* in which the archetype of the human-animal creature is explicitly revisited and updated, thus taking over the defining features of the classic prototype of the werewolf, while setting it in contemporary society. As an epitome of the figure of the double, the werewolf shifts from a nineteenth-century archetype in the Gothic tradition, in which it mainly embodied the social outsider, to a postmodern interpretation, whereby the lycanthrope personifies the furious release of repressed anxieties regarding gender dictates and social conventions in the wake of new masculinities. Accordingly, in King's contemporary portrayal, the werewolf arises as a notorious relic from the past—an embodiment of dominant masculinities and domestic gender conventions—which still threatens to emerge through contemporary reactionary discourses. If the effects of the full moon used to pave the way for releasing the repressed self of the romantic social outcast, in King's novella, it is implied that the moon rather contributes to unleashing the individual's inner self, which remains concealed behind social appearances and conventions. As is stated in King's novella, "they speak of a man-wolf, but think only in terms of the wolf, not the man" (2019: 110), hence suggesting that, for King, the werewolf conforms to a personification of the double whereby the human truly ends up being the criminal, while the beast stands for the reflection of his true self. In King's novella, as a pervasive trope, the moon turns into the spotlight where the postmodern individual finds his reflection in his double, until he realises that this alter ego or other is in fact himself.

References

Chu, Judy, Michelle Porche, and Deborah Tolman. 2005. The Adolescent Masculinity Ideology in Relationships Scale Development and Validation of a New Measure for Boys. *Men and Masculinities* 8 (1): 93–115.

Connell, Raewyn. 2005. *Masculinities*. New York: Polity Press.

Curran, Bob. 2009. *Werewolves: A Field Guide to Shapeshifters, Lycanthropes and Man-Beasts*. Franklin Lakes: New Page Books.

Davis, Jonathan. 1994. *Stephen King's America*. Ohio: Bowling Green State University Popular Press.

Elliott, Karla. 2016. Caring Masculinities: Theorizing an Emerging Concept. *Men and Masculinities* 19 (3): 240–259. https://doi.org/10.1177/1097184x15576203.

Fincher, Max. 2016. Werewolves. In *The Encyclopedia of the Gothic*, ed. William Hughes, David Punter, and Andrew Smith, 733–735. Oxford: Wiley Blackwell.

Hoppenstand, Gary, and Ray Browne. 1987. The Horror of It All: Stephen King and the Landscape of the American Nightmare. In *The Gothic World of Stephen King: Landscape of Nightmares*, ed. Gary Hoppenstand and Ray Browne, 1–19. Ohio: Bowling Green State University Popular Press.

Indick, Ben. 2007. King and the Literary Tradition of Horror and the Supernatural. In *Stephen King: Bloom's Modern Critical Views*, ed. Harold Bloom, 5–16. New York: Chelsea House Publishers.

King, Stephen. 2000. *Danse Macabre*. London: Warner Books.

King, Stephen. 2019. *Cycle of the Werewolf* [1983]. Illustrations by Bernie Wrightson. New York: Gallery, 13.

Magistrale, Tony. 1988. *Landscape of Fear: Stephen King's American Gothic*. Ohio: Bowling Green State University Popular Press.

Magistrale, Tony. 2002. Toward Defining an American Gothic: Stephen King and the Romance Tradition. In *Stephen King: Bloom's BioCritiques*, ed. Harold Bloom, 95–105. Philadelphia: Chelsea House Publishers.

Magistrale, Tony. 2006. *The Moral Voyages of Stephen King*. Rockville: Wildside Press.

Otten, Charlotte. 1990. Introduction. In *A Lycanthropy Reader: Werewolves in Western Culture*, ed. Charlotte Otten, 1–17. New York: Dorset Press.

Patton, Niall. 2004. Self-Inflicted Eye Injuries: A Review. *Eye* 18:867–872. 10.1038/sj.eye.6701365.

Silver Bullet. 1985. *Directed by Dan Attias*. Paramount Pictures: Los Angeles.

Vogler, Christopher. 1998. *The Writer's Journey: Mythic Structure for Writers*. Studio City: Wiese Productions.

Wrightson, Bernie. 1993. Bernie Wrightson on His Art. In *The Stephen King Companion*, ed. George Beahm, 276–277. London: Warner Books.

PART II

The Moon and Gender Poetics

CHAPTER 6

"The Terror of the Rustics"; or, Witches and Werewolves: Lunar and ecoGothic Monstrosities in Catherine Crowe's "A Story of a Weir-Wolf"

Nicole C. Dittmer

The witch and her associated counterpart the werewolf are sympathetic and symbolic figures of both the natural environment and inherently female "nature". As two characterisations that function under the mode of the Lunar Gothic, each depicts the underlying sexual passions and violence of women, perpetuated by Victorian medical and pseudo-scientific discourse. As a writer of both social and supernatural stories, Catherine Crowe formulates the significance of nature's lunar cycles and society's concerns about formidable women. Published in *Hogg's Weekly Instructor* in 1846, Crowe's short tale "A Story of a Weir-Wolf" exhibits the popular depiction of women and nature through the connection of such lunar monstrosities as witches and werewolves and their night-time excursions. While these gothic-infused works contain supernatural and fictitious characteristics, the short story coalesces with popular Victorian discourses

N. C. Dittmer (✉)
The College of New Jersey, Ewing, NJ, USA

E. Gomel, S. Bacon (eds.), *Lunar Gothic*, Palgrave Gothic,
https://doi.org/10.1007/978-3-031-92621-1_6

about female nature to manifest tales of real-life events affected by transgressive behaviour.

Categorised as a dualistic entity, nature, as Carolyn Merchant (1980) posits, is a wild and uncontrollable force historically aligned with women. Nature, then, was determined as both nurturing and supportive while also functioning as a destructive and threatening force. As associated with nature, women were similarly forced into stereotypical roles as either the maternal angel or the monstrous, and animalistic, witch. These popular perspectives that intertwine femininity and nature as ontological bifurcations manifest as monstrous figurations of werewolves (or, in this case, *wif*-wolves) and witches in Gothic literature of the Victorian period. This dualistic understanding of nature is both nurturing and destructive, a concept that parallels the societal roles assigned to women. In this dichotomy, both nature and women are portrayed as chaotic and wild, embodying societal fears of the feminine. The witch and the *wif-wolf* emerge as reflections of this duality, representing the monstrous potential of women when they step outside societal norms. Victorian Gothic literature, then, serves as cautionary tales, warning against the perceived dangers of female autonomy and desire. Crowe's exploration of these themes through the Lunar Gothic invites a deeper analysis of the fears and tensions that shaped the Victorian understanding of womanhood.

This chapter, then, examines how lunar monstrosities are material amalgamations of societal fears against the transgressive and potentially feral attributes of women and their connection to nature. Investigating Crowe's (2023: 46) depiction of alchemical witchcraft, accusations of lycanthropy, and moonlit "heathen forms of worship", I argue that, when read alongside nineteenth-century texts about inherent "womanhood", these female figurations are representations of the blurred distinction between nature and culture vying for independent expression. The witch and the *wif-wolf* serve as potent symbols within the realm of the Lunar Gothic, each embodying societal fears regarding female nature and its inherent connection to the natural world. As both sympathetic and monstrous figures, they reveal the complex interplay between femininity, sexuality, and societal constraints, particularly within the context of Victorian medical and pseudo-scientific discourse. Examining Catherine Crowe's "A Story of a Weir-Wolf", I unravel the cultural anxieties surrounding agentic women and their association with lunar cycles and nature.

Nature and Women/Witches and Wolves: Popular Perspectives of the Nineteenth Century

Medical sciences and popular culture of the nineteenth century centred their rhetoric about the threat of degeneration in the biologics and inherent disposition of women. Perceived as potentially dangerous commodities, women's bodies were essentialised and cast into positions of domestic and reproductive fulfillment. It is in this prescription of forced womanhood that society hoped to regulate the temperance and carnality of women's nature. While reductionistically figured as maternal and reproductive beings, women were faced with identities founded on the sole process of procreative maternity. Identified as wild and chaotic, women were supposed to be driven by emotion and desire, and therefore this social construct of womanhood was considered a necessary measure to regulate and channel women's excess passions. In the mid-nineteenth century gender-specific classifications were implemented to create behavioural guidelines that aligned men with culture and women with nature. Partly informed by the theories of experts such as Jean-Baptiste Lamarck (1744–1829), Thomas Laycock (1812–1876), and Charles Darwin (1809–1882), that women were only controlled by their instincts, societal institutions sought to repress female nature by replacing it with social rules.

Historically, the witch has been viewed as a transgressive individual bound to the Devil due to an intrinsic vulnerability. While not always a woman, the witch is considered a predominantly female figure based on a relationship with nature and sin. As Heinrich Kramer and James Sprenger (1971: 43) so succinctly determine in their fifteenth-century text, the *Malleus Maleficarum*, women are "an evil of nature", although they are perceived as a "necessary evil" prone to the "lust of the flesh". Created as a witch identification guide, also known as "The Hammer of Witches", Kramer and Sprenger's text clearly outlines that female agency is determined as an evil behaviour informed by their "insatiable" carnal lust (1971: 43). While harbouring an inherent, and supposedly flawed, nature, women were then identified as uncontrollable objects of excessive passions and malicious intent. Promoted by such texts as "domestic dangers", independent women that "think alone" were targeted as "evil" witches who faced social regulation or eradication (Kramer and Sprenger 1971: 43). An amalgamation of chaos, lust, and destruction, the witch became a material-semiotic figuration throughout the centuries to warn of the consequences of unrestrained female nature.

Later in the mid- to late nineteenth century, Charles Darwin, on the heels of Lamarck's theory of evolution and environmental affectations, concluded that women were less prone to aggression and used "coy" passivity to attract attention. Arguing that this technique was a strategic female inclination for social manipulation, Darwin's impression, similar to Kramer and Sprenger's witch figure (1971: 43), identified women as "natural temptation(s)" and inherently tactical. Female sexuality and a metamorphic biology were considered the source or "assumed origin of animality" and chaos, and identified as the reason for institutional regulation (Dittmer 2022: 43). Therein, questions of women's instinctual nature and intent increasingly proliferated throughout the nineteenth century, re-enforcing the previously implemented restrictions of constructed womanhood.

Prior to Darwin's observations about women and nature, French naturalist and biologist Jean-Baptiste Lamarck hypothesised how nature informs the behaviour of "higher level species" (1830: 52). In doing so, he created the foundation for environmental affectation in which Lamarck determines that the environment influences the evolutionary development of an individual, thus also recreating their ontological structure. Although Lamarck's theories were formulated through his zoological observation of animal hierarchies, he alludes to the possibility of such affectations in human development. Inspired by these earlier theories, Victorian neurophysiologist Thomas Laycock incorporated such ideas of women/nature into his medical advancements of female biology.

Laycock's theories intertwined the perspectives of Lamarck and Victorian society's fears of female reproductivity by positing that women have a dichotomous biology. Women, according to Victorian standards, are either destructive villains or virtuous victims and both are susceptible to their reproductive functionality (Dittmer 2022: 7). Through Laycock's investigation of female ontology and reflex theory, he determines that nature is an influential force responsible for affecting the psychosomatic functions of women. Promoting the philosophy that the mental emotions of the "human female" are similar to the "lower animals", Laycock (1840: 72) perpetuated the belief that women are "closer to nature than men", and therefore should be treated as unpredictable and dangerous (Merchant 1980: 144). Although nineteenth-century society no longer perpetuated fears of fifteenth-century witchcraft, it re-focused the corruption of female sexuality onto such figures of unmarried or hysterical women. As Elizabeth Reis (1999: xiii) so notably posits, while the target of the witch or witchcraft accusation changes, the foundational belief, or cause, remains unchanged. Therein, in alignment with this observation, it is quite clear that Victorian accusations of witchcraft transformed into fears of uncontrolled women, as both were informed by innate female nature.

Basing his theorems on the hypotheses of Pythagoras, Laycock circulated the popular medical belief that the lunar cycles influence female biology—as mostly observed in the events of puberty, menstruation, pregnancy, and menopause—and therefore function as a direct source of psychosomatic affectation for female instability. Laycock ascertains that with each moon cycle, there are additional lunar elements that inform the female mind-body and influence such passions as sexual desire or hysteria. These "solar influences", including the "equinoxes" and "solstices", were assumed to create chaos and destructive reactivity in women, thus maintaining the belief that women were affected by nature, therefore remaining a part of it (Laycock 1840: 146). This assumed relationship between female biology and the lunar cycles demonstrates how the early nineteenth-century medical industry, while claiming progress, maintained the antiquated notion that women, while not restricted by the social constructs of Victorian womanhood, faced the challenges of potential monstrosity.

Stemming from cultural, medical, and legal rhetoric, literature of the nineteenth century incorporated language focuses on the chaos and destruction of female nature. This feedback loop of psychosomatic abnormalities and degeneration perpetuated negative discourse about women's nature and informed the fiction of the period. Gothic fiction, in particular, as inspired by cultural and social issues, both informed and was informed by these popular perspectives and used such figures as witches and werewolves to warn of the dangers of women and nature. Both the witch and lycanthropic characters, then, in the nineteenth-century Lunar Gothic are figurations of nature, desire, and the rejection of socially induced repression. These monsters of excess and corruption are hyperbolic figures of uncontrolled sexuality and reclamation of female agency.

Lunar Gothic and Feral Women: Crowe's Victims and Villains

Demonstrating how Gothic-adjacent literature is in a perpetual discussion with popular Victorian rhetoric, Crowe's tales of witches, werewolves, and supernatural entities illustrate how these night creatures respond to societal fears of monstrous women. As Carol Karlsen (1987: xii) so clearly points out, "witchcraft confronts us with ideas about women". The classification of "the witch", then, creates a material-semiotic figuration that fully embodies the collective fear of women, their societal place or role, and "with women themselves", such as their intrinsic "nature" (Karlsen 1987: xiii). The witch figure has historically represented a deviation from societal norms. In Crowe's narrative, it is the female character Manon who embodies the traits associated with witchcraft—envy, malice, and a willingness to manipulate others for her gain. This reversal of expectations serves to critique the tendency to project societal fears onto women, who are often vilified for behaviours that challenge established norms. Through the lens of witchcraft, Crowe emphasises the fragility of social structures that dictate women's behaviour. Manon's actions, driven by jealousy, expose the underlying tensions within the narrative—how women's desires can be perceived as threats to societal order. This dynamic speaks to the broader Victorian context, where women were often seen as the corruptors, and creators of moral decay, particularly when they expressed their sexuality or agency.

In Catherine Crowe's short tale "A Story of a Weir-Wolf", she intertwines characteristics of the Gothic and societal fears of the period through witch accusations of her two primary characters. Inspired by a fatal witchcraft event that occurred in 1588, Crowe reimagines the accusations and execution of a young woman-turned-wolf into a tale of betrayal and rage with subtle hints that initiate a witch hunt.[1] Written at a time when Laycock published his *Treatise of the Nervous Diseases of Women* (1840: 23), a text, as mentioned above, that promotes the connection of women's nature to the "lesser animals", "A Story of A Weir-Wolf" incorporates suspicion of female intentions, nature, and sexuality with figurations of a witch and a suspected werewolf.

Taking place in a forest village in Auvergne, France, Crowe's story focuses on the relationship of two cousins: Francoise, a seventeen-year-old daughter of an alchemist, and Manon, the beautiful vain daughter of a prosperous family. At her father's request, Francoise is sent to live with Manon's family during the summer months. Initially excited and intrigued

[1] Crowe's 1846 tale was possibly based on the case of Arline of Barioux in Auvergne, France, in 1588. During this trial, the woman was accused of lycanthropy and burned at the stake. See Henri Boquet's (1602) *Discours execrable des Sorciers* and Alexi Easley and Shannon Scott's (2023) *Terrifying Transformations: An Anthology of Victorian Werewolf Fiction, 1838–1896.*

by her cousin's visit, Manon's hospitality rapidly wanes as Francoise becomes the centre of attraction for Victor. Dejected and jealous of her cousin, Manon, "under the influence of the evil passions raging within her", accuses Francoise of witchcraft and lycanthropy, thereby sentencing her to imprisonment and potential execution (Crowe 2023: 52). Throughout the trial, direct witchcraft accusations are made against Francoise and evidence is supplied to support such claims; however, it is Manon who demonstrates the characteristics of the witch figuration.

Described as in possession of a "beautiful face" that is "nothing superior" to other women, Francoise becomes the target of Manon's rage and jealousy when she enchants the noble, Victor, suggesting that a supernatural element is involved. The son of a high-born family, Victor is desired by Manon who feels entitled to his attention as she "never neglected an opportunity" to have "homage" paid to her beauty (Crowe 2023: 48). However, at his initial glance at Francoise, Victor claims that "[h]is heart seemed taken by storm; he could not drive the beautiful features from his brain", creating the illusion that he is "enslaved" and not in control of his own faculties (Crowe 2023: 48). According to Kramer and Sprenger (1971: 24), witches have the power to bewitch and "turn the minds of men to inordinate love or hatred" with a "mere look". Creating the suspicion that Francoise is potentially a witch, Crowe positions her character as the centre of the accusations and social problems. However, while using Francoise as the direct subject of the witch hunt, she is a decoy, as there are subtle hints that allude to Manon as the true witch/weir-wolf. For example, it was stated that "it was highly probable that these great people believed in witchcraft" and all suspected the enchantment of Victor, as Francoise Thiolouze and her alchemist father were "what the Scotch call, no *canny*", or individuals depicted as harmful or evil (Crowe 2023: 52). While not acting on their suspicions prior to this accusation, it was only when Manon declared her cousin a witch that the villagers took action and took notice of Francoise. While Crowe ensures that the reader focuses on the implied coercion of Victor under suspicion of Francoise as a witch, it is Manon who uses her words to enchant the villagers, of which "the idea was seized on with avidity", to ensure that her cousin is destroyed (Crowe 2023: 53).

A traditional belief about witches is that they were granted the power of the Devil and had the potential to destroy lives. A witch, according to Norman Cohn (2000: 50), was "wholly malignant, wholly set on destruction", and performed *maleficarum* to bring harm to those of her own choosing. In Crowe's tale, this intent on destruction is invoked through Manon's passion and rage. Convinced that she "was much the handsomer of the two", Manon was known by the villagers as "such a woman you might live with well enough as long as you steered clear of her vanity" (Crowe 2023: 48). This vanity, identified as "the strongest passion of her nature", once challenged, "aroused a latent venom that was sure to make you smart" (Crowe 2023: 48). Therefore, Francoise's "soft blue eyes and auburn hair" that was designated as "tame and ineffective" by Manon transformed the cousins into "implacable enem[ies]", due to the former's ability to coerce Victor (Crowe 2023: 49). With Crowe's description of their physical attributes, she pays homage to the Victorian standards of the light "angel" aesthetic versus the dark "villain", or witch. Francoise, albeit boring in the eyes of her cousin, presents the image of the desirable Victorian woman, hence the real reason for her enchantment of the nobleman. Manon, on the other hand, invokes the sentiment of the hardened, problematic woman with her shining black hair and "dark flashing eyes"—a symbolism that was popular later in the nineteenth century, with Cesare Lombroso's phrenological studies of the criminal woman (Crowe 2023: 48). As an author whose interest resides in the supernatural and real-world events, Crowe purposefully creates a dynamic of opposing womanhood between the two characters that mirrors the restrictions of women in Victorian society while implementing the confusion and suspicion of witchcraft.

Evil witches, as Elaine Breslaw (2000: 4) submits, were "deviant people" who disliked order and threatened to "disrupt the harmony of their community". Known as women who are incapable of social camaraderie, they are often argumentative, confrontational, and aggressive, these assumed witches also "demand more than their due" (Breslaw 2000: 4). For example, when Manon observes Francoise and Victor visiting the woods and the alchemist's house, she declares to the village that "they must have bewitched him, between them; she and that old conjurer" (Crowe 2023: 52). In that same moment, it is noted that in reality Manon has "entertained no such idea" but it was her "evil passions" that drove her to make false witchcraft claims (Crowe 2023: 52). In her desire to obtain Victor, and failing to do so, Manon threatens Francoise with a revocation of social acceptance. This follows Breslaw's (2000: 4) claim that labelling someone "a witch or sorcerer" caused the person to become a "visible, physical presence", one who is blamed for any social issues or malignancies. Likening Manon to this assumption of the historical witch figure in correlation with the Victorian perspectives of the uncontrolled passionate woman, Crowe creates an inconspicuous witch figuration that speaks to contemporaneous social constructs of womanhood.

The Nightly Hunt: The Woods, The Witch, and The Wif-Wolf

Throughout history, the witch and the werewolf, most notably the *wif-wolf*, have an intrinsic relationship to non-human nature. These figurations, as Merchant (1980: 127) submits, are "classical symbol[s] of the wilderness and violence of nature". Both the lycanthrope and the witch are associated with the environs and inhibited by the metamorphic biologies of nature. This relationship of seeing women "as closer to nature" than men proliferates in the medical and cultural rhetoric of the nineteenth century, therefore informing works of the Victorian Gothic to align monstrous women with hostile and "natural" environs (Merchant 1980: 5). The forest landscape, as an area antithetical to the order of men and culture, is a gendered environment that exhibits chaos, instability, and terror, a place in which feral women and violent beasts are harboured.

In "A Story of a Weir-Wolf", the forest setting symbolises the untamed aspects of femininity. The wilderness serves as a refuge for both witches and werewolves, mirroring the societal fears surrounding women's perceived chaos. Manon's ability to navigate the forest and her indifference to its dangers further exemplify her alignment with the natural world, positioning her as both a victim and a villain within the narrative. The climactic hunt for the werewolf encapsulates the story's tension between civilisation and the wild. Crowe employs the motif of the hunt to explore themes of power, agency, and the intersection of femininity and monstrosity. Manon's determination to confront the werewolf reveals her complex relationship with nature and her desire for control in a world that seeks to regulate her. The *wif-wolf*, often seen as a manifestation of uncontrolled desire, serves as a potent symbol of the feral aspects of femininity. By portraying the *wif-wolf* as both a threat and a reflection of societal fears, Crowe complicates the binary between good and evil, highlighting the experiences of women who challenge social norms.

Crowe's tale sets up the connection between women-nature-witch-wolf when the villagers of Loques are deceived into believing the witchcraft accusations about Francoise. When on trial, the huntsmen of the village claimed to have "frequently met" Francoise and Victor "in remote parts of the domain"; however, when discovered, "she suddenly changed herself into a wolf and ran off", offering support that she is a witch (Crowe 2023: 53). Similar to what Cotton Mather (1693: 33) claimed during the Salem Witch Trials, that women, or witches, "transubstantiate themselves into wolves", Francoise's character now faces those accusations while solidifying the relationship between women and nature. As Crowe (2023: 53) explains, "weir-wolves" were the "terror of the rustics", as it is a known "trick of the witches" to change into such creatures as "wolves, cats, and hares", with the werewolf being the worst. Werewolves, or *wif-wolves*, are material-semiotic figurations of woman-nature and animal-human whose transgressions and metamorphic capabilities are informed by an innate sexuality and rebellion. Born from the reductive essentialisms of constructed womanhood, *wif-wolves* in the Victorian Gothic are hyperbolic figures utilised to emphasise the agency of women and their sexuality in ways "that both inscribe and resist" social discourses about "their supposed intrinsic monstrosity" (Dittmer 2022: 141). It is because of this belief that the villagers feared the appearance of the "one particularly large wolf" who they decried as the "representative of the metamorphosed Francoise" (Crowe 2023: 53).

Known as an area of ungodliness, or the place of wild beasts, the forest lends itself to such societal aberrations as witches and werewolves (Nash 2014: 3). As an environment that is wild, dangerous, and chaotic, the forest mirrors the supposed instability and wildness of women's nature. As Robert Frazier Nash (2014) argues, there are two reasons why the wilderness is feared: first, there is a physical and mental threat to an individual's survival, and second, there is a "moral vacancy" within its borders (Dang 2022: 118). The wilderness, or in this case, the forest, is believed to have offered shelter to such monsters as witches, heathens, and wild animals. As a place which Elizabeth Parker and Michelle Poland (Dang 2022: 118) call an "anti-Christian space", the forest is viewed as an environment with "either no god or the *wrong* god or gods". The forest, then, as a place where female monsters and feral beasts reside, is a space designated as not controlled, chaotic, and dangerous, an area that symbolises the "allegedly unappeasable nature of women" (Reis 1999: 93). Therefore, such residents of the forest as witches and werewolves were figured as archetypal monsters of the Gothic that unified corruption and non-human nature to highlight the "unholy merging of woman, flora, and fauna" while responding to the nineteenth century's medical internment of female nature

(Parker 2020: 184). The witch and the werewolf, then, depict a symbiotic relationship to the environment, thus demonstrating a mutual woman–nature connection.

Crowe's depiction of women's relationship with nature is exhibited through Manon, her reaction to the environment, and her involvement with the witch/wolf hunt. When we are introduced to Manon, she demonstrates an almost inhuman response to the weather. While Francoise argues that the "heat of the sun is insupportable" and she must escape into the shelter of the house, Manon retaliates with "I don't mind the heat" and the reader is quickly informed that "nobody appeared disposed to brave the heat but Manon" (Crowe 2023: 45). While the other villagers avoid such temperatures, it is only Manon that can withstand the hellish climate. Speaking to earlier claims about witches being instruments of the "devil's machinations", and possessing the ability to withstand inhumane elements, Crowe's character once again alludes to the possibility that she is the witch/wolf figure while demonstrating women's agency and power with her connection to nature. For example, Manon continues to demonstrate her strength, albeit "witchiness", when she voluntarily offers to hunt for the elusive werewolf under the full moon.

Described as a "girl of strong passions" and in possession "of a fearless spirit", Manon's "whole nature was aroused" when presented with a nightly challenge (Crowe 2023: 57). Crowe's reference to the lunar hunt provides a perfect Gothic setting while it also, once again, alludes to Manon's true identity as a witch, and it presents the affective relationship between the environment (moon/forest) and the corrupted woman (Manon/witch/wolf). Claiming her guilt over the accusations towards her cousin, the impending *auto da fe*, and resulting "witchburning", Manon overlooks her "personal danger" and "feminine fears" to search for the real wolf to "prove the falsity of the accusation" (Crowe 2023: 58). Opting to "shoot the wolf herself", Manon demonstrates her prowess in a "natural" environment by stalking the beast "with a beating heart", through the "broad glades" and the "wide woods" (Crowe 2023: 58). Exhibiting expertise in this chaotic region, Manon's movements, behaviour, and abilities mirror those of the wolf she hunts, creating the implication of a double. Concluding the story with the release of Francoise and the death of both the wolf and Manon, Crowe once again implies the direct correlation of woman-nature and the rejection of constructed womanhood.

Conclusion

In conclusion, Catherine Crowe's "A Story of a Weir-Wolf" intricately weaves the dual narratives of women and nature within the context of the Victorian Gothic, using the figures of the witch and the *wif-wolf* to challenge societal constructs of femininity. Through the lens of lunar cycles and Victorian medical theories, Crowe examines how these monstrous representations embody the fears and frustrations of a society grappling with the perceived threats posed by women's inherent passions and desires. The tension between nurturing and destructive qualities—so deeply ingrained in both female nature and the natural world—reflects the broader cultural anxieties about the autonomy of women in a restrictive, and repressive, framework. "A Story of a Weir-Wolf", then, engages with the complexities of female identity in the Victorian era, revealing the ways in which societal fears manifest in narratives about witches and werewolves. The tale underscores the dangers of projecting societal anxieties onto women, illustrating how these figures become both victims and agents of their destinies.

Through the lens of the Lunar Gothic, Crowe crafts a narrative that speaks to the broader implications of femininity, sexuality, and the natural world. The witch and the werewolf, as embodiments of transgression and desire, ultimately challenge the confines of constructed womanhood. In reclaiming their agency, these figures invite a reevaluation of the narratives surrounding women in the Victorian context, revealing the enduring power of monstrous femininity.

As Crowe illustrates through her characters, particularly the juxtaposition of Francoise and Manon, the line between victim and villain blurs, revealing the complexities of female identity during this tumultuous period. Manon, embodying the traits of the archetypal witch, manipulates societal perceptions to enact vengeance on her cousin, thus serving as a stark reminder of how jealousy and ambition can lead to ruin—a narrative steeped in the fears of unchecked female agency.

Ultimately, the connections between lunar monstrosities and the natural world serve as a powerful critique of the reductive and essentialised classifications imposed on women in Victorian society. Crowe's work not only underscores the cultural and medical rhetoric that sought to confine women within rigid domestic roles but also champions the possibility of reclaiming their narrative power through the very monstrosities society deems threatening. In this interplay of myth and reality, Crowe's characters reflect the ongoing struggle for agency, illuminating the intricate dance between nature and culture, desire and repression, as they emerge from the shadows of the Lunar Gothic.

References

Baptiste, Jean. 1830. *Philosophie Zoologique* [1809]. Paris: J. B. Balliere

Boquet, Henri. 1602. *Discours execrable des Sorciers.* Paris: Court de Bauiere pres.

Breslaw, Elaine. 2000. *Witches of the Atlantic World.* New York: NYU Press.

Cohn, Norman. 2000. The Non-Existent Society of Witches. In *Witches of the Atlantic World*, ed. Elaine Breslaw, 49–59. New York: NYU Press.

Crowe, Catherine. 2023. A Story of a Weir-Wolf [1846]. In *Terrifying Transformations: An Anthology of Victorian Werewolf Fiction, 1838–1896*, ed. Alexis Easley and Shannon Scott. Kansas City: Valancourt Books.

Dang, Trang. 2022. Elizabeth Parker and Michelle Poland. *The Ecogothic: An Interview With Elizabeth Parker and Michelle Poland* 3:113–128.

Dittmer, Nicole C. 2022. *Monstrous Women and Ecofeminism in the Victorian Gothic, 1837–1871.* Lanham: Rowman & Littlefield.

Easley, Alexis, and Shannon Scott. 2023. *Terrifying Transformations: An Anthology of Victorian Werewolf Fiction, 1838–1896.* Kansas City: Valencourt Books.

Karlsen, Carol F. 1987. *The Devil in the Shape of a Woman: Witchcraft in Colonial New England.* London: Peter Smith.

Kramer, Heinrich, and James Sprenger. 1971. *Malleus Maleficarum [1486].* London: Arrow Printing.

Laycock, Thomas. 1840. *A Treatise on the Nervous Diseases of Women.* London: Longman, Orme, Brown, Green, and Longman.

Merchant, Carolyn. 1980. *Death to Nature: Women, Ecology, and the Scientific Revolution.* New York: HarperCollins.

Nash, Roderick Frazier. 2014. *Wilderness and the American Mind.* 5th ed. New Haven; London: Yale University Press.

Parker, Elizabeth. 2020. *The Forest and the Ecogothic: The Deep Dark Woods in the Popular Imagination.* Cham: Palgrave Macmillan.

Reis, Elizabeth. 1999. *Damned Women: Sinners and Witches in Puritan New England.* Ithaca: Cornell University Press.

CHAPTER 7

Children of the Night's Light: Moon as a Structuring Element of Vampire Fiction—From Polidori's *The Vampyre* to the *Twilight* Series

Patrycja Pichnicka-Trivedi

With examples such as the *Moonlight* television series (2007–2008), Stephanie Meyer's *New Moon* (2006) and Chris Weitz's *The Twilight Saga: New Moon* (2009), J. R. Rain's Samantha Moon book series (with novels such as *Moon Dance* (2009) and *Vampire Moon* (2010)), the moon seems to be popular within vampire lore. Moonlight, even when it is not specifically mentioned or made visible in the vampire stories, is a core structural element of the narrative. Not only does it form the typical background, scenery present in both horror tales and in vampire romances, it is a defining feature for the vampire, who usually appears at the same time as the moonlight, or in the moonlight, and who is often like moonlight, with the most obvious example of this being Edward Cullen shining like the moon in the *Twilight* saga. However, not only vampires are linked to the moon.

P. Pichnicka-Trivedi (✉)
University of Warsaw, Warsaw, Poland
e-mail: patrycjapichnicka@uw.edu.pl

E. Gomel, S. Bacon (eds.), *Lunar Gothic*, Palgrave Gothic,
https://doi.org/10.1007/978-3-031-92621-1_7

Also other actors of the narrative can be conceptualised in relation to the moon and defined by moon-related terms. In classic vampire narratives the contrary figure of the "Hunter" (slayer) is defined as anti-lunar, and a solar "Hero", while the "Victim" is often as much a lunar creature as the vampire themselves. This applies even more to the apotheosis of the "Victim", the "Vampire Lover".

Methodology

The popular figure of the vampire was adopted from Eastern European folklore into Western culture, upon the "discovery" of Eastern Europe (Wolff 1994: 2015) in the eighteenth century. The fictional vampire is a modern, Western creation (Groom 2018) and so is the wider vampire narrative which is treated here as a (meta)narrative, in the way that their materials were treated by Vladimir Propp ([1928] 1968), Joseph Campbell (1949), or Claude Lévi-Strauss (1958), or again by Roland Barthes (1977).

The basic structure of the vampire narrative—as part of my previous research—is one that centres around "Good" (the hero) fighting "Evil" (the monster) and the "Stake of Conflict" (the victim). From this analysis the moon was both a building tool and a pivotal point of the structure. The first view of the vampire, and/or its lair, by the protagonist (and/or the victim) frequently happens in a moonli environment. This sees the actors of the narrative being described, even defined, in relation to the moon in its two aspects. The first of these is the moon as a symbol of the night, and more so, of literal and metaphorical darkness—the presence of the moon therefore helps to define actors as night and/or dark creatures. The second defining aspect is the moon itself—the moon defines some actors as lunar creatures.

This chapter will analyse the emergence of both these aspects and their semiotic significance by considering a brief history of the appearance of the moon in vampire fiction, starting with what is widely considered as the first vampire novel in English, John William Polidori's *The Vampyre: A Tale* (1819).

Night Vampires

Eastern European folklore vampires (*upyrs*, *upiórs*) were not necessarily creatures of the night (Kozak 2021). The link only becomes solidified with the intervention of Western literature where having the vampire appear predominantly—or at least it being the time when it attacked its victims—at night worked better within the thematic scope of the Gothic novel popular at the time. Consequently, vampires became inextricably linked to the night, and dark and disturbing environments.

However, in the first vampire novels, vampires are not completely restricted to the night. In John William Polidori's novel "The Vampyre: A Tale" (1819), the vampire Lord Ruthven appears in London society during the day, but performs his blood-sucking deeds under the light of the moon. His alignment with the dark, and the moon, is emphasised when he is fatally wounded—but revived by the power of moonbeams. The Count in Bram Stoker's *Dracula* is strong at night and thrives in the moonlight, but still walks the streets of London in daylight. It is only Friedrich Wilhelm Murnau's film *Nosferatu* (1922) that makes sunlight anathema to the vampire, causing Graf Orlok to disintegrate into a pile of ash. Here the separation of good/fair/light and evil/dark/night finds its peak and its narrative expression.

More recent adaptations of Stoker's *Dracula* usually follow Murnau's example of making the vampire solely a creature of the night, as seen most obviously in the Hammer Dracula films but also in post-2000 iterations such as Dacre Stoker and J.D. Baker's *Dracul* (2020), Dacre Stoker and Ian Holt's *Dracula the Un-dead* (2009), Barbara Hambly's *Renfield: Slave of Dracula* (2006), and George DeVein's *Renfield's Journal: Dracula's Protege* (2018). The ubiquity of Dracula's entanglement with the lunar world expressed as extreme allergy to sunlight is central to many other well-known works like Stephen Sommers' *Van Helsing* (2004), Elisabeth Kostova's *The Historian* (2005), Gary Shore's *Dracula Untold* (2014), or the animated Netflix serial *Castlevania* (2017–2021). The Netflix series *Dracula* from 2020 shows the vampire Count as sensitive to sunlight though only because of his own self-suggestion. However, when he finally dies it is in a visual eruption of sunlight. The Dracula from *Penny Dreadful* (2014–2016) cannot stand the sun and brings darkness to the earth, while in contrast the popular *Van Helsing* series (2016–2021) saw only Dracula herself as safe in the sun while all other vampires were killed by it. The list continues in other popular series such as *True Blood* (2008–2014) based on *The Southern Vampire Mysteries* book series written by Charlaine Harris (2001–2013); *The Vampire Diaries* (2009–2017), and its spin-off *The Originals* (2013–2018)—though magical rings can protect vampires from being burnt—*From Dusk Till Dawn* (2014–2016) where the title itself suggests the nighttime nature of its snake-like vampires; *30 Days of Night*

(2007), which includes the Steve Niles and Ben Templesmith comics, and its various spin-offs and online iterations; and Guillermo del Toro and Chuck Hogan's *The Strain* book trilogy (2009–2011), and subsequent television series (2014–2017), where vampires resort to using an atomic bomb to block out the sunlight. *The Moth Diaries* (Klein 2002; Harron 2012) connects vampires to nighttime, moths, and the moon. The *Underworld* franchise (2003–2016) continues such associations and so do *Daybreakers* (2010), *I Am legend* (2007), *Let Me In* (2010), *Afflicted* (2013), *Kiss of the Damned* (2013), the series *Blood Ties* (2006–2008), and *Only Lovers Left Alive* (2013).

The list of examples could be hugely multiplied. They show how the nighttime has become the domain of the vampire, and the equating of darkness with "evil" sees many vampires as the opposite of the heroes, who represent all that is good. From Stoker's *Dracula* and other nineteenth-century works, those heroes are predominantly male, heterosexual, white, Western, middle-class, healthy, "normal", "natural" monster hunters. Day is their domain and in regard to the vampire genre they have been rather aptly labelled as the "The Crew of Light" (Craft 1984). Their job is to kill the "creatures of the night".

This creates the previously mentioned tripartite framework within Gothic narratives of the "Monster", the "Victim", and the "Hero". In the nineteenth century, the vampire was inevitably cast as the Monster; the Western, white, male hunter/slayer as the Hero; and usually a white, innocent/virgin female as the Victim. The plot was thus that a dangerous Other was attacking Western society by seducing its women, who needed to be protected from depravation by the brave men, and killed if necessary. The vampire was seen as dangerous, unscientific, and even unhuman and represented all kinds of diverse differences (sexual, gender, ethnical etc.), which were seen as abject (Kristeva 1980) transgressions. It also represented the differences between the West and the East where vampire narratives expressed Western ideas of modernity, science, whiteness, maleness, heteronormativity, and humanity understood as anthropocentrism. Light and civilisation was then seen to be carried by white, middle-class, Western males to the wild dark domains of the non-Western world.

Moon Vampires

As mentioned previously, Polidori's *The Vampyre* is arguably the first literary vampire to have a strong association with the moon. The corpse of Lord Ruthven is revived by moonbeams, a feature that often appeared in the nineteenth-century theatrical works inspired by the novel, including Charles Nodier's 1820 stage adaption. Subsequently, the moon has become a necessary attribute in many vampire narratives since. It provides the only light to observe the nefarious plans of Dracula and other aristocratic vampires in the Hammer Studio movies and Roman Polanski's *Dance of the Vampires* (1967). It is an important motif or central feature in the *Underworld* franchise, *Only Lovers Left Alive*, Sommers' *Van Helsing*, and *The Moth Diaries.* It permits the viewer to see the bloody deeds of the vampires in *30 Days of Night.* In Dufaux, Penet, and Bastide's comic *Koba* (2014), vampires' naked bodies are exposed to receive the white light of the moon. The comic adaptation of *Dracula* by Hippolyte (2003–2004) not only shows the moon many times, but is created in the moon's colours: white, whitish blue, light yellow, and crimson (like the blood moon) on a black background.

Vampires frequently appear for the first time in moonlight in their respective stories or moonlight is used to reveal their true nature. Often, their castle or lair is first uncovered by moonlight: in Peru, Martino and Digikore Studios' comic *Nosferatu* (2011–2012), Nosferatu's cave is discovered in the light of the moon by two young boys deep in the Indian jungle. In the Netflix series *V-wars* (2019) the vampiric virus is released from icebergs in a moonlit environment.

In contrast, the opponents of the vampires are defined by diametrically opposed terms.

The aforementioned group of vampire hunters—the Crew of Light—is also known as the "solar heroes" (Janion 2002). Indeed, much of their power is of a solar character. They often rely on the sun's rays as their most powerful weapon—or UV light as a "man-made" version of that. In the Netflix series *Dracula*, the Count dies bathed in an ocean of light because he drank the blood of the solar hero(ine), Zoe/Agatha Van Helsing. In *The Strain* it is the "solar" explosion of an atomic bomb, detonated by the appropriately named Dr. Goodweather, that saves the world and kills the Master. In Jessica M. Thompson's *The Invitation* (2022) the female Hero burns the vampires in their mansion/lair in a huge fire, fire being representative of the sun and of purification.

The solar element in Western culture is male, like Apollo and Helios. Indeed, solar heroes use phallic weapons and resources: from the obvious stake, through emasculative decapitation, to bomb explosions. The lunar element is female, like Diana and Luna. The moon has associations with the female reproductive cycle and it represents female nature: it only shines with reflected sunlight, just as women were supposed to lack originality and only imitate male attributes. "Woman, in her proper function, had existence only as the passive reflection of male creativity. The sun was Apollo, the god of light, the moon Diana, his pale echo in the night" (Dijkstra 1986: 122). In this sense, a woman's greatest achievement was to imitate (white) men. However, it could also be her greatest transgression and greatest sin, if she tried to get something that was not meant for her, i.e., agency. This was the sin of Lucy Westenra in *Dracula*: she then turned into a vampire and was brutally, and "justly", killed by the offended Crew of Light. It was exactly the same with those perceived as "lower" races whose only possible hope was to follow the example of white men. They could only be an imitation, just as the vampire was only an imitation of a living being.

In more psychoanalytic terms the moon, due to its reflective aspects, is also associated with mirrors and the alter ego. Subsequently, while the slayer/hunter was a patriarchal, heteronormative, middle-upper class, white, Western male, who protected women, and conquered other lands (Thompson 2000: 202), the vampire was his dark alter ego.

Accordingly, the fictional vampire frequently does not have a shadow or a mirror reflection. Carl Gustaw Jung ascribed shade to one of the degrees of unconsciousness, associating it with alienation. Homi Bhabha (1994) wrote about the social dimension of the construction of the alter ego where it is a recognition and disavowal of the colonising process. The coloniser recognises himself in those he colonises but denies the similarity, creating the "difference" between them—for which the coloniser blames the colonised and imposes on them an impossible assimilation. Within the dynamics of the domination–subordination relationship similarity is needed, as it allows for the coloniser to view the colonised as being on the same level, furthering allowing comparison. It then gives them permission to impose on the dominated the moral and epistemological categories of the dominator, evaluate them according to those categories, and legitimise the supremacy of the dominator. However, it is the difference that makes this morally acceptable, and thus the difference between the colonised and the coloniser must be produced. This idea of similarity and difference creates a necessary dynamic in the relationship between the vampire, the slayer, and the victim. The victim is similar and yet different from both vampire and slayer, being prone to the influence of both.

Both the monster and the hero want domination over the body of the victim. They both use coercion, violence, and penetration—be it vampire's fangs, blood transfusions, or the stake—in an attempt to mark their domination, represented in erotic terms using phallic weapons. Their actions are not essentially different, but they are presented as such because of who is performing those actions. It is the identity of the agent (whether they are vampires or hunters) and of the object (whether they are vampires or humans) that decides the moral quality of the action. Within the tripartite configuration of actors in vampire narratives, the vampire is not only the alter ego of the Hunter, but is also that of the Victim. It is most obviously seen in Joseph Sheridan Le Fanu's *Carmilla* (1872), in which the sensual seductive vampiress is a mirror reversal of the innocent Laura (this is highlighted by their common maternal descent). Carmilla is a figure of impure sexual desire and an impure will to dominate—supposedly improper impulses that have apparently been eradicated from women in the process of domestication and civilisation. However, in the paranoid patriarchal optics, those instincts are always somewhere nearby—repressed yet ready to return if men are not vigilant enough (Dijkstra 1986: 341–2). In this sense, Carmilla represents the return of Laura's repressed impulses.

Following this, even the male vampire, like Dracula, can symbolise the dark side of femininity that needs to be purified by the solar men. Women in nineteenth-century culture were indeed seen as a kind of Other: less civilised, more emotional, and more carnal than rational and spiritual men, and more biological ("animal"). Women were then necessarily "protected" from their impure impulses by men. Their irresponsible longing for emancipation was exploited by the vampire—and of course punished by the heroes. The linkage between the vampire and the female victim was again embodied in the moon.

Evolution: *Midnight Son*—The Solar-Lunar Vampire

The Moon and the Sun have remained key elements of definition for each of the figures of the vampire narrative in the twenty-first century. In fact, the two come together in the recent iteration of the undead, that of the "Good Guy Vampire" (Carter 1992) that can be defined in terms of both the lunar monster and the solar hero to offer his Victim/Lover a new-old form of love. These types of vampires are often configured as a "Bad Boy" type in being a slightly transgressive figure, but one that is overall positive or even heroic.

The more recent evolution of the figure of the vampire has seen it being more closely associated with the Romance and Detective genres. The first one puts the vampire into the role of a romantic, Byronic hero, assigning it the ability to love. The process started in the second half of the twentieth century with examples seen in less mainstream films and literature, for instance in the 1964 novel *The Shiny Narrow Grin* by Jane Gaskell which featured a relationship between a rebel girl and a vampire. More well known was the vampire Barnabas Collins from *Dark Shadows* (1966–1971) which saw him pursue the reincarnation of his true love who he had lost in his human life—a motif now assumed to be part of the vampire genre and popularised by the film *Bram Stoker's Dracula* by Francis Ford Coppola from 1992. Between 1969 and 1971 many vampire romances were published, authored mostly by women—Dorothea Nile, Barbara Michaels, Virginia Coffman, Elna Stoneand—revolving around the love story of a male vampire and a female human. In the novel *Pages from a Young Girl's Journal* by Robert Aickman (1973) a vampire changes his female human lover without her knowing but (fortunately) to her great satisfaction. In 1976 Anne Rice's *Interview with the Vampire* was published. By the 1990s "Vampire Romance" was already an official publishing category (Carter 2011: 354) and the adaptation of literary undead lovers into televisual heartthrobs—as seen in *True Blood* (2008–2014) and *The Vampire Diaries* (2009–2017)—saw the vampire able to be both an uncivilised (lunar) monster and a societal role model (solar) hero almost simultaneously.

In detective/action narratives vampires are more concentrated on fighting a world-threatening evil. While most vampire stories involve a certain amount of detection, usually in relation to discovering who the vampire is or where their lair is located, it took much longer for the undead to become the detectives themselves. In 1967 Gordon Linzner wrote his stories about agent James Blood (in reference to James Bond), a vampire serving an organisation that fights evil. In 1969 Vampirella appeared in a comic book, being the first well known "Good Female Vampire" (even though ultimately she turns out to be an alien rather than a vampire). Comic books served detective vampires rather well with Doctor Morbius appearing in 1971—who is actually a rather bad vampire, but often fights even worse villains—and Blade appearing in 1973. Vampires (or dhamphirs in Blade's case) tracked down and killed other vampires.

In the late twentieth century, vampires became police or private detectives. One of the most well-known vampires of that kind is the hero of the Canadian series *Forever Knight* (1992–1996) that told the adventures of vampire police detective Nick Knight. At about the same time Tanya Huff's series about Victoria Nelson—which began in 1991—concentrated on a paranormal detective supported in her works by a vampire named Henry Fitzroy. The series was adapted into the television series *Blood Ties* (2007–2007). Almost the same role is assigned to vampire Jean-Claude in Laurell K. Hamilton's Anita Blake series which began in 1993. In 1999–2004, the TV series *Angel*, a spin-off from *Buffy the Vampire Slayer*, featured the eponymous vampire as an undead detective. The series combined many of the previously mentioned themes as the vampire Angel both solved individual criminal cases and fought to save the world from being overwhelmed by evil.

In all these cases, the Good Guy Vampire becomes as sublime as the Hunters in classic vampire narratives. They struggle heroically with themselves as they restrict their own desires even at the cost of becoming weaker: they do not hunt people (except if they are very bad ones), they acquire their diet of blood from hospitals, willing donors, animals, or blood substitutes. They willingly sacrifice themselves for love and/or society.

In these new types of vampire narrative, the moon continues to play a crucial role: the romantic opening love scene in *True Blood* between Bill and Sookie sees a young blonde virgin in a long white nightgown running in the moonlight, before being tempted and seduced by the vampire. In Francis Ford Coppola's *Twixt* (2011), the crucial events happen in the misty moonlight, when the tolling of the mysterious town clock takes the protagonist back in and/or outside time. Most famous is perhaps the figure of Edward Cullen and his vampiric family from the *Twilight* franchise. As mentioned before, Edward himself is as pale and as radiant as a full moon. It is also not coincidental that two of four titles of the novels are associated with the moon: *New Moon* and *Eclipse*.

The latest (and last?) book of the series expresses best the essence of the new Good Guy Vampire: *Midnight Sun* (2020). In the novel, night and day, moonlight and sunlight are linked, just like the solar hero and lunar vampire characteristics are converged in the figure of Edward, the hero of this narrative.

The monster has become the sensitive solar hero, but the vampire narrative continues to perform the norms that it performed in the nineteenth century. Men maintain their phallic dominance and women are submissive and maternal. If the relationship with a vampire can be seen as being sexually transgressive, it is not socially transgressive. In fact, sexual transgression is yet another tool of male control. It is up to a male to decide about sex: it is Edward who decides when Bella will lose her virginity, and while he hurts her during intercourse when it eventually occurs, she begs for more. Edward constantly complains about the risk Bella faces because of him, but when his trials to end the relationship are sham. He manipulates and makes Bella lie for him. Unsurprisingly, there is a lot of violence in such narratives—but the violence is romanticised into an ideal of true love. If the woman is to be (sexually) emancipated, her partner decides about the borders of this freedom: he protects the women from bad vampires just like hunters protected women from vampires in general. Exactly as the traditional solar Hunters did, the new types of vampires objectify female bodies: things to be possessed and controlled.

The Vampire Hero as seen in figures like Edward Cullen is more often than not a vampire hunter as well and is perfectly solar in the most classical way. He is most often male, white, and an upholder of (Western/American) colonial endeavours and neo-liberal ideals. This is seen in *Twilight* in the love triangle between Edward, Bella, and Jacob and the relations between the Cullens and the Quileute tribe. Both of these represent the relations between white people and Native Americans in regard to land/property, with the love triangle conflating the body of the white woman (Bella) with America itself. Jacob, the Quileute man, has historical and cultural ties to the land, and, as a childhood friend, he has long-lasting ties to Bella. Edward is a coloniser coming from Europe, and he also appears in Bella's life out of nowhere. Unsurprisingly, Bella chooses the rich, white, educated doctor's son over a poor Native boy (Leggat and Burnett 2010).

In the franchise, Jacob is often fetishised, but almost always orientalised (Said 1978). In comparison to the Vampire Hero, Jacob is seen as hot-blooded, reckless, risk-taking, passionate, sexually aggressive, and metaphorically and literally animalised. In contrast, Edward is his opposite, solar like Apollo, god of the sun (Spooner 2013). He is an incarnation of patriarchal-colonial power, just dressed up in new (superficially) liberal form: he is cool (literally), composed, restrained, civilised. He is god-like in opposition to animal-like Jacob.

The original meeting between the Quileute tribe and the vampires follows a similar pattern to the rivalry between Jacob and Edward. The Native Americans are living a peaceful life in the woodlands when white invaders from Europe arrive. This first encounter begins in violence and bloodshed, with the vampires claiming the land as theirs. It is only after the Quileute gain their shapeshifting abilities—which appear when they are under threat—and begin fighting back that an uneasy "peace" is reached and the original inhabitants of the land are allowed to stay on a "reservation" outside of town. This kind of "allowance" mirrors that imposed upon the First Nations of America. When the good vampires, the Cullen family, arrive, they sign a very similar unequal "treaty" with the Quileutes.

Even if, at the end, the Cullens and the Quileutes become allies and Jacob "imprints" with Renesmee, Bella's and Edward's quickly growing daughter, the alliance seems dominated by the vampires, and Jacob and Renesmee's relationship feels more like a consolation prize. Within it, Jacob looks more like a faithful servant/carer than a lover.

Curiously, within the oppositional duality of Edward–Jacob, neither figure is dependent upon the moon or its environment—Edward is able to walk around in daylight and Jacob, as a shapeshifter rather than a werewolf, is not influenced by the full moon in any way. However, it is Edward's ability to be both a solar hero and be aligned with the moon that makes his ascendency almost irresistible. As mentioned previously, Edward himself is as pale as a full moon and shines with the same brilliance when his surface (skin) reflects the light of the sun. With this, the narrative of his ascendency to solar hero is told through the phases of the moon, as shown in the various titles of the books and films in the franchise: Part I: Twilight—as darkness falls and we enter the environment of the moon; Part II: New Moon:—the moon appears at its smallest as Edward is absent from much of the story; Part III: Eclipse—the moon is consumed by darkness but emerges reinvigorated as the Cullens overcome rival "bad" vampires; Part IV: Breaking Dawn—the moon is about to disappear but is replaced by a new hope and a new age as the Volturi are overcome and Renesmee grows up; Part V: Midnight Sun—the moon is seen in its full splendour as the main event: the moon has become the sun.

Conclusion

As argued here, the moon is a crucial element of vampire fiction. It is not only an ambiance-maker but a pivotal element of narrative structure. The moon has continued to be a hugely important presence in vampire narratives and the genre as a whole throughout the ages. It has facilitated the evolution of the vampire and the tripartite structure—solar Heroes, lunar Monsters, and the moon-seduced Victims—that is central to the majority of vampire narratives. More so, it is a defining aspect of the eternal struggle between the light and the dark, life and death which is central to the vampire narrative and the evolution of the undead into being able to embody both sides of this duality. Here then, in the twenty-first century, it is the symbiosis of the solar and lunar Hero that defines the modern vampire and how it combines the Gothic nature of the darkness with the rationality of the day to bring us a monster that controls the power of the sun and the mystery of the moon.

References

Barthes, Roland. 1977. Introduction to the Structural Analysis of Narratives. In *Image-Music-Text*. London: Fontana.

Bhabha, Homi K. 1994. *The Location of Culture*. London & New York: Routledge.

Campbell, Joseph. 1949. *The Hero with a Thousand Faces*. Princeton: Princeton University Press.

Carter, Margaret L. 1992. What Is a Good Guy Vampire? In *Good Guys Wear Fangs*, ed. Mary Ann B. McKinnion, vol. 1, vi–ix. Plymouth: KnightWriter Press.

Carter, Margaret L. 2011. Vampire Romance. In *Encyclopedia of the Vampire: The Living Dead in Myth, Legend, and Popular Culture*, ed. Sunand T. Joshi and Santa Barbara, 353–358. Denver, Oxford: Greenwood.

Craft, Christopher. 1984. *Kiss Me with Those Red Lips*: Gender and Inversion in Bram Stoker's *Dracula*. *Representations* 8:107–133.

Dijkstra, Bram. 1986. *Idols of Perversity. Fantasies of Feminine Evil in Fin-de-Siècle Culture*. New York, Oxford: Oxford University Press.

Groom, Nick. 2018. *The Vampire. A New History*. New Haven; London: Yale University Press.

Janion, Maria. 2002. *Wampir. Biografia symboliczna*. Gdańsk: Słowo/Obraz/Terytoria.

Kozak, Łukasz. 2021. *Upiór. Historia naturalna*. Warszawa: Evviva l'Arte.

Kristeva, Julia. 1980. *Pouvoirs de l'horreur. Essai sur l'abjection*. Paris: Editions Seuil.

Leggat, Judith, and Kristin Burnett. 2010. Biting Bella: Treaty Negotiation, Quileute History, and Why "Team Jacob" Is Doomed to Lose. In *Twilight and History*, ed. Nancy R. Reagin, 26–46. Hoboken: Wiley.

Lévi-Strauss, Claude. 1958. *Anthropologie structurale*. Paris: Plon.

Meyer, Stephanie. 2020. *Midnight Sun*. New York; Boston: Little, Brown and Company.

Propp, Vladimir. 1968. *Morphology of the Folktale*. 2nd ed. Austin: University of Texas Press.

Said, Edward. 1978. *Orientalism*. New York: Pantheon.

Spooner, Catherine. 2013. Gothic Charm School; or How Vampires Learned to Sparkle. In *Open Graves, Open Minds: Representations of Vampires and the Undead from the Enlightenment to the Present Day*, ed. Sam George and Bill Hughes, 4489–4492. Manchester; New York: Manchester University Press. Kindle.

Thompson, Ewa M. 2000. *Imperial Knowledge: Russian Literature and Colonialism*. Westport, CT: Praeger.

Wolff, Larry. 1994. *Inventing Eastern Europe. The Map of Civilization on the Mind of the Enlightenment*. Stanford: Stanford University Press.

CHAPTER 8

"Crackle and Drag": Sylvia Plath's Lunar Gothic in "The Moon and the Yew Tree", "The Rival", and "Edge"

Cathleen Allyn Conway

Introduction: Plath and the Moon

In Sylvia Plath's poetic landscape, the Moon is mother and Madonna; nurse and midwife. The presence of the moon as a figure of femininity, death, and witchcraft looms large in Plath's imaginary, characterised as a bald and wild woman, merciless yet luminous, overseeing the creation of life and the transition to death, and as such, is both inherently and overtly Gothic.

Despite Plath's use of the Gothic throughout her published and unpublished works, there is little scholarship that explicitly argues for her inclusion in the canon as a Gothic writer. Plath creates her own "Moon language", which transcends word classes in Plath's lexis: "moon" becomes prefix, suffix, noun and adjective, a colour, a verb, and an emotion.

This usage, alongside her recurrent use of Gothic imagery and tropes, creates its own mythology—one in which the Moon is the

C. A. Conway (✉)
Independent Researcher, London, UK

E. Gomel, S. Bacon (eds.), *Lunar Gothic*, Palgrave Gothic,
https://doi.org/10.1007/978-3-031-92621-1_8

Mother-Maiden-Crone archetype rolled into one—firmly establishing her work within the Gothic mode. Gina Wisker writes that "Plath is a missing historical link" as a "mid-century exponent of female literary Gothic", "using Gothic strategies and tropes when confessional poetry and romantic fictions predominated" (Wisker 2004: 105); however, extensive Gothic interrogations of Plath's poetry and prose remain unexplored. Mythic and psychoanalytic studies probe Plath's use of certain tropes, but there is a propensity for critics to focus on her death and presume that all works that use the Gothic as a field for play must actually be premonitions of her suicide.

Although throughout Plath's oeuvre the Moon is impeccable, steely, plague-pitted, generous, indefatigable, and a liar, I argue there is a narrative thread within this sampling of poems in which the Moon is characterised and active in the context of the themes of anxiety, darkness, and grief that Plath explored in her poems, and that Plath uses an "imagined" horror to communicate the real-life horrors she wrote about and experienced as a mentally ill and domestically abused woman in the twentieth century, one who, like her Moon, "is used to this sort of thing./Her blacks crackle and drag".

The moon functions as both trigger and timekeeper: releasing the werewolf during its "full moon monthly transformations" (Hubner, 2018: 117), for example, or acting as a deadline or celestial calendar. For Plath, the moon is a companion, oracle, and guide. In her *Journals*, she repeatedly checks in on the Moon, reports how it looks, orients herself with it, in relation *to* it:

> I twisted the lock; there were only four possible combinations of handle and lock positions, and still the door stuck, white, blank, and enigmatic. I glanced up. Through the glass square, high in the door, I saw a block of sky, pierced by the sharp black points of the pines across the street. And there was the moon, almost full, luminous and yellow, behind the trees. I felt suddenly breathless, stifled. I was trapped, with the tantalizing little square of night above me, and the warm, feminine atmosphere of the house enveloping me in its thick, feathery smothering embrace. (Plath and Kukil 2000: n.p.)

In this excerpt from her July 1950 entry, Plath is locked inside and unable to figure out the combination to open the door. In frustration, she looks up to see the moon, which she describes as almost beckoning her outside. The moon is a point on Plath's personal compass; she always includes what it looks like and what it is doing.

Unsurprisingly, she carries this praxis into her poems, continually a location or orientation point, a form of timekeeping, as seen in "Three Women"—"There is the moon in the high window. It is over" (Plath 1981: 181)—or an assurance of its continued action and presence, as seen in "Stings": "As the moon, for its ivory powders, scours the sea" (Plath 1981: 215).

In *Bitter Fame: A Life of Sylvia Plath*, Anne Stevenson correlates two sides of Plath's personality to the sun and moon, with the "moon side" being a "disguised" "inner self"—"that troubled, vital, inaccessible part of her": "Plath's true subject was this inner self, not her outer experiences and achievements. Eventually she would yearn to kill her false self so that her real one might burn free of it" (Stevenson 1998: 23).

This tension between Plath's light and dark sides is evidenced across her work, and manifests most overtly in her twin impulses to be a wife and mother and the greatest poet of her generation, which is arguably her "moon side". The full embodiment of the Moon as a character is best evidenced in "The Rival" (1961), "The Moon and the Yew Tree" (1961), and "Edge", the last poem she wrote, two days before she died on 7 February 1963.

"The Rival"

"The Rival" was published in *The Observer* on 21 January 1962. In *Red Comet: The Short Life and Blazing Art of Sylvia Plath*, Heather Clark writes:

> Plath explained the poem as 'a contrast between two women: the speaker, who is a rather ordinary wife and mother, and her "rival"—the woman who is everything she is not—who obsesses her. This woman terrifies the speaker and dominates her thoughts, seeming almost superhuman…and, in the third section, grows impressive and omnipresent as a sort of goddess.' [*The New Yorker*] would reject the poem in late September. (Clark 2020: 664)

Although Clark argues "'The Rival'…was a personification of Plath's perfection-demanding demon" (Clark 2020: 664), it could be read as more of a split-self of Plath's twin impulses: home and family, and a desire to live a romanticised, nomadic life of travel, poetry, and its perceived glamour. Plath often deployed doppelgängers in her work to battle the opposing forces she put into her poems; and this use of "the 'unheimleich', the unfamiliar entering the everyday, and bodily estrangement, are features of Plath's domestic Gothic" (Wisker 2004: 106).

In "The Rival" we see these two warring selves, the "rather ordinary wife and mother" and the almost "goddess"-like Rival, of which we know nothing and everything. The Rival is essentially the opposite of what the speaker fears—as Wisker writes, "Knowing what we fear, we know what we desire: safety, mother, friends. Our worst fears arise from dangerous domestic disillusionment" (Wisker 2004: 106), and in this we see the speaker waking "to a mausoleum", to post of the "dissatisfactions" and "news" of the Rival, wherever she is. In this we see what disgusts and terrifies the speaker: the ordinariness of her domestic existence, the challenge to her constructed identity, "warding off fear" (Wisker 2004: 105–106) through sneering critique of the Rival, who seemingly has everything the speaker wants and is still unhappy.

Plath repeatedly personifies the Moon as female, literally and figuratively, as distant, cold, and cruel in her indifference, but she is also emotive. In "The Rival", Plath draws comparisons between the Rival and the Moon, at first suggesting this is a compliment. She writes:

> If the moon smiled, she would resemble you.
> You leave the same impression
> Of something beautiful, but annihilating. (Plath 1981: 166–167)

In identifying the Rival as an avatar for the speaker's shadow self, we see that the poem's narrative voice describes something she herself wants. As Wisker explains: "Imagery of split selves exposes the constructedness, the performativity of gendered roles, the oscillation between versions of self, showing in post-existentialist, post-modern fashion how ontological security is a tenuous construction" (Wisker 2004: 104).

Both the Moon and the Rival are "beautiful, but annihilating", as it seems the poem's speaker also wishes to be. But then we see the other areas in which the speaker recognises that the Rival is not a doppelgänger, because the speaker discards those aspects of the Rival she views as unbecoming:

> Both of you are great light borrowers.
> Her O-mouth grieves at the world; yours is unaffected,
> And your first gift is making stone out of everything. (Plath, 1981: 166–167)

Plath's journals give some indication that a biographical reading of this poem is valid in that she often wrote of the warring desires within her—"who is that blond girl: she is a bitch: she is the white goddess" (Plath 2000: 289); "How can I find myself & be sure of my identity?" (Plath 2000: 460)—and it is not unreasonable to presume she was working out these impulses through verse, attempting to orient her Wife Self (the speaker) with her Poet Self (the Rival) in triangulation with the Moon, her one fixed point.

Although Plath does give a gentle criticism of the Moon in calling her a "light borrower", we suspect this is forgivable in context, as the poem's speaker acknowledges that the Moon is capable of grief and empathy, whereas the Rival, on the other hand, is a Medusa, turning everything to stone.

The introduction of the Medusa allusion adds additional weft, as this is one of the few poems in which the Moon is considered destructive. In *The Monstrous-Feminine: Film, Feminism, Psychoanalysis*, Barbara Creed writes: "Wife, mother, daughter, virgin, whore, career woman, femme fatale—these are the most popular stereotypes of woman that have been addressed by feminist theorists" (Creed 1993: 151) and we see how Plath plays on these tropes, as the Rival is a femme fatale, and the speaker is wife and mother. Creed tells us that in myth, the goddess Athena—"Mother-Goddess of the ancient world" and "daughter of Metis, the goddess of wisdom, also known as the Medusa"—"embossed her shield with the Medusa's head…to strike terror into the hearts of men" (Creed 1993: 166), and explains that "the Medusan myth is mediated by a narrative about the difference of female sexuality as a *difference* which is grounded in monstrousness" (Creed 1993: 2). The Rival, in being Medusan, is monstrous and transgressive, "almost superhuman…and, in the third section, grows impressive and omnipresent as a sort of goddess" as Plath herself describes.

Plath later writes that "The moon, too, abases her subjects,/But in the daytime she is ridiculous" (Plath 1981: 166–167), which contextualises the Moon as divine, an object of worship and leadership. She is only cruel because it is sometimes required of her, Plath's speaker argues, and knows her powers are limited to the night. The Rival, on the other hand, refuses to acknowledge limits, as her "dissatisfactions…Arrive through the mailslot with loving regularity" (Plath 1981: 166–167) and "No day is safe from news of" (Plath 1981: 166–167) her.

But the Medusa allusion is a further connection to an element of vampirism that rings through the poem. Creed writes that "ancient cultures also associated the full moon and woman's monthly bleeding with the snake" (Creed 1993: 64), which correlates with Medusa having snakes instead of hair, and being used to signify a female sexuality that terrifies men. This is further compounded with the menarche, as Creed writes: "Many early myths state that the young girl begins to bleed when the snake-goddess, or god which lives in the moon, bites her" (Creed 1993: 64). This act of a bite, at night, and a penetration of two fangs that make the victim bleed is also seen in vampire folklore and literature, as Creed explains:

> The vampire story contains many symbolic elements which have persisted over the centuries. The vampire is one of the undead, a figure who rises from the grave on the full moon in search of young virgins, almost always female. ... Common symbolic elements in this narrative are: womb-like coffins, the full moon, snake-like fangs, two bite marks, dripping blood, transformation. ... The perfect time for one of the undead to suck blood from the living was on the night of a full moon. (Creed 1993: 62, 63, 64)

The Rival herself is a broad-strokes vampiric personality within the poem, but Plath adds further vampiric imagery: "I wake to a mausoleum; you are here,/Ticking your fingers on the marble table" (Plath 1981: 166–167) places both the reader and the poem's speaker into a tomb, where The Rival is waiting. What does she want? Plath tells us she is "dying to say something unanswerable" (Plath 1981: 166–167)—is she a literal vampire who wants blood? Is she a metaphorical vampire who wants the domesticity the speaker has?

Creed's work on vampires complicates the Rival further, suggesting that:

> the female vampire's world signifies darkness, the undead, moon, the tomb/womb, blood, oral sadism, bodily wounds and violation ... through an interplay of these oppositions, the vampire myth becomes a narrative about the construction of the maternal world as pagan and abject. (Creed 1993:71)

While the characterisation of the Rival in-poem is contextual, the symbolism of the tropes Creed lists is undeniable. The speaker wakes in a tomb, the Rival is an abject transgressor, and the Moon is celestial feminine divine—all demonstrate that the Gothicism of the poem is built into its foundations.

Wisker writes that "Plath's work is recognised anew as ironic, revelatory, aware of paradoxes, using fantasy, the surreal and horror to express and critique contradictions of the everyday and the self" (Wisker 2004: 105) and this praxis is evident in "The Rival". The polarisation of these two warring selves, the one who wants the home and the one who wants the world, is locked into battle in this poem. The speaker's criticism of the Rival, and the acknowledgement that wherever the Rival may roam—"Walking about in Africa maybe, but thinking of me" (Plath 1981: 166–167)—the fact she still thinks of the speaker, and the delivery of this information in the final line, suggests the speaker sees herself as triumphant, at least this time.

"The Moon and the Yew Tree"

Plath wrote the poem "The Moon and the Yew Tree", on 21 October 1961, while living with Ted Hughes at their home, Court Green, in Devon. It was sent for consideration to *The New Yorker* in December 1961, and was posthumously published in the 3 August 1963 issue. According to Clark: "Hughes wrote that he suggested the poem as an exercise one night when she could not sleep. He told her to write about what she saw when she looked out the window—St Peter's Church, a graveyard, and a large yew tree" (Clark 2020: 665). However, Stevenson wrote in *Bitter Fame*: "Ted Hughes had set her the subject as an exercise after they observed the full moon setting over the yew in the churchyard early one morning. By midday she had shown him the result" (Stevenson 1998: 23).

While the inception of the poem differs, both biographers agree that Hughes felt the poem was depressing. The poem as site of contention is not limited to the conflicting origin stories, however. As the Gothic is a discourse of intertextual hybridity and appropriation, it is significant to note that even the origin story of "The Moon and the Yew Tree" contains the tropes of the Gothic. It can be read as Court Green becomes a castle; Plath as isolated heroine, in distress one night because she cannot sleep—or not? because gaslighting a heroine is central to a Gothic narrative—and Hughes in the role of Gothic villain or antihero, taking credit for the creation of the poem by claiming he "set" Plath an "assignment" as though he were her teacher and her his student.

It is easy to imagine Plath in the dark, staring out her bedroom window, remarking on the "light of the mind, cold and planetary" (Plath 1981: 172–173)—but it is *her* mind, alight and large, in the cold dark—not Hughes'. As with many appearances of Hughes in relation to Plath's work—particularly once she was no longer alive to speak for herself and he took control of her estate—it is a form of confinement of Plath, her voice and her legacy, in which Hughes through word, deed, and reaction suggests there is only one way to interpret her work: his way. This makes "The Moon and the Yew Tree" additionally ironic in that Plath situates the poem in the confined space of the mind, which cannot be breached, and within this space is a wild moon Madonna, dragging "the sea after it like a dark crime" (Plath 1981: 172–173).

Plath writes that "The moon is no door. It is a face in its own right,/White as a knuckle and terribly upset" (Plath 1981: 172–173), explicitly laying out that the Moon is not a portal or a gateway. Stevenson suggests this "churchyard with its father-yew and mother-moon had become yet another reenactment of Sylvia's imprisoning drama" (Stevenson 1998: 229), but later in the poem, Plath writes: "The yew tree points up. It has a Gothic shape./The eyes lift after it and find the moon" (Plath 1981: 172–173). In this description, the Gothic is not a literary mode but an architectural one, with the tree pointing to the moon as if it were the cathedral and the moon a rose window, or an altar.

She continues this motif in the third stanza, invoking a divine feminine: "The moon is my mother. She is not sweet like Mary./Her blue garments unloose small bats and owls" (Plath 1981: 172–173). Judith Kroll writes in *Chapters in a Mythology: The Poetry of Sylvia Plath* that for the speaker, "the true religion is a pagan one of ecstasies, oracles, prophecies and omens" (Kroll 2007: 39), despite the "stark, unromanticised world" that is the poem's landscape. Rather than rely on notions of the sublime, Plath locates the Moon as Madonna, dressing her in blue—a darker, night-sky ultramarine known as "Marian blue" was often used for depictions of the Virgin in Renaissance artworks in Europe—through which these robes of night sky come nocturnal flying animals that carry their own Gothic significance.

According to Clark, the poem "has a sense of loneliness and yearning for communion" (Clark 2020: 670), and Stevenson says the moon is a "neutral, impersonal force to which she was drawn in these black moods" (Stevenson 1998: 71). But in the final stanza, there is a sense of coming together with the speaker and the Moon, a sense of mutual understanding. After describing the Moon's face as an "O-gape of complete despair" and informing us, in a short, sharp sentence, "I live here", the speaker describes the Christianity in the poem's view: church-bells, a cemetery, saints, pews. The speaker informs us that:

> The moon sees nothing of this. She is bald and wild.
> And the message of the yew tree is blackness—blackness and silence. (Plath 1981: 172–173)

The speaker does not appear to yearn for communion, as Clark argued, because she *is* communing. The Moon speaks to her through the movement of the night and the sky. The tree itself communicates a "message" of "blackness and silence" that the speaker does not question, implying an understanding. While Stevenson argues that the force of the moon is "neutral" and "impersonal", a manifestation of Plath's dark moods, the counterargument is that the speaker is telling readers what the Moon sees, or does not see, because she knows. She tells the reader the moon is "bald and wild", uninterested in the blue saints and their "delicate feet", "Their hands and faces stiff with holiness". Plath's bald and wild Moon is neither neutral nor impersonal: she may not be sweet, but she is herself, "a face in its own right,/White as a knuckle and terribly upset" (Plath 1981: 172–173).

And while the speaker may yearn for the tenderness of Mary, "The face of the effigy, gentled by candles,/Bending, on me in particular, its mild eyes" (Plath 1981: 172–173), she knows she has a higher purpose. Here in the blue-light, where the "trees of the mind are black" (Plath 1981: 172–173) and the "grasses unload their griefs at my feet as if I were God" (Plath 1981: 172–173), we see that the speaker has constructed this internalised mind-space and is safe there, but is also depended upon as well as revered.

Wisker argues that "Conventional Gothic entrapment in the family home replaces incarceration in castles and flights along dangerous tunnels. Gothic spatial descriptions destabilise" (Wisker 2004: 107), and in "The Moon and the Yew Tree", Plath gives us a universal fear of being alone and existentially anxious at night while the world sleeps. Plath knows what we fear and what we desire—"safety, mother, friends"—and this is evident here, because "our worst fears arise from dangerous domestic disillusionment" (Wisker 2004: 106). The speaker is confined—to the mind, to this space, to domesticity; Plath herself was confined to Court Green, a sleepless night, and Ted Hughes—and "simply cannot see where there is to get to" (Plath 1981: 172–173) as the Moon, Plath's ever-present guide, hovers above, waiting for the speaker to figure it out.

"Edge"

"Edge" is one of the last two poems Plath wrote before her suicide in 1963. Clark describes the poem as "a cold, expressionless portrait of a dead mother with her dead children…a mother on her own, trying to protect her children" (Clark 2020: 871). It is also one of those poems in which Plath's death overshadows the work to a degree that skews the poem's reading. As Clark writes:

> Though surrealist in tone, no other poem in Plath's oeuvre…has been as biographically determined as 'Edge', which gives the uncanny impression of having been published posthumously. Widely believed to be Plath's last poem, 'Edge' has been interpreted literally as a suicide note. (Clark 2020: 871)

The significance of being "one of the last" is problematic on a number of fronts, as it leads to analysis of Plath's psyche rather than her work. It is also a biased reading—another one of the last poems Plath wrote was "Balloons", a poem in which she tenderly describes her babies playing with the deflating balloons in their flat. Wisker addresses this problem astutely:

> In the decades following her death, critics of Sylvia Plath's poetry tended to read the life and the poetry backwards, as if death's fixed point puts everything into perspective, defining her as only a highly-talented, golden girl suicide, and limiting the ways we read her work, as evidence of a trajectory leading inevitably to that death. (Wisker 2004: 104)

In this poem, the Moon appears in the final stanza, observant, aware, but not impassive. Nor is the mother the moon, as was the case in "The Moon and the Yew Tree", but a "perfected" "dead woman". The speaker acknowledges that only a dead woman can be perfect, which "indicts a sexist culture and literary tradition that equated perfect womanhood with passivity and compliancy" (Clark 2020: 875).

The poem simmers with a cold, bitter rage, and this is reflected in its short lines and enjambments, Plath's use of present tense, and the curt final sentences in the last segment of the poem. As readers, we see the speaker unfurl their observations in a caustic flow as Plath addresses familiar themes: motherhood, domesticity, mythic engagement, the divine feminine, and feminine ambition. As Clark writes, "the poem's savage irony checks the despair. The message of 'Edge' is not, as in the 'The Moon and the Yew Tree', 'blackness and silence', but fury" (Clark 2020: 875), and the speaker's engagement with the Moon in particular gives us a sense of Gothic finality.

Clark notes that in an early draft of the poem, "The woman is perfected./Her dead/Body wears the smile of accomplishment" was initially "Down there the dead woman is perfected", as if "viewing the scene from high up, alongside the indifferent moon" (Clark 2020: 872). Clark again reads the moon as indifferent, similar to "The Moon and the Yew Tree", but "indifference" is inaccurate, as seen in the poem's final four lines:

> The moon has nothing to be sad about,
> Staring from her hood of bone.
> She is used to this sort of thing.
> Her blacks crackle and drag. (Plath 1981: 272–273)

The Moon, in her "hood of bone", is "used to this sort of thing"—she is familiar with the scene described in the preceding lines, and she should be. Clark describes the poem's dead woman as "not perfect, *perfected*—like a work of art, an experiment, something controlled, without agency" (Clark 2020: 871), the presentation of women throughout mankind. No, the Moon is not sad, but she is also not indifferent, lacking concern, because as Creed notes, the Moon is cyclic: "the moon, snake and woman's cycle—move through stages in which the old is shed and the new reborn: the moon moves through its cycle from the old to the new moon; the snake sheds and renews its skin; woman sheds and renews her blood" (Creed 1993: 64).

Plath references cycles of death and rebirth throughout her poetry and prose; indeed, "Lady Lazarus" explicitly states three incidents of death and resurrection that correlate to her biographical history of suicide attempts. A thematic reading across Plath's poetry gives readers a sense that the Moon knows that the dead woman will rise, like Lady Lazarus, and the cycle will begin anew. Creed makes the point that in *The White*

Goddess, Robert Graves "argues that 'twenty-eight is a true lunar month not only in the astronomical sense…but in the mystic sense that the Moon, being a woman, has a woman's normal menstrual period ("menstruation" is connected with the word "moon") of twenty-eight days'" (Creed 1993: 64). The Moon waxes and wanes, growing full and decreasing to new, just as the womb prepares for pregnancy and then sheds on a similar cycle. Within the context of Plath's poem, why would the Moon be surprised by a cycle of rebirth? Why should she show concern? The familiarity of the old turning into the new is not unfamiliar to the Moon.

The final two lines demonstrate a more active presence of the Moon in the poem. The short, one-sentence lines and use of active, present tense suggest that Moon is not passive, as Clark suggests, but in a state of motion, not dissimilar to the action we saw in "The Moon and the Yew Tree": "She is used to this sort of thing./Her blacks crackle and drag" (Plath 1981: 272–273). The Moon is going about her business.

Again Plath has dressed the Moon in the night sky—except instead of being "bald and wild" as described in "The Moon and the Yew Tree", she is wearing a "hood of bone", and "blacks" that "drag", not unlike the hooded cloak of the Grim Reaper. The Moon's cloak drags as she moves across the sky—either an indication of how long the night can feel, or the slow creep of Death itself. Wisker writes that Plath "spotlights the liminal, the boundaries, the animate/inanimate, life and death held in balance. Facing up to the fearful attractiveness of death and its stasis, its artistic completion, provides the energy to rise anew" (Wisker 2004: 115). The Moon may be used to this sort of thing, she may have nothing to be sad about, but that does not mean she is not invested, or in active motion. It does not mean that she will not rise again.

Conclusion

Reading across Plath's poems, we can see a construct of the moon emerge, a recurring character in her work: She is "my/Indefatigable cousin" (Plath 1981: 242), "impeccable" (Plath 1981: 37) with "steely patinas" (Plath 1981: 51); sometimes she is seen in a phase when her "crook whitens" (Plath 1981: 153), but more often she is "rictus" (Plath 1981: 163), "embalmed in phosphorus" (Plath 1981: 209), or "diminished and flat, as after radical surgery" (Plath 1981: 192). Plath's moon has a "concern" that is more personal (Plath 1981: 176); she intervenes in moments of despair, illness, or death and decay, seemingly taking pleasure in it: "The moon lays a hand on my forehead,/Blank-faced and mum as a nurse" (Plath 1981: 157); "But their bones showed, and the moon smiled" (Plath 1981: 209). The moon is a "liar" (Plath 1981: 174) and "merciless" (Plath 1981: 192), and "would drag me/Cruelly, being barren./Her radiance scathes me. Or perhaps I have caught her./I let her go. I let her go" (Plath 1981: 192).

In respect of Stevenson's postulate that the sun and moon represent Plath's inner "light" and "dark" sides, we must acknowledge what Wisker calls "a favourite Gothic trope, the split female self", which she argues "is at the heart of Plath's writing": "She problematises ambiguities inherent in women's sexually and socially-constructed roles—mother, wife, lover, whore, creative artist—showing each to be a version of self, each a performance" (Wisker 2004: 110). The Gothic mode allows both writers and readers a site of connection as well as a discourse through which they can communicate the unspeakable, and provides tools to transgress the boundaries of what it is "acceptable" for women to write about. Plath's poems often wrestle with this desire to both adhere to and redefine the gendered roles for women of her era.

Plath's use of the Gothic demonstrates there is much more to her than her death, or Sun and Moon selves in constant battle, despite critics seeking to reduce Plath "to a brilliant, complicated, dark and unstable poet" (Wisker 2004: 105). It could be suggested that Plath's repeated use of the Moon as a personified entity in her poems, despite its potentially "spooky" presentations, is actually a symbol of calm and stabilisation. No matter where Plath's speakers are—walking about in Africa, maybe; trapped in the cold and planetary light of the mind; or a mother folding her children in like petals—the Moon is ever-present, watching with care.

References

Clark, Heather. 2020. *Red Comet: The Short Life and Blazing Art of Sylvia Plath.* London: Jonathan Cape.

Creed, Barbara. 1993. *The Monstrous-Feminine: Film, Feminism, Psychoanalysis.* London; New York: Routledge.

Hubner, Laura, and Springerlink Online Service. 2018. *Fairytale and Gothic Horror: Uncanny Transformations in Film.* London: Palgrave Macmillan.

Kroll, Judith. 2007. *Chapters in a Mythology: The Poetry of Sylvia Plath.* Stroud: Sutton Pub.

Plath, Sylvia. 1981. *The Collected Poems.* Cambridge: Harper and Row.

Plath, Sylvia, and Karen V. Kukil. 2000. *The Unabridged Journals of Sylvia Plath, 1950–1962.* New York: Anchor Books.

Stevenson, Anne. 1998. *Bitter Fame: A Life of Sylvia Plath.* London: Penguin.

Wisker, Gina. 2004. Viciousness in the Kitchen: Sylvia Plath's Gothic. *Gothic Studies* 6 (1): 103–117. https://doi.org/10.7227/gs.6.1.10.

PART III

Lunacy and Transformation

CHAPTER 9

Illuminating the Darkness: Lunar Representation in Children's Literature

Lauren Christie

Introduction

For millennia, the moon has been considered a powerful symbol of transition and change. Acting as a source of energy for the tides, a source of light within the darkness and providing folkloric inspiration, the moon has played a crucial role across science, nature and culture. The significance of the moon within culture can be evidenced in literature, as the Gothic genre often references the moon in an uncanny way, associating this symbol with graveyards or through provoking anxieties generated by a Sublime environment. However, despite its more sinister associations with cemeteries and terror, the very nature of the moon is that through the reflective power of the sun, it provides light in a period of darkness. Critic Oliver Morton, notes, "what people see when they look at the Moon is indeed, for the most part, a reflection of themselves—of their preoccupations, and theories, their dreams and fears. It has been used for such reflection, or projection, in science and fiction alike" (Morton 2019: 20). As Morton

L. Christie (✉)
University of St Andrews, St. Andrews, UK
e-mail: lec28@st-andrews.ac.uk

E. Gomel, S. Bacon (eds.), *Lunar Gothic*, Palgrave Gothic,
https://doi.org/10.1007/978-3-031-92621-1_9

demonstrates, the reflective properties of the moon can be construed either as literal, by way of providing light in darkness, or as symbolic, offering the observer a philosophical chance to explore their inner thoughts and feelings—their dreams and their innermost fears. Pursuing the concept of the moon in this context presents a complex layering of understanding. For example, in addition to the basic function of providing light, Morton urges the observer to reflect on a more philosophical basis, thereby associating this symbol with a deeper level of significance. As this chapter will later discuss, the different phases of the moon and the periods of light and darkness play an equally significant role in reflecting the transitional journey of ageing for children, challenges they may face as they age, periods of light and darkness within their emotional state, and physical body changes. For this reason, it can be argued that the genre of children's literature likewise possesses transformative and reflective abilities in its power to mould itself to reflect an evolving audience.

The present chapter will examine ways in which the moon is portrayed through two examples of children's literature and will begin by exploring the diversity and extensive application of this symbol. The first textual example that this chapter will cover is Chae Strathie's *The Loon on the Moon*, a picture book targeted towards early age readers. By selecting an example that features the moon as a significant presence through a child-friendly format, this chapter will highlight ways it is portrayed to a young audience in a positive and playful way. As explored through the text, the moon can often convey a sense of hope and imagination, identifiable as the Loon embarks upon its creative journey across outer space, down to earth and into the dreams of young children; the strong connection between imagination and the moon is evident through the significance of the "dream steam" that the Loon collects, and the role that this plays in lighting up the moon.

By way of contrast, the chapter will then progress to consider ways in which the moon is presented to an older childhood/adolescent audience in J. K. Rowling's *Harry Potter and the Prisoner of Azkaban*. It can be argued that as children develop, the corresponding literature often becomes darker, providing the reader with implied situations or threats as an acknowledgement that as readers age, encounters with fearful objects or scenarios that are of a diverse nature and appearance become inevitable. Threats and embodiments of fear can manifest from any situation and are personalised for every reader. Authors often maintain this subtle threat throughout texts written for older readers, urging them to question their own relationship with fear. In the case of Rowling's book series, there is a notable shift in tone as the novels advance—the first two novels are written with a light and curious purpose, and then gradually adopt a darker tone. Providing the audience with a group of fictional characters that explore their emotions in parallel with the readers presents an opportunity to generate a strong bond between reader and fiction through association. Generations of young readers literally grew up through the book series, ageing with the characters and therefore experiencing many similar momentous life events and emotions alongside Harry and his friends.

The moon plays a significant role in both literary examples explored within this chapter, largely due to its symbolic association with the ageing and transformative experience of humanity. These moments of symbolic significance can, for example, emphasise the darkness of uncertainty and anxiety that may come from monumental changes in childhood—both physical and emotional—brought about through ageing. Throughout this chapter the moon will be primarily explored as representative of ageing and innocence when discussing Strathie's picture book, and as a symbol of chaos when considering Rowling's novel. Acting as a central focus within storytelling, the moon has frequently been applied to represent a wealth of symbolism and deeper meaning. Storytelling, coincidentally, is a hugely impactful way of helping progress young children during early developmental years. It is therefore fitting that a symbol which is firmly associated with storytelling through historic examples of folklore has also become embedded in many examples of children's literature, stories which are shared during a young age. Jules Cashford notes:

> The evidence of stories and images from around the world suggests that most, if not all, ancient cultures passed through a stage of interpreting certain aspects of their reality through the Moon. Indeed, the extraordinary and far-reaching powers attributed to the Moon—powers over birth, fecundity, growth, destiny, death and rebirth—amount almost to a world view at the beginning of human history. (Cashford 2003: 8)

As Cashford discusses, the moon has an identifiable cultural significance in relation to history, folkloric roots and the power that it can wield over nature. On a metaphorical level upon considering birth and death as mentioned above, Cashford continues to describe the "provocative metaphor of the Moon's cycle and phase, exploring ways of thinking about permanence, time and mortality. The essential myth of the Moon is the myth of transformation" (Cashford 2003: 8). As evidenced, it is important that younger readers are encouraged to consider "time and mortality" through the journey of the moon by way of emphasising the temporary state of different life phases and difficulties. Although questions around mortality may not be considered an obvious inclusion for children's literature, this is widely applied across the genre, and is covered in great depth throughout the *Harry Potter* series:

> Of the many human longings explored by Rowling, the fear of death is the central element in each, and Rowling appropriates elements of folklore and myth in the satisfying of those "primordial human desires." How one responds to the fear of death is the central conflict of the story; the fundamental difference between Harry and Voldemort is how each one approaches the reality of their own mortality. (Prinzi 2009: 8)

As evidenced in this example, Travis Prinzi acknowledges ways in which Rowling impactfully incorporates "realistic" topics such as death and mortality into her folklore and fantasy. Through this argument, Prinzi also succeeds in emphasising the diverse application of the moon as a central focus to the story. For example, whilst Strathie's picture book explains different phases of the moon to an extremely young readership, Rowling's inclusion of a werewolf urges a deeper consideration of the moon on a more extensive level for an older audience. As this chapter will later explore, the moon also plays a crucial role in chaos and bodily transformation (through werewolves), implying further symbolism in reflecting children as they age. Regarding the basic functionality of the moon, it can be considered soothing due to the strict adherence to a pattern that moves through the same exact cycles on a monthly basis. Examining this from a metaphorical viewpoint, Cashford notes,

> The Moon tells one fundamental story: birth, growth, fullness, decay, death and rebirth. It is the story of transformation. Like human beings, the Moon is born out of the dark and grows to the peak of its powers when, unaccountably, like them, it begins to wither and decay.... But on the third day the Moon comes back to life; it rises again: it is a "New Moon". (Cashford 2003: 15)

If the moon is to be regarded as "a story of transformation" then there remains somewhat of a contradiction between its function in nature and the transformational state of its different phases. On one hand, as Morton explains, "from one full Moon to the next takes 29 days, 12 hours, 44 minutes and 3 seconds" (Morton 2019: 8); the moon is calming and predictable. For an object within nature to be so predictable in behaviour, down to the minutes and seconds of each phase, one may presume that the observer can depend on the reliability of each phase. Indeed, the inevitability of the moon's transitional phases and "re-birth" mirrors the inevitability of ageing. However, as will be discussed later in the chapter, it is ironic that a symbol which is presented as fully predictable and reliable in terms of phases and timing is the same symbol which invokes chaos and anarchy when considering its function in triggering bodily transformation for werewolves.

As can be observed through the turbulent physical and emotional transformation of humans into werewolves (as will be later explored through Rowling's novel and the role of the moon in adolescent literature), these different phases of the moon can equally represent the emotional transformation of children as they age, and their declining reliance on their own imagination. The transitional journey of the moon presents several opportunities for symbolic consideration. For example, as the moon appears in its young state, the young child is likewise new and naïve to the ways of the world; the child then progresses to develop and age, gaining further wisdom and knowledge as they do so whilst reflecting the similar phases and cycles of the transitional moon. As demonstrated in Strathie's picture book, literature targeted towards a younger age group is often replete with examples of imaginary fantasy, wielding the power to transport generations of young children to different worlds and introducing them to fanciful creatures. Supporting this relationship between encouraging a strong imagination and early development, Prinzi argues, "Imaginative literature is a doorway to other worlds, to more permanent things…to the changed mind that can see the present world as more than bare scientific fact" (Prinzi 2009: 46). There is a wealth of literature supporting the application of imagination and storytelling as an early developmental tool. Critic Alison Hawkins explains, "Storytelling constitutes a vital part of early language development, passing on words and sentences, facial expressions, and differing voice tones to everyone from newborns and infants to older children and teens. Communications through talking and listening form the foundations of early literacy, and literacy development" (Hawkins 2024: 167). If, as Hawkins believes, children can learn from these early interactions between adult and child, sharing stories and observing expressions through reactions, then this experience of storytelling has the potential to become embedded in the impressionable memories of young children. Therefore, if storytelling is to play such a pivotal role in forming young children's impressions and values towards life, then literature should be the mode through which many symbolic ideas or messaged are conveyed. Cashford noted earlier that the moon can be considered a "myth of transformation" (Cashford 2003: 8) which mirrors the transformation of a child as they age. If, as Hawkins suggests, storytelling plays such a vital role in language development for the early years, then this is something that needs to be widely practised within early years pedagogy with attention paid towards the content within these stories.

Similar to the nurturing of literacy development through storytelling, it can also be argued that sharing stories and engaging with play likewise strengthens the power of their children's imaginations:

> Children don't need to learn how to play because it is integral to the process of growth and development.... As a child traverses the childhood years, play and development evolve organically in symbiosis with each other: play nurtures development, and the natural course of development is reflected in the child's play. (Whitaker 2024: 19)

In this quotation Julia Whitaker argues for the natural connection between healthy, regular play during childhood and growth and development; for this reason alone, children's fiction authors commonly encourage a sense of fun and play within a storytelling space for young readers. Educationalists are frequently observing changes in early development through connecting this with the power of storytelling and play; therefore it is vital that regular research is conducted on the stories that are shared, and examples of topics that can awaken the imagination.

The transformative state of the moon, and the movement through different phases, can be mirrored through the journey of young children as they age. If the moon symbolises ageing and innocence—both an abundance of innocence for a young audience and loss of innocence as children age—then there is an identifiable connection between the different lunar phases throughout the monthly cycle as being reflective and imitative, and the wealth of evidence supporting the theory that children learn best during early developmental years through imitation; they absorb every story time and every fantasy adventure. The most obvious example of learning through imitation is the power of sharing a story and imaginative play with children. Virginia Radcliffe describes "in imaginary play, we can be anyone, do anything, go anywhere" (Radcliffe 2024: 114). Stressing the connection between the imagination and early development offers the opportunity to awaken a child's mind, and what better way to do so than by presenting them with a picture book which explores the mysteries of the moon and outer space. Exploring the significance of the moon through a picture book for early childhood demonstrates the playful depiction and role of the moon as igniting the imagination of young children, thereby demonstrating the faith that children place in imaginative powers and the trust in their own sense of self.

Radcliffe stretches the understanding of storytelling and the imagination towards imaginative play when considering early developmental benefits. She continues to add,

> Play is arguably the most authentic expression of identity, the essence of who we are. Children have a fierce need to play because they are at the start of their great journey of Life. Play is how they investigate the world and explore their place in it, what they think about, and what matters to them. (Radcliffe 2024: 113)

Strathie's picture book provides a strong example of the culmination of storytelling, early development and the imagination. Referencing dreams, imaginary worlds and creatures, and explaining to young readers the importance that imagination can have—both literally through the power levels of the moon and symbolically through the connection with their development—offers a moving depiction of ways in which the imagination can be inspired through storytelling. Strathie's picture book isolates the moon as a central focus throughout the story, using creative licence and brightly illustrated aliens to explain the different phases and transitions of the moon to a young audience in a relatable and memorable way. As demonstrated in early developmental phases as they learn, the moon represents imagination and creativity, and therefore the early representations of the moon often instil a sense of curiosity and wonder.

The Loon on the Moon follows the journey of the "Loon" who lives on the moon and is solely responsible for travelling down to earth and collecting "dream steam", which is generated from the imaginative adventures of childhood dreams. Strathie's picture book concentrates on exciting a young imagination through use of brightly coloured aliens, imaginative worlds and the wonder of storytelling. Furthermore, the book explains that the different phases of the moon are generated by the power of the imagination gathered from the dreams of children, and as the power levels of this imagination fade, so does the brightness of the moon (an impactful way of explaining different phases of the moon to a young audience). The picture book details the journey of the Loon as he travels between houses, gathering imaginative "steam" to then return home to the moon. Detailing the return journey, and specifically the outcome of this visit, Strathie explains:

> He zooms back up again and uses the dream steam to power the engine…
> that lights up the lightbulbs…
> that make the moon glow. (Strathie 2010: 5–6)

Due to this explanation as to the purpose of the Loon's visit to earth to collect the "steam" from children's dreams, the multiple connections between imagination and dreams are clearly emphasised, as is the role that this imaginative steam has in ensuring the ongoing survival of the moon. What is most powerful about this picture book is the overall relationship between the power of imagination, the moon and the purpose of both. As Strathie explains, due to an overall lack of available dream steam from the children on earth, the consequences appear to young readers as being severe:

> No dream steam meant no power, which meant no moon!
> … the Loon only had enough power to light up three-quarters of the moon…
> until finally the light in the moon went out altogether. (Strathie 2010: 17–18)

Aligning the significance of a diminishing level of dream steam with the changing phases of the moon simultaneously presents a powerful message and a way of explaining a complex state of nature to a younger audience. Furthermore, this connection implies not only that the lack of dream steam is the cause for the light of the moon fading until it eventually reaches its state of a new moon, but Strathie equally succeeds in emphasising the significance of retaining a child-like state of imagination. As the picture book concludes, Strathie explains that the Loon can succeed in re-lighting the "moon lightbulbs" to make it fully glow again by documenting his adventures throughout outer space, and the planets and aliens he encounters in order to share his stories. As the Loon later revisits earth to share his stories of outer space he notices an increase in dream steam from their imagination, which succeeds in re-lighting the moon. Strathie's decision to use stories to reignite the imagination of children all around the world (and to simultaneously also reignite the moon) returns to the initial connection between the imagination and literature. Furthermore, as the Loon chooses to document his travels in outer space, including each of the planets and aliens that he encounters throughout the picture book succeeds in educating young readers on not only the different phases of the moon, but also the importance of the moon as a central symbol within nature and informing them of the different planets within the solar system. Strathie's picture-book is therefore utilised as both inspiration and explanation for younger readers, with the moon being central to the story; he succeeds in inspiring young readers to continue reading stories and using their imagination, but also explaining to them the solar system and different moon phases through brightly illustrated imaginative creatures.

In contrast to Strathie's picture book, Rowling's novel explores the moon through a darker light. Although both textual examples are entirely dependent on the moon, in one instance the symbol represents the importance of retaining a childlike imagination and curiosity, and the other represents chaos and focuses on highlighting the presence of the shadows in the world as children age. As previously argued, there is an implied assumption that once children age, they begin to distance themselves from the immersive world of storytelling and imagination; they stop believing in magic and instead focus on the expected realities of life. Arguing this point further, critic Alistair Pugh observes:

> While play is now widely accepted as the "work of childhood," there is still an expectation among many parents…that older children and young people will…finally get down to some "real, serious work"…. We need to start again. And at the heart of any new approach there must be an acknowledgement that playfulness is just as much the work of adolescence as it is of childhood. (Pugh 2024: 135–136)

Through his observation of the transitional nature of ageing, and the perceived limited timeline around what it means to be considered a child, Pugh is arguing that one of the main causes of a loss of play and the retreat of the imagination is societal expectations, rather than a true "loss" of this innocence through ageing. Pugh argues that this level of imagination and immersive sense of playfulness should be embraced as a fundamental quality throughout different stages of life. Furthering Pugh's argument, Ike Odina notes, "Anecdotally, and as a collective, we appear to have adopted the notion that play only pertains to very young children; that it features less and less as we advance in years" (Odina 2024: 175). Isolating the moon as a central symbol, Pugh and Odina's viewpoints can be demonstrated through the diverse application of the moon in literature for different ages. Whilst Strathie's picture book is the most striking example of literature that aims to inspire imagination and storytelling, Rowling also turns towards fantasy and creates an entire magical world born from the powers of a strong imagination.

Harry Potter and the Prisoner of Azkaban is the first novel in Rowling's *Harry Potter* series that is significantly transformed in tone; whereas the earlier novels in the series convey a young adventurer theme, *Azkaban* is notably darker and more complex. Critic Vandana Saxena argues, "as the protagonist and the reader grow, the books grow in complexity—what seemed like a straightforward struggle between good and evil in the early books becomes a means to reflect on institutional politics, terrorism, changing power equations and moral relativism" (Saxena 2012: 11). Considering the incorporation of darker tones and more complex social politics, Rowling's novels reflect ageing in relation to what the readers may be exposed to within their reality. As the series progresses, the novels reveal deeper levels of complexity around Potter's challenges and enemies when there are further politics and ethical quandaries involved.

This argument will explore the significance of the moon in context through one of Rowling's more creative characters, the werewolf, Professor Lupin. Lupin acts as a confidant and mentor to Harry Potter, arguably a figure that Harry can look upon with dependency and trust. However, as revealed towards the end of the novel, Lupin's body and emotions are unpredictable as he is at the mercy of the transitional moon, which can be viewed as parallelling Harry's turbulent emotional state as he ages. Both Harry and Lupin are considered outcasts, a feeling that they express throughout the book series; furthermore, they are both equally at the mercy of chaotic emotions and transformation, respectively through adolescence and lycanthropy. Presenting this connection highlights a darker function of the moon, one which has the power to transform a trusted figure in Harry's life into a different state—physically as he changes into wolf form, but also in how he becomes unpredictable and therefore potentially less of a stable influence on Harry's turbulent life. Furthering this point, Saxena argues,

> It is not the shape-shifting itself that causes anxiety, but the shape-shifting of a werewolf which undoes the illusion of active control over one's own body. A werewolf monster complicates the elements of folkloric man-wolves. The transformation is involuntary, painful, dangerous and contrary to "human" nature. (Saxena 2012: 160)

Saxena highlights the significant difference between the act of shape-shifting and shape-shifting into a werewolf. Due to the involuntary and violent physical transformation, these shape-shifters can be some of the most threatening. Acting as a further contrast to the first two novels in Rowling's series which are significantly more light-hearted (reflecting a targeted younger readership), the third novel focuses on the importance of light and dark, and most importantly, what may reside within that darkness. *The Loon on the Moon* explores the lighter side of the moon, through the significance of wonder and imagination. For Rowling, there are connections with the moon which indicate something darker, for example through the crucial role of the moon in werewolf transformation, but also the treatment of light and dark through the shadows and fear. Three key figures which represent this darkness and the fear of uncertainty throughout the novel are Boggarts (a fearful magical object which literally resides in the darkness), Dementors (fearful prison guards of Azkaban prison), and Professor Lupin's unpredictable werewolf state. When considering the darker phase of the moon, it is vital to analyse the use of light and darkness and the role of the moon in a novel which assumes a darker tone to reflect an ageing audience. There are numerous examples throughout young adult fiction or older junior fiction where the protagonist is inevitably faced with a moral predicament, where they must deicide a pathway that can determine their moral fate. Therefore, connecting the opposition between light and dark, the lunar phases of the moon and an older childhood/adolescent audience who may experience turbulent emotions and transitions, Rowling's novel presents the reader with darker and more complex social situations, relationships and environments.

Rowling introduces new levels of darkness in her third novel not only through Lupin and his constant battle with the moon, but also through characters that threaten Harry's safety at Hogwarts. Bridging the gap between Harry's turbulent emotions and physical changes as he ages, this novel also explores fear of the unknown through the concealed appearance of the Dementors and Boggarts. Discussing this darkness in the novel, Prinzi argues,

> In alternating between two worlds, Rowling is able to introduce us to the "shadows," to the paradoxes of good and evil that exist both in the world around us and in ourselves. Shadows confuse things and provide little in the way of hard-and-fast rules and descriptions of life; but then again, this is far more realistic. (Prinzi 2009: 41)

Throughout this novel, Rowling draws upon both the difficulties faced by Harry within one world—his home life—through the abusive relationship with the Dursleys and the physical threats towards his safety in the magical world. The Boggarts and Dementors pose such an acute threat due to the fact that neither of them possesses an obvious physical form. Introducing Dementors for the first time, Rowling explains:

> The thing beneath the hood, whatever it was, drew a long, slow, rattling breath, as though it was trying to suck something more than air from its surroundings. An intense cold swept over them all. Harry felt his own breath catch in his chest. The cold went deeper than his skin. It was inside his chest, it was inside his very heart. (Rowling 1999: 66)

The levels in which these monsters are concealed by their hood upon Harry's first encounter directly addresses the fear of the unknown: Harry is unsure as to what is threatening him precisely, but he is aware of the darkness and malice surrounding this creature. The lack of description provided regarding their appearance is likely to spark the imagination of younger readers as they attempt to "fill in the gaps" with their own perceived appearance. Maintaining a sense of mystery around the Dementors enables Rowling to generate a threat of the unknown towards Harry, until a later disclosure of their appearance, purpose and origin. Boggarts are introduced in a similar way; this magical figure possesses no true appearance, but instead reflects that which truly frightens its observer. However, regarding their remedy, it is notably laughter that helps to defeat a Boggart:

> Boggarts are defeated not with the *ridikulus* incantation itself, but with the effect it produces: laughter. "The Boggart in the Wardrobe" does nothing less than equip readers with a method for dealing with fear: imagine the cause of that fear as something to be laughed at. In doing so, we strip the

> object of its power—or better said, we refuse to *give* it power, because in many cases, the object has no power other than the power we give it in allowing it to scare us. (Prinzi 2009: 65)

Rowling's decision to employ laughter as the way to defeat this frightful creature directly reflects a more simplistic view of "good" and "bad" that young children are exposed to. Despite the complexities present throughout this novel, the simple way to defeat Boggarts, creatures which physically transform into whatever the victim is most afraid of, is to laugh. Drawing upon the powerful relationship between fear and laughter allows Rowling to subtly imply that in moments of difficulty and darkness, lightness and laughter may be the answer.

For centuries, werewolves have been regarded through folklore and literature as something unclean and to be feared. For example, Fincher notes, "In fairy tales such as Charles Perrault's 'Little Red Riding Hood,' the wolf is symbolic of evil, embodying deception. In Christian theology, the wolf is most closely associated with the idea of the Devil" (Fincher 2016: 733). Jacques-Lefevre observes the more brutal nature of the werewolf by explaining, "The form of the werewolf is never stable. Neither wolf nor man, he is at the same time both the one and the other in a continuous mutation…a figure of disorder, of trouble which must absolutely be warded off" (Jacques-Lefevre 2002: 189–191). Selecting a werewolf as a central character not only brings into question the role of the moon throughout this novel, but also the dangers that are concealed through the shadows of the night. Furthermore, the physical transformation that Lupin is forced to experience mirrors physical changes throughout adolescence, but also the turmoil of psychological changes through ageing. Saxena explains, "An adolescent can be seen as an 'other,' an outsider to the categories of child and adult, embodying the gap between the two states of being in the chronology of growth" (Saxena 2012: 5). Fundamentally, Harry does represent a hero, but he is also a teenager, and therefore the novels depict this turbulent shift and chaos as he ages and grapples with changing emotions and a sense of self.

Harry Potter and his friends first encounter Lupin on their way to Hogwarts at the start of term. During this enclosed train journey, Harry is targeted by Dementors who board the carriage and attack him, and it is only through Lupin's quick and knowledgeable actions that he is able to repel the Dementors, thus revealing himself as someone who ends up growing to become one of Harry's guardians at Hogwarts. At no point does Harry appear to be threatened by Lupin during their initial encounters; however, he does appear to be curious about Lupin's dishevelled state: "The stranger was wearing an extremely shabby set of wizard's robes which had been darned in several places. He looked ill and exhausted. Though he seemed quite young, his light-brown hair was flecked with grey" (Rowling 1999: 59). Throughout the novel Lupin is often referred to as possessing a sickly pallor, with torn clothes and a weary demeanour when he remains in his human state, a further consequence of Lupin attempting to conceal his werewolf nature to the pupils. The reasons behind this fragile appearance become clear when Harry (and the reader) is made aware of the reality behind Lupin's condition, and the lengths to which Lupin and his friends have gone over the years to help support and conceal his condition:

> The Shrieking Shack was never haunted… the screams and howls the villagers used to hear were made by me…I was a very small boy when I received the bite. My parents tried everything, but in those days there was no cure. The Potion that Professor Snape has been making for me is a very recent discovery. It makes me safe, you see. As long as I take it in the week preceding the full moon, I keep my mind when I transform. (Rowling 1999: 258)

Throughout the novel, the Shrieking Shack is referred to as a hub for paranormal activity. However, as Lupin explains in this quotation, this rumour was created to provide Lupin with a refuge during the full moon. This quotation also informs Harry of Snape's role in this situation as he helps Lupin control his state through use of a potion. It is commonly believed that when werewolves transform, they lose all sense of conscious reasoning and succumb to animalistic desire. Having been unable to secure his potion towards the end of the novel, Lupin transforms upon sight of the full moon in front of Harry and his friends. Discussing this encounter, Saxena explains, "Lupin attacks Harry in his transformed state. Clearly, a werewolf is too dangerous to be included in the human community. It connotates wildness, violence, unbridled instinct and cannibalism" (Saxena 2012: 159). Saxena's description of Lupin's transformed state in this quotation directly aligns with stereotypical understandings of werewolves, through the "wild and violent" nature of those plagued with this condition. However, through noting the "unbridled instinct", Saxena appears to be referencing the deeper significance of an inner turmoil between good and evil that society experiences, choosing morally what is considered "right" over "wrong" in order to live within and contribute towards what is to be classed as a "civilised" society. Divulging his background to Harry, Lupin explains,

> My transformations in those days were—were terrible. It is very painful to turn into a werewolf. I was separated from humans to bite, so I bit and scratched myself instead. The villagers heard the noise and the screaming and thought they were hearing particularly violent spirits. Dumbledore encouraged the rumour. (Rowling 1999: 259)

Due to Lupin's direct narrative, Harry and the reader become aware of the pain and suffering Lupin has experienced in the past as he lives with his condition, and the extent to which he has attempted to control his state as he ages. The true nature of his curse is exposed at the point where Lupin begins to transform under the light of the full moon:

> A cloud shifted. There were suddenly dim shadows on the ground. Their party was bathed in moonlight…Harry could see Lupin's silhouette. He had gone rigid. Then his limbs began to shake…. There was a terrible snarling noise. Lupin's head was lengthening. So was his body. His shoulders were hunching. Hair was sprouting visibly on his face and hands, which were curling into clawed paws. (Rowling 1999: 278–279)

During this moment of transformation, Rowling's excessive detail adheres to common lore about the appearance and behaviour of werewolves. Furthermore, this moment reminds the reader not only of the brutal reality of what it means to transform into a werewolf and live with this curse, fully at the mercy of the lunar calendar, but also the significant role of the moon throughout the novel.

Conclusion

To conclude, this chapter set out to explore lunar representation in children's literature, with a specific focus on the role of the moon within folklore and storytelling, and specifically, contemporary examples of children's literature. Observing the central role of the moon within science, nature and culture, this chapter began by outlining ways in which generations of cultures have attempted to understand the surrounding world based on the rhythms of the lunar patterns and the behaviour of nature in response. Furthermore, research from early developmental studies with children highlighted the significant connection between storytelling, play and encouraging imaginative thought. Similar to the evolving nature of the moon, and the transitional state of a werewolf, children are constantly in a state of flux, learning more about their emotional capacity and physical changes on a regular basis; for this reason, it can be argued that the phases of the moon can likewise mirror the different phases that children experience as they age.

Presenting the moon as a central focus within storytelling offers a powerful opportunity for children to exercise their imaginative powers whilst simultaneously learning about the world around them, for example through Strathie's picture book. Rowling's novel provides an equally powerful example of literature that explores the light and darkness to be found in life, particularly as the protagonist and reader both age. Despite the genre being firmly rooted in fantasy fiction, Rowling delves into tribulations that can be experienced within reality, demonstrated through Harry and his peers as they learn how to process a variety of emotions and challenges, friendships and relationships. Isolating the role of the moon throughout this novel succeeds in raising the question of light and darkness, and threats that may lurk within the shadows, but also by presenting a werewolf as a central character. For these reasons, *Harry Potter and the Prisoner of Azkaban* is arguably the first of Rowling's novels that has adopted a darker tone, offering the reader the opportunity to connect with a character who is at the mercy of the moon (and therefore unpredictable emotions and physical changes similar to a young readership), but also to encounter dangerous threats that reflect situations that young people experience that may be unavoidable and appear insurmountable. Rowling explores the concept of implied threat and fear of the unknown through the Boggarts and Dementors, neither of which instantly reveal their appearance, therefore enabling Harry and the reader to explore their own personal relationships with fear.

The textual examples selected for this chapter, combined with an exploration into research surrounding folklore and storytelling, has enabled an examination of the significance of lunar representation within children's literature. Analysing the transitional nature of the moon and different lunar phases enabled parallels to be drawn between this natural process and the different phases of a child's development. With the transitioning reader in mind, this chapter has explored the diversity through which the moon can be presented. Through Strathie's picture book, the moon is depicted as a champion for the importance of creativity and exploration to develop a young mind. In contrast, Rowling's novel for an older readership presents the moon as a symbol of ongoing chaos and transition, as evident through Lupin's transition into a werewolf and through the developing readership. Rowling's novel provides space for both reader and the characters to explore complex emotions and physical change, and to confront any darkness they may encounter in life with confidence. Connecting these turbulent phases to the moon as a central focus throughout the novel acts as a stark reminder to the reader that, similar to the different phases of the moon, many periods of difficulty will pass as they enter the next phase of their lives.

References

Cashford, Jules. 2003. *The Moon: Myth and Image*. London: Octopus Publishing Group Limited.

Fincher, Max. 2016. Werewolves. In *The Encyclopaedia of the Gothic*, ed. William Hughes, David Punter, and Andrew Smith, 733–735. Oxford: Blackwell Publishing Ltd.

Hawkins, Alison. 2024. Children Listen Anywhere: Storytelling in Early Years Practice. In *Play and Health in Childhood: A Rights-Based Approach*, ed. Julia Whitaker and Alison Tonkin, 166–168. London: Routledge.

Jacques-Lefevre, Nicole. 2002. Such an Impure, Cruel and Savage Beast: Images of the Werewolf in Demonological Works. In *Werewolves Witches and Wandering Spirits: Traditional Belief & Folklore in Early Modern Europe*, ed. Kathryn A. Edwards, 181–197. Missouri: Truman State University Press.

Morton, Oliver. 2019. *The Moon*. London: The Economist Books, Profile Books Ltd.

Odina, Ike. 2024. Never Too Old: Rediscovering the Joy of Play in the Teenage Years. In *Play and Health in Childhood: A Rights-based Approach*, ed. Julia Whitaker and Alison Tonkin, 175–177. London: Routledge.

Prinzi, Travis. 2009. *Harry Potter and Imagination: The Way Between Two Worlds*. Pennsylvania: Zossima Press.

Pugh, Alistair. 2024. Playful Participation in Curriculum Design. In *Play and Health in Childhood: A Rights-based Approach*, ed. Julia Whitaker and Alison Tonkin, 135–139. London: Routledge.

Radcliffe, Virginia. 2024. Licketyspit, Early Years Theatre and Play—The Home of Storyplay. In *Play and Health in Childhood: A Rights-based Approach*, ed. Julia Whitaker and Alison Tonkin, 112–115. London: Routledge.

Rowling, J. K. 1999. *Harry Potter and the Prisoner of Azkaban*. London: Bloomsbury Publishing Plc.

Saxena, Vandana. 2012. *The Subversive Harry Potter: Adolescent Rebellion and Containment in the J.K. Rowling Novels.* Jefferson: McFarland & Company.
Strathie, Chae. 2010. *The Loon in the Moon*. London: Scholastic Children's Books.
Whitaker, Julia. 2024. What is Play? In *Play and Health in Childhood: A Rights-based Approach*, ed. Julia Whitaker and Alison Tonkin, 17–31. London: Routledge.

CHAPTER 10

Lunar Becomings in "The Yellow Wallpaper"

Jacqueline Weal

In 1892, in the context of the *fin de siècle*, the *New England Magazine* published Charlotte Perkins Gilman's most well-known short story, "The Yellow Wallpaper", which follows an unnamed narrator's changing condition as she endures Silas Weir Mitchell's infamous rest cure. Under the moon, the narrator undergoes a steady metamorphosis into a beastly figure that crawls on all fours, biting and shredding her surroundings; in this way, Gilman alludes to the mythical lore of werewolves, as Gothic creatures of nocturnal becoming. Given its rich history and subtext, "The Yellow Wallpaper" has been analysed from a myriad of perspectives but its lunar transformations deserve a closer look. The story reveals metonymic connections between the moon and madness that are further linked to werewolves through intertextuality. A brief overview of critical discourse on the narrator's transformation confirms its animalistic qualities; however, this chapter explores the story as a werewolf narrative specifically, and even more specifically, as a becoming-animal, becoming-multiple and breaking-free.

Gilles Deleuze and Felix Guattari's theory of "becoming-animal" from *A Thousand Plateaus* illustrates how the narrator in Gilman's story

J. Weal (✉)
Langara College, Vancouver, BC, Canada

E. Gomel, S. Bacon (eds.), *Lunar Gothic*, Palgrave Gothic,
https://doi.org/10.1007/978-3-031-92621-1_10

functions like "anomalous" individuals in wolf packs situated at the bounds of society (1987: 243–45). Typically, werewolves have served as symbols of anti-social human behaviour, but a positive take sees becoming-animal as emancipatory. During her lifetime, Gilman fought valiantly for women's rights and freedoms, manifested in the nineteenth-century figure of the New Woman, as embodying a deviation from patriarchal norms. As the child of a single mother, she was often left with friends and family so her mother could work. After marrying and giving birth, Gilman herself underwent Weir Mitchell's rest cure, whose advice to live domestically and forego creative work nearly drove her mad. Subsequently, she separated from her husband and joined "feminist and social reform groups" in which she found fulfillment (Wagner 2014: 369–70). Gilman's collaborative efforts evoke Deleuze and Guattari's emphasis on wolves as pack animals and collectives that are always shifting and on the move. In "The Yellow Wallpaper" the narrator's transformation, or becoming-animal, is like a breaking-free, with the moon an agent of change; furthermore, the multiplicity of creeping women that she conjures up and then releases from behind the titular wallpaper is like a metaphorical pack of were-women: her imagined community.

The narrator goes through several changes over the course of a three-month stay in the country: her health deteriorates, her relationships weaken and her self-awareness intensifies. Before the story begins, she experiences the monumental shift of becoming a mother for the first time, and thereafter, due to a catch-all diagnosis of "a slight hysterical tendency" and the presumed inability to tend to their child, she is prescribed the rest cure by her husband-cum-doctor: the purpose of their trip to the country (Gilman [1892] 1997: 1). Early on, we learn that she is conflicted over what she "personally" thinks she needs to thrive, in contrast to what her husband, John, expects of her (Gilman [1892] 1997: 1). She believes "congenial work, with excitement" and "companionship" will improve her condition, whereas John requires her to be compliant, to follow strict dietary rules and to withstand severe isolation (Gilman [1892] 1997: 1, 4). His rest cure reduces her to a zombie-like state, alive but not living. She is deprived even from using her imagination, be it for writing or for commenting on the "ghostliness" of their rented "estate" (Gilman [1892] 1997: 1–2). As an avid reader of Gothic fiction, Gilman would have been familiar with the "tradition of the rational scientist confronting the supernatural", and thus she depicts John as an extreme rationalist at odds with the romantic sensitivities of his wife (Horowitz 2010: 180). John, along with the medical establishment, represents the symbolic order of male-created discourse. As such, the narrator's secret chronicling of the rest cure can be interpreted as breaking-free from the "phallocentric norms of language"; in her journal, she rambles, leaves gaps and changes topics on a whim, marking "a clear break" from John's rational discourse (Zeidanin 2021: 1418). Indeed, John frequently draws on medical authority to assure his wife that the rest cure is the correct remedy, while threatening to "send [her] to Weir Mitchell" if she does not "pick up" more rapidly (Gilman [1892] 1997: 6). Despite John's reassurances, the narrator is uncertain as to whether his treatment is helping or hurting; she only knows that she cannot survive in a state of passivity and so she rebels, first cautiously, then aggressively. Her rebellion, or becoming-animal, is triggered by the moon, the "light of gothic possibility" (Horowitz 2010: 184).

Lunar Transformations

Since antiquity, the moon has been connected to madness and transformation but also to uncanny monsters of the Gothic genre: vampires, witches and werewolves are all creatures of the night. In his book *The Moon and Madness*, Niall McCrae examines the relationship "between the full moon and transformation" into "a dangerous 'other', most notably a werewolf", showing how this union has been a constant in fiction throughout the ages (2011: iii). And yet, he also considers how people who suffered from illnesses and "psychosis" were "strong candidates for being considered werewolves" too, thus revealing the blurred boundary between fact and fiction when it comes to metamorphosis under the moon (McCrae 2011: iv). Following the Lunatic Acts of 1845, descriptions of "lycanthropy as a form of insanity" became widespread, so that by the time Gilman was writing her story, the idea was commonplace (Du Coudray 2006: 56–57). The word lunatic itself comes from the Latin word for moon, *luna*, indicating deep historical and linguistic ties between werewolves, madness and the moon. In addition, McCrae traces an ancient "male-female dualism" linking the sun to men and the moon to women; this idea, in turn, aligned men with rationalism and daylight, and women with imagination and moonlight, resulting in metonymic connections between women, insanity, and monstrosity which can be found in literary fiction and medical discourse alike (2011: 2). "The Yellow Wallpaper" draws on this nexus of connections, albeit with a subversive twist: the narrator's perception of reality is strongest at night, while John is frequently shown to be irrational. Gilman's application of lunar and werewolf intertextuality heightens the impact of the narrator's transformation, moving the story through realism—autobiography, journal writing and social critique—into the realm of Gothic and horror. This blending of Gothic conventions with "realistic details" creates an "uncanny effect" that opens up the narrative to a multiplicity of interpretations and makes the story difficult to categorise (Horowitz 2010: 176). Accordingly, through its generic wavering and lunar associations, "The Yellow Wallpaper" develops from a place of instability, not the least of which is the narrator's predicament.

So enters the moon, and a proclivity for "excited fancies" (Gilman [1892] 1997: 4). In the attic room, where John has effectively imprisoned her, the narrator fixates on the wallpaper, projecting her desires onto the walls. Ironically, this fixation operates like a stabilising force, giving her the control that she lacks in the rest of her life. The narrator shares her obsession in asides that resemble unconscious thoughts, as she becomes increasingly preoccupied by the light. She remarks upon sunlight, daylight, crosslights, twilight, candlelight, lamplight and, of course, moonlight. In particular, she recognises how the light affects her interpretation of the paper's pattern, noting that in "certain lights…where the sun is just so", a "formless sort of figure" appears (Gilman [1892] 1997: 6), and then "when the crosslights fade and the low sun shines directly upon it", the paper radiates (Gilman [1892] 1997: 7). The narrator explains that the pattern "by daylight [has] a lack of sequence, a defiance of law", subverting the notion that daylight equates to rationalism, and she is proud to be the only one who notices how "it changes as the light changes" (Gilman [1892] 1997: 9). These subtle daytime shifts give way to drastic changes at night, when the narrator's vision is at its sharpest, causing her to wonder if her condition is changing and if the moon is a factor:

> I hate to see *it* sometimes, *it creeps* so slowly, and always comes in by one window or another. John was asleep and I hated to wake him, so I kept still and watched the moonlight on that undulating wallpaper till *I felt creepy*. (Gilman [1892] 1997: 8: emphasis added)

Here, the moonlight is anthropomorphised, "creeping" in through the windows and making the narrator feel "creepy", implying a synergy between her "nervous troubles" and the moon (Gilman [1892] 1997: 3). Upon her arrival at the estate, the narrator describes it as being "quite alone, standing well back from the road… [and] miles from the village"

(Gilman [1892] 1997: 2); she also notes that her attic room has windows looking "all ways" (Gilman [1892] 1997: 3). Nineteenth-century asylums were similarly isolated and built on "elevated rural sites", thus helping to create the "conditions for a moonlight effect" where the moon's influence on mood is greatest (McCrae 2011: 146–47). This is precisely the case for the narrator. When John awakens, she shares her concerns with him, but he dismisses her, suggesting they "talk about it in the morning" and not during the moon's "shining hours" (Gilman [1892] 1997: 9). Yet her nocturnal fixation continues:

> By moonlight—the moon shines in all night when there is a moon—I wouldn't know it was the same paper. At night in any kind of light, in twilight, candlelight, lamplight, and worst of all by moonlight, it becomes bars! The outside pattern I mean, and the woman behind it is as plain as can be. (Gilman [1892] 1997: 10)

The narrator notices how the woman is "subdued" by day and comes alive at night, in a classic Gothic inversion recalling werewolf transformations under the full moon (Gilman [1892] 1997: 10). The paper seems to "move" as the woman "shakes it", trying to break-free (Gilman [1892] 1997: 12). At first the moonlight displays a "formless sort of figure", or a lack, which transforms into a plainly visible woman who is the narrator's reflective double, foreshadowing her metamorphosis. Her fixation with the moon manifests the latent reality of her imprisonment, which causes a visceral reaction; like the woman in the wallpaper, she too becomes increasingly agitated and ironically begins to enjoy the paper that she previously called the worst she had ever seen (Gilman [1892] 1997: 3). Now, it is something "to look forward to" as she is excited by the liberatory possibilities it reveals (Gilman [1892] 1997: 10). For Deleuze and Guattari, such possibilities, or "lines of flight", are bound up with becoming-wolf (1987: 32).

Becoming-Animal

Critics have long recognised the bestial nature of the narrator's metamorphosis, though without linking it explicitly to werewolves. Judith Fetterley notes how the narrator identifies with the "monstrous disruptive self" implicit in the paper (1986: 162), and Mary Jacobus compares her to Bertha Mason in *Jane Eyre*, as "an embodiment of the animality of woman unredeemed by (masculine) reason" (1986: 4). More specifically, Catherine Golden sees her as possessing the "mind-set of a domesticated feline…marking her territory [and] gaining dominance over patriarchy by taking control of her environment" (2007: 16–17). Niles Tomlinson reads a cat-like "animality" in the narrator as unsettling anthropocentric hierarchies (2010: 243). Analysing the narrator's creeping, Leticia Rocha Duarte and Cynthia Beatrice Costa observe how she watches John and Jennie "like a hunter watches a prey", and although she is "not a wild animal", in their view, she "ascends to an animality that defies male certainties" (2021: 275–78). Along with this critical overview, it is worth touching on the period in which Gilman was writing, as her contemporaries, the suffragettes, were repeatedly compared to werewolves, not only in fiction but on satirical postcards and in the news media. Jazmina Cininas maintains that the "female werewolf absorbed misogynist anxieties surrounding the…New Woman", a female "prototype" affiliated with "bad" mothers, "moral degeneracy" and domestic defiance (2017: 37–39), all of which are qualities that can be ascribed to Gilman's narrator, within the historical context. Chantal Bourgault du Coudray also confirms that the "ferocious female werewolf persisted in fiction throughout the period of the *fin de siècle*" (2006: 61). Once again, these examples illustrate how werewolf discourse straddled the boundary between fact and fiction, while also making apparent that the werewolf was a ubiquitous figure in Gilman's cultural milieu, and thus it is unsurprising to find its tracks in her story.

The narrator's becoming-animal is fraught and painful like werewolf transformations in folklore or Gothic literature. After the moonlight increases her self-awareness, the narrator's metamorphosis becomes physical. She experiences feral changes, such as increased nocturnal activity; heightened senses, particularly sight and smell; a lowered stance, from stooping to creeping; and growing aggression, in ripping and biting. Not only does she use night vision to decode the wallpaper, she becomes obsessed with its smell, which "creeps" through the house disturbing her and taking on a life of its own (Gilman [1892] 1997: 11). She spends hours shredding the paper until she and the creeping woman have "peeled off" the bulk of it and then gnaws on the hard wood of the bedstead, injuring her teeth in the process (Gilman [1892] 1997: 13–14). The narrator refers to scratching, ravaging and digging activities that seem to have preceded her arrival, though Gilman hints that she may have participated in these activities by noting how the paper was torn precisely to the narrator's height, both when she first notices it and again when she admits to ripping it herself (Gilman [1892] 1997: 3, 14). As part of John's treatment, she is forced to consume "rare meat" (Gilman [1892] 1997: 7), evoking "Lycaon, the first werewolf in Western literature"; after he served bloody body parts to his guests, Lycaon was transformed into a werewolf by the gods as punishment, losing his voice and humanity as a result (Cohen 2020: 45–46). In Gilman's story, the narrator loses her voice, too, but in an ironic reversal her lycanthropic transformation gets it back. The narrator goes through emotional and attitude shifts, as well, becoming mistrustful, vigilant and bold, while using "language [that] suggests violence" (Horowitz 2010: 185). As the narrator's double, the creeping woman's actions speak for the both of them, and much like a wolf or wild animal, she "hides under the blackberry vines" whenever a carriage approaches the house (Gilman [1892] 1997: 12). The narrator becomes equally vigilant and mistrustful of approaching humans, locking the attic door to keep out Jennie and John and expressing mistrust in their motives. Now, she believes John only pretends "to be loving and kind" and she interprets Jennie's offer to keep her company as being "sly" (Gilman [1892] 1997: 13). But while the narrator is cautious on the one hand, she is bold on the other, declaring that she ripped down the wallpaper "out of pure spite" and then brazenly threatening to murder anyone who goes near it: "no person touches this paper but me—not *alive*!" (Gilman [1892] 1997: 13) Gilman emphasises the narrator's violent language in italics, showing the monstrous extent of her change from a meek and uncertain wife at the beginning of John's treatment, to a feral, restless and even blood-thirsty creature now. Werewolves are often read as manifestations of Freud's "return of the repressed", which goes some way in explaining the narrator's cathartic emotions and animalistic behaviour as a rebellion against the subjugation of the rest cure.

Film adaptations of "The Yellow Wallpaper" remediate its werewolf intertextuality, capturing the narrator's wolf-like characteristics in the *mise en scène*. In a sequence from the BBC adaptation (1989), the narrator is shown awake during the night, gazing out of her attic window, when the camera cuts to a forest and she finds herself standing amongst the trees: there, she spots an unkempt woman in a yellow dress slowly creeping under the moonlight. In a similar scene near the end of the film—her ragged visage and messy hair now resembling those of François Truffaut's wild child—the narrator transforms into a crawling woman, initially creeping over an unconscious John, and then, through a dissolve, creeping in the forest. The viewer swiftly recognises her as the wolf-like doppelgänger from the earlier scene. Carolina Nunez-Puente reads the film through a queer lens, specifically, but seems to observe wolf-like traits in the narrator, nevertheless, by noticing her "panting"; her powerful "Medusian look", like an animal's fierce gaze; and her "convergence with nature" when she crawls through the forest like a wolf in a fairytale (2019: 11–17). A more recent adaptation (2021) emphasises the narrator's growing rebellion in repeated shots of the outdoors. She is shown outside day and night: in one scene spotting a rodent with its babies and killing them with her bare feet, as though they were prey; and in another scene, bringing her infant son into the moonlight and covering him up with grass and leaves in order to hide him. Repeatedly, we see her outside sleeping, slinking about or draped over rocks. In the film's final sequences, which are cross-cut with the narrator crawling on the lawn, she maniacally rips the wallpaper, gouges the floor, bites and shakes the bedstead, and jumps up and down on the mattress, until John breaks into the room and faints, in slow motion, before the frame cuts to black. While the recent adaptation portrays the narrator as having committed suicide, both films are largely faithful to Gilman's text, ending with the protagonist—called Charlotte and Jane, respectively—crawling on all fours, strongly alluding to wolves and werewolves.

Without question, the werewolf intertextuality in Gilman's story is not simple mimicry. Importantly, it manifests liberatory possibilities for the narrator. Becoming-animal helps her to overcome, rather than succumb to, the rest cure, moving towards a sort of *anti*-rest cure. Tracing the growth of werewolf literature in the early to mid-nineteenth century, Joseph Crawford (2020) underscores how stories "repeatedly associated lycanthropy with…madness" but he also quotes from Sabine Baring-Gould's later *Book of Were-wolves* (1865), showing an etymological link between wolves and restlessness: Baring-Gould notes, "the word *vargr*, a wolf, had double significance, which would be the means of originating many a were-wolf story. *Vargr* is the same as *u-argr*, [or] restless" (1865: 105). Significantly, restlessness does not equate to madness; to be restless can also mean to be discontent, a definition that best suits the shifting ontology of the narrator in Gilman's tale: from rest to restlessness, to bestial, the narrator is clearly discontent with the status quo. For Deleuze and Guattari, becoming-animal is a "coming and going", not teleological, but like the moon, always waxing and waning (1987: 25). It is a shape-shift that happens "between" identities and does not settle, in the same way that werewolves are always changing back and forth between states, liminal and ontologically unstable (1987: 239). The narrator's becoming is not straightforward either, as her future is undetermined; however, we can speculate that she will not be fixed to an assigned domestic role, confined to a bed, locked in an attic, or trapped by her husband-doctor and the symbolic order. Her metamorphosis seems to take her closer to "*jouissance*" as the abundance of moonlight in the attic acts as stimulant, visible in her increased activity and suggesting a breaking-free from social, medical and marital constraints (Tomlinson 2010: 243). As Duarte and Costa put it, "liberation and creeping come together" at the end of the story (2021: 278). Appropriately, then, the narrator's wolf-like transformation is characterised by discontent or restlessness, and the effects of that restlessness spread outward.

Becoming-Multiple, Breaking-Free

Adjacent to the narrator's changes are disruptions to her environment and relationships. These changes are contingent and metonymic, which means that almost everything around her is reassembled. When John shows her the attic room that he has selected for them, the narrator asks to stay in a room downstairs with "chintz" wallpaper and windows covered in roses (Gilman [1892] 1997: 2). John will "not hear of it", rejecting the idea to "repaper" the attic and refusing to indulge in the narrator's "fancies" (Gilman [1892] 1997: 2, 4). Later, when the room is mostly "bare again", the narrator embarks on renovations of her own, attempting to move the remaining furniture and tearing "off all the paper" she can reach until she finds the room to be "pleasant" again, almost like a blank slate (Gilman [1892] 1997: 14). Her relationship with John morphs from one of compliance into one of deception, a trait regularly associated with werewolves. Like a wolf in sheep's clothing, she tricks him into thinking that she is following his rules while she conjures up companionship to improve her health, which was denied to her through enforced isolation. For Deleuze and Guattari, becoming-animal always "involves a pack, a band, a population, a peopling, in short, a multiplicity": a "wolfing" is a method "of expansion" (1987: 239). In "The Yellow Wallpaper", the creeping women proliferate until the narrator imagines that she, too, is part of a pack. Energised by the moon, she conjures up multiple women, first within the wallpaper and then reflected outside, through the windows, where she sees several women creeping "so fast" (Gilman [1892] 1997: 14). In this way, the narrator generates a community of wolf-like women who reflect her predicament back to her, and who also offer a method of creative expression after she is forced to quit, or hide, her writing. In addition, the metaphorical pack of werewolf-women reveals an alternative mode of being involving collective action, where the narrator and the woman in the wallpaper work together to free each other: "I pulled and she shook, I shook and she pulled" (Gilman [1892] 1997: 13). Thus, her former, isolated self is transformed through this imagined connection with other monstrous women attempting to break-free. For Deleuze and Guattari, there is a politics to becoming-animal of "groups that are oppressed, prohibited, in revolt, or always on the fringe of recognized institutions" (1987: 247). Accordingly, the werewolf-women are analogous to nineteenth-century suffragettes or New Women, oppressed groups that rebelled against traditional, patriarchal institutions, just like the narrator rebels against her husband and the rest cure. As noted previously, Gilman herself was involved in feminist movements, implying a doubling between her and the narrator, as "The Yellow Wallpaper" is at least semi-autobiographical. The changes in the narrator ignite a chain reaction, in which becoming-animal is also a becoming-multiple; the sublime proliferation of were-women functions as a liberating force in the story and resonates beyond the text.

"The Yellow Wallpaper" is freeing in its deconstruction of dualisms too, or the ways in which the story embraces contradiction over fixed categories. Deleuze and Guattari suggest, "the only way to get outside the dualism is to be-between, to pass between…never ceasing to become" (1987: 277). Comparably, du Coudray says that dualisms "cannot fully contain or explain the werewolf"; drawing on Slavoj Žižek, she reasons that the "surplus" or "excess" aspect of monstrosity can be liberating (2006: 60–61). In the story, oppressive dualisms are displayed and then torn down, like the wallpaper. Sun–moon, rational–imaginative, domestic–wild, mad–sane: each of these binaries is dismantled, questioned or put into motion by the story's end. For example, while the narrator is initially active under the moon, later she is active in the day too—"I always lock the door when I creep by daylight"—and her double, the creeping woman, also "gets out in the daytime", thereby overturning the correlation between daylight and an intrinsically male rationalism (Gilman [1892] 1997: 12). Prior to John breaking into the attic, the narrator exclaims, "it is so pleasant to be out in this great room and creep around as I please! I don't want to go outside" (Gilman [1892] 1997: 14). It seems counterintuitive that she would want to stay inside in the room that she previously hated, especially because her transformation is wolf-like. Gothic houses, however, provide a space of possibility "between inner and outer", before the heroine inevitably breaks-free (Holland and Sherman 1977: 283–84). So although the narrator remains inside the attic initially, this does not mean that she has been domesticated; after all, the attic is in a rented house and not in John's patriarchal home, and thus it is temporary. Moreover, in this space she feels liberated to creep as she wishes, and "creeping signals the corrosion of a hierarchal system", in which "humans are not only elevated above" animals, "but man is privileged over woman" (Tomlinson 2010: 238). Her aggressive creeping, contra to John's fainting, troubles the gender binary, calling to mind the Gothic convention of the femme fatale triumphing over an ineffectual hero. Gilman additionally blurs the boundary between madness and sanity via the narrator's journal, which remains lucid. For example, even at her most desperate, she is cognisant that ending her life would be a mistake: "I know well enough that a step like that is improper and might be misconstrued" (Gilman [1892] 1997: 13). On the whole, then, the narrator's contradictions show a complexity that collapses dualisms and hierarchies, while eliciting empathy for her situation: becoming-animal puts everything asunder, instigating movement along contradictory lines. This fluidity is evident even in the wallpaper's rhizomorphic design, where it turns somersaults, grows "new shoots" in the fungal pattern and reveals "unheard of contradictions", further proof of its Gothic excess and a mirror-image of the narrator's breaking-free (Gilman [1892] 1997: 9, 11, 3).

Becoming-animal opens up space for multiplicities—for species other and alike—staging crossings between humans, animals and monsters. For Deleuze and Guattari, like the rhizome, with its horizontal shape and offshoots, becoming-animal assumes "diverse forms" that break-free from traditional, hierarchal structures (1987: 7). However, as evidenced in nineteenth-century scientific discourse, some entrenched hierarchies were difficult to uproot. Although the narrator's transformation performs an emancipatory function in "The Yellow Wallpaper", the cross-species association of women with animals was also used as a means to control and demean. With Darwinian evolution, some theorists saw women as a subspecies of men, closer to animals and the natural world on the hierarchical chain of being (Cininas 2017: 37). Similarly, speculation in degeneration theory suggested "if humanity had evolved from the animal", it could also devolve "in the same direction", and because of the common association of men with progress, women were considered most likely to regress (Du

Coudray 2006: 40). Therefore, the physicians who treated patients for hysteria sought to regulate the woman's body as a method of control (Horowitz 2010: 127). Like the narrator's husband in the story, doctors were trained to "assume a tone of authority" over female patients so that they would obey, like an animal (Smith-Rosenberg 1972: 675). John condescendingly refers to his wife as "a blessed little goose" (Gilman [1892] 1997: 4), which can be read as an insidious and demeaning way of asserting authority. Similarly, an eminent nineteenth-century gynecologist compared his power over female patients to that "obtained over a wild beast" (Smith-Rosenberg 1972: 676). Within this historical context, the figure of the werewolf still held recuperative value, specifically because of its liminality; for Barbara Creed, the werewolf signifies the "collapse of the boundaries between human and animal", destabilising hierarchical categories and amplifying ambiguity (1993: 10). It follows that the werewolf intertextuality in Gilman's story works as a feminist appropriation of liminality, breaking-free from the degrading discourse. The narrator's transformation a metaphorically collapses the boundary between human and animal, while also moving between body and mind, as she becomes increasingly self-aware and comfortable in her own skin and within her environment. Du Coudray states that "the werewolf's monstrous boundary crossings suggest new possibilities for the constitution of subjectivity and identity" (Du Coudray 2006: 131). In the "Yellow Wallpaper", the narrator's imagined pack of werewolf-women helps to constitute an emergent sense of self within a collective movement, or her feminist awakening.

Understanding becoming-animal through an ecofeminist perspective also foregrounds human-animal likeness while undermining portrayals of women and animals as unthinking beasts to be controlled and domesticated. Indeed, there are versions of female werewolves that demonstrate "a sense of connection" with their environment and an openness to species interconnectivity (Du Coudray 2006: 137). As Polly Atkin says, ecofeminism "does not reject the notion of synergy between women and animals, but questions the framing of that synergy" with what it has been "used to justify" (2020: 212). In her later Gothic story "When I was a Witch" ([1910] 1980), Gilman portrays another unnamed narrator who undergoes a change under the moon, when she discovers that she has mysteriously acquired the powers to make her wishes come true. Like the narrator in "The Yellow Wallpaper", her transformation happens while she is in a state of "simmering rage", in this case due to her frustration with injustice in the urban environment ([1910] 1980: 21). Through the story's premise, Gilman depicts interdependence and concern for animals, women and the working class, and although the narrator's supernatural powers expire before she can help women, she nevertheless manages to enact meaningful change while she still has them. Her empathy for a "starved black cat", the "poor wretch" of a horse and a little "chained" dog compels the narrator to take action using her witch-like magic for emancipatory purposes (Gilman [1910] 1980: 22–25). The rising "wave of humane feeling" that comes from this positive change leaves her with a satisfied sense of pleasure (Gilman [1910] 1980: 26). As an advocate for social reform herself, Gilman believed the subjugation of women amounted to an "obstruction of social evolution"; in her view, "increased interdependency was a mark of evolutionary progress" including "cooperative action for the common good" (Magner 1992: 125, 121). Her politics were notably anti-hierarchical and collective, which is to say, they were unconventional for the time. This is evident in "The Yellow Wallpaper", where the narrator's metamorphosis signifies that she is no longer held in thrall by John and his medical treatment, or by the implicated binaries and hierarchies that were used to oppress women: instead, she is free to become something new.

Conclusion

Importantly, it is the moonlight that catalyses all of this becoming, beginning with the narrator's growing self-awareness and setting into motion her becoming-animal. Gilman connects this lunar transformation to werewolves through intertextuality, which brings forth an expansion, evident in a proliferation of werewolf-women. Gilman's purpose in writing "The Yellow Wallpaper" arose from a yearning: the desire to create art and use her voice for social change. After undergoing the rest cure, in her words, she "came so near the borderline of utter mental ruin that [she] could see over", and so she cast aside Weir Mitchell's advice, like the narrator rejects John's treatment, and "went to work again" ([1913] 1999). In both cases, social constraints led to a breaking-free and becoming-multiple: Gilman through her political work; the narrator with her imagined community. "The Yellow Wallpaper" concludes with imagery of restlessness: the narrator creeps continuously, and freely, around the attic and over John, with no end or destination in sight. For Deleuze and Guattari, becoming-animal "has no beginning or end; it is always in the middle, between things" (1987: 25). Similarly, the narrator and her pack are like a multiplicity travelling along the margins, on the move, and ready to inspire movement in others. Years ago, Gilman let loose the creeping women in the yellow wallpaper—and arguably they are still in motion today.

References

Atkin, Polly. 2020. 'Stinking of Me': Transformations and Animal Selves in Contemporary Women's Poetry. In *In the Company of Wolves: Werewolves, Wolves and Wild Children*, ed. Sam George and Bill Hughes, 211–226. Manchester: Manchester University Press.

Cininas, Jazmina. 2017. Wicked Wolf-Women and Shaggy Suffragettes: Lycanthropic Femmes Fatales in the Victorian and Edwardian Eras. In *Werewolves, Wolves and the Gothic*, ed. Robert McKay and John Miller, 37–64. Cardiff: University of Wales Press.

Cohen, Jeffrey Jerome. 2020. Monster Culture (Seven Theses). In *The Monster Theory Reader*, 37–56. Minneapolis: University of Minnesota Press.

Crawford, Joseph. 2020. No More than a Brute or a Wild Beast': *Wagner the Werewolf, Sweeney Todd,* and the Limits of Human Responsibility. In *Company of Wolves, Werewolves, Wolves and Wild Children*, ed. Sam George and Bill Hughes, 101–112. Manchester: Manchester University Press.

Creed, Barbara. 1993. *The Monstrous-Feminine: Film, Feminism, Psychoanalysis.* New York: Routledge.

Deleuze, Gilles, and Felix Guattari. 1987. *A Thousand Plateaus: Capitalism and Schizophrenia,* translation by Brian Massumi. Minneapolis: University of Minnesota Press.

Du Coudray, Chantal Bourgault. 2006. *The Curse of the Werewolf: Fantasy, Horror and the Beast Within*. London: I.B. Tauris & Co. Ltd.

Duarte, Leticia Rocha, and Cynthia Beatrice Costa. 2021. Creeping into Freedom: Woman's Body in 'The Yellow Wallpaper. *Revista de Estudos Literarios Da UEMS—REVELL* 2 (25): 261–281.

Fetterley, Judith. 1986. Reading about Reading: 'A Jury of Her Peers,' 'The Murders in the Rue Morgue,' and 'The Yellow Wallpaper. In *Gender and Reading: Essays on Readers, Texts and Contexts*, ed. Elizabeth Flynn and Patrocinio Schweickart, 147–164. Baltimore: The John Hopkins University Press.

Gilman, Charlotte Perkins. [1910] 1980. 'When I Was a Witch'. In *Charlotte Perkins Gilman Reader: 'The Yellow Wallpaper' and Other Fiction*, ed. Ann Lane, 21-31. New York: Pantheon Books.

Gilman, Charlotte Perkins. 1997. "The Yellow Wallpaper" [1892]. In *"The Yellow Wallpaper" and Other Stories*, 1–15. New York: Dover Publications Ltd.

Gilman, Charlotte Perkins. [1913] 1999. "Why I Wrote "The Yellow Wallpaper". The Department of History, prepared by Catherine Lavender. New York: The College of Staten Island of the City University of New York. https://web.archive.org/web/20140804112304/http://csivc.csi.cuny.edu/history/files/lavender/whyyw.html. Accessed 24 July 2024.

Golden, Catherine. 2007. Marking Her Territory: Feline Behaviour in The Yellow Wallpaper. *American Literary Realism* 40 (1): 16–31. University of Illinois Press. https://www.jstor.org/stable/27747270. Accessed 29 June 2024.

Holland, Norman, and Leona Sherman. 1977. Gothic Possibilities. *New Literary History* 8 (2): 279–294.

Horowitz, Helen Lefkowitz. 2010. *Wild Unrest: Charlotte Perkins Gilman and the Making of "The Yellow Wallpaper."*. New York: Oxford University Press.

Jacobus, Mary. 1986. "An Unnecessary Maze of Sign-Reading." In *Twentieth-Century Literary Criticism*, ed. Thomas J. Schoenberg, vol. 201, Gale, 2008. *Gale Literature Resource Centre*. gale.com/apps/doc/H1420082952/LitRC?u=vanc85972&sid=ebsco&xid=7b40f146. Accessed 5 July 2024.

Magner, Lois. 1992. Darwinism and the Woman Question: The Evolving Views of Charlotte Perkins Gilman. In *Critical Essays on Charlotte Perkins Gilman*, ed. Joanne Karpinski, 115–128. New York: G.K. Hall & Company.

McCrae, Niall. 2011. *The Moon and Madness*, forward by Dr. Paul Crawford. Luton: Andrews UK Ltd.

Nunez-Puente, Carolina. 2019. A Queer Eye for Gilman's Text: *The Yellow Wallpaper*, a Film by PBS. *In Atlantis.* 41 (1): 11–30.

Smith-Rosenberg, Carroll. 1972. The Hysterical Woman: Sex Roles and Role Conflict in 19th-Century America. *Social Research* 39 (4): 652–678.

The Yellow Wallpaper. 1989. Director, John Clive. British Broadcasting Corporation. London.

The Yellow Wallpaper. 2021. Director, K. Pontuti. Hysteria Pictures. United States of America.

Tomlinson, Niles. 2010. Creeping in the 'Mere': Catagenesis in Poe's 'Black Cat' and Gilman's 'Yellow Wallpaper'. *ESQ: A Journal of the American Nineteenth Century Literature and Culture.* 56 (3): 232–268.

Wagner, Corinna. 2014. Charlotte Perkins Gillman. In *Gothic Evolutions*, 369–370. New York: Broadview Press.

Zeidanin, Hussein. 2021. The New Versus True Woman in Charlotte Perkin Gilman's *The Yellow Wallpaper* and Ellen Glasgow's *Dare's Gift. Theory and Practice in Language Studies* 11 (11): 1416–1420. https://doi.org/10.17507/tpls.1111.08.

CHAPTER 11

Lunacy: Anxieties of Modernity in Luigi Bazzoni's *Footprints on the Moon*

Fernando Gabriel Pagnoni Berns

The Gothic mode is superficially associated with "women in white gowns fleeing dark mansions" (Crow 2015: 139) amidst the night. Also, with the past haunting the present in the form of ghosts and spectres. Yet, the Gothic is also strongly attached to the blurring of categories, boundaries and distinctions. The Gothic is all about impurity of forms, the interstitial bleeding into the narrative (Bienstock Anolik 2019: 9), and emphasises the mixing of reality and fiction via narrative interventions where even readers and viewers are in the dark about what is really transpiring in the story.

Hybridity shapes Italian Gothic film *Le orme* [aka *Footprints on the Moon*] (Luiggi Bazzoni, 1975). Labelled a *giallo* on most websites and academic texts such as Alexandra Heller-Nicholas' *The Giallo Canvas: Art, Excess and Horror Cinema* (2021: 123), the film denies classification: there is no black-gloved killer assaulting beautiful women in expressionist, colourful ways, nor sharp blades shinning in the light of a lamp. Bazzoni's film blends together psychosexual drama, horror, science fiction and art house style to tell the story of Alice Campos (Florinda Bolkan), who is

F. G. Pagnoni Berns (✉)
Universidad de Buenos Aires, Buenos Aires, Argentina

E. Gomel, S. Bacon (eds.), *Lunar Gothic*, Palgrave Gothic,
https://doi.org/10.1007/978-3-031-92621-1_11

haunted in her dreams by the vision of astronauts being left stranded on the moon. Further, she has lost track of three days. To get some relaxation she goes to an eerily deserted seaside resort town where she thinks she has never been, yet where everyone seems to remember her visiting the week before. In the mixing of film genres, the film is ultimately an exercise in Gothic style.

Yet, the film retains something from the *giallo* cycle, in particular its anxieties regarding modernity. The *giallo* is informed by a space that lies between modernism's experience of time and deep memory, and postmodernism's discontinuous spatial experience (Kannas 2020: 184). The collapse of borders separating geographies (Alice works as a translator), eras, reality and fiction stages a confrontation with modern Italy as a cosmopolitan space for tourism and globalisation. Rural, traditional Italy is slowly disappearing, leaving in its place an unrecognisable geography. The everyday becomes discontinuous and tenuous, arguably, part of the Gothic mode that privileges the ephemeral rather than fixity.

In this scenario, the motif of being stranded on the moon reconnects the Gothic with lunacy, meaning the mental affliction caused by the period following the full moon (Brunner 2010: 128). The moon theme highlights the Gothic narrative of ephemeral borders and the dissolution of anything solid. As Italy becomes as much alien as the moon itself, the fear of being left behind increases anxieties over the passage of time.

In this chapter, I will make a close reading on how the lunacy sustaining *Le orme* answers Gothic social and cultural anxieties regarding mental stability in the face of discontinuous spatial experience.

Gothic Experiences of Ephemeral Italy: The Gothic and *Gialli*

Classical Italian horror cinema comprised three main cycles. First, the Gothic years (roughly, from the mid-1950s to the 1970s), sustained on ruined castles and abbeys and embedded with asphyxiating atmospheres of dread, repressed sexuality and perversity. The second cycle was the famous *gialli* (plural for *giallo*), a *filone* (a form of Italian subgenre) predicated on anxieties about modernity, the ruined buildings now replaced in the 1970s by the cosmopolitan city and social mobility. The third cycle (the 1980s) was of decomposition, with gore taking centre stage in films of zombies and cannibals.

Each cycle was not an autonomous category. The Gothic stage and the *giallo* cycle shared elements in common, even when they looked very different. One trope in common is the obsession with reality as a fragmented, almost-oneiric ontology, with the gaze as the main vehicle used to mark the destabilisation of the real.

Italy is currently well known for its horror cinema. When the first Italian horror films opened, however, the country lacked a tradition of fantastic cinema (Bondanella 2009: 306). The first ventures into horror were mostly ignored by audiences who saw with suspicious eyes Italian names in the cast credits and in the director's chair. For Italian audiences, Italian horror films were likely not to be very good, so they mostly turned them down.

The first Italian horror films were Gothic spectacles led by vampires living in ruined castles. These films were never really popular among Italian audiences, thus preventing the development of a strong horror cycle until the 1960s. The utilisation of vampirism can be understood as a commercial device, as vampires were recognised global monsters. For some, however, there was a more complex reason for the use of Gothic images in the first Italian horror films. The Gothic landscapes could be interpreted as a response to the changing landscapes of Italy, symbols of a stagnant past desperately trying to survive in a country which, almost in the blink of an eye, shifted from feudal-like agriculture and farming to industrial labour in what had been called the "economic miracle" (Sorlin 1996: 115).

The Italian economic miracle of the postwar period refers to the striking (in terms of quality and speed) reconstruction of Italy after the years of the Second World War and the fascist regime of Benito Mussolini. This period, roughly encompassing 1958–1963 (even if the period of high economic growth ran right from the early 1950s up to the first years of the 1970s), was possible in part thanks to the contribution of funds from the Marshall Aid programme, which supported Italian economic policies. Italy made good use of these funds, especially making investments in the most underdeveloped regions of the south: "Italy became an industrialised nation, at least in parts of the north and centre, and centuries-old social categories—the rural day-laborer, the sharecropper—all but disappeared across much of the country" (Sorlin 1996: 115), thus changing the traditional social landscape. This shift from a (mostly) agricultural country to an industrialised one brought urbanisation at a never before seen scale which, in turn, produced massive internal migration (approximately 10 million Italians moved from the rural areas to the urbanised centres).

Further, the Italian miracle was part of a global "golden age" of capitalism, "which created a new world market for consumer goods and forced Italians into a modern, industrial world" (Foot 2003: 138).

This increasing prosperity brought a new consumerist society, a real novelty at the time; many Italians (or at least those belonging to the middle class) were able to acquire consumer goods such as cars or home appliances like fridges, televisions or washing machines (Foot 2003: 138). Schooling and increasing secularism, together with urbanisation and industrialisation, transformed the Italian landscape, producing "a shift of power away from the traditional 'structures in dominance'—that is, the essentially regionalist bourgeoisie and intellectual class—toward the 'emergent structure' centered on the technocrats," the latter a new class whose essential features were "a new mobility across the national space" (Restivo 2002: 46). Furthering the presence of Italy across the globe, vernacular cinema contributed to the country's international fame: Italian cinema "was extraordinarily robust, and the art films that defined the Italian cinema internationally were only a part of its flourishing and robust film industry" (Restivo 2002: 8–9). The neorealist movement of filmmaking was embraced at film festivals and the art house circuit, and accepted by general audiences as well. As a consequence of this economic and cultural boom, Italy became a well-renowned destination for global tourism, which accumulated political and economic importance in the country steadily over the course of the twentieth century, coming to a peak in the years following the late 1950s. The European postwar era, rife with trends in international leisure and travelling, influenced Italy, emphasising socio-cultural and economic shifts to new levels which, in turn, enhanced consumer society. The country was literally "transformed by highways and tourism" (Hendrix 2003: 35) and the invasion of hundreds of tourists from the entire globe brought to Italy new anxieties concerning the rapidly changing social, cultural and geographical landscapes. Even if the changes were for good, many Italians, arguably, were anxious about the future of their country within this highly fluid scenery.

This new reality gave rise to the *giallo* cycle, the latter predicated on two main bases: modernity and the gaze. Koven (2006) identifies this cosmopolitanism with violent impulses, the feelings tied to the anxieties brought by the encroaching modernity in postwar Italy. As consequence, there are two interconnected tropes within the *giallo* cycle: the gaze as an unreliable source and gender confusion. Both tropes are rooted in this sense of an invading modernity: Italian locals were witnesses to their country being completely transformed, seemingly in the space of just a few years, while the increasing flux of tourism brought new and modern perspectives on gender to obscurantist Italy, including new fashion trends like long-haired men and women wearing pants. It is not by chance that the *giallo* cycle was, thus, populated by tourists coming in and out of Italy, their foreign gaze offering novel points of view. As such, the *giallo* cycle was populated with witnesses that were baffled by the ambiguity of their gaze, many times unable to distinguish if the figure or voice they saw or heard was that of a woman or a man.

Yet, *giallo* was not entirely new, but a derivation of the detective story, with more emphasis on the crimes than on the investigative procedural or the resolution. As Mikel Koven argues, the detective story, in turn, has its roots in the Gothic:

> the Gothic is linked to the horror story; the Gothic developed into the detective story; therefore there is a link between the detective and the horror story. This is by no means an attempt to alleviate the genre ambivalence in the *giallo* between horror and crime cinema, but to the contrary, to highlight this 'border crossing' between the two. (2006, 74)

Thus, the Gothic and the *giallo* share many elements in common, the role of the gaze in the deconstruction of reality being a key aspect.

Le orme, thus, is a film pivoting between the Gothic cycle and the *giallo*, as the story depicts a woman drowning in confusion and dragging the viewer with her. Neither she nor the viewer knows if what they are seeing is truly taking place or if it is just part of a sick mind unable to differentiate the truth from lies. The boundaries dividing illusion from reality collapse, providing in return uncertainty, the epistemological ruins of reality. In this scenario, the presence of the moon is not mere background but a key interpretative element that evokes political surrealism via oneiric shock.

Fragmented Temporalities, Fragmented Spaces

Fittingly, *Le orme* begins with a shot of the moon, a spaceship slowly approaching the orb. Equally slowly, the spaceship lands on the moon's surface, the latter looking as fake as did the first depictions made by Georges Méliès and his *Le Voyage dans la Lune* (1902). Méliè's' film, in turn and as argued by Frank Kessler, was inspired by a long-standing tradition of *féeries*, "a form of theatrical entertainment combining visual splendor, fantastic plots, amazing tricks, colorful ballets, and captivating music" (2011: 115). The moon, as depicted in the féeries, shared the same fantastic (and inadequate) topography used by Méliè's film. Still, it is important to state that Bazzoni's film was made in 1975, with humanity reaching the moon in 1969. Real images of how the moon looked were common by the 1970s, yet the director preferred a fantastical version, with this natural satellite's landscape dotted with thin mountains of sharp peaks. As such, an effect of alienation is created, where the viewer feels an "unsettling uncertainty that evokes an odd familiarity in the midst of strangeness" that, according to Tom Gunning, is typical of the experience of the modern (Gunning 2018: 69). Already in the first scenes, Bazzoni plays with the viewer and the sense of reality as it is visually presented. Depicting a more realistic moon would not change the narrative at all; however, the director preferred to use a contrived, old-fashioned image, which foreshadows things to come and warns viewers not to believe everything they are looking at.

The moon landing scene ends when an astronaut abandons a companion on the lunar surface before climbing back into the spacecraft and taking off. The film continues with a black-and-white sequence that looks like it was lifted from a 1950s science fiction film. Some enigmatic scientists, communicating through intercoms, inform Dr. Blackman (Klaus Kinski) that the experiment has gone well and that it is "starting again". This abruptly cuts to the next scene, now in colour, where Alice Campos (Florinda Balkan) wakes up in her flat in Italy. Alice's apartment is the epitome of modernity: her cordless phone is very modern (for the 1970s), she lives in a large loft with almost no furniture, and much of the house is robotic, with the curtains rising automatically at the push of a button. Alice's home is the miracle house of the future as promised in the 1950s with its consumer fantasies (Samuel 2009: 80). The house is painted in a clinical white, with no traces of colour and with very little furnishing: the only furniture is strictly functional, leaving most of the space in a sterile white emptiness.

If the apartment is a modernistic and futuristic fantasy, Alice is the depiction of the modern woman, as she lives alone while pursuing a lucrative career of great responsibility as a translator for transnational councils. Further, she wears her hair short and smokes—markers of "modernity" for traditional Italians. The modernist obsession of the *giallo* is also present in Jean, Alice's best friend, an African-American woman who wakes her up by calling Alice from the airport. Before mentioning the reason for her call, Jean comments on how much she marvels at modern airplanes and the speed they reach. This line of dialogue would not seem to carry any weight in the subsequent narrative; however, it does emphasise Italy's obsession with modernity, speed and how everyday life is transformed. Jean mentions how incredible it is to move from one part of the world to another in just a few hours. The African-American is also a mark of the entrance of the diaspora in an Italy closed to the world only a few years before. Alice's almanac, in turn, is written in different languages, including Italian and German: Alice's house is, following a term coined by Michel Foucault (1984), a heterotopia. Foucault's heterotopia is a site where real social, cultural and spatial life is depicted as ultimately entangled in relations of power where different forms of being occupy and cohabit a space together. Alice's surname, Campos, hints at a South American origin (Bolkan is Brazilian, but her character is Portuguese).

The mystery starts when Alice finds pieces of a postcard in her trash can: it depicts the Garma Hotel, a place she has never visited. How did the card reach her house? Why it is in pieces? Alice is disturbed, not only due the torn card, but because, as the day goes on, she remembers the dream she had the night before: an astronaut abandoning his companion on the moon and fleeing. For some reason that she cannot decipher, the dream disturbs her. More disturbing for Alice is to learn that three days have disappeared from her life: according to her boss, Alice left a translation session at an astronautics congress (thus connecting this with her dream) without giving any explanation and leaving her work unfinished. Her boss assures her that "it's not the first time you've caused us problems", without specifying what those problems were. Alice, however, does not remember any of these events. Those days have simply disappeared from her memory. All the scenes described take place through a frenetic editing where dialogue scenes are alternated with brief scenes of cars, roads and government buildings where people walk without pause. It is a modern world far removed from the Italy that lived on agriculture only a couple of decades previously. The confusion besieging Alice, the film seems to suggest, is perhaps related to the frenzy and exhaustion produced by modern life.

Alice's efforts to remember are striking: the flashbacks are in black and white, thus linking her memories with her dreams, one and the other being indistinguishable to the viewer. The talk that Alice translated, meanwhile, revolved around the dangers of modern life: the current pollution problems, promoted by the pace of modern life, which promises a dystopian future where life will be practically impossible. It seems that modernity is at the core of Alice's problems and fatigue. Finally, Alice remembers a panic attack she suffered during the session and her need to flee the translation booth. Although in the 1970s "panic attacks" had not yet been defined as such, it is clear that Alice is a victim of one: a panic attack is defined as the abrupt onset of an episode of intense fear or discomfort and this is how Alice describes her uneasiness. She ran from the place, but the rest of the three days' absence remains in darkness, hiding in her memory.

Alice explains her situation to Mary (Ida Galli), a friend who, the film hints, is a psychologist. It is she who diagnoses Alice as a woman on the verge of burning out: "You needed to rest, and this conditioned your will. There is no doubt you are totally exhausted and you know it". The conversation takes place with both women walking away, skyscrapers in the background, the incessant sound of car horns passing through the congested avenues. Bazzoni begins the conversation with a general shot of a cosmopolitan city, where speed reigns supreme. Thus, Alice's problems are suggested by a modernity that overwhelms her and in which it is normal to feel depressed and exhausted. The dialogue makes it clear that Alice takes pills to get through the day: "It's all these tranquilizers you take", argues Mary. The dialogue could take place in any other scenario, yet the director chose to depict said conversation with both women diminished by the presence of enormous buildings. Alice climbs up to her auto in a parking lot crowded with cars, their owners as anonymous as Alice is in the big city. Before leaving her, Mary mentions that Alice's illness comes from the latter's insistance on being the best in her work. *Le orme* then reveals cultural anxieties about how to be a modern woman in cosmopolitan Rome in the mid-1970s, and the dehumanising demands of the job market.

Suspended from her job due to her past irregularities, Alice faces days with nothing to do, something that bothers her very much as this inaction is clearly alien to her busy lifestyle. With nothing better to do, Alice decides to take a few days away at the mysterious Hotel Garma. Faithful to *giallo* narratives, Alice comes to the little known town of Garma (even the employers at the airport are unaware of a place called Garma) via airplane—modern mobility, as previously mentioned, being key for the narrative. The Garma Hotel is a gigantic, Gothic and luxurious building, located in a small, almost deserted village—the filming took place in Phaselis, Turkey, but the movie does not make explicit where exactly Garma is located, thus solidifying a sense of deterritorialisation. The name "Garma" avoids national roots, yet the film shows Turkish-language posters, emphasising that Garma is a non-place in Italy but not of Italy.

Alice tries to rest, but just minutes after arriving at the hotel, she finds guests who insist they have met her before. Alfredo Laurenti (John Karlsen) asserts he spoke with Alice the previous week. Paola (Nicoletta Elmi), a girl who befriends Alice—the girl introduces herself as Mary, yet her name is Paola—insists that Alice's name is Nicole. All this opens the film up to a blur of identities. Actress Nicoletta Elmi is, herself, a hinge between two eras: the young girl worked in the Italian Gothic period in films like *Gli orrori del castello di Norimberga* [The Torture Chamber of Baron Blood] (Mario Bava, 1972) and in *gialli* like *Rosso Profondo* [Deep Red] (Dario Argento, 1975) or *Chi l'ha vista morire?* [Who Saw Her Die] (Aldo Lado, 1972), thus suturing together two cycles based on the distortion of reality in terms of both time and space. This distortion is channelled through the gaze, especially that of Alice. Looking is key for the narrative, as Alice is intently observed throughout the film: during her role as translator, she is observed by Marie Leblanche (Rosita Torosh), a woman who wants Alice's job; and at the hotel, Alice is intently observed by the other guests.

The film's narration is deliberately fragmented, elliptical and even opaque, leaving audiences in the dark about what is really taking place in the hotel. Is Alice losing her grip on reality? Has she been at the hotel before, as many characters claim? Does Alice have a doppelgänger running asunder around out there? Chatting with the other guests at the hotel about what she did the previous week as Nicole, Alice tries to uncover a previous life or identity. Alice's identity depends on what the other characters saw her doing, rather than on her own memory. Alice is a *flâneur* when "the emptiness of modernity, its meaninglessness and therefore the meaninglessness in the lives of modernity's residents, demanded a search for some kind of meaning" (Koven 2006: 93) through watching to "occupy his gaze and thus complete his otherwise incomplete identity" (Koven 2006: 93); yet, Alice's act of *flânerie* is Gothic in nature, as she tries to complete her identity via the gaze of the other guests, thus breaking down the boundaries separating the subjectivity of the Self from the interpretation of the other guests. Alice even resorts to violence against Paola to obtain information about her previous life. The gaze is key also for Henry (Peter McEnery), a man who lives near the hotel and has an interest in Alice: the man works in biology and, as he states, only sees life "through the lens of a microscope".

Gender ambiguity is another important narrative device for *gialli*. According to Jacqueline Reich, *giallo* films are defined in part by the killer's gender ambiguity. The *giallo* is "a genre dominated by sexually ambiguous villains and monsters offering diverse points of cross-gender identification" (Reich 2001: 8 9). As previously stated, this ambiguity comes from modernity as well, where young women wearing pants and young men wearing long hair were a novelty for traditional Italy: only with the transnational flux of tourism did Italy uneasily accept this scandalous lifestyle. In *Le orme*, Alice is informed by the hotel concierge that someone has called looking for her. When questioned if that person was a man or a woman, the concierge is not sure, as the voice was weirdly androgynous. This gender ambiguity follows Alice as well: a hairdresser states he has met her before, when she arrived at his salon the previous week to change her style to "look more feminine". Modern notions of womanhood clash with traditional ideals of femininity, modern women struggling in balancing being professional and feminine at the same time. Alice's doppelgänger (Nicole) seems to be a divided part of her, one who wants to embrace a more traditional feminine persona.

Recurring dreams (or are they flashbacks? It remains ambiguous) about astronauts on the moon hint at another possibility: that the scientists Alice sees in her dreams are real and, for an unknown motive, kidnap people to mess with their memories. The moon landing is a metaphor for Alice's wreaked memories and identities, and for her incapacity to see clearly. The moon has been historically linked to lunacy (madness). As Niall McCrae states, "the idea of lunar influence on behavior can be traced back to antiquity" (2011: 1), including the triggering of madness. It was firmly believed that the moon could turn people mad. Occult tradition emphasises the role of the moon and its influence on earthly matters: "Though bright and nurturing, the dark side of the Moon incites lunacy, a well-known association reflected in the common saying that 'it must be a full Moon' when unusual or mysterious things happen" (Bremmer 2022: 128), with the satellite a gateway to other realms.

This relationship between the moon, the oneiric and lunacy did not go unnoticed by one of the most popular historical avant-garde movements: surrealism. Like the Gothic and the *giallo*, the avant-garde artists of the interwar period focused, in part, on deconstructing the gaze. They not only wanted to take art out of the galleries, schools and museums, and break "modernism's aesthetics of self-sufficiency" (Lisi 2013: 5), but also to bring art back to its vital praxis (everyday life). Chief among the many purposes of the avant-garde movements was a complete restructuration of the gaze, inviting viewers to see everyday reality in other ways. For avant-garde artists, empiric, rational reality was just a bourgeois construction that art should help to dismantle. The experimental practices of deconstruction attempt to undercut the claims of representation while claiming that "all hope for securing the 'foundations' of knowledge is futile—that 'foundations' must be replaced by 'abysses,' that 'representations' must always be 'put into question'" (Murphy 1999: 291). Thus, reproducing reality via mimetic tools of representation is never a subversive movement, as realism always "serves merely to stabilize and legitimize that reality against which it protests" (Murphy 1999: 9). Thus, experimental artistic movements aimed for viewers to see reality differently, looking directly to esoteric realms, invisible spheres or, simply, to what is socially ignored and marginalised in daily life, via avant-garde practices of spectator–art relationships in order to deconstruct the scopic gaze.

Like many other historical avant-garde movements, surrealism "encourages all viewers to redirect their gaze from outward to inward" (Conley 2013: 114) with a subjective exteriorisation of the internal world of both artists and spectators. Yet, surrealism also invoked political engagement to change social reality. As Adam Lowenstein astutely observes:

> Surrealism has little to do with the popular image of Surrealism as an art movement characterized by romantic investments in psychic automatism, dreams, and liberating love. As early as 1929, Walter Benjamin was calling for the 'dissection' of this 'romantic dummy' version of Surrealism in order to expose what is 'usable inside': the cult of evil as political device (2005: 18).

Thus, "Surrealist art's bizarre, tormented refigurations of the human body should not stand merely as abstract explorations of the unconscious" (Lowenstein 2005: 18–19); they also respond to socially and culturally horrid realities such as economic depression, warfare and social unrest. Bazzoni's use of surrealist, fragmentary filmmaking evokes a political commitment to social unrest, as Italy's landscape and economic/urban/cultural reality transformed into another reality. Thus, the Gothic devices of fragmentary realities, the *giallo* preference for the unstable gaze, and the surrealist assault on the social structures were all friendly neighbours.

In this scenario, the moon is integral to avant-garde experimentations and surrealism in particular. The avant-garde used the moon as "oneiric fatalism" (Havard 1988: 231) with the nocturnal being a reverse of daily life. The moon is key for one of the masterpieces of surrealism, opening Luis Buñuel and Salvador Dalí's *Un chien andalou* (1929). Surrealism characterises a dramatisation of the nocturnal dream world and the unconscious (Warren Friedman 2018: 19), offering a reverse of daily, sunny coherence. Thus, it is not by chance that Bazzoni chose the moon as the particular place to interpret a fall into madness which, in turn, is a surrealist consequence of modernity sweeping Italy and transforming the country. This is not to say that those visual and societal transformations were inherently bad; addressing the "economic miracle" transforming Italy is not the same as making a value judgement. It was a schizophrenic transformation that shattered time and space, turning Italy into a space where boundaries collapsed into uncertainty.

Le orme's end, faithful to its surrealist roots, offers little in terms of explanation. Alice starts to remember that she and Henry visited the hotel many years before, as teenagers in love. Somehow, however, she forgot all about that time of her existence, modern life destroying all romantic, vital aspects of life. Yet this explanation is slightly refuted when Alice hears Henry talking on the phone with an anonymous person, stating that she will not escape this time. Thus, the film hints at the possibility that a conspiracy was, in fact, behind all of Alice's problems, and the scientists are actually a real menace. There is no clear resolution, as Alice accidentally kills Henry during a fight and runs away from the hotel. As she runs, she is hunted down and captured by two astronauts, their white costumes evoking doctors' white uniforms. The film ends just as it started, with a wide shot of the moon in a nocturnal sky.

Conclusions

Luigi Bazzoni's *Le orme* is a surrealist statement about a woman falling into mental illness, the astronauts standing for men in white dragging her into a sanitarium. Maybe the whole Hotel Garma is a huge asylum, a place for the mentally ill. Certainly, Kier-La Janisse included the film in the groundbreaking book *House of Psychotic Women* (2012). Yet, this chapter argues that Bazzoni's *Le orme* is, also, a political film that dialogues with its cultural and societal context of the Italian economic miracle. Thus, the Gothic and the *giallo* cycles were functional, with both being engaged with narrative devices of ambiguity and fragmentary storytelling, with fiction and reality collapsing into each other. The recurrent presence of the moon, in turn, evokes surrealism, not only in its oneiric but also in its political dimension, inviting viewers to see as Alice sees: through the veil of confusion, where reality is no longer a coherent entity but a space where past and present are mixed in a heterotopia. Alice is, maybe, a psychotic woman as argued by Kier-La Janisse, yet her illness is not only a subjective production, but the consequence of what is being obscured: anxieties concerning the state of Italy after a transformative economic miracle that left the country as alien as the moon.

References

Bienstock Anolik, Ruth. 2019. *American Gothic Literature: A Thematic Study from Mary Rowlandson to Colson Whitehead*. Jefferson: McFarland & Company.

Bondanella, Peter. 2009. *A History of Italian Cinema*. New York: Continuum.

Bremmer, Marlene. 2022. *Hermetic Philosophy and Creative Alchemy: The Emerald Tablet, the Corpus Hermeticum, and the Journey Through the Seven Spheres*. New York: Inner Traditions.

Brunner, Bernd. 2010. *Moon: A Brief History*. Yale University Press.

Conley, Katharine. 2013. *Surrealist Ghostliness*. Nebraska: University of Nebraska.

Crow, Charles. 2015. Fear, Ambiguity, and Transgression: The Gothic Novel in Unites States. In *A Companion to the American Novel*, ed. Alfred Bendixen, 129–146. Malden: Wiley.

Foot, John. 2003. *Modern Italy*. New York: Palgrave Macmillan.

Foucault, Michel. 1984. "Of Other Spaces: Utopias and Heterotopias," translated by Jay Miskowiec, *Architecture/Mouvement/Continuité*. http://web.mit.edu/allanmc/www/foucault1.pdf. Accessed 28 August 2019.

Gunning, Tom. 2018. Uncanny Reflections, Modern Illusions: Sighting the Modern Optical Uncanny. In *Uncanny Modernity: Cultural Theories, Modern Anxieties*, ed. Jo Collins and John Jervis, 68–90. New York: Routledge.

Havard, Robert. 1988. *From Romanticism to Surrealism: Seven Spanish Poets*. Totowa: Barnes & Noble.

Heller-Nicholas, Alexandra. 2021. *The Giallo Canvas: Art, Excess and Horror Cinema*. Jefferson: McFarland & Company.

Hendrix, John. 2003. *History and Culture in Italy*. Maryland: University Press of America.

Kannas, Alexia. 2020. *Giallo!: Genre, Modernity, and Detection in Italian Horror Cinema*. Albany: State University of New York Press.

Kessler, Frank. 2011. A Trip to the Moon as Féerie. In *Fantastic Voyages of the Cinematic Imagination: Georges Méliès's Trip to the Moon*, ed. Matthew Solomon, 115–128. Albany: State University of New York Press.

Koven, Mikel. 2006. *La Dolce Morte: Vernacular Cinema and the Italian Giallo Film*. Lanham: The Scarecrow Press.

La Janisse, Kier. 2012. *House of Psychotic Women: An Autobiographical Topography of Female Neurosis in Horror and Exploitation Films*. London: FAB Press.
Lisi, Leonard. 2013. *Marginal Modernity: The Aesthetics of Dependency from Kierkegaard to Joyce: The Aesthetics of Dependency from Kierkegaard to Joyce*. New York: Fordham University Press.
Lowenstein, Adam. 2005. *Shocking Representation: Historical Trauma, National Cinema, and the Modern Horror Film*. Columbia: Columbia University Press.
McCrae, Niall. 2011. *The Moon and Madness*. London: Andrews.
Murphy, Richard. 1999. *Theorizing the Avant-Garde: Modernism, Expressionism, and the Problem of Postmodernity*. Cambridge: Cambridge University Press.
Reich, Jacqueline. 2001. The Mother of All Horror: Witches, Gender, and the Films of Dario Argento. In *Monsters in the Italian Literary Imagination*, ed. Keala Jewell, 89–105. Detroit: Wayne State University Press.
Restivo, Angelo. 2002. *The Cinema of Economic Miracles: Visuality and Modernization in the Italian Art Film*. Durham: Duke University Press.
Samuel, Lawrence. 2009. *Future: A Recent History*. Austin: University of Texas Press.
Sorlin, Pierre. 1996. *Italian National Cinema: 1896–1996*. London: Routledge.
Warren Friedman, Alan. 2018. *Surreal Beckett: Samuel Beckett, James Joyce, and Surrealism*. New York: Routledge.

PART IV

Lunar Cultures and Identity

CHAPTER 12

The Moon as Mirror in The Hungry Moon, Waking the Moon, and Moondial

J. Simpson

The Folkloric Moon as Anti-Modernist

As a celestial body that shines by night rather than day, producing its wan light by reflection rather than combustion, the Moon is the perfect vessel for the Gothic. For most of recorded history in the West, the Moon has represented the irrational, the supernatural, the superstitious. Its invocation often represents the pre-Christian, due to its association with a nightside pantheon of dark goddesses (and a few gods) as contrast to solar deities and spirits, which are more often associated with logic and reason. It also symbolises the dark, the feminine, the chthonic, and the underworld. Symbolically, the Moon threatens the thin veneer of society, subverting the myth of progress and challenging the positivist illusion that science, logic, and reason will cure society of all its ills. As Marquette University note in their *Glossary of the Gothic*:

> Gothic literature, however, often challenged the ability of reason and rationality to explain every aspect of the unknown. Rationality breaks down when society is shown to be beyond predetermination by mere equations.

J. Simpson (✉)
Portland, OR, USA

E. Gomel, S. Bacon (eds.), *Lunar Gothic*, Palgrave Gothic,
https://doi.org/10.1007/978-3-031-92621-1_12

> The Gothic explores the unreasonable and chaotic universe, rife with twisted desires where 'progress' and the veneer of reason and rationality only conceal repressed desires paradoxically brought about by such values. It shows how the power of science can indeed transform life but not always positively and without cost. (Marquette University n.d.)

With its shifting, cyclical appearance and its association with the night time, when all things blasphemous and unholy are thought to walk the Earth, the Moon often symbolises the irrational, undermining the logocentrism of Western thought and casting an epistemological pall over the very idea of knowledge. In this capacity, the Moon serves as a counterpoint to the solar logos, as noted by psychologist and literary theorist Steven Moore while discussing the symbolic resonance of the Moon in alchemy and the works of C. G. Jung in *The Recognitions*, the debut novel by William Gaddis:

> Similarly, alchemists invested the moon with various roles and properties; Jung contrasts male/solar with female/lunar consciousness, and it is easy to sympathize with Wyatt's attraction to (and need of) the latter: 'Its light is the "mild" light of the moon, which merges things together rather than separates them. It does not show up objects in all their pitiless discreteness and separateness, like the harsh, glaring light of day, but blends in a deceptive shimmer the near and the far, magically transforming little things into big things, high into low, softening all colour into a bluish haze, and bleeding the nocturnal landscape into an unsuspecting unity'. (Mysterium Coniunctionis qtd. in Moore 2015: 47).

He goes on to list a number of other Jungian binaries associated with the Moon: "sun/moon; sol (gold)/luna (silver); Logos/Eros; Christianity/paganism; consciousness (rationality)/unconsciousness (irrationality); reason/intuition; separation/unity; activity/passivity; intellect/emotion; day/night", all of which help to further illuminate the Lunar Gothic and its ability to subvert and critique modernity (Moore 2015: 47).

These lunar associations—which make up the bulk of the shadowy, insubstantial body of the Lunar Gothic—are central to many different schools of psychology and modern philosophy, particularly feminism and, later, postmodernism, as argued by twentieth-century philosophers Jacques Derrida and Jacques Lacan. These feminist readings suggest that there is more going on in lunar literature and symbolism than might be noticed with a surface reading or cursory glance. Consider the association with the feminine and irrationality, for example. Far too often, accusations of mental illness were levelled against women for simply behaving in ways other than what patriarchal society deemed appropriate. As Sophia N. Rosenthal observes in her thesis *Letting in the Night: The Moon, the Madwoman, and the Irrational Feminine in Jane Eyre and Wide Sargasso Sea*, you can see how the Lunar Gothic's association with women and mental illness is often women behaving in ways outside of the expectations of a patriarchal society. Referencing Phyllis Chesler's *Women and Madness*, Rosenthal explores some of the mythic roots of women performing roles other than wife, mother, or lover.

> In her introduction, before any modern concepts of madness are introduced, she narrates how 'Artemis [...] had Demeter consecrate her to the moon, so that no matter how far she'd have to wander, she would never forget, never betray her origins' (Chesler 1972: xviii). Artemis, the Greek goddess traditionally associated with childbirth, the hunt, and, yes, the moon, is the only one of Demeter's daughters who never marries, instead becoming a wanderer and creating her own tribe of women, Chesler claims. She is consecrated to the moon, establishing its role as a connection to the matriarchal goddess, in this case Demeter, that can neither be broken nor betrayed, no matter what paths the wandering heroine takes; she is free to roam as she likes, as long as she does not forget her essence. (Chesler qtd. in Rosenthal 2017: 10)

Pathologising traits traditionally associated with femininity as mental illness reflects a wider trend in Western civilisation of demonising nature, thus justifying its conquest and exploitation. As Peter Hinchley argues in his paper *Goddess Worship, Nature and Animality*:

> From this perspective, civilisation appears as a masculine imposition upon female nature, quite the reverse of the old goddess worship. This Old World was extinguished in the succeeding Bronze Age as Indo-European warrior nomads from the east established a patriarchal, stratified and war-orientated culture. The female deities, or more accurately the Goddess Creatrix in her many aspects, were largely replaced by the predominantly male divinities of the Indo-Europeans. The polytheism of gods and goddesses was replaced by the monotheism of God, the single white male. (Critchley 2010: 6)

The Lunar Gothic not only disrupts Western notions of logic, reason, science, and nature, it also challenges the linear conception of time and "the myth of progress", as author Tom Wessels (2013) phrases it, with the neoliberal condition being the ultimate foregone conclusion. As Juan Carlos Duran notes in his thesis *Linear Time* vs *Now Time*: *Towards a Critical Conception of Time in Marx, Benjamin and Rosenzweig*:

> The idea of modern progress establishes a civilizing tendency of development in history that prioritizes the future and rejects the past. The linear time conceives of traditional constitution of life of the oppressed people of the past as obsolete and old, and associates 'modern' behaviors in order to establish a bourgeois and utilitarian relation with nature devoid of metaphysics and myth. (Durán 2020)

The Moon, with its association with cyclical and non-linear time, challenges the supposed primacy of the neoliberal condition, asserting that an alternative may be possible.

In this chapter, the Lunar Gothic's ability to reflect, interrogate, and critique anxieties around women, sexuality, nature, otherness, time, and the limits of rationality will be explored via three works of fiction, Ramsey Campbell's *The Hungry Moon* (1986), Elizabeth Hand's *Waking the Moon* (1995), and the BBC adaptation of Helen Cresswell's *Moondial* (1988).

The Devouring Darkness of *The Hungry Moon*

Published in 1986 by Ramsey Campbell, *The Hungry Moon* tells the story of Moonwell, a hidden hamlet in the Peak District of Northern England existing in the shadow of a nearby nuclear base. For generations, the residents have followed local customs so ancient their origins are lost to the mists of time: decorating the mouth of the cave with flowers on Midsummer, or Summer Solstice, in exchange for another year of peace and bounty. That peace is disrupted with the appearance of Godwin Mann, an American fundamentalist preacher, and his ragtag band of roaming disciples. Mann claims to have been called to Moonwell to put a stop to their ancient customs, which he feels are Pagan. Unfortunately for Mann, the residents of Moonwell—and their ancient ancestors—have very good reason for their continued supplication.

The Hungry Moon largely follows a sprawling ensemble of characters that live in, or come into proximity with, Moonwell, although the novel spends the bulk of its time focusing on four main characters, all of whom are considered outsiders in some regard. There is Nick Reid, a reporter from Manchester who happens upon Moonwell, and falls under its spell. Diana Kramer is an American who came to the town to teach primary school. Finally, there are Geraldine and Jeremy Brooks, a young childless couple from a nearby city who opened a used bookstore in a decommissioned church. The bulk of the novel's drama comes from these four characters interacting with the locals, usually to illustrate their hypocrisy and small town intolerance.

As the novel progresses, the residents of Moonwell fall increasingly under Mann's charismatic spell, which helps to stoke a spirit of fundamentalism, intolerance, and, ultimately, xenophobia in the town into a blazing bonfire. As the tensions mount, Mann's followers descend on the used bookstore, burning every book they deem offensive or objectionable. In this chilling act of mob rule, the first face of *The Hungry Moon*'s Lunar Gothic is made clear—the insularity and small-mindedness of people living in small towns. As Jeremy the bookseller puts it, "My God, that American talks about evil, but that's evil if anything is, people trying to suppress anything they find disturbing, as if shoving it out of sight will make it go away" (Campbell 2019: 70). Once Moonwell is fully under Mann's sway, he plans a symbolic act to illustrate his dominion. He descends into the cave from which the town draws its name, symbolising a triumph over the darkness by the light, thus proving there is no need for the ancient customs. Unfortunately for all involved there was *every* need for said customs. The Druids knew *exactly* what they were doing when they called down their ancient Lunar deity, nicknamed by local custom "Harry Moony", to make their last stand against the Romans, as the village elder Nathaniel Needham tells Diana Kramer:

> Some of them [the Romans] thought on the way to the cave that there was more moonlight under the trees than there ought to be. One soldier even thought that the rays coming down through the branches looked like a spider's web.... Only there must have been more to it than moonlight, because they saw the thing in the forest running across the web the rays made, to get to the baby in the cave.... The light got brighter...until the moonlight hurt their eyes. It looked like a spider as big as a man, a beautiful spider made out of moonlight, or it may have looked like a maggot that was growing more legs than a spider, or a man with arms and legs that stretched out over the forest and a face just like the moon's face except it was moving.... But the soldier who'd seen the light turning into a web saw it scuttle over the edge of the cave, down to the baby, and the light seemed to flare up out of the cave as if the moon had fallen in. (Campbell 2019: 90)

The yearly cave decorations kept Harry Moony imprisoned in the darkness. The lack of offerings allows Harry Moony to take over Mann's body, making his escape and hurtling the novel towards its climax.

Once the entity is freed from the well, Moonwell descends into literal and symbolic darkness. Inside the town, all illumination is gradually devoured by the inky void. Outside of town, Moonwell's very existence seems to be dissolving, falling out of Nick Reid's mind as soon as he passes the town limits. He arrives just in time for the novel's stunning ending, with Mann's human disguise falling away completely. The possession has not restricted itself to Mann, either, moving through several of his followers like an infection before finally taking over most of the town. The darkness' ultimate triumph is only prevented with the death of a child, acting as a kind of sacrifice that returns the town to its natural state. When the darkness lifts and Moonwell is returned to public consciousness, every resident of the town has gone totally blind.

The Hungry Moon both reflects and subverts traditional Gothic themes. Most notably, the Druids are a perfect receptacle for the Romantic energies supposedly vanquished by the Enlightenment. In fact, there is a long history of the Druids being used as bogeymen and as a tool for propaganda. Many believe that is where our ideas about the Druids come from in the first place, with the Ancient Celts serving as a convenient scapegoat to justify Roman occupation of England. Historian Barry Cunliffe observes, "Some have argued that Caesar wanted to present the Druids as dangerous extremists, and thus it was in the interests of effective propaganda to give the impression that they were directly responsible for human sacrifice" (Cunliffe 2013: 76). The Druids were depicted as murderous savages, thus justifying the need for Roman occupation as a civilising force as is so often used as a justification for colonialism. Cunliffe also notes,

> But in the new Imperial age, there was a new imperative—to depict the Druids as the leaders of a vicious sect that revelled in human sacrifice—thus providing a moral justification for conquest. While, in the Posidonian tradition, the Celts and Druids were presented in the comforting, if patronising, guise of 'the noble savage', under the Imperial tradition they had become the enemy who must be destroyed in the name of civilisation. The demonisation of others to justify aggression is a familiar political ploy. (Cunliffe 2013: 7)

It also conveniently overlooks the inherent hypocrisy of Rome's own brutal capital punishments, which they justify by their legal status. These contradictions and subtle tensions are fertile ground for the Gothic to flourish.

The fact that *The Hungry Moon* concerns itself with an entire community rather than a single house or family aligns the story with many of the themes found in Folk Horror, as well, shedding some light on the social concerns of its time. The cloistered insularity, fundamentalism, and xenophobia raging through the inhabitants of Moonwell symbolise what horror historian Bernice Murphy terms "urbanoia", referencing theorists Linnie Blake and, separately, Carol J. Clover:

> Trading on assorted cultural myths—of inbreeding, insularity, backwardness, sexual perversion (especially incest and bestiality), these rural 'white trash' are familiar popular culture icons...which serve as 'symptoms of social, cultural, and economic processes having profound impact upon rural regions in the USA...' [Blake]. More recently, in a reading of the 'hillbilly horror' film that links the sub-genres post-2000 resurgence to the Bush administration's 'War on Terror', Blake notes that 'the United States has a very long history of representing the inhabitants of its own isolated rural places or backwoods communities as monstrous, grotesque, diseased and polluted.' The result of this 'urbanoia' as Carol J. Clover puts it, is the assumption, 'People from the city are people like us. People from the country...are people not like us'. (Blake, and Clover qtd in Murphy 2013: 134)

The anxieties and tensions symbolically reflected by Folk Horror and the Rural Gothic are traditionally associated with Pagan beliefs and customs, which often serve as a shorthand for rural superstitions and customs misunderstood by city dwellers. The fact that both Paganism *and* Christianity pose a grave threat makes *The Hungry Moon* a particularly loaded, layered, and nuanced text that speaks volumes about our current historical moment. The seismic tremors Campbell sensed while attending a Billy Graham rally in the 1980s have since become a grinding, gnashing earthquake, subsequently urging for greater examination of the Folk Horror and Rural Gothic aspects of *The Hungry Moon*'s Lunar Gothic and its themes of class conflict, xenophobia, fundamentalism, and religious intolerance.

The Devouring Goddess of *Waking the Moon*

Waking the Moon largely follows three main characters: Sweeney, Angelica, and Oliver. The trio meet while attending the University of the Archangels and Saint John the Divine during a course on Magic, Witchcraft, and Religion under the instruction of Professor Balthazar Warnick, where they form an unlikely friendship. The unlikeliness stems from the fact that Angelica and Oliver—apart from being seemingly rich and impossibly beautiful and glamorous—are treated like campus royalty, particularly by Professor Warnick.

This reverence stems from the fact that Angelica and Oliver belong to a secret order known as the Benandanti, a shadowy cabal dedicated to keeping an ancient Moon Goddess at bay. The Goddess, known as Othiym Lunarsa, is no matronly nurturer, however. Instead, this ur-Goddess represents primeval darkness and chaos, as Sweeney perceives directly in a vision on the way to meet the Benandanti:

> Above us floated that gorgon's face, vast and ravenous and patient. Once more the moon burned upon her brow with a hard silver gleam. Her hair flowed across the sky, her mouth gaped wider and wider until I thought it would swallow us. But what was most terrible was her eyes. Because they were not a gorgon's eyes. Instead, when the heavy lids lifted, there in that dreadful white face shone eyes warm and blue and brilliant as the heart of summer. (Hand 1995: 115)

It soon comes to light that Oliver and Angelica are thought to be the culmination of an ancient prophecy, which seems closer to coming true when an ancient moon-shaped pendant, known as a lunula, is unearthed in an archaeological dig. This prophecy culminates with the ritual sacrifice of a bull, followed by Oliver and Angelica ritualistically coupling in front of the bull's corpse. This bloody ritual climaxes with Oliver committing suicide by castrating himself, bringing the novel's first act to a close.

The story's second half picks up many years later. Following the bloody ritual, Sweeney ended up being expelled from the University of the Archangels. She is living a quiet life, working at the Anthropology Department of the Natural History Museum. Meanwhile, Angelica has become a feminist icon, writing several best-selling books about women's spirituality and ancient matriarchal societies. Sweeney has not had any contact with her college friends since being expelled, until one day her friend Baby Joe gets in touch to let her know their old friends are getting picked off one by one. It is eventually revealed that Angelica is sacrificing everything she has ever loved to return Othiym Lunarsa to Earth, ushering in a new age where women will reign supreme. The final sacrifice of Angelica's son, sired by Oliver on the night of his suicide, will allow Othiym Lunarsa to physically manifest on Earth. Only a last minute intervention from Oliver, who had been transformed into a woman following his castration and botched suicide attempt, thwarts the chaotic Goddess from returning. She takes Angelica with her as she is plunged back into the void.

Elizabeth Hand's *Waking the Moon* trades the Folk Horror and Rural Gothic aspects of *The Hungry Moon* for the cloistered confines of Dark Academia. Although the story largely concerns itself with the three precocious college students, the decade-spanning, globetrotting story of a primordial Goddess and the patriarchal secret sect that kept her contained for millennia reflects the tensions and anxieties around feminism in the 1990s. As a feminist icon and role model, Angelica encourages her followers to incorporate a full range of female emotions and experiences. As she says during a talk show appearance,

> But until we as women acknowledge our own personal need for power and our own capabilities for aggression and independence, we will never be whole. We'll continue to be good mothers and daughters, we'll continue to be muses, we'll continue to be victims—but we won't be whole and strong. We won't be the Supreme Goddess that we can be. We need to acknowledge all the aspects of the Goddess within us; we need to embrace the chthonic darkness, to welcome and awaken the Moon; and then we will be whole again. (Hand 1995: 334)

The Gothic genre, as a whole, exists as a response to the rational impulse of the Enlightenment. With its crumbling ruins and wandering specters, its ancestral curses and rampant decadence negates the presumptive triumph of logic and science over every aspect of life. The Gothic illuminates what society would prefer to keep repressed and hidden, bursting forth with the daemonic energies of Stevenson's Mister Hyde. The Gothic exists to remind us that nature, including human nature, is not so easily repressed. The Lunar Gothic of *Waking the Moon*, in particular, reflects the subtle energies and currents of the Female Gothic. It is a dark parable of the psychic damage of a society that refuses to engage with anything remotely "feminine", which includes the body, nature, and emotions other than anger. This repression disfigures absolutely *everybody*, man, woman, and otherwise alike. As Angelica states during her talk show appearance, women need to be allowed to express the full force of their being, to exhibit their full humanity rather than merely the roles allowed by patriarchy. Yes, women are goddesses of the hearth, of love and desire, of healing and service. Girls and women can also be valkyrie. Women can be war goddesses or agents of chthonic chaos. Girls and women are capable of *anything*, and we will never have a healthy society until we acknowledge this indisputable reality.

While being symbolically rich and potent, both *The Hungry Moon* and *Waking the Moon* ultimately reify the patriarchal position. Although the Druids embody the Romantic impulses supposedly vanquished by the Enlightenment, ultimately they were right to be afraid of the dark. Likewise, the chaotic Goddess of *Waking the Moon* is a threat to civilisation, order, and perhaps life itself. In light of this reality, the patriarchal order of the Benandanti have a point, elitism and classism aside. The third work to be considered illustrates the redemptive power of the Lunar Gothic.

The Lunar Bridge of *Moondial*

In Helen Cresswell's *Moondial*, adapted for the BBC in 1988, the Moon does more than reflect. It serves as a bridge to the past, adopting the Gothic mechanisms of the time-slip and the ghost story to critique the notion of linear, mechanical time.

Moondial tells the story of Minty (Siri Neal), a teenage girl who gets sent to live with an ageing relative following her mother being involved in a car accident. Bored and worried, Minty begins exploring a nearby mansion estate. While investigating, she discovers a sundial in a rose garden flanked by statues of Kronos/Saturn and Eros/Cupid. She soon discovers it is no ordinary sundial but, in fact, a moondial. When the Moon falls on the dial, it allows her to travel back in time, where she becomes acquainted with two children from previous eras. First she meets Tom (Tony Sands), a cocky, charismatic kitchen boy from the Victorian era who thinks that Minty is a ghost. She soon learns she is not the only one, as Tom tells her he sometimes sees a misty hooded figure in the garden. On her next trip, she goes back even further in time, where she meets the other "ghost", a young girl named Sarah (Helena Avellano). In her own time, Sarah is forced to wander the garden alone at night, cloaked in a deep hood due to a birthmark on her face. Her governess, the cruel and vain Miss Vole

(Jacqueline Pearce), says that she is marked by the devil, a rumour that quickly gets picked up by the superstitious villagers. Miss Vole also keeps all the mirrors in the house covered, as she tells her that seeing her own reflection would cause the Devil to drag her to hell.

Minty and Tom soon resolve to help Sarah, travelling from their respective eras to let the girl know of the governess' treachery. As the final confrontation draws near, a sinister double of Miss Vole, Miss Raven, appears as a lodger at Minty's aunt's house. Miss Raven, an amateur ghost hunter, seems intent on keeping Minty from helping Sarah on Halloween. Fortunately, her plot comes to nothing, allowing Minty and Tom to travel back to the Edwardian era, showing Sarah that her reflection is nothing to be afraid of, thus setting the past right for both Sarah *and* Tom.

With its focus on family and dreamy estate setting, the Lunar Gothic of *Moondial* functions more as a Gothic fairy tale rather than a social critique. Ironically, this unlocks the revolutionary potential of the Gothic genre more than the previous two texts, both of which are more overtly and explicitly political. Linear time, or mechanical time, imposes the notion that modernity is inevitable, that things cannot be other than how they currently *are*. The cyclical time of the Lunar Gothic threatens both the supposed triumph of late-stage capitalism following the fall of the Berlin Wall and the collapse of the Soviet Union and the market logic that makes speculation and profit possible. It is also the engine that propels the forces of Enlightenment, positing that modernity is an evolution and thus superior, which makes anything in the past regressive and a step backward.

Economists Jeff Sugarman and Erin Thrift state that the Industrial Revolution separated time from nature, making it into another commodity to be exploited:

> The rapid proliferation and domination of industry that followed during the nineteenth century was accompanied and abetted by the technologizing of time. The significance of organizing and conducting industrial production under the control of clock time constitutes what Lewis Mumford (1934/1963) identified as the most important technology of the industrial revolution. In the wake of the industrial revolution and its rationality of systems of production, human life not only was reshaped in its relation to labor but also reordered in its relation to time. (Sugarman and Thrift 2017: 3)

The proliferation of mechanical time has spread into every aspect of life. Time is money, after all. Market logic supersedes morality, imagination, even love. It short-circuits any notion of resistance. The mythical time offered by the Lunar Gothic of *Moondial* serves as a reminder that there are always points of resistance. Time does not only move in a straight line. It moves in circles and spirals, loops, and swirls. The Lunar Gothic explored in *The Hungry Moon*, *Waking the Moon*, and *Moondial* offers a vision of a different, older relationship with the natural world; with our emotions; with the parts of our minds we had overlooked or forgotten about. The Moon, as part of our folkloric and folk Gothic pasts, offers a glimpse of an at times frightening, even dangerous, past that flows beneath the modernity of the twenty-first century, but it is one that might just connect us back to ourselves and the world we depend upon for our survival.

References

Campbell, Ramsey. 2019. *The Hungry Moon*. London: Flame Tree Press.

Chesler, Phyllis. 1972. *Women and Madness*. New York: Avon Books.

Critchley, Peter. 2010. *Goddess Worship, Nature and Animality*. [e-book]. http://independent.academia.edu/PeterCritchley/Papers. Accessed 28 October 2024.

Cunliffe, Barry. 2013. *Druids: A very short introduction*. Oxford: Oxford University Press.

Durán, Juan Carlos. 2020. *Linear Time Vs Now Time: Towards A Critical Conception Of Time In Marx, Benjamin And Rosenzweig*. Open Access Theses & Dissertations. 3160. https://scholarworks.utep.edu/open_etd/3160. Accessed 28 October 2024.

Hand, Elizabeth. 1995. *Waking the Moon*. London: HarperPrism.

Marquette University. n.d. *Glossary of the Gothic: Rationality*. https://epublications.marquette.edu/gothic_rationality/. Accessed 28 October 2024.

Moondial. 1988. *Created by Helen Cresswell*. London: BBC.

Moore, Steven. 2015. *William Gaddis: Expanded edition*. London: Bloomsbury Academic.

Murphy, Bernice. 2013. *The Rural Gothic in American Popular Culture: Backwoods Horror and Terror in the Wilderness*. London: Palgrave Macmillan.

Rosenthal, Sophia. 2017. Letting in the Night: The Moon, the Madwoman, and the Irrational Feminine in Jane Eyre and Wide Sargasso Sea. *Scholarship @ Claremont*. http://scholarship.claremont.edu/scripps_theses/901. Accessed 28 October 2024.

Sugarman, Jeff, and Erin Thrift. 2017. Neoliberalism and the Psychology of Time. *Journal of Humanistic Psychology* 60 (6): 807–828. https://doi.org/10.1177/0022167817716686.

Wessels, Tom. 2013. *The Myth of Progress: Toward a Sustainable Future*. Lebanon: University Press of New England.

CHAPTER 13

The Wolf, the Woman and the Moon: Modern Gothic and Grotesque in Hūshang Golshiri's "The Wolf"

Nahid Shahbazi Moghadam

Introduction

In the early twentieth century, modernism heralded what Mikhail Bakhtin referred to as "a new and powerful revival of the grotesque", emerging alongside "the realist grotesque" (1984: 46). Bakhtin posits that the modernist grotesque, while drawing influence from existentialism, was rooted in Romanticism and its dark individualistic representation of the grotesque (1984: 46). Emphasising the mode's darker aspects—congruent with the alienation and uncertainty pervasive in modernist works—the modern grotesque diverges from Bakhtin's celebrated regenerative aspect of the grotesque and its jovial communal laughter and culminates in what Wolfgang Kayser classifies as the "'fantastic' grotesque with its oneiric worlds" (1963: 186). Kayser primarily relies on this iteration of the grotesque to proffer his final definition of the mode as "an attempt to invoke and subdue the demonic aspects of the world" (1963: 188).

N. Shahbazi Moghadam (✉)
Semnan University, Semnan, Iran
e-mail: n.shahbazi@semnan.ac.ir

E. Gomel, S. Bacon (eds.), *Lunar Gothic*, Palgrave Gothic,
https://doi.org/10.1007/978-3-031-92621-1_13

The modernist grotesque predominantly focusing on characters' inner lives rather than physical deformities or external monstrosities, and delineates abstract states and psychological intricacies, accentuating alienation, madness, death, and identity crises. Bernard McElroy observes that the modern grotesque has transitioned from "the external realm" into human interiority, manifesting "the fears, guilts, fantasies, and aberrations of individual psychic life", thus representing an "internal" rather than "infernal" world, whose "originator [is] neither god nor devil but man himself" (1989: 21). Expounding further on the essence of the modern grotesque, McElroy recontextualises John Ruskin's pivotal emphasis on the grotesque as a "play with terror", redefining it in modern terms as an engagement with the horrors of human "external powerlessness and psychic dissolution" rather than "supernatural demons and devouring chimeras" (1989: 22).

Similarly, the Gothic has transcended its definitive generic categorisation, emerging as a potentially ubiquitous phenomenon across a spectrum of literary and artistic works in the twentieth century and beyond. Despite its etymologically implied opposition to modernity, the Gothic has demonstrated a capacity for diverse and evolving manifestations.[1] Indeed, the Gothic, "a tradition of representation, evidently still in making", is characterised in its modern incarnations by a "reflexive self-consciousness", facilitating its resurgence in contemporary settings as "a disturbing…form of open-endedness based on a deliberate foregrounding of reiteration… [which] is the modern form of haunting" (Smith 1996: 4). Consequently, not only is the Gothic now recognised as "deeply bound up with the contradictions basic to modern existence" but also as "endemic to the modern" (Hogle 2014: 6, 7).

Notably, the Gothic retains its primary preoccupations with "the limits of rationality and passion" (Bruhm 2002: 259), persisting as "the barometer of anxieties plaguing a certain culture at a particular moment of history" (2002: 260). What distinguishes contemporary works from their predecessors is the emphasis on "characters' psychological complications" and their struggle with an unsettling temporal dissonance (encompassing past, present, and future) and the experience of loss, particularly the dissolution of self (2002: 267). Akin to the grotesque, the modern Gothic is more concerned with abstract manifestations of horror, delving into the

[1]See David Punter's *The Literature of Terror* (Volume I, chapter 1) and *The Cambridge Companion to Modern Gothic* (Part I, Chapter 1 by Jerrold E. Hogle).

inner darkness of human nature alongside psychological and existential fears, rather than adhering to traditional Gothic tropes of supernaturalism in haunted castles set in distant times and locales. Consequently, the Gothic and grotesque further align with modernism in their portrayal of uncertainty, alienation, and cognitive dissonance.

Hūshang Golshiri (1938–2000), a distinguished fiction writer and literary critic, was instrumental in introducing modernist trends into Persian literature. Renowned for his psycho-experimental novel *Prince Ehtejāb* (1968), Golshiri was well read not only in Persian literature but also in Western fiction, particularly the French New Novel (Sabā 2000; Mirabedini 2002). Upholding exacting standards for storytelling, Golshiri conceived of fiction as "an existential necessity…a primal urge rooted in the human soul" and perceived life itself as a narrative, a "narrative structure" comprising "our acts of cognition", "our communications", and "our effective responses to the world" (Milani 2008: 860). As a novelist and short story writer, he experimented "with the formal and technical aspects of fiction writing" (Ghanoonparvar 1985: 356), consistently "explor[ing] new literary techniques with each piece he wrote" (Mirabedini 2002). As a critic, he focused on critically surveying and reassessing modern Persian literature through his writings, speeches, and workshops. Golshiri belonged to the 1960s generation of modernist Persian writers, whose "social commitment" culminated in their "conscious literary commitment" (Hillmann 1982: 8). Following a transformative period of imprisonment, however, he distanced himself from overt political concerns (Golshiri 2021). Asserting that politically motivated literature is not genuine literature (Golshiri 1999: 438), he remained committed solely to his fight against censorship and lifelong advocacy for writers' freedom of expression. Despite being "well versed in the committed literary theory" (Talattof 2000: 72), he was unequivocal about his disinterest in forms of social realism confined "to a judgmental depiction of the world" (Mirabedini 2002). Concurrently, he dissuaded younger writers from merely practising experimentation and imitating "techniques of magical realism, or stream of consciousness, without reference to their own culture and time" (Mirabedini 2002).[2]

[2] In a lecture on the relationship between modern and classical Persian literature, Golshiri elaborates on the necessity of a return to the classics once modernism has refreshed and released literature of nonessential bounds (Golshiri 1999: 445–463).

"The Wolf" was initially published in Golshiri's collection *My Little Prayer Room* (1975). The English translation first appeared in *Stories from Iran: A Chicago Anthology* (1992), subsequently featuring in *Modern Literature of the Non-Western World* (1997), and his English-language collection *Black Parrot, Green Crow* (2003). The narrative exemplifies Golshiri's mastery of modern storytelling techniques, employing an ambiguous and largely unreliable narrative voice to recount an eerie tale through flashbacks. It chronicles a medical doctor's appointment to a village clinic situated in a remote, mountainous rural area adjacent to a cemetery. The locale, notorious for its harsh winters and heavy snowfall, is pregnant with the threat of wolves throughout long winters. The doctor is accompanied by his young wife, Akhtar, and through flashbacks, a local resident who runs the village school provides an equivocal narrative of Akhtar's gradual self-isolation from the community, paralleled with a growing obsession with a wolf whose recurrent appearance at their dwelling is at the core of the story. As such, the story offers a nonconventional and modern treatment of the Gothic. This study aims to read and discuss "The Wolf" as a tale of modern Gothic, taking into consideration the modernist narrative style and the elements of the grotesque as depicted in the story.

Mysterious Intrusion and Categorical Transgression

The central image of "The Wolf" envisions a young woman gazing out the window of her residence adjacent to the cemetery, observing a solitary wolf staring back and howling in the moonlight. Notably, this image is depicted sparingly throughout the narrative. In one instance, the doctor awakens in the night to find his wife at the window and "the wolf sitting right on the other side of the fence in the dim light of the moon and howling occasionally at the moon" (Golshiri 1991: 345).[3] On another occasion, the narrator describes Akhtar's drawings of the wolf, in one of which "the wolf's shadow was greatly exaggerated, in such a way that it covered the entire clinic and cemetery" (Golshiri 1991: 348). Intriguingly, the image's centrality permeates the entire narrative, haunting both within and beyond the story world. As the drawing suggests, the wolf's shadow

[3] All references to "The Wolf" (translated by Paul Losensky) are taken from Mage Publishers' first edition, second printing of *Stories from Iran: A Chicago Anthology 1921–1991*, edited by Heshmat Moayyad (1991).

not only extends over the cemetery and clinic, where the doctor's residence is situated, but also eclipses life in his household and the entire village.

Regarding the depiction of animal motifs, grotesque fiction is not confined to legendary beasts and hybrid monsters, as "real animals also frequently recur in the grotesques" (Kayser 1963: 182). Kayser asserts that "modern man may experience the strangeness of something totally different from himself and suggestive of abysmal ominousness" in encounters with real animals, particularly "the nocturnal and creeping animals which inhabit realms apart from and inaccessible to man" (1963: 182). Real animals, alongside imaginary beasts, may be portrayed in the grotesque to "combine aversive appearance with real or imaginable dangers" and "direct our attention to the undignified, perilous, even gross physicality of existence" (McElroy 1989: 11). In this context, the grotesque element of categorical transgression may manifest not in the physical and visible hybridity of human with nonhuman—whether animal/floral life or inanimate objects—but in the way that "an animate being" disrupts conceptual understanding of its existence as "it violates our standing biological or ontological concepts and expectations" (Carroll 2003: 298).

In "The Wolf", as the title intimates, the animal motif serves as the narrative's centrepiece, revolving around Akhtar's progressive fixation on the solitary wolf's recurrent nocturnal visitations at her window. Though not inherently nocturnal, wolves are classified as crepuscular, a characteristic mirrored in the story's wolf, which frequently materialises by the clinic and cemetery in darkness and is ultimately glimpsed on the mountain pass on the evening of Akhtar's disappearance. The wolf is portrayed as a menacing presence, disrupting the tranquillity of the rural life: "who would have thought that a wolf, large and solitary, I believe, sitting opposite the window and staring, would little by little become a problem for the doctor and for all of us besides?" (Golshiri 1991: 345) The narrator's statement evinces an ominous undertone, intensifying the aura of mystery and threat engendered by the wolf's presence.

Scholarly analyses of Golshiri's "The Wolf" have interpreted the wolf figure through various lenses. The wolf's presence is discussed as element of magical realism within an otherwise realistic narrative, symbolically embodying a malevolent, deceitful spirit (Shiri 2007: 147). A Freudian psychoanalytical interpretation posits the wolf figure as representative of the id (Kāzemi et al. 2017: 55). While symbolic significations and psychoanalytical implications are indeed present, to regard the wolf as purely negative or as an incarnation of evil is to overlook the quintessence of its portrayal, which is, first and foremost, the very essence of the grotesque itself. As depicted, the wolf exemplifies the definition of the grotesque as "a corporeal, or flesh-made metaphor which produces…intellectual uncertainty, emotional disharmony, and hermeneutic indeterminacy" (Chao 2010: 14). The "emotional disharmony" here pertains to the impossibility of ascribing definitive attributes to the wolf (e.g. an evil spirit) and the sentiments it evokes (both within the main characters and readers). This is best epitomised in Akhtar's oscillating feelings between fear and attraction. The "hermeneutic indeterminacy" and "intellectual uncertainty" can be observed, respectively, in the narrative's open-endedness and the wolf's evasion of categorisation within its own species.

The narrator observes that wolves are considered a natural threat, particularly during the cold season in mountainous regions: "in the winter, if the snow falls, the wolves come closer to the settlement. It's the same way every year" (Golshiri 1991: 344). Typically, wolves attack in packs; however, the sense of dread and danger in this narrative focuses solely on a single wolf, a solitary figure appearing repeatedly at the same location. This depiction renders the wolf incongruous with its species, imbuing the story with its grotesque essence; had the narrative centred on a pack of wolves threatening human life, it would lack the incongruity necessary to create a Gothic atmosphere. Moreover, the wolf is characterised beyond cognitive expectations of typical lupine behaviour. When the doctor, overwhelmed by its constant returns, sets a trap baited with meat, the wolf eschews the lure: "From the footprints, we realized that the wolf had come up to the side of the trap and sat right next to it. Then the trail of footprints went straight up to the fence around the clinic" (Golshiri 1991: 347). The narrator concedes, "I've never before heard of a hungry wolf passing up all this meat" (Golshiri 1991: 347).

The wolf's enigmatic state of being is further intensified by references to its eyes. The significance of eyes in grotesque depictions is noted by both Kayser and Bakhtin. In discussing grotesque body parts, Bakhtin associates eyes with individuality, which he considers "not essential to the grotesque" due to his focus on the mode's regenerative and comic form (1984: 316). Kayser suggests that "the isolation of the eyes has an ominous and alienating effect" and refers to them "as an expression of the soul, as a link with the world; …as the actual seat of life" (1963: 73). The concept of eyes conveying individuality is particularly pertinent to this discussion, as it aptly defines the wolf as a solitary figure and alludes to the nature of Akhtar's obsession developed through visual connection. Assuming eyes as expressive of the soul, the wolf's eyes render its ambivalences and shape the characters' feelings and reactions. Here, the eyes are not isolated but appear as isolated "shining red eyes" on a black page in one of Akhtar's drawings (Golshiri 1991: 348). Furthermore, the wolf's eyes distinctively recur throughout the narrative and are highlighted in the focal image of the "staring" wolf. The narrator twice refers to "the wolf's glistening eyes" when describing the driver's wife, Sadiqeh, initially noticing Akhtar's obsession with the wolf's eyes, and Akhtar seeing the wolf at the window at midnight (Golshiri 1991: 344, 346). Akhtar herself describes the wolf's eyes, in her conversation with the narrator, as "two burning coals" (Golshiri 1991: 346).

Aligning with Carroll's definition of a grotesque being, the wolf's appearance and demeanour are not only disconcerting and unsettling for a lupine creature, but also convey a liminal state of existence, as the wolf is variously confused with and identified as a dog. Identity confusion, a trope masterfully employed by pioneering authors such as Edgar Allan Poe and E.T.A. Hoffmann, is prevalent in Gothic and grotesque fiction. In Hoffmann's works, according to Kayser, "doubts concerning…identity are never fully resolved" (1963: 73). In this narrative, the doctor's wife indicates that the wolf resembles "a German shepherd sitting upright on its front legs" as she recounts to the narrator how her fear dissipated after the initial midnight encounter at the window (Golshiri 1991: 346). Later, when she and her husband meet the wolf on the snowy mountain pass and she attempts to persuade him to exit the vehicle and repair it, Akhtar reiterates: "It's the same one. Believe me, it is completely harmless. Perhaps it's not a wolf at all, maybe it's a German shepherd or some other dog. Get out and see if you can fix it" (Golshiri 1991: 350). Curiously, the narrator also observes that the school children's copies of one of Akhta's sketches, which she had previously confirmed to him as depicting a wolf, all resemble "German shepherds, with ears drawn back and tails that wrapped around their haunches" (Golshiri 1991: 349). Significantly, the story concludes with the narrator commenting on the final sketches Akhtar entrusted to Sadiqeh for the school children: "I couldn't tell Sadiqeh, or even the doctor, but after all, what appeal could sketches of dogs, such ordinary mutts, have for the village children?" (Golshiri 1991: 351) The disparate perceptions of the wolf, and what the divergent views signify about the ambivalence surrounding the wolf's identity—oscillating between a dangerous beast and a harmless ordinary dog—warrant further examination, particularly in relation to Akhtar's growing obsession.

Haunting Obsession and Alienation Vs. Hunting and Humiliation

Akhtar, the doctor's wife, is portrayed as mirroring the wolf as a solitary and divergent figure. She is initially introduced as a nineteen-year-old bride, "short and thin, so thin and pale that it seemed as if she'd collapse any minute" (Golshiri 1991: 344). The pallor is reiterated when the narrator, accompanying the doctor to check the trap, glimpses her at the window: "The woman's eyes were wide open, staring. Her pale skin had become paler" (Golshiri 1991: 347). Following her disappearance, her husband is twice described as pale: "he turned pale, exactly the same sickly color of his wife's face" (Golshiri 1991: 350). Beyond suggesting a fragile mental state, her pallor and diminutive stature evoke a sickly childlike appearance, contrasting her with the womanly, maternal image typically associated with village life and rural settings. The narrator learns from his wife about Akhtar's unusual concern regarding her ability to bear children, an atypical worry for a young, newly wed woman:

> My wife informed me that she had gone to look for the doctor's wife. She said, 'She's not doing well.' She said, I believe, that the doctor's wife had told her that she was afraid she would not have children.
>
> My wife had consoled her. They had been married for a year. (Golshiri 1991: 346)

Akhtar's fear of sterility and her frail physique are intricately linked to her isolation and subsequent obsession. A sense of insignificance, embodied in her frailty, engenders a degree of neglect, against which her desire for motherhood serves as a counterpoint. At times, the narrative tone reveals a rather indifferent and oblivious attitude towards her; upon learning of the doctor's car being stranded in the snow and listening to his account, "no one thought of his wife until the very moment he said 'Akhtar, so where is Akhtar?'" (Golshiri 1991: 343–344) Also, discussing his offer for her to teach at the school, the narrator admits, "the truth of the matter is that the doctor had suggested it to keep his wife occupied" (Golshiri 1991: 344). Evidently, her daily activities are limited; she is occasionally seen "behind the windowpanes" and "only when it is sunny would she leave the side of cemetery and walk about the village, ...along the path to school...[and]...to the canal bank together with the women" (Golshiri 1991: 344). This routine is significantly disrupted by the onset of winter:

"after the first snow fell, she disappeared. The women would see her sitting beside the heater reading something or pouring herself tea" (Golshiri 1991: 344).

The advent of winter further isolates Akhtar, a condition exacerbated by the wolf's appearance. Sadiqeh initially suspects that Akhtar approaches the window "when the wolves start howling" and subsequently notices "the wolf's glistening eyes" and "how the doctor's wife stared at the wolf's eyes" (Golshiri 1991: 344). Akhtar herself discusses the wolf with the narrator on several occasions. Once, responding to the narrator's inquiry about her drawing a wolf on the classroom board, she states: "However much I wanted to draw something else, it wouldn't come to me. I mean, when I put the chalk to the board, I drew it automatically" (Golshiri 1991: 348). Earlier, describing the wolf's eyes as "exactly like two burning coals", she confesses:

> 'I myself don't know why, when I see it, see its eyes or that stance...you know, it's exactly like a German shepherd, sitting upright on its front legs and staring for hours at the window of our room.'
>
> I asked, 'So why do you?'
>
> She grasped my meaning and said, 'I told you, I don't know. Believe me, when I see it, especially its eyes, I can no longer budge from the window'. (Golshiri 1991: 346)

Akhtar's alienation is thus intensified by her obsession with the wolf to the point of abjection. The abject, as Julia Kristeva posits, "the jettisoned object, is radically excluded... towards where the meaning collapses" (1982: 2). Here, it is not the feminine maternal body that is abjected, nor even Akhtar's childlike and frail figure per se, but rather its indication of a divergence from community norms, foreshadowed in her physical frame and later manifested in her obsession. Kristeva elaborates that the abject revolves around "what disturbs identity, system, order. What does not respect borders, positions, rules. The in-between, the ambiguous, the composite" (1982: 4). Akhtar's desperation and concern about childbearing signify her internal conflict between a desire for normalcy and an urge to explore the unknown, the self, the instinctual, and the boundless.

If the wolf is associated with the instinctual, the realm of the mysterious and threateningly unknown, then Akhtar's obsession indicates a compulsion to trespass known boundaries, to transgress. At a metaphoric level, the depiction of the moon during the wolf's nocturnal visits, its staring and howling at the lunar orb, bears significance in relation to Akhtar's problematic state. Long associated with the cycle of nature, femininity, death, birth, and becoming (Eliade 1996: 154–155), the moon is also portrayed in Persian classics as a source of inspiration, a muse-like figure (Kuryluk 1987: 216). If the wolf's presence reinforces the flight to instinct or the unknown, the moon replaces the desire for motherhood as a new form of feminine and instinctive boundlessness, the becoming, the urge for which intensifies the obsession with the wolf as a form or medium of transgression. Akhtar, whose name interestingly translates to "star" in Persian,[4] ultimately disappears in a rather ethereal sense; no remains of her are found.

Akhtar's husband, though most intimately affected by the wolf's appearance and his wife's obsession, remains a peripheral figure until midway through the narrative, when he is portrayed as overwhelmed by the unfolding events. As recounted, he first becomes aware of the wolf when he awakens in the night to find his wife at the window. In his account of the incident, he refers to his wife as being "fearless" (Golshiri 1991: 345). It is well into the story that we learn he has purchased a trap to catch the wolf. The following day, he anxiously confides in the narrator that his wife "is going crazy" and that he was roused by the wolf's call to find her "fiddling with the door latch", flashlight in hand (Golshiri 1991: 347). When the doctor and narrator inspect the empty trap, with Akhtar observing from behind the window, the doctor desperately implores the narrator: "I don't understand, you at least say something to this woman" (Golshiri 1991: 347). Paradoxically, it is not the wolf but the doctor who finds himself ensnared, though by the wolf's presence which the narrator refers to as "a problem for the doctor" (Golshiri 1991: 345). The trap serves as the first explicit manifestation of the doctor's struggle to eliminate the wolf. Arguably, he develops a peculiar and ambivalent attitude towards the creature, as if his feelings are directed not merely at an animal, but at an enigmatic existential threat that has alienated his wife. He appears to cultivate an eccentric hostility, a form of rivalry, towards the apparent intrusion of the wolf which disturbs his domestic tranquillity.

The doctor's predicament aptly illustrates McElroy's aforementioned redefinition of the grotesque as a play with the horrors of human "external

[4] The word "Akhtar" is an older equivalent of "star" in Persian than the contemporary "setāreh".

powerlessness and psychic dissolution" (1989: 22). His failure to eliminate the wolf seemingly parallels a growing estrangement in the couple's relationship, though the narrator dubiously suggests "none of them remembered the wife and husband ever having raised their voices to one another" (Golshiri 1991: 349). Unable to trap the wolf, he is "forced to get the police" (Golshiri 1991: 348). By this juncture, his reactions to the wolf's presence blend dread and aggression, his fear and abhorrence culminating in intense hostility. Three days later, when the wolf is ostensibly killed, the doctor has the news relayed to his wife, who disbelieves it and is said to have "only smiled" at the news (Golshiri 1991: 348). The narrator also admits, "I didn't believe it myself" and later cautions the doctor about heavy snow in the pass, advising him "not to go" to the city (Golshiri 1991: 349). Regardless, the doctor departs with his wife for the hospital, despite being a medical professional himself and her condition not appearing grave. On the journey, his hesitation to repair the car leads to his wife's exit and disappearance; "before he could realize it, she was out of the car... then it seemed that he had closed the door out of fear, or Akhtar had closed it before" (Golshiri 1991: 350). Twice thwarted, he is ultimately compelled to confront the wolf and potentially save himself and his wife, but he is described as remaining in the vehicle as his wife alights and vanishes.

The doctor's portrayal and his desperation effectively epitomises "the death of the hero, even of the heroism" that characterises modern literature (Clark 1991: 29). His futile struggle to hunt the wolf and his wife's enigmatic disappearance leave him in a state of profound confusion and loss. As he prepares to depart the village on that fateful evening to take Akhtar to the city, he confides in the narrator: "she is not well. I don't think she can stand it here" (Golshiri 1991: 349). Even prior to her disappearance, he has relinquished hope of reclaiming her. While Akhtar's experience is depicted as a gradual alienation from her surroundings and an intensifying obsession with the wolf, the doctor undergoes the ultimate degradation. Not only does he fail to hunt the wolf, he also proves inept at protecting his estranged wife. Following her final disappearance, he is consumed by degrading shame and remorse. His humiliation is palpable towards the narrative's conclusion, evident in the narrator's confusing and dubious account of the events.

Unresolved Eeriness and Narrative Incongruities

Grotesque fiction, particularly in works bordering on the Gothic, often relies on external factors, namely the setting, to create an atmosphere of mystery and fear. In "The Wolf", as discussed, a solitary wolf repeatedly appears at the doctor's lodging, "two rooms in the clinic…on the far side of the cemetery…exactly one block away from the settlement" (Golshiri 1991: 344), in desolate surroundings characterised by harsh winters and heavy snowfall. As Mirabedini asserts, in this story, as in others from the same collection, Golshiri harnesses nature's capacity for mystery to engender an atmosphere of fear and aggression (1999: 687). The overall setting—the clinic rooms adjacent to the cemetery, the howling wolves, the wolf's nocturnal visits under the light of the moon, and the wintery isolation—creates an eerie ambiance, which is further mystified through the incongruously unreliable narrative tone. The narrator's account is both emotionally and intellectually unsettling, leaving the reader in a state of confusion and uncertainty regarding a clear understanding of the incidents. The language of the narration can be considered a powerful verbal manifestation of the grotesque, its detached and confusing tone clashing with the gravity of the subject matter.

The story's opening observation that "sometimes a dog, a sheep, or even a child would disappear" when wolves approach the village during the cold season (Golshiri 1991: 344) initially appears to foreshadow Akhtar's ultimate disappearance. However, this seemingly straightforward possibility is subsequently complicated by the narrative's cultivation of doubt and confusion. As previously noted, the narrator seems to criticise the doctor for his hasty and reckless decision to journey to the city despite the snow and warnings. Concurrently, he equivocates, suggesting that "perhaps the doctor was right" (Golshiri 1991: 349) and describing him as "a responsible man" (Golshiri 1991: 349). Earlier, upon hearing of the doctor taking his wife to the city, he relates: "Sadiqeh said his wife was ill. The doctor had told her so. I didn't believe it" (Golshiri 1991: 348). Also, regarding the final incident on the mountain pass, since "the doctor was not able to speak properly", he "gathered" that the windshield wipers malfunctioned; "then the motor shut off" (Golshiri 1991: 350). However, he twice mentions that there was "nothing wrong with the windshield wipers" when they were checked after the incident (Golshiri 1991: 343, 350). Furthermore, the narrator portrays the doctor as devastated by Akhtar's disappearance, "choking on his sobs" (Golshiri 1991: 343). Yet, in recounting his efforts to calm the grieving man, he subtly notes the doctor's composure and puzzlingly mentions, "I don't know why the doctor kept saying, 'Believe me, it wasn't my fault'" (Golshiri 1991: 349).

The narrator's occasionally detached tone suggests a certain emotional distance from the events, leaving the reader uncertain about the narrative's overall mood and, more significantly, the reliability of his account. The narrator's tone is especially remarkable in his attitude towards Akhtar. In their initial conversation at the school, he appears caring and considerate, offering that they "come to village and take a house" away from the cemetery (Golshiri 1991: 346). However, his overall tone regarding her appearance and obsession conveys a degree of scorn. Discussing her sketches, he repeatedly mentions her hiding them when others enter her room and somewhat dismissively states, "there is nothing special about the woman's drawings" (Golshiri 1991: 348). Referring to Akhtar's note accompanying the final model drawings for the school children, he indicates being "still more confused" by "a *hastily* written note...saying *something like* 'As an offering to our school'" (Golshiri 1991: 350–351, emphasis mine). The entire text is a tapestry of confusing and contradictory observations, deliberately fostering an atmosphere of uncertainty and mystery.

The narrative language ingeniously constructs a verbal grotesque, accentuating the dissonance between the story's content and its narration by juxtaposing a nonchalant tone with the gravity of the events depicted. In an analysis of Nikolai Gogol's "The Overcoat" in relation to the grotesque in the story, "the narrator's distorted language" is described as "filled with the many irregularities of colloquial speech and the sort of puns and language games we associate with folklore or urban gossip" (Roney 2009: 167). The effect of such a language of narration, which bears resemblance to the language style of "The Wolf", is that it "evokes both empathy and disgust from its readers, a characteristic response to the grotesque" (Roney 2009: 167). The ambivalent and seemingly frivolous narrative tone in "The Wolf" stands in stark contrast to the sinister and enigmatic progression of events, engendering the grotesque through the collision of incongruous form and content, thereby evoking contradictory emotional responses. This phenomenon aligns with Philip Thomson's definition of the grotesque as "the unresolved clash of incompatibles in work and response", supplemented by a secondary definition of "ambivalently abnormal" (1972: 27). In this narrative, the storytelling approach is instrumental in amplifying the contradictory aspects inherent to the grotesque; as McElroy astutely observes, "the equilibrium between the fearsome and the playful is not contingent upon the subject matter but rather on the artist's disposition and the response he appears to be cultivating in the reader or viewer" (1989: 14). Consistent with his distinctive prose style, Golshiri employs an unreliable narrator and experimental linguistic deviations, manifested in both word choices and narrative structure (Sāleh 2010: 47). The narrator's colloquial language and his catchphrases such as "I believe", which recurs more than 15 times to indicate pervasive doubt, are instrumental in rendering the ultimate effect of the narrative account as profoundly more impactful. Encapsulated within a deliberately intricate style, the denouement remains as unresolved and unsettling as the sequence of events preceding it.

Conclusion

As a vanguard of modernist fiction in his homeland, Golshiri crafts a multifaceted narrative in "The Wolf", inviting diverse interpretations as it unfolds an open-ended tale through the lens of an unreliable narrator. His adept employment of modernist narrative techniques effectively amplifies the story's grotesque essence, blurring the lines between reality and perception, and leaving the reader in a state of unresolved tension—mirroring the characters' own experiences within the tale in regard to the wolf and the lunar-inflected space it appears from. The narrative is replete with incongruities: the wolf's nebulous existence and its intrusion into the human sphere, the ambivalent dispositions of the doctor and his wife, and the dissonant narrative tone collectively engender alienation and degradation for Akhtar and the doctor, respectively. Akhtar, already isolated from her community, experiences further alienation with the appearance of the wolf and her burgeoning obsession with its presence. The doctor, despite his efforts, suffers humiliation as he fails to intervene effectively, ultimately bearing witness to his wife's enigmatic disappearance into the desolate wilderness. The narrative's deft portrayal of a setting bereft of definite references to time and place heightens the plausibility of underlying metaphoric significance, fostering potential symbolic and mythic interpretations. The intricate interplay of the imagery of the wolf, the moon, and Akhtar coalesces into a metaphoric representation of primal femininity, symbolically illustrating Akhtar's tumultuous inner landscape and suppressed desires as she grapples with the constraints of a normative existence within a patriarchal society, epitomised by her husband's paradoxical blend of aggression and impotence. Whether one examines the triangular relationship between the wolf and the couple through a macrocosmic lens or within the microcosm of the individual narrative, "The Wolf" emerges as a modern Gothic tale. It revolves around internalised fears and psychic complexities, unfolding within an eerie atmosphere punctuated by mysterious occurrences. The masterful crafting of this narrative not only showcases modernist storytelling but also weaves together elements of the grotesque and the Gothic, creating a richly layered text that invites multiple readings and continues to resonate with its enigmatic power.

References

Bakhtin, Mikhail. 1984. *Rabelais and his World*. Translated by Hélène Iswolsky. Bloomington: Indiana University Press.

Bruhm, Steven. 2002. The Contemporary Gothic and Why We Need It. In *The Cambridge Companion to Gothic Fiction*, ed. Jerrold E. Hogle, 259–276. Cambridge: Cambridge University Press.

Carroll, Noël. 2003. The Grotesque Today: Preliminary Notes toward a Taxonomy. In *Modern Art and the Grotesque*, ed. Frances S. Connelly, 291–312. Cambridge: Cambridge University Press.

Chao, Shun-Liang. 2010. *Rethinking the Concept of the Grotesque: Crashaw, Baudelaire, Magritte*. Routledge.

Clark, John R. 1991. *The Modern Satiric Grotesque and its Traditions*. University Press of Kentucky.

Eliade, Mircea. 1996. *Patterns in Comparative Religion*. Translated by Rosemary Sheed. Lincoln & London: University Press of Nebraska.

Ghanoonparvar, Mohammad R. 1985. Hushang Golshiri and post-Pahlavi concerns of the Iranian writer of fiction. *Iranian Studies* 18 (2–4): 349–373. https://doi.org/10.1080/00210868508701662.

Golshiri, Hūshang. 1991. "The Wolf," translated by Paul Losensky. In *Stories from Iran: A Chicago Anthology 1921–1991*, edited by Heshmat Moayyad. Waldorf: Mage Publishers.

Golshiri, Hūshang. 1999. *باغ در باغ* (Bāgh dar Bāgh) [Garden in Garden]. Tehran: Niloofar.

Golshiri, Hūshang. 2021. Interview with Hūshang Golshiri. September 1999. BBC Persian Broadcasting Company. https://youtu.be/DDxsBKsWXlc?si=31QgCDN3_X0EB8bh. Accessed 28 October 2024.

Hillmann, Michael C. 1982. The modernist trend in Persian literature and its social impact. *Iranian Studies* 15 (1–4): 7–29.

Hogle, Jerrold E. 2014. Introduction: Modernity and the Proliferation of the Gothic. In *The Cambridge Companion to the Modern Gothic*, ed. Jerrold E. Hogle, 3–19. Cambridge: Cambridge University Press.

Kayser, Wolfgang. 1963. *The Grotesque in Art and Literature*, translated by Ulrich Weisstein. Bloomington: Indiana University Press.

Kāzemi, Merāj, Nāser Maleki, and Bahman Fallāh. 2017. *اثر هوشنگ گلشیری» گرگ«خوانشی روانکانه از داستان کوتاه* (Khāneshi ravānkāvāne az dāstān kūtāh-e gorg asar-e Hūshang Golshiri) [Psychoanalytical Reading of Hūshang Golshiri's "The Wolf"]. *New Literary Studies* 195 (29–4): 49–66. https://doi.org/10.22067/jls.v49i3.64091.

Kristeva, Julia. 1982. *Powers of horror: An essay on abjection*, translated by Leo S. Roudiez. New York: Columbia University Press.

Kuryluk, Ewa. 1987. *Salome and Judas in the Cave of Sex*. Evanston: Northwestern University Press.

McElroy, Bernard. 1989. *Fiction of the Modern Grotesque*. Hampshire: The Macmillan Press Ltd.

Milani, Abbas. 2008. *Eminent Persians: The Men and Women Who Made Modern Iran, 1941–1979*. Vol. II. New York: Syracuse University Press.

Mirabedini, Hasan. 1999. *صد سال داستان نویسی ایران* (Sad sāl dāstān nevisi-e Iran) [One hundred years of Persian Fiction]. Tehran: Cheshmeh.

Mirabedini, Hasan. 2002. Hushang Golshiri. In *Encyclopedia Iranica*, ed. Ehsan Yarshater. Vol. XI. 114–18. Columbia University Centre for Iranian Studies. http://www.iranicaonline.org/articles/golsiri-hušang.

Roney, James N. 2009. Reading Gogol's Grotesque 'Overcoat'. In *The Grotesque*, ed. Harold Bloom and Blake Hobby, 167–176. New York: Bloom's Literary Criticism.

Sabā, Sādeq. 2000. Obituary of Hushang Golshiri. *The Guardian*. https://www.theguardian.com/news/2000/jun/20/guardianobituaries.books. Accessed 28 October 2024.

Sāleh, Golriz. 2010. *قاعدهکاهی در نثر گلشیری* (Qāede kāhi dar nasr-e Golshiri) [Rule reduction in Golshiri's writing]. Language Studies 1 (1), 43–56.

Shiri, Ghahremān. 2007. *جایگاه نماد و کنایه در داستانهای گلشیری: دلالتهای ضمنی در پس زمینه روایت* (Delālathāye zemni dar pas zamine revāyat: Jāygāh-e namād va kenāye dar dāstānhāy-e Golshiri) [Implied significations in context of the narrative: symbol and irony in Golshiri's stories]: Journal of Literature and Humanities Faculty of Isfahān University 47 (2), 139–170.

Smith, Allan Lloyd. 1996. Postmodernism/Gothicism. In *Modern Gothic: A Reader*, ed. Allan Lloyd Smith and Victor Sage, 6–19. Manchester: Manchester University Press.

Talattof, Kamran. 2000. *The Politics of Writing in Iran: A History of Modern Persian Literature*. New York: Syracuse University Press.

Thomson, Philip. 1972. *The Grotesque*. London: Routledge.

CHAPTER 14

The Moon in *Requiem for a Beast*: An Apophasis of Colonial Transgression and Indigenous Suppression

Phil Fitzsimmons

Introduction

An Overview of the Context

This chapter deals with the representation of the moon-Minotaur double, as portrayed in one of Australia's most controversial books. In 2008 Matt Ottley's multimodal children's book, *Requiem for a Beast*, won the Australian Book Council Picture Book of the Year award (ABCPBY), which at the time of its publication was advertised as a multimodal illustrated book for children. For a short time after it was published this book attracted very little attention. However, this soon changed.

The initial reviews were mostly benign, such as Heath Graham's (2007) sparse comments which gave virtually no details regarding the content and focus of the text. However, when Tracy Grimshaw condemned the book on national television (Grimshaw and Lumb 2008), there was an ensuing

P. Fitzsimmons (✉)
NSW, Cooranbong, Australia

E. Gomel, S. Bacon (eds.), *Lunar Gothic*, Palgrave Gothic,
https://doi.org/10.1007/978-3-031-92621-1_14

cry of outrage from parents. While *Requiem* was a departure from the other dystopic and Gothic text types that had won the book council's award in previous years, no parents or cultural groups had complained prior to this point. This silence seemed to indicate that few adults were aware of the actual overall nature of Australian children's literature, and the content and focus of previous winners. It would appear that the adult silence is a critical part of Ottley's book.

There had been several award winners that had certainly cut through the literary conservatism that schools used to guard school-aged readers. In 1994 Isabelle Carmody's *The Gathering* and Gary Crew's *Angel's Gate* jointly won the ABCPBY award, both of which had at their core the Gothic notions of evil, possession and the haunting presence of past crimes. Both were thinly clad pointers to the enduring horrors of colonialism and had received national and international acclaim. Thus revealing that, for the most part, the Australian population appears to have believed, and still believe, that because of its intended audience children's texts are perceived to be ahistorical and written for phonics instruction only, which is the lowest common denominator of the meaning making process. *Requiem* was another steppingstone in the Australian context in which children's texts have had a long history of providing an opportunity for the dark nature of Australia's metanarrative to be given voice: "… to emerge from beneath the surface of culture, beneath the territory of its laws and prohibitions, from the semiotic possibility of a language and its unwritten track of history" (Sempruch 2008: 108).

An Overview of the Undercurrents

While the British sense of supremacy and its initial colonial system are deeply embedded in the national psyche and social structures, Australian children's literature is one of the deepest and longest-lived reactive agents against this still unacknowledged "persistent neurosis" (Gibson 1988: 50). While it may seem counterintuitive, Australian children's literature is underpinned by what is deemed to be the ongoing metanarrative of the initial convict sense of estrangement and resistance against the "dominating order of the empire" (Mukherjee 2022: 225). Further emphasising the ruthless power of the British colonisers and their continuing psychical presence of oppression, the representation of children in the Australian canon is often portrayed as having an imprint of wild independence, and an inexplicable dark and haunting sense of existential absence. Although this presence-absence twinnage has a spectrum of forms, it often tends to be grounded in a storied life bereft of authentic familial relationships, in the depths of the Australian desert or forests. While there are also narrative instances and ensuing influences of an "absent mother", it is more likely it is the "absent father" syndrome that creates social and psychological issues in Australian children's literature. These texts, "...have never articulated an easy articulation of a hopeful future, ...always at risk of being defeated or destroyed by the continent" (Hately 2015: 74).

While Ottley's graphic novel continues the Gothic relationship between the outcomes of English colonisation and the desert landscape, he takes this perspective a step further. Through the multiple lenses that form indigenous memories, these are framed in a kaleidoscopic and labyrinthine pattern of an indigenous child who is one of the "stolen generation". This term refers to those countless Aboriginal children forcibly removed from their families between 1910 and the 1970s and placed in white families or in boarding schools run by Christian denominations. The latter proved to be institutions that ran on physical, emotional and sexual abuse. The reason for this removal was ostensibly for the benefit of the indigenous children, to "protect them and save them from a life of neglect" (O'Laughlin 2020). While the practice was theoretically finished in 1969, as reported by Young (2014), forced removal of children has currently recommenced, under the guise of counteracting Aboriginal disadvantage. While clearly this whole saga of dislodgement has racist foundations that commenced in the early days of colonisation, despite the cultural trauma inflicted on these "stolen children" and their parents, what is not understood by governments is the trauma inflicted on the entire Aboriginal society. This policy dismantles the Aboriginal clan networks, which are "complex, intricate and intricately tied to the land" (Kelly and McConvell 2018: 24). At the very least this sophisticated and socially accessible knowledge engendered through the overall system of matriarchy allows for "permissible marriages" (Sutton 2018: 192) within the clan, across clans and intertribal marriages.

Many indigenous children are consequently caught in the disconnected literal and psychohistorical borderlands of disconnected remembering. *Requiem* is therefore a visual and textual "prosthetic narrative, one that invites people to take on memories of a past through which they did not live" (Landsberg 2004: 8). Furthermore, as a spatially grounded prosthetic, *Requiem* leads the reader through a multi-framed and doubled journey by connecting childhood, the Aboriginal sense of the Dreamtime within contemporary Australia, and the deep Aboriginal sense of connection to the land through the ancient mythic narratives of the Minotaur and the moon.

The moon in Ottley's text is a double facet. As a key representative element in any Western narrative, or any narrative that moves through cycles, it represents a feminine entity as well as a "memory of place,…and its history of growth and expansion, change, ruin" (Godfrey 2016: 32). Hence, in this text the moon is coded as a mother forced to watch her traumatised children through lunar cycles of hope and despair. However, Ottley further emphasises this connection to the Australian indigenous understanding in which the moon is a "father" (Bathal and Mason 2015: 4.15), and a giver of life. In the darkness of its cycle, it was still deemed to be giving opportunity to view the constellations much more clearly and therefore an indicator of resurrection (Bathal 2015: 4.15).

Structurally, this shifting cycle is indicated by the illustrated presence or absence of light, and the use of text only and illustrations. This underpinning sub-narrative is also linked to the changing seasons of the monsoonal sections of the Australian Northern Territory. Linked to the Australasian sense of the outback as a point of desolation and deprivation experienced by the first colonists, the far north remains as a marker of a "persistent sense of dislocation" (Collins et al. 2019: 16).

As a parallel double-double, the ever-present Minotaur in *Requiem* not only indicates the presence of male conquest and power, but also a reference to the unforgiving Australian landscape. This representation acknowledges a society "haunted by the unacknowledged history of colonization" (Collins et al. 2019: 17), the ambiguity of the relationship between the ever-present monsters in Australian folklore, and the fear of the indigenous "others within" its desert heartland.

Layered over the top of this interconnected fragmentation is the framework of a Requiem mass, which infuses the text with a sense of death and judgement, but also, in its internal repetitions, it has the overall intent of "offering insights into how the particular composer is thinking, musically, theologically and philosophically, and invites careful attention" (Jeffers 1988: 63). While referencing the care that the Christian church should have provided for the "stolen generation" this framework acts as an ever-present reminder that they instead destroyed the interconnectedness of several generations of indigenous clans. Hence, the social-emotional support they did not supply is represented as silence and indivisibility, and especially in the spaces illustrated as darkness and shadows.

In contrast to the religious deficiency of the Christian church, the following sections reveal Ottley's use of the moon as both literal and visually explicit "flashbulb" moments, or what Fred Botting calls "photoflashes" or "puncta points" (2008: 74): "...flashbulb moments, granting an individual the ability to serve as a witness and the way such witnessing allows the community as a whole to enter into the trauma process" (2008: 592).

These are elements in which reality and language are unable to provide an adequate description of horror because of the pain or fear. Instead, a representation "functions as disorientating puncta where sense is disturbed by something unknown" (Botting 2008: 74). In *Requiem*, the unimaginable and cultural pain is framed as a "doubled" visual retelling, redirection and reapplication of the ancient image of the Minotaur with the Aboriginal sense of the moon. This twinned visual represents the combination of ancient but contradictory cultural understandings, pointing to contemporary instability and a clash of cultures within cycles of darkness and light. In this interplay, the moon is always present, but like the "stolen generation", in a simultaneous state of "absence and presence".

Under the symbolic sliding canopy of the twinned motifs of the Minotaur and the moon, these co-axial visuals motifs also create the beginning of intertextual and hypertextual threads. Differing slightly in form and focus at key points, this book is an ongoing reflexive sequence of "autre-biography" that forms a connected thread of colonial settler memory autobiography, which emphasizes the themes of gender, identity and power. In other words, the moon–Minotaur connection becomes critical narrative pointing to in a stream of cultural memories in crisis.

The Moon as a Silenced Child and Voice of the Ancient Beast

Reflecting the "red thread bricolage" of labyrinthine narrative that visually and textually spirals through *Requiem*, and the presence of an indigenous culture with its different social imaginary of time and relationships, stepping into the pages of this multimodal children's book is akin to entering the forms and frames of "being and non-being" in several forms. This ambivalent and yet still co-existent state is created in this text through a visual-textual sense of the "unheimlich" in which a subjective sensing of the known crosses over and melds with the unknown. This unheimlich co-mingling of direct illustrative contrasts and doubling intensifies the embodied feelings and cultural tensions that also give rise to a final understanding of the monstrous representation. As is often the case in Australian children's literature, and certainly found in Ottley's work, there is also a parallel set of twinned visual elements that not only highlight the darkness and anxieties of the current culture, but simultaneously emphasise the disruption of order created by the central monstrous figure. An inkling of social order is emphasised through a doubled disorder. Parallel visual elements, which are often found in textual metonymic threads of the Australian monstrous as co-signifiers, represent the web of uncanny elements in *Requiem* that indirectly point to the varied influences of horror in Australian life in general, and that also "live[s] very close to home" (Botting 2008: 114).

The Moon and Monster Double as Paratext

This sense of the "close to home" monstrous is firstly framed as paratext on the covers of *Requiem*. With the purpose of paratext to enact a self-questioning process regarding the possibilities of what follows beyond the initial paratextual triggers, on the covers of this hinged text there are three key conjoined "sense making" inferences on the front and four visual frames on the back. Each illustration mirroring a depth of dark ambiguity.

The first telling element is embedded in the title of the book itself; indeed the phraseology *Requiem for a Beast* represents the epitome of a Gothic double, and the ambiguity of the Australian relationship to its Christian heritage. As it references a particular form of signage in a Catholic or Church of England funeral, as well as the biblical antichrist, it creates a sense of a doubled institutional injunction: the religious and institutional demand of grief following death, and the possible suffering created by an unknown and forgotten biblical satanic entity. Both these aspects underpinned the arrival of the First Fleet, as *Terra Australis* was deemed to represent the biblical apocalypse (Trigg 2005). The other conjoined aspect on this cover is the portrayal of an indigenous toddler standing to the left and below an image of an Australian Brahman bull. These images are uniquely associated with the tropical north of Australia, with the bull motif an indicator of the imported American breed introduced into the "top end" in the early 1900s. Unlike the British settlers, these cattle were suitable to cope with the harsh tropical climate.

Also, the term Requiem is a specific reference to the Latin used by the Roman Catholic Church and the Anglo Catholic Church of Great Britain.

A requiem is a funeral mass for the dead or dying and the term requiem in Latin can be translated as "rest" or "repose". This also suggests a link to Australia's colonial past and the First Landing and the hope that transportation would go a long way in solving the issues of prison overcrowding, while at the same time decimate the lawless Irish that had created social problems in London, and all the "filthy and unnameable criminal class" (Hughes 1988: 1). However, there is another doubled meaning in that the first convict settlers barely survived the first four decades, with the indigenous tribes around Sydney Harbour providing assistance to those who had arrived on the first thirteen ships. However, the first expansionist movements and lack of any attempt at understanding by the colonists soon led to conflicts with the indigenous population, commonly called the "Sydney Wars" (Gapps 2018). The indigenous population commenced a highly successful guerilla campaign for decades, almost succeeding in defeating the colonialists.

In a visual narrative on the front cover, indicating the social darkness of colonisation that indigenous Australians often describe as invasion, an indigenous child is positioned in the very bottom left-hand corner of the cover. From a spatial literacy perspective, in this position the child is coded as feminine weakness, and in a textual place corresponding to an impending sense of desolation and despondency. The child is also looking directly out of the page signifying a demand. The apparent direct eye contact is semiotically an imperative, demanding the reader-viewer to ask a raft of personal questions that include questioning what is the child's place and standing in the world at large. Positioned well above and to the right of the child, the bull is asserting dominance. However, its head is in the lower left quadrant and slightly tilted to the right and only its left eye can be seen staring out of the page. Towering over the child, its overall bodily positioning suggests dominance and power, while the head, facial position and eye contact are indicative of uncertainty and mistrust.

Drawing on the seminal work on visually and bodily positioning undertaken by McQuire (1998), the figures in this paratext, and their placement, symbolically form a relationship with the title representing a doubled form of *momento mori*. Firstly, it is a representation of a white Australian "memoire dispositif" that pushes the notion of Aboriginal people into the realms of the distant past that has no connections to contemporary Australia. As an indigenous civilisation that is at least forty thousand years old these illustrations also represent an unheimlich memory, one that is "worth preserving, bringing close, and making familiar what must nevertheless remain unfamiliar, alien and discontinuous" (Kristeva 1982: 152).

As a literal and metonymic visual hinge, the imagery on the front cover is then linked though an image of a full moon, situated under the "vampiric like" wings of a standing Minotaur. Also, below the clearly defined horizon line on which the beast is standing are three images as a braided thread. With all images above a horizon line generally coded as male, the image of the full moon and the beast creates a sense of ambiguity, which is the very essence of Gothic texts. However, the moon in this instance is also a reversal of the typical meaning of the Australian indigenous belief structure which saw the moon as a male emblem (Bathal and Terry 2011). As a powerful motif in this culture, young women are counselled not to look at a full moon in case they become pregnant. However, from a Western perspective, the moon is narratively in a feminine position referencing a colonial sense that the beliefs and identity of those who hold a different understanding deserve oppression and subjugation. It also reveals the fear that the British colonisers held that this distant land was the complete ideological and religious inversion of their God-fearing homeland in the Northern Hemisphere, one equated with Gothic darkness to the point that it was viewed as the site of the entrance to the biblical abyss (Trigg 2005). Thus the figure of the standing Minotaur looking up to the top left-hand corner, a placement representing feminine uncertainty. This is a further "red thread" reference to the beast at the bottom of the mythical labyrinth, which is structurally coded as vaginal. Further to this, the moon–Minotaur connection in *Requiem* represents the constant sense of captivity of Aboriginal childhood within white culture and the British practice of brutally enforcing colonial rule, especially by condoning and engaging in sexual abuse (Stoler 2002).

The Moon–Monster Double Framed as Elements of a Requiem Mass

The Double as "The Final Judgement"

Following the flow through the sequence of a requiem mass, Ottely commences the body of his narrative with the first section of the generic section of a funereal mass, known as *Dies Israe*. Literally translated as final judgement, the day of wrath or the day of ashes, Ottley is indicating all that follows in his narrative is clothed in an overarching sense of absolute doom and destruction.

This first section opens with a double page spread revealing the tropical plains of northern Australia, with a single sentence: "It's our memories that make us" (Ottley 2008). As with those sections dealing with indigenous memories, there are no page numbers, indicating the loss of indigenous memory related to Aboriginality and within the Australian population. These pages are also suggestive of not only the wide-open spaces, lushness and timelessness of the top end in the fertile wet seasons, but also the indigenous notion of "deep time" in contrast to the white focus of "clock time". These illustrations inferring rain cycles, heat and wide-open spaces stand in direct contrast to the mythologised English countryside that the early settlers bought with them. Instead, through the lens of culture shock they instead saw only a "wilderness of ruins" (Spicer 2020: 128). These two double pages also echo the cartographic and epistemological framework that the British brought with them and sought to overlay onto the Australian continent. They saw this perspective as their God-given right to bring domination and order to an unknown land, which became an axiological driver of overpowering people and place. As expressed in the openness of these illustrations, the sense of ownership of the land also stood in direct contrast to the beliefs of the indigenous people, who saw themselves not owning the land but being an integral component of it. For the Aborigines "being on country" meant immersion in the deep memories of their ancestors, and the deep history that they saw everywhere in the landscape around them.

Shifting from a brightly lit country through to the final frames of night and clearly outlined gathering storm clouds, Ottley's initial pages reveal an all-enveloping darkness of night, suggesting much more than the simple close of day. In the bottom array on the left-hand side that highlights a place of both the feminine and depression, there is a full moon shining through the clouds. Although an emblem of the indigenous male, this symbol becomes a visual carrier to the next panel and a reference to the enduring matriarchal nature of indigenous communities. In a brief comment made by a female Aboriginal elder, that she is "supposed to be a fully initiated elder, but that knowledge of that memory is gone" (Ottley 2008), this reversal signifies that a change will eventually happen. In the same sentence the British geographical consciousness that conquered Australia is framed as an outcast female, a cartographic ontology that considered rape and desecration as a natural and expected outcome.

This visual introduction then shifts into a brief narrative of an indigenous boy who is awakened in the night by the roar of a bull. Giving chase over a ridge, the landscape vanishes, becoming "a place of immeasurable barrenness, to the shimmering edge of the world" (Ottely 2008: 9). This section then moves into another series of visual panels revealing the desolate landscape and a small school. With a panel showing a hand opening the school door, an indigenous child is seated, and looking out the window he sees a horned rider. Through the pounding of hooves, a voice screams to the boy to run and he is then pushed out a window. Through shards of shattered glass, a reflection of the Minotaur is seen and the boy cries for his mother. This section clearly aligns the Minotaur with the colonial-like institutional forces still in operation in the Australian context that encapsulate the "white masculine ideologies of colonial occupation, domination and control" (Gibson 1994: 49).

In the following section there are several pages of text and visuals detailing a stockman's life, drug addiction, the blurred image of a child and confrontation with a large brown bull. Through a series of vertical panels, the image of the child framed on the front cover comes into focus. Gradually the last panels of this section telescopically move into the eye of the child, and in the internal darkness of an eye a blurred image of a full moon takes over the entire last page. Metonymically connecting the full moon, loss of self and repression of memory as prefigured in the paratext, this journey into the centre of the child's eye intertextually deepens the initial interrogatives related to place and identity. In a Gothic sense, this form of visual internalisation acts as a refocusing mirror and "signifies an alienation of the human subject from the culture and language in which s/he is located" (Botting 1999: 8).

The Double as "Resurrection of the Monster"

Under the heading of *Mors Stupebit et natura*, the fourth movement of a Requiem hymn, the narrative shifts into another textual pastiche. With this section having the overarching meaning of "death and nature will be dazed when the creature rises again", the clear reference to the monstrous nature of what happened to the stolen generation and the first arrival is established. The illustrations that start this section, however, are in the glare of the Australian outback and see the arrival of a young adolescent male.

The section begins with a set of visual frames showing a young indigenous boy entering an outback town on a bus, clearly about to begin working on an outback cattle farm. Waiting to be picked up by his new employer, as he walks around the town there are clear intertexual references to previous elements in the narrative. Walking past a school, an indigenous teenage boy is seated at a desk in front of it with photos of a group of young indigenous children. He stops and stares, apparently recognising a face and a memory.

Through the use of the Gothic signage of shadows and darkness in this site, Ottley visually implies an oppositional double. With the town shown in the bright light of day the first inference is that all its boundaries are included "as members of our culture" (Kress and van Leeuwin 1996: 116). However, in the context of the book and illustrations that accompany it, the shadows also act as a delineation of boundaries and limits of "white" socio-cultural order. Thus, within these frames portraying normal white life, there are boundaries placed on indigenous Australians curtailing cultural acceptance, and a true sense of personal and social identity. Within this setting clearly marked as a privileged space, he is coded as a stranger in his own traditional land. This visual narrative then shifts into an explicit text-only description of the truth of colonial power and its creation of the stolen generation. In visual spatial-literary terms, this form of shift in narrative framing, or storied insertion, indicates a heterotopic boundary marker. In what appears a deliberate sense of ambiguity, the inference is that the subjects or objects highlighted in this space are designated an in area of crisis and marked as monstrous. At this point it is not clear if the boy or the township is marked as such. As Botting states, these are places or states where ambiguity and textual transference occur within ordinary settings: "...the 'other' or 'different' spaces which traverse, demarcate, bolster, and disrupt the homogeneity of all the sites and borders composing everyday material existence" (Botting 2018: 21). This "marking of difference' comes into distinct clarity in the final paragraphs linking to the initial section of paratext, through the statement regarding the boy's childhood and those of the other stolen generation: "the darkness and loneliness of those years.... They no longer knew their place in the world" (Ottley 2007: 45). The starkness of these words and the final clause, "there is another darkness coming, see those clouds out there" (Ottley 2007: 45), written on white pages, connects to the aesthetic whiteness of the town. This speaks to the uninterrupted "whiteness" of even the indigenous sacred places and desecration of the landscape. The last comment is a reference to the lunar cycles, and the certain knowledge that the light of "father moon" will return, the "whiteness" thus remaining the deep-seated social imaginary for most Australians.

The Double as the Final Judgement

Moving into this section under the section heading of *Lacrymosa*, often loosely translated as "weeping in the final judgement", the text reverts to a narrative with three sections. The first is akin to a graphic novel, then a section of text describing a visit to a museum, with the final section a graphic summation of the entire book drawing back into the threads of the paratext. In this section there are no page numbers, and there is a blending and blurring of personal narratives, from the perspective of an indigenous mother and an indigenous child. The core thread in this section is the lapsing into the dream states of salient memories. In tandem with this narrative flow are the aesthetic shifts from the brightness of the Australian outback into ever increasing pages of darkness in the memory phases. While the bull is a constant figure that gradually morphs into a Minotaur, it is only in the last page of darkness that the moon reappears. Each re-enters the memory of a dream.

The first section commences with a shift back into the desert landscape, revealing the young male, confronting a large Brahman bull. As the bull escapes, he follows behind, "deeper into the day,...and himself" (Ottley 2007: n.p.). The pages then enters a dark section, in which an indigenous stockman named Rudy has entered this deserted place, and his horse begins to buck wildly. Through a series of illustrations on a black background, Rudy merges with his horse, melding into a screaming Minotaur. Following on, the next section shows an indigenous mother searching for her child, and is framed in a rectangular box that increases in height and width across the page and increasingly telescopically and microscopically zeroes into the mother's face and eyes. This section then once again shifts to the young stockman "entranced by the heat, and lead by the beast into "a world of remembering" (Ottley 2007: n.p.).

There is no illustration or reference to the moon, until the end of the section where it becomes conjoined with the initial paratext of both the bull figure riding a horse and the upright roaring Minotaur. Botting terms this form of narrative construction as:

> a murmuring absence,…a thin line, an abyss…out of which things may emerge, a space not of simple absence, limit, opposition, inversion, transition, or discontinuity, but where a language to infinity may appear in a flash, darkly, and brilliant in a moment of transgression. (2022: 32)

In the same way that the mother was framed in multiple telescopic strips of illustration, the moon appears as a single and centred entity followed by the Minotaur figure. These ever-growing panels end with a hand holding an axe, dripping in blood, which is centred in this strip, and between panels revealing the moon above the Minotaur figure. This is immediately followed on the final page of this section by the roaring of the Minotaur as seen in the paratext on the back cover. As illustrated there, the moon is shown next to the Minotaur, and below this image the indigenous child is also seen holding onto the threads, and a single word: "Roaring" (Ottley 2007: n.p.).

Despite the roaring and size of the Minotaur, the vector line of this full-page illustration directs the eye of the reader diagonally from the moon in the upper left-hand quadrant down to the child holding the thread in the bottom right corner of the page. This vector shifts from a space on a page designated as feminine, through to a space designated as male. While the child revealed to be below the horizon line is in area representing alienation, this position also suggests the possibility of hope. Thus symbolically inferring that the "moon father" of the indigenous child is about to assert his dominance, and that the bull is in the throes of defeat. Just as the previous segment revealed the boy as having to kill the Brahman bull, so too this moon vector infers dislocation and death of the colonising forces.

The Double as the Sacrifice

This final section is headed as *Pie Jesu*, which translates as "pious Jesus" and infers Christian salvation. The final illustrated panel of the child holding a thread now links to this final section. Just as Theseus followed the red thread and escaped out of the labyrinth, so too the inference is that the indigenous nations will survive. However, like Theseus' duplicity in sacrificing the woman who aided his escape, so too the "stolen generation" are culturally welded to a general population that has largely ignored their voice.

However, this final part provides hope.

The ensuing section begins as text only and describes how the young stockman survives the bull's attack, although injured. However, in this melee the bull breaks its pelvis and the young boy decides to kill it rather than let it suffer. Sticking a knife into the back of its neck, he cuts its spinal cord with blood oozing between his fingers, and the bull dies. Searching for the boy in the desert, an older indigenous stockman rides up and pulls him onto the back of his horse. It is then that the "moon shines through a veil of rain mist illuminating the landscape ahead, and just below the horizon a light flickers into existence—the camp fire". The final double spread ends the narrative, with illustrations of an oncoming thunderstorm and the words: "There is another darkness coming…. We all have to stand in the rain, however long it lasts" (Ottley 2007: n.p.)

A Final Voice of Silence

As *Requiem for a Beast* is arguably one of the most radically constructed and certainly the most controversial children's books to be published in Australia, like its twinned focus on the "stolen generation" and Aboriginal identity, it has slipped into the socio-political void of "disremembering". The final panel is without a moon, but pictures a gathering storm as a double that both affirms this state and offers some hope. While the suggested silence of this panel implies "a portrayal of indifference" (Correia 2017: 93), the approaching storm is also emblematic of: "The relation established between consciousness and phenomena, allowing the examination of the position of the characters before the fundamental things in human existence and to show their search for the essence and the truth" (Correia 2017: 93).

References

Bathal, Ragbir and Mason Terry. 2011. Aboriginal Astronomy and Landscape Painting. *Astronomy and Geophysics,* 52 (4). https://academic.oup.com/astrogeo/article/52/4/4.12/217904. Accessed 28 October 2024.

Botting, Fred. 2008. *Limits of Horror, Technology, Bodies, Gothic.* Manchester: Manchester University Press.

Botting, Fred. 2018. Literature-Outside-Space: Foucault, Sade, and Tales of Terror. In *Spaces of Crisis and Critique*, ed. David Hancock, Anthony Faramelli, and Robert White, 17–38. London: Bloomsbury.

Botting, Fred. 2022. Monstrocene. In *Dark Scenes from Damaged Earth: The Gothic Anthroprocene*, ed. Justin D. Edwards, Rue Graulund, and Johan Hoglund, 314–318. Minneapolis: University of Minneapolis Press.

Collins, Felicity, Jane Landman, and Susan Bye. 2019. Introduction: Australian Cinema Now. In *A Companion to Australian Cinema*, ed. Felicity Collins, Jane Landman, and Susan Bye, 1–27. Wiley Blackwell: Hoboken.

Correia, Alda. 2017. *Narrative and Space: Across Short Story Landscape and Regional Places*. New York: Peter Lang.

Gapps, Stephen. 2018. *The Sydney Wars: Conflict in the early colony, 1788–1817*. Sydney: New South Press.

Gibson, Ross. 1988. 'Formative Landscapes.' In *Back of Beyond: Discovering Australian Film and Television*, ed. Scott Murray, 45–59. North Sydney: Australian Film Commission.

Godfrey, Laura Gruber. 2016. *Hemingway's Geographies: Intimacy, Materiality and Memory*. New York: Springer.

Grimshaw, Tracy and Kirstine Lumb. 2008. Award Winning Children's Book Causes Controversy: The Children's Book Council of Australia has created a stir by giving its picture book of the year award to the controversial title, Requiem For A Beast. *A Current Affair*. Tvnews.tex20083303656. https://search-informit-org.databases.avondale.edu.au/doi/10.3316/tvnews.tex20083303656. Accessed 28 October 2024.

Hately, Erica. 2015. Productive Anxieties Lostness in *The Arrival* and *Requiem for a Beast*. *Papers* 23 (1): 73–86.

Hughes, Robert. 1988. *The Fatal Shore: The Epic of Australia's Founding*. London: Vintage Books.

Jeffers, Ron. 1988. *Translations and Annotations of Choral Repertoire*, Sacred Latin Texts. Vol. 1. Corvallis: Earthsongs.

Kelly, Piers, and Patrick McConvell. 2018. Evolving Perspectives on Aboriginal Social Organization: From Mutual Misrecognition to Kinship Renaissance. In *Skin, Kin and Clan: The Dynamics of Social Categories in Indigenous Australia*, ed. Patrick McConvell, Piers Kelly, and Sabastian Lacrampe, 21–42. Canberra: Australian National University Press.

Kress, Gunther, and Theo van Leeuwin. 1996. *Reading Images: The Grammar of Visual Design*. New York: Routledge.

Kristeva, Julia. 1982. *The Powers of Horror: An Essay on Abjection*. New York: Columbia University Press.

Landsberg, Allan. 2004. *Prosthetic Memory: The Transference of American Memory in the Age of Mass Culture*. New York: Columbia University Press.

McQuire, Scott. 1998. *Visions of Modernity: Representation, Memory, Time and Space in the Age of the Camera*. London: DAGE.

Mukherjee, Mousumi. 2022. Decolonising Education: Critical reflections from India. *Aula de Encuentro* 1:215–237.

O'Laughlin, Michael. 2020. *The Stolen Generation' Australian Museum*. https://australian.museum/learn/first-nations/stolen-generation/. Accessed 28 October 2024.

Ottley, Matt. 2007. *Requiem for a Beast: A Work for Image, Word and Music*. Sydney: Hachette Livre Australia.

Ottley, Matt. 2008. *Requiem for a Beast*. Sydeny: Lothian Books.

Sempruch, Justyna. 2008. *Fantasies of Gender and the Witch in Feminist Theory and Literature West Lafayette*. West Lafayette: Purdue University Press.

Spicer, Christopher. 2020. *Cyclone Country: The Language of Place and Disaster in Australian Literature*. Jefferson: McFarland & Company.

Stoler, Ann Laura. 2002. *Carnal Knowledge and Imperial Power: Race and the Intimate in Colonial Rule*. Berkeley: University of California Press.

Sutton, Peter. 2018. Patricion Subsets of the Ashburton River District in Western Australian. In *Skin, Kin and Clan: The Dynamics of Social Categories in Indigenous Australia*, ed. Patrick McConvell, Piers Kelly, and Sabastian Lacrampe, 179–218. Canberra: Australian National University Press.

Trigg, Stephanie. 2005. *Medievalism and the Gothic in Australian Culture*. Melbourne: University of Melbourne Press.

Young, Matt. 2014. Australia in the Grip of a New Stolen Generation, Indigenous Children Forcibly Removed From Homes. *Daily Telegraph*. https://www.dailytelegraph.com.au/lifestyle/australia-in-the-grip-of-a-new-stolen-generation-indigenous-children-forcibly-removed-from-homes/news-story/88e06e6db098dfddf39e8412674734c0?utm_campaign=BoostedContent&gad_source=5&gclid=EAIaIQobChMI1KK2hb2-iAMVfSWDAx0ghQbDEAAYBCAAEgK8fPD. Accessed 28 October 2024.

CHAPTER 15

Moon, Music, and Melancholia: Gothic Aesthetics in *Kuroshitisuji's* Lacrimosa

Jasdeep Kaur Chandi

Introduction: Many Faces of the Moon

Lunar symbolism is ubiquitous. It is present in everyday narratives, from mythology to folklore, from children's bedtime stories to a love-sick poet's romantic prose. However, the meanings associated with lunar symbolism alter with the kind of narratives in which it is present. In Hindu mythology, the moon is associated with the lunar deity *Chandra* or *Soma*, popularly known as Chandra Dev. According to one of many Hindu narratives, Chandra, or Soma, is a "male" God but also a part of *Navagraha* (Nine Planets) and is "depicted as a white deity, holding a mace in one hand, seated in a three wheeled chariot, drawn by three or more horses" (Dalal 2010: 394). Although Dalal (2010) mentions that the Hindu lunar deity's chariot is drawn by horses, the artwork associated with Chandra or Soma, usually depicts antelopes or deer (see Fig. 15.1).

Buddhist scriptures also mention "Candra", a lunar deity, "depicted as rising in a chariot pulled by seven geese" (Kotyk 2022: 21); at the same time, they also consider the "moon as a physical place housing devas" (Kotyk 2022: 9). In Roman and Greek mythologies, the divine

J. K. Chandi (✉)
Guru Gobind Singh Indraprastha University, Delhi, India

E. Gomel, S. Bacon (eds.), *Lunar Gothic*, Palgrave Gothic,
https://doi.org/10.1007/978-3-031-92621-1_15

Fig. 15.1 Soma/Chandra: The Hindu lunar god in a chariot being pulled by an antelope. (Unknown 1700) (Artist unknown, 1700–1725. Image in the public domain)

embodiment of moon is represented as Goddesses *Luna* and *Selene*, respectively (see Fig. 15.2).

According to Japanese lore, the moon goddess is a "benevolent deity" and has been associated with symbols of the waters of life, death, "immortality, the renewal of time, the serpent, and the rejuvenation" (Waida 1977: 411). In ancient Japan, the moon also served as a cultural symbol representing the "after life" and "enlightenment" (Mitani 2011). There are multiple representations and conceptualisations of moon throughout history. While comparing the symbolism of moon to that of the sun, Slaughter (1902: 296) states,

Fig. 15.2 Selene: The Moon Goddess from "Flora, seu florum…", by Giovanni Battista Ferrari 1646. (Copyright Wellcome Library reproduced under Creative Commons: https://wellcomecollection.org/works/pbpp6t6d)

> The moon, on the contrary, whose mildness of luster enticed attention, whose phases were an embodiment of change, whose strange spots seemed shadowy pictures of things and beings terrestrial, whose appearance amid the darkness of the night was so welcome, and who came to men susceptible, from the influences of quiet, and gloom, of superstitious imaginings, from the very beginning grew into a familiar spirit of kindred form with their own, and though regarded as the subordinate and wife of the sun, was reverenced as the superior and husband of the earth. With the transmission of this myth began its transmutation. From the moon being a man it became a man's abode; with some of it was the world whence human spirits came; with others it was the final home whither human spirits returned. Then it grew into a penal colony, to which egregious offenders were transported; or prison cage in which, behind bars of light, miserable sinners were to be exposed to all eternity, as a warning to the excellent of earth.

The "transmutation of myth" about the moon, specifically in relation to lunar symbolism and iconography presents an interesting conundrum that has been continually utilised in fictional narratives, particularly those within the fantasy and Gothic genres. In one of his creative presentations the artist Michael Betancourt depicts the moon as a "site of fantasy run amok" where "it is 'loony"', 'madness', but also banal, prosaic and ambivalent, filled with objects that masquerade as the un/familiar and uncanny since distinctions between the living and the non-living are unclear" (Betancourt 2015: 412). To be more precise, there exists a duality in the representation of the moon; male and female, subject and object, madness and enlightenment, familiar and uncanny, that serves to facilitate the plot setting required of fantasy and Gothic storytelling. This duality is typical within contemporary Japan's popular media, in particular anime, possibly owing to the cultural significance of moon viewing or *Tsukimi*[1] in Japanese culture. The moon becomes a subject in *shōjo* anime like *Sailor Moon* (1992) and an object in *shōnen* anime like *One Piece* (One Piece Wiki n.d.). Typically, in fictional stories, the moon is a site of departure where humans go after death (Slaughter 1902), a source of power for fantastical creatures like werewolves (Levi 2006) and magical girls (Napier 1998), and at times, a symbol of sorrow as depicted in the story of *Princess Kaguya* (Hui 2019). More specifically, while describing a *mise-en-scène* in a Gothic novel, the authors often used "moonlight" as a "prop" to create a strange,

[1] Tsukimi is a moon-viewing festival celebrated in Japan. The tradition of viewing the full moon and its reflection in water dates back to the Heian era (794–1185).

dangerous, and spectral atmosphere. Gothic stories are usually characterised by "ruined castles, dungeons, trapdoors, skeletons, flesh and blood ghosts and perpetual *moonshine*" (Bridgwater 2013: 163, emphasis mine) and "mountain crags, heart-stopping abysses, *moonlit* ruins" (Bridgwater 2013: 169, emphasis mine). In this sense, the moon has a deeper significance in Gothic narratives; however, the mere presence of moon cannot effectively create a Gothic ambience. For example, the moon can serve as a Gothic motif expressing death and sorrow provided it is accompanied with other elements within the text. In audio-visual texts like anime, a lyrical narrative, chilling visuals, and aural composition can create a Gothic atmosphere surrounding lunar imagery. It is at this intersection of moon symbolism and other narrative elements that this chapter is focused. In this chapter, I will analyse the latent presence of the moon in the second ending theme song (ED) titled Lacrimosa (Sono Shitsuji 2009) of the *shōjo* Gothic anime *Kuroshitsuji* or *Black Butler* (Kuroshitsuji 2008c) (Kuroshitsuji 2008b). I will then discuss how the convergence of symbolism and the lyrical narrative of this ED supplements the overarching Gothic narrative of the anime. However, before proceeding to the thematic analysis of the song and its lunar imagery, it is necessary to provide a brief overview of the anime *Kuroshitsuji* and its Gothic style.

The "Gothic" in *Kuroshitsuji*

Kuroshitsuji, more famously known as *Black Butler*, is an anime adaptation of Yana Toboso's manga of the same name. The plot of *Kuroshitsuji* is set in late Victorian England. The narrative of the anime revolves around a twelve-year-old aristocrat, Earl Ciel Phantomhive and his butler Sebastian Michaelis, named after Ciel's late dog. The Gothic elements of *Kuroshitsuji* are epitomised by the demise of Ciel's entire family on his birthday, his subsequent abduction and abuse by a demon-worshipping cult, followed by a Faustian pact with the devil, wherein he trades his soul for vengeance against his family's killers, who are yet to be identified (Bilkhu 2023). The demon with whom Ciel enters this pact is, in fact, his flawless butler Sebastian. The master–servant duo, with their recruited allies, then go on to solve mysterious cases at the Queen's behest, including murder mysteries like those of *Jack the Ripper* (Kuroshitsuji 2008a) and the *Demon Hound of Houndsworth* (Kuroshitsuji 2008b) (Kuroshitsuji 2008a).

The visual aesthetics of the anime further complements its Gothic genre with comedic elements. Loh (2012: 111) classifies Kuroshitsuji as a "postmodern gothic" or more specifically, having a "shōjo gothic style" with an "aestheticization of demonic and the deathly, and its penchant for roses, Rococo motifs and the color black". In *Kuroshitsuji*, the conventional Gothic motifs like the haunted house, coffins, and skulls are "simulated" and "exaggerated", thereby transitioning to a "cliché" of symbols while delivering a dark-comedic narrative (Loh 2012: 113). Comparing the audio-visual anime with traditional Gothic novels, Loh argues that, in Kuroshitsuji,

> rendering banal of the Gothic illustrates a process of simulation, whereby Gothic tropes are stripped of their repressed, unconscious depth, and 'flattened' out into superficial images that are more fantastic than frightening and that self-consciously evoke their own superficiality. (Loh 2012: 114)

In that context, the Gothic in *Kuroshitsuji* does not evoke an "uncanny" atmosphere using conventional Gothic motifs as much as their pastiche offers a dark humour. The Gothic style in *Kuroshitsuji* is based on "simulation, recontextualization and reinscription" of European aesthetics and the culture of the Victorian era (Loh 2012: 121). The recontextualisation of the age-old Faustian narrative that serves as the basic premise of *Kuroshitsuji* (Bilkhu 2023), the setting of the narrative in Victorian Europe (Bilkhu 2023; Loh 2012) and the fact that the Faust myth was particularly popular in that era (Sivrioğlu 2017; Bilkhu 2023) also underlines the "simulation" style of this Gothic anime (Loh 2012). The presence of dark comedic elements within the Gothic genre also establishes that Gothic motifs can have functions that serve to elicit other emotions than the expected unsettling feelings of fear and dread. Still, sorrow, anxiety, death, melancholia, madness, and loneliness remain the most significant themes that are often typically associated with Gothic narratives (Howells 2013; Wright 2004); *Kuroshitsuji* is no exception.

The assertion that the Gothic style of *Kuroshitsuji* is an intentionally exaggerated simulation of the Gothic trope that gave it a distinct comedic character leaves little room for consideration that traditional Gothic motifs evoke "Gothic" feelings other than those commonly linked to them. Contrarily, I suggest that the Gothic tropes in this anime evoke ambivalent feelings, where at one end the narrative across the series is embedded with dark humour, while at the other end it stimulates Gothic emotions using a blend of melancholic music and latently present Gothic motifs—typically in the closing theme songs (EDs). In addition to the basic premise of the story built on the child-demon pact, gruesome murders, the presence of a demon-worshipping cult, and supernatural entities, conventional Gothic affects become profound not because of the episodic storyline as much as by the additional ending theme sequence, entitled Lacrimosa (Sono Shitsuji 2009). It is in this ending sequence that the overarching Gothic narrative of *Kuroshitsuji* becomes apparent and presents feelings of melancholia and sorrow by amalgamating signature *Yuki Kajiura* music (Jocoy and Hoffer 2023) and latent lunar symbolism with other Gothic motifs.

Lyrical Narrative, Visual Representation, and Lunar Imagery in Lacrimosa

One of the first things that comes to mind while reading the term Lacrimosa is Mozart's classical composition, which is a part of the *Requiem*—a musical service to honour the dead. Lacrimosa is a Latin word that translates to "weeping" or "tears" in English. Contextually, the original Lacrimosa, i.e., Mozart's Lacrimosa is based on "Western/ Christian Music traditions" and the themes of "death", "mourning", "grieving", and "judgement after death" are profoundly present throughout its lyrics (Keller 2019: 251). Although there is no direct relationship between Mozart's Lacrimosa and the Lacrimosa used in *Kuroshitsuji* or any overt mention by the latter's music composer about the possibility of an association between the two, a subtle influence of the former on the latter can still be observed, as will be revealed later in this section. Thus, it is useful to begin this discussion with a brief introduction to Mozart's Lacrimosa.

The Lacrimosa that is used in *Kuroshitsuji* as the second ending theme song in its first season, was in fact, released as a single by Kalafina—a Japanese vocal group formed by the renowned music composer Yuki Kajiura. Kajiura composed the music and wrote the lyrics for Lacrimosa. Known for a signature eclectic musical style, Kajiura's music is characterised by "nonsense language" also popularly referred to as "Kajiurago" and "ethereal chants" inspired by neo-medieval Gregorian chants (Jocoy and Hoffer 2023). Kajiura's musical composition is focused on "narratives based on certain themes and particular types of characters" of anime, not on its popularity" (Jocoy and Hoffer 2023: 4). In that sense, her music and lyrics serve as an extension to the larger storyline of the anime. Lacrimosa is no exception in that context. Although the duration of the complete song released by Kalafina is approximately four minutes and twenty seconds (Kalafina Official YouTube Channel, dir 2016), only a portion of the song (one minute and thirty seconds), accompanied with visuals, was used as the ending theme of *Kuroshitsuji* (Sono Shitsuji 2009). The overall visual representation of this one-minute song accompanies Ciel's corpse being carried in a boat by his butler Sebastian while crossing the sea. This short visual representation is an extension of the storyline that hints towards the beginning of the story as well as one of its potential endings—the final result of the demonic pact where the child sold his soul to the devil in exchange for his revenge.

I will now analyse the lyrical narrative of the song as well as the accompanying visuals to elucidate the Gothic themes intertwined within the narrative. Since there are no official translated lyrics available and I am not proficient in *Kanji* or Japanese, I limit myself to analysing the lyrics translated into English available on different websites run by Kajiura, Kalafina, and Kuroshitsuji fans. For the analysis, I used translated lyrics acquired from four different websites; the rationale for employing various versions of the translated lyrics is to ascertain whether the overall meaning post-translation is consistent. On initial close reading of the four versions of lyrics, the meaning appeared to be approximately similar. Likewise, on an initial analysis of the visuals of the ending theme song, I identified four key frames in the visuals. The time frame for the four frames are as follows:

I divided each version of the translated lyrics into four sections by using Table 15.1. Subsequently, I proceeded to study the images and lyrics concurrently, specifically examining the lyrical and visual narrative within the song frame by frame.

Table 15.1 Four key frames in Lacrimosa as per their duration

Frame	*Duration (minutes)*
First frame—Visual I	0:00–0:32
Second frame—Visual II	0:32–0:48
Third frame—Visual III	0:48–01:01
Fourth frame—Visual IV	01:01–01:30

Frame by Frame Description of Four Key Frames in Lacrimosa: Interpretation and Symbolism

First Frame

Visual Description: The song starts with the focus on Sebastian. The visual zooms out, depicting Sebastian the butler rowing a boat in a dark sea. Ciel's corpse lying in a white bed of roses and Sebastian in his signature black costume, Ciel's body is also dressed in black clothes. The reflection of moon contrasts with the dark sea.

Translated Lyrics—First Version (source: [outori 2010] emphasis mine)
In darkness harmonizing
Despair and Future
were coldly shone upon
by the sorrow-disclosing **moonlight**

Translated Lyrics—Second Version (source: [canta-per-me-net 2015] emphasis mine)
The **moonlight**, which
Exposes sadness
Coldly illuminated
Despair and the future
That are friendly with
Each other within the darkness

Translated Lyrics—Third Version (source: [freedomwriter126 2011] emphasis mine)
Trembling **moonlight** canters on a desperate crusade
Shadows scatter from its cold despair
Shattering the night pearls of sorrow hang in the air
From the **moon's** hollow cheek they cascade

Translated Lyrics—Fourth Version (source: [Smule n.d.] emphasis mine)
In the growing night
The **moonlight** shines down on my fears
And adorns all my wretched sorrow

Let it sing with fright
Entwine and immerse in our lives
We can't stop their dance in the dark

Second Frame

Visual Description: The visual zooms in on Sebastian's side profile placed within a black background. The visual then pans to depict Sebastian throwing petals of white roses, seemingly to Ciel's corpse lying in the boat.

Translated Lyrics—First Version (source: 'outori 2010] emphasis mine)
By the evidence you were given
You walk through the stillness of the pale night

Translated Lyrics—Second Version (source: [canta-per-me-net 2015] emphasis mine)
Turning the secret
that you gave me into a sign
I go through the silence
Of the pale night

Translated Lyrics—Third Version (source: [freedomwriter126 2011] emphasis mine)
Locked away in my heart
Veiled in whispers your secret lies (hidden)
Unbidden, I carve my soul into the vanishing silence

Translated Lyrics—Fourth Version (source: [Smule n.d.] emphasis mine)
The secrets you gave me
Unravel into new meanings
I can't see through the night
Even so I will run blind

Third Frame

Visual Description: The visual starts by zooming in on Ciel's folded hands, then moves to focus on his corpse, specifically his face, lying in a white bed of roses. Ciel is seen to be wearing his gold ring, a mark of being the Earl, and his eye mask is absent.

Translated Lyrics—First Version (source: [outori 2010] emphasis mine)
Lacrimosa
The faraway broken and vanished,
Dazzling world, I want to love it once more

Translated Lyrics—Second Version (source: [canta-per-me-net 2015] emphasis mine)
Tearful, once more,
I want to love
The glaringly bright world
That shattered in the distance
And vanished

Translated Lyrics—Third Version (source: [freedomwriter126 2011] emphasis mine)
Lacrimosa, please don't cry
Look toward the brightening sky
For want of love for all that lies
Behind turrets of oblivion

Translated Lyrics—Fourth Version (source: [Smule n.d.] emphasis mine)
Lacrimosa once again
I will love this world's beauty
That is now gone
Dead to my eyes
It vanished that day
Shattered at the dawn

Fourth Frame

Visual Description: The visual now reveals the whole image, where Sebastian's back is shown, along with the boat he is rowing. The reflection of the moon again visible in the dark sea. The image zooms out to show a seascape and a bright full moon in the dark night. After a second, the screen turns black.

Translated Lyrics—First Version (source: [outori 2010] emphasis mine)
I <u>hide</u> the dreams in my eyes
Until in my <u>dirtied heart</u>
Tears will be falling

Translated Lyrics—Second Version (source: [canta-per-me-net 2015] emphasis mine)
<u>Hide</u> your dream in your eyes
Until tears come falling
Onto your <u>sullied heart</u>

Translated Lyrics—Third Version (source: [freedomwriter126 2011] emphasis mine)
<u>Hide</u> those dreams inside your eyes
Pound your heart to your <u>battle cry</u>
We synchronize, dare to defy
All that denies the sweet sanctity of our bond

Translated Lyrics—Fourth Version (source: [Smule n.d.] emphasis mine)
Don't let dreams show in your eyes
<u>Hide the</u> <u>light</u> <u>deeper inside</u>
With all the tears
You should have cried
Tormented heart,
<u>You're tainted</u> by your own <u>fears</u>

In the first frame, the lyrics and visuals together create a picture that conveys extreme sadness. The Gothic motif of "moonlight" is profoundly present in the first frame, as reflected in the dark sea, together with its apparent usage in the lyrics. The adjectives to define the moonlight, according to the varied four versions, for example, "sorrow-disclosing moonlight", "coldly shining", and "trembling moonlight", all imply deeper emotions of sorrow and despair. Additionally, the use of dark hues in the visuals creates a sombre and melancholic ambience, underlining the utilisation of conventional Gothic tropes. Sebastian's sombre and sad expression in the second frame, accompanied with the lyrics, for example "veiled in whisper your secret", "stillness of pale night", conveys a narrative shrouded in mystery. The presence of white roses and petals in the three frames underlines a funereal mood. Lyrics with visuals in the third and fourth frames together suggest a dialogue taking place between Ciel and Sebastian. The lyrics in the third frame imply a longing for the world even after death, and despite the cruelty and abuse Ciel faced, his hope to live again is apparent in the accompanying lyrics. In turn, Sebastian's response, in the form of phrases—"hide the light deeper inside" and "hide those dreams inside your eyes"—reflects a strong denial to let Ciel live again, thereby abiding by the pact between them. The visual in the fourth frame finally reveals the brightly shining moon, further suggesting that Sebastian is rowing the boat towards the moon. As iterated earlier, there are multiple symbolic presences within the Lacrimosa that assist as an extension of the larger Gothic narrative of *Kuroshitsuji*. Throughout the one-minute and thirty second duration of the piece, Sebastian and Ciel's corpse are accompanied by conventional Gothic tropes such as dark surroundings, roses, ocean waves, and "perpetual moonlight" in the anime music video. The duality of lunar symbolism that was discussed in the beginning of this chapter is also visible in the visual representation and lyrical narrative of the Lacrimosa. On one hand, the perpetual moonlight and its reflected image in the water contrast strikingly to the dark atmosphere symbolising sorrow. On the other hand, the full moon at the end of the song along with Sebastian's image of rowing the boat towards the moon symbolise the soul traversing the dark sea to the afterlife.

An additional theme that emerged during the analysis is the convergence of Japanese and Western cultural influences on the overall visual narrative of the song. According to a Greek myth, Charon, a mythological figure, serves as the ferryman of the Underworld, who transports the souls of the dead to the "other side" by crossing the rivers Acheron and Styx.[2] The Greek myth is visually represented throughout the song, where Sebastian takes on the role of a ferryman similar to that of Charon, taking Ciel's corpse (soul) to the Underworld by rowing the boat across the dark sea, symbolising the rivers Acheron and Styx. Simultaneously, according to the Japanese cultural tradition, lunar symbolism serves as a motif for the "waters of life". Waida defined the "waters of life" as "the waters of rejuvenation which could restore strength, vitality, and youth to the weary and

[2] According to the Encyclopedia Britannica (2024), "the duty of Charon was to ferry over the Rivers Styx and Acheron those souls of the deceased who had received the rites of burial".

old" and argued that "waters of life might have also been understood as the waters of immortality" (Waida 1977: 408). They further suggest that the moon is the "lord of life and death, controlling both the waters of life and waters of death" (Waida 1977: 411). One of the interpretations that these converged myths offer, specifically in relation to the fourth frame, is that Sebastian (as Charon) is rowing the boat through the dark sea (Styx) towards the moon (waters of immortality), offering a new perspective and a more open ending to the Gothic storyline. In this sense, the integration of cultural motifs and myths, render a culturally hybrid yet "odourless" (Iwabuchi 2002) visual narrative through the otherwise melancholic composition of the Lacrimosa (Green 2021: 154).

As mentioned previously there are some instructive connections, even if not intentional, to Mozart's Lacrimosa and these will be looked at now and how they relate to the anime ending theme. The translated lyrics of Mozart's Lacrimosa are as follows:

> That day of tears and <u>mourning</u>,
> From the dust of earth <u>returning</u>
> Man for <u>judgement</u> must prepare him,
>
> Lord, have mercy on him,
> Gentle Lord Jesus,
> <u>grant them eternal rest</u>,
> Amen.
> (Keller 2019: 251; emphasis mine)

Aside from the same title for the musical composition, Mozart's and Kajiura's Lacrimosa exhibit further parallels. Like Mozart's Lacrimosa, whose overall theme is focused on death, grieving, and judgement, Kajiura's Lacrimosa is also a mourning song embedded with themes of hopeless longing, despair, and tragedy. Supplemented with dark visual aesthetics and narrative, the Lacrimosa in *Kuroshitsuji* is also a song for the departed soul. Musical chords play a significant role in the portrayal of emotions where major chords reflect positive emotions and minor chords reflect negative emotions (Bakker and Martin 2015; Berkemeier 2021; The Music Studio 2023). Mozart's classical composition is set in d-minor, reflecting feelings of sorrow (Keller 2019). Similarly, Kajiura's composition for her Lacrimosa largely uses minor chords, thereby manifesting a sombre, melancholic, and funereal sound. The subtle influence of Mozart's

Lacrimosa on Kajiura's piece becomes apparent as the visual and narrative elements reach their conclusion.

To summarise the analysis, there are three significant characteristics that emerged in relation to the Gothic style implemented in *Kuroshitsuji*, particularly vis-à-vis its ending theme song the Lacrimosa. Firstly, multiple layers of symbolic motifs are observed within the song, including roses, dark hues, moonlight, the moon, reference to the Greek myth of Charon, and Japanese reference to the "waters of life". The presence of these motifs suggests an additional narrative to the original storyline of *Kuroshitsuji*, offering its viewers a potential end of the story. Secondly, lunar symbolism in the Lacrimosa has a dual meaning in regard to sorrow and the "hope for immortality". This dual symbolism of the moon in the song, reinforced by melancholic music and other layers of symbolism generate the dark emotions required of a Gothic narrative. Lastly, the presence of culturally hybrid elements, i.e., the interweaving of the Greek myth of Charon with the Japanese significance of "waters of immortality", adds layers of hybrid identities to the storyline, thus, delivers a cross-cultural but "odourless" Gothic narrative (Iwabuchi 2002). This echoes Loh's argument that the "cross-cultural dimension" in *Kuroshitsuji* is a "postcolonial practice of cultural hybridity concerned with undermining and yet affirming hierarchies of consumption" (Loh's 2012: 115).

Conclusion: Converging Lines of Music, Lunar Symbolism, and Gothic in Lacrimosa

The Moon has long served as a traditional Gothic motif. The beginning of the chapter provided a brief overview of the different cultural associations vis-à-vis lunar representations. The moon has multiple, cross-cultural, meanings and interpretations associated with it that often require additional aesthetics and motifs to create a Gothic narrative. In this sense, the meaning derived from lunar symbolism can be both associative and relative. Some of these meanings, particularly in relation to audio-visual Gothic texts, can be created via music and lyrics. Like the moon and moonlight, the perception of "sound" and "music" has always been a crucial part of Gothic novels to achieve a haunting yet romantic narrative (Noske 1981). In this regard, music acts as a significant element in creating atmosphere and emotion within Gothic texts. The use of Kajiuora's Lacrimosa as *Kuroshitsuji*'s ending theme delivers a spectral and mournful tone that aligns with the main plot of the series, but at the same time, its melancholic sound offers a relational meaning to the lunar imagery used in the anime ending theme. Since the main theme of this song is about death and offers its viewers a glimpse into one of the potential endings of the main storyline, the moon acts as a significant source of symbolism in the overall Gothic narrative of *Kuroshitsuji*. In that context, *Kuroshitsuji* may not be an example of Lunar Gothic in its entirety, but like many Gothic texts, the lunar symbolism remains a powerful motif to enhance the themes of death, mystery, and darkness present in the anime.

References

Bakker, David Radford, and Frances Heritage Martin. 2015. Musical Chords and Emotion: Major and Minor Triads Are Processed for Emotion. *Cognitive, Affective, & Behavioral Neuroscience* 15 (1): 15–31. https://doi.org/10.3758/s13415-014-0309-4.

Berkemeier, Stephen. 2021. *How Chords Portray Emotion (with Chord and Emotions Chart)*. Tabletop Composer. https://www.tabletopcomposer.com/post/chord-relationships-and-emotion. Accessed 28 October 2024.

Betancourt, Michael. 2015. The Semiotics of the Moon as Fantasy and Destination. *Leonardo* 48 (5): 408–418, 435.

Bilkhu, Joti. 2023. Black Butler: The Child Detective Hunts Jack the Ripper. *Journal of Anime and Manga Studies* 4:61–86.

Bridgwater, Patrick. 2013. *The German Gothic Novel in Anglo-German Perspective*. Leiden: Rodopi.

canta-per-me-net. 2015. *Canta-per-Me.Net—A Yuki Kajiura Fansite » Lyrics & Song Info » Lacrimosa*. https://canta-per-me.net/lyrics/lacrimosa/. Accessed 28 October 2024.

Dalal, Roshen. 2010. *Hinduism: An Alphabetical Guide*. Penguin Books India.

Encyclopedia Britannica. 2024. *Charon | Myth & Symbols | Britannica*. https://www.britannica.com/topic/Charon-Greek-mythology. Accessed 28 October 2024.

Ferrari, Giovanni Batista. 1646. *Flora, Seu de Florum Cvltvra Lib. IV / [Giovanni Battista Ferrari]*. Welcome Collection. https://wellcomecollection.org/works/tecfwkdt/images?id=fj7qmcpf. Accessed 28 October 2024.

freedomwriter126. 2011. Lacrimosa English Lyrics. *Freedomwriter126's Blog* (blog). https://freedomwriter126.wordpress.com/lyrics/lacrimosa-english-lyrics/. Accessed 28 October 2024.

Green, Laurence. 2021. *From Score to Song—The Rise of the 'Star Composer' and the Role of Music in Contemporary Anime*. SOAS, University of London.

Howells, Coral Ann. 2013. *Love, Mystery and Misery: Feeling in Gothic Fiction*. A&C Black.

Hui, Christine. 2019. Sun Flowers And Moon Powers: Princesses and Magical Agency in Tangled and The Tale of the Princess Kaguya. *Frames Cinema Journal*, 16.

Iwabuchi, Koichi. 2002. *Recentering Globalization Popular Culture and Japanese Transnationalism*. London: Duke University Press.

Jocoy, Stacey, and Heike Hoffer. 2023. Composer Kajiura Yuki and Neo-Medieval Anime Soundtracks. *Mutual Images Journal* 11:3–25.

Kalafina Official YouTube Channel, dir. 2016. *Kalafina—Lacrimosa*. https://www.youtube.com/watch?v=6kgJBzCXr4Y. Accessed 28 October 2024.

Keller, Veronika. 2019. Sounds of Tears: Mozart's Lacrimosa in Different Media. In *Playing the Field: Video Games and American Studies*, ed. Sascha Pöhlmann, 249–258. Oldenbourg: De Gruyter. https://doi.org/10.1515/9783110659405-017.

Kotyk, Jeffrey. 2022. The Moon as a Celestial Body and God in the Buddhist Worldview: From India to China. In *Worldmaking in East Asian Buddhism*, ed. Jin-Hua Chen, 2–28. Singapore: World Scholastic Publishers.

Kuroshitsuji. 2008a. Directed by Tomihiko Ōkubo. Sono Shitsuji, Suikyō. MBS.

Kuroshitsuji. 2008b. Directed by Tsukushi Daisuke. Sono Shitsuji, Yūkyō. MBS.

Kuroshitsuji [Black Butler]. 2008c. Directed by Toshiba Shinohara. MBS.

Levi, Antonia. 2006. The Werewolf in the Crested Kimono: The World-Human Dynamic in Anime and Manga. *Mechademia* 1:145–160.

Loh, Waiyee. 2012. Superflat and the Postmodern Gothic: Images of Western Modernity in Kuroshitsuji. *Mechademia* 7:111–127.

Mitani, Toru. 2011. Moonlight in Japanese Zen Buddhist Temple Gardens: An Analytical Simulation. *Journal of Landscape Architecture* 6 (1): 46–53.

Napier, Susan. 1998. Vampires, Psychic Girls, Flying Women and Sailor Scouts: Four Faces of the Young Female in Japanese Popular Culture. In *The Worlds of Japanese Popular Culture: Gender, Shifting, Boundaries, and Global Cultures*, ed. Dolores P. Martinez, 91–109. Cambridge: Cambridge University Press.

Noske, Frits. 1981. Sound and Sentiment: The Function of Music in the Gothic Novel. *Music & Letters* 62 (2): 162–175.

One Piece Wiki. n.d. *Moon*. One Piece Wiki. https://onepiece.fandom.com/wiki/Moon. Accessed 28 October 2025.

outori. 2010. *[翻訳] Kalafina—Lacrimosa*. https://outori.livejournal.com/345683.html. Accessed 28 October 2024.

Sailor Moon. 1992. Directed by Junichi Sato. ANN (TV Asahi).

Sivrioğlu, Şeyda. 2017. *The Faustus Myth in the English Novel*. Newcastle: Cambridge Scholars Publishing.

Slaughter, J. W. 1902. The Moon in Childhood and Folklore. *The American Journal of Psychology* 13 (2): 294–318.

Smule. n.d. English Lacrimosa Kuroshitsuji (Annalie)—Lyrics and Music by Kalafina Arranged by AdorableDoge. *Smule*. http://www.smule.com/song/kalafina-english-lacrimosa-kuroshitsuji-annalie-karaoke-lyrics/631555197_509685/arrangement. Accessed 28 October 2024.

Sono Shitsuji, Inō. 2009. Directed by Takahiro Okao and Mika Iwamoto. MBS.

The Music Studio. 2023. How Chords and Key Impact Emotion in Music. *The Music Studio* (blog). https://www.themusicstudio.ca/how-chords-and-key-impact-emotion-in-music/. Accessed 28 October 2024.

Unknown. 1700. *Chandra, The Moon God; Folio from a Book of Dreams (Image 2 of 3)*. Los Angeles County Museum of Art. https://commons.wikimedia.org/wiki/File:Chandra,_The_Moon_God;_Folio_from_a_Book_of_Dreams_LACMA_M.83.219.2_(2_of_3).jpg. Accessed 28 October 2024.

Waida, Manabu. 1977. Symbolisms of the Moon and the Waters of Immortality. *History of Religions* 16 (4): 407–423. https://doi.org/10.1086/462776.

Wright, Angela. 2004. 'To Live the Life of Hopeless Recollection': Mourning and Melancholia in Female Gothic, 1780-1800. *Gothic Studies* 6 (1): 19–29. https://doi.org/10.7227/GS.6.1.3.

PART V

Lunar Futurities

CHAPTER 16

“Blood Moon”: Lunar Monstrous Spaces in Gothic Science Fiction

Elana Gomel

The Cosmic Haunted House

Situated at the intersection of two different forms of speculative fiction, Gothic Science Fiction (hereafter SF) is a genre that combines two seemingly incompatible forms of affect: cognitive defamiliarisation and visceral fear. Traditional SF is famously defined by Darko Suvin as a rationalistic genre, appealing to the reader’s intellect rather than their emotions (Suvin 2016). Gothic, on the other hand, is the literature of terror, meant to create an atmosphere of dread and confusion, and to terrify, horrify, or frighten the reader (Punter 1996). Gothic, or “dark”, SF is a hybrid genre which explores the culturally constructed borderlands of rationality and horror.

The relationship between Gothic and SF goes back to the very beginning of the genre. Mary Shelley’s *Frankenstein* (1818) is simultaneously a Gothic novel and the first SF text ever written. Brian Aldiss argued in his groundbreaking history of SF that the genre emerged out of the eighteenth-century Gothic and appropriated many of its tropes in its attempt

E. Gomel (✉)
Tel-Aviv University, Tel-Aviv, Israel

E. Gomel, S. Bacon (eds.), *Lunar Gothic*, Palgrave Gothic,
https://doi.org/10.1007/978-3-031-92621-1_16

to bring scientific enlightenment to the superstitions inherited from the Dark Ages (Aldiss 1973).

While Gothic and SF were intertwined throughout the Victorian age, with such novels as Bram Stoker's *Dracula* (1898) or R.L. Stevenson's *Dr. Jekyll and Mr. Hyde* (1886) classified as both, their paths diverged in the twentieth century. SF carved out its own quasi-scientific ethos, while Gothic gave rise to supernatural horror, splatterpunk, and related genres. But recently, the two have converged once again. The resulting hybrid is known as "cosmic horror" (Vieira 2003), weird fiction (Marshall 2017), or even "Posthuman Interstellar Gothic" (Milette 2020). I will use the term "Gothic SF" for the genre as a whole, and Lunar Gothic for the particular sub-genre which is my subject in this chapter.

The settings for Gothic SF may be an abandoned spaceship, a ruined space station, a zombie-infested planet, or some combination thereof, as in the paradigmatic *Alien* series of movies. But it is really surprising how often the setting is not the unknown reaches of outer space but something much closer to home: the Moon.

It is surprising since our satellite is the best explored body in the Solar System and the only one where humans have actually landed. So, it seems to offer less latitude for Gothic mysteries of the unknown. And yet, in such novels as Sharman DiVono *Blood Moon* (1999), Johan Harstad's *172 Hours on the Moon* (2012), Rick Chesler's *Luna* (2013), Peter Clines' *Dead Moon* (2019), and many others, the Moon becomes a stage for familiar Gothic tropes—ghosts, zombies, doppelgängers, and dark labyrinths.

The reason for this, I will argue, lies in the double cultural meaning of Luna: as the focus of a long tradition of mysticism predating science; and as the setting for the greatest triumph of space technology. Thus, the Moon becomes a monstrous space, a cultural oxymoron, in which the boundaries of science and superstition, knowledge and fear are mapped out and (re)negotiated.

As Bernd Brunner writes in his cultural history of our satellite:

> The importance of the moon has less to do with its proximity to Earth than with its centrality in the human imagination. The moon's face has been known to inspire admiration, sadness, joy, even longing, and under certain conditions, fear.... Close, yet really far away—the moon is a paradox. And when we study it, we are studying an aspect of ourselves. (Brunner 2010: 74)

The Moon is the space-age equivalent of the haunted castle that defined the early tradition of Gothic: "The major locus of Gothic plots, the castle, was gloomily predominant in early Gothic fiction. Decaying, bleak and full of hidden passageways" (Botting 2014: 2). This is the Moon of Lunar Gothic, except that the past encoded in its "hidden passageways" is the geological past of our own planet where life's precarious existence is shadowed by the spectre of extinction. The Moon is a witness to profound geological upheavals of the past that had almost destroyed the emerging life on Earth, and yet at the same time had created the conditions for its development. The family trauma that so often lies at the heart of Gothic is replayed on a cosmic scale in the history of Earth and its satellite.

The bleak sterility of the Moon brings home the most frightening aspect of evolution: its contingency. The Moon, so close and yet so remote, so similar to Earth and yet so profoundly different, shows that the existence of life or humanity is a happenstance, a random event that did not have to occur. Earth could have been as lifeless as the Moon. The Gothic castle is haunted by the past, by what was. The Moon is haunted by what might have been.

In this chapter, I am going to discuss several texts of Lunar Gothic that bring together a space-age setting and the horrors of the unknown, the incomprehensible, and the supernatural. Since my focus is on narrative techniques, I will discuss novels only, though such movies as *Moon* (2009) and the South Korean TV series *The Silent Sea* (2021) certainly belong in the tradition of Lunar Gothic. Moreover, their visual vocabulary is strikingly similar to that of the novels discussed below. But for reasons of space limitations, my focus will be on Lunar Gothic novels of two kinds: those set on the Moon in the near future; and those set on Earth but depicting some sort of catastrophe sparked off by the malevolent influence of our satellite.

In novels of the first kind, ghosts flitter through the gleaming corridors of high-tech space stations and habitats, giving a lie to the triumphalism of the Space Age. In novels of the second kind, the ancient magic of the Moon wreaks havoc on our technological civilisation. In both cases, my main focus is on the relation between space, time, and actant. In Lunar Gothic, I will be arguing, these three main components of narrative are blended together, creating the monstrous spacetime, which is the focus of these novels. In Lunar Gothic, the Moon itself is the main character, warping space and distorting time, generating monstrous chronotopes of the genre.[1]

Ghosts of/in the Moon

The first novel of Lunar Gothic is also one of the first novels of SF. H. G. Wells' *The First Men in the Moon* (1901) belongs to the great period of Wells' SF writing in the late 1890s–early 1900s, which defined the genre. However, of the string of novels published in this period, *The First Men in the Moon* is less known than *The Time Machine* (1896) or *The War of the Worlds* (1898). Partly it may be the result of an artistic mismatch between the two parts of the novel. The first, in which the narrator, Mr. Bedford, meets the eccentric inventor Mr. Cavor, is Wells at his most whimsical and satirical, as the entrepreneurial Bedford decides to invest in Cavor's invention: a material that blocks gravity. But the lightheartedness of this part gives way to the gloomy visions of the second part, in which Cavor and Bedford arrive on the Moon in a gravity-repelling sphere and find it populated by a grotesque alien race: the Selenites.

The description of the Selenites and their strange bio-civilisation is a tribute both to the scientific knowledge of Wells—a trained biologist—and to the power of his imagination. The Selenites, an ant-like species with multiple castes and body plans, are the first SF attempt to represent a genuinely alien form of intelligence. They are progenitors of such alien lifeforms in subsequent SF as Stanislaw Lem's "doublers" in *Eden* (1957) or Ted Chiang's Hectapods in *Stories of Your Life* (2002). But at the same time, descriptions of their dark subterranean mazes, the "huge, shadowy caverns", presided over by the grotesque Grand Lunar, "an opaque, featureless bladder with dim, undulating ghosts of convolutions writhing visibly within", are cast in the modality of cosmic horror, foreshadowing Lovecraft's outer monstrosities (Wells 326). And the novel ends on a profoundly Gothic note, as Cavor, stranded on the Moon and broadcasting his dispatches, falls silent:

> For my own part a vivid dream has come to my help, and I see, almost as plainly as though I had seen it in actual fact, a blue-lit shadowy disheveled

[1] For the notion of chronotope as the spacetime of a fictional world, see Mikhail Bakhtin's "Forms of Time and of the Chronotope in the Novel" («Формы времени и хронотопа в романе»), 1937.

> Cavor struggling in the grip of these insect Selenites, struggling ever more desperately and hopelessly as they press upon him, shouting, expostulating, perhaps even at last fighting, and being forced backward step by step out of all speech or sign of his fellows, for evermore into the Unknown—into the dark, into that silence that has no end.... (Wells 1901: 342)

Critics do not quite know what to make of the novel. Taunton sees it as part of the "disenchantment of the moon" under the twin influences of scientific rationalism and capitalism (Taunton 2016: 6). But he also points out that it is simplistic to see the trajectory of the Moon's representations in this period as one of the uninterrupted shift from the "romantic" to the "scientific" view of our satellite, as "increasing scientific knowledge of the moon tends to dispel its mythical and poetic power". Instead, he proposes that "scientific knowledge and the literary imagination coexist and at times feed one another" (Taunton 2016: 1).

This coexistence does not mean, however, that the proportion of "scientific" and "romantic" is the same in all the Lunar Gothic novels written at the time. Rather, it may indicate that even the most fantastic texts use quasi-scientific rhetoric to naturalise their representations of our satellite. A case in point is another significant lunar novel, published roughly at the same time as Wells'. Jerzy Żuławski's trilogy *Trylogia księżycowa* (1901–1911) is a towering achievement of SF that profoundly influenced the genre's development in Eastern Europe, though it was unknown in the West until recently.[2]

The trilogy is composed of three novels: *Na Srebrnym Globie* [On the Silver Globe], *Zwycięzca* [The Conqueror], and *Stara Ziemia* [The Old Earth]. The novels describe the progressive stages of the earthlings' arrival on the Moon, the establishment of a colony, and the eventual return of some of them back to humanity's home. A rich and complex text that combines elements of bio-horror, adventure, and dystopia, *The Lunar Trilogy* deserves a more extensive discussion. My purpose here is just to indicate how the elements of rationalistic quasi-scientific ethos and Gothic ambience interact in the description of the Moon itself.

When the one-way vessel with the five explorers crashes on the Moon (no magical Cavorite to bring them back), the Polish narrator Jan Korecki

[2] The title is normally translated as The Lunar [or Moon] trilogy. The title of the Russian translation is *On the Silver Planet*, while the title of the recent English translation is The Lunar Trilogy. I will be using both the Russian and English translations for reference.

describes the horror that awaits them on the lifeless and frozen planet: "That white light makes everything around us look mysterious and lifeless" (Żuławski 2020: 23). Two of the expedition members eventually die of their injuries sustained in the landing, and the only woman, Martha, who joined in order to be with her lover Thomas Woodbell who eventually also dies, becomes distraught and apathetic, while the two remaining men, Jan Korecki and Peter Varadol, vie for her affection. This rivalry becomes important as Martha is the Eve of this horrifying world. Eventually the stunted descendants of her union with Varadol populate the dark side of the Moon and create a superstitious and violent society, preyed upon by the monstrous Moon race of the Szerns.

But before the three surviving members of the original expedition arrive at the dark side, they have to traverse the barren craters and "the infinite deadly plain" of the airless Moon. The vivid descriptions by Żuławski rival Wells', but as the odyssey progresses, they become more and more detached from the actual science of selenography, descending into the poetics of nightmare. Particularly interesting are the frequent references to blood. This literalisation of the imagery of the "blood Moon" is something that we encounter in Lunar Gothic again and again, as the superstitious belief that the Moon regulates the female menstrual cycle is projected upon the barren landscape of rocks and regolith: "At the same time, the light on the Moon changed from orange into red, and it looked like someone poured blood on the dark desert in front of us" (Żuławski 2020: 82).

Another Gothic trope that reappears in the descriptions of the moonscape is ruins. The fashion for picturesque ruins was foundational in the poetics of the Gothic as it emerged in the eighteenth century. Later, ruined cities built by nonhumans become a staple of Lovecraftian cosmic horror. Żuławski's Moon combines elements of the traditional Gothic with the SF imagery of lost and abandoned cities of other civilizations: "And there, look, a spacious building, with a low colonnade at the front.... I swear this kind of gorge, buried with lots of boulders now, was once a street.... Now its fallen and dead.... City of corpses" (Żuławski 2020: 95).

And in a final Gothic twist, actual ghosts seem to materialise on the Moon, as Thomas Woodbell, before dying, claims to have seen the mutilated corpses of the other spacemen who died before him walking in the ruined city. The experience convinces him that the Moon is where science and superstition, rational and irrational, coexist: "I know...you all believe, and I used to believe...once...that the only truth is the knowledge...based on experience which can be put in mathematical formulas but there are things that are inconceivable and strange..." (Żuławski 2020: 120).

But it is not just space that becomes distorted and monstrous on the Moon; time does as well. The narrator constantly refers to the difficulty of measuring and experiencing temporality on the lunar surface where time passes "without end, without change, without seasons, with no years or months..." (Żuławski 2020: 23). The chronotope of the Moon is one in which the basic scientific parameters of space and time buckle and collapse under the pressure of Gothic and horror imagery.

Before and After

The year 1969 was a pivotal one for Lunar Gothic. One would expect that after the triumph of science and technology embodied in humans landing on another celestial body, the scientific ethos would prevail in fictional representations of our satellite (Taunton 2016). But in fact, the opposite happens. Just as fictional moon landings become more technologically plausible, they also increasingly emphasise the imagery of horror, disorientation, claustrophobia, and madness. In fact, the post-landing Lunar Gothic derives its frisson precisely from the juxtaposition of these two strands. This is clear in the visual vocabulary of movies such as *Apollo 13* (1995) and *Moon* (2009), in which sterile high-tech environments of moonbases and spaceships become the stage for hauntings, monstrous visitations, or uncontrollable violence. And the same dynamics structures Lunar Gothic novels.

Sharman DiVono's *Blood Moon* (1999) starts with a mystery: a Far Side moonbase under construction falls silent, and a team led by Po Tseng, a NASA scientist, is sent to investigate. The team finds most of the crew members dead, gruesomely murdered, and the only survivor, Bob Faden, clearly insane. Tseng is conducting the investigation, while gradually losing contact with NASA headquarters and trying to keep her own people from succumbing to the horror of what they uncover.

The combination of detective story and SF is a well-known sub-genre, whose origins go back to the scientific ethos of the Sherlock Holmes stories. Holmes, despite Doyle's own unshakeable belief in the paranormal, is a rationalist who rejects supernatural explanations out of hand. No matter how bizarre, the solution to the murder mystery must be within the realm of the scientifically possible.

But this is not what happens in *Blood Moon*. Despite the technological paraphernalia of the investigation, from the very beginning there are hints of the supernatural. Tseng and her crew find the base disfigured with satanic and occult symbols and inscriptions. Of course, it is possible that this was part of the insanity that struck the original crew, and this is how the investigators originally regard it: "Satanic cults. Ritual killing" (DiVono's 1999: 89). But this rationalistic explanation is hard to reconcile with the clouds of flies infesting the supposedly sterile base and with the horrifying injuries found on the dead bodies, some of them appearing to be self-inflicted.

As the investigation continues, the novel becomes a sort of police procedural in space. But the supernatural creeps in, first as a supposition that it is not actual ghosts or demons that destroyed the base but rather the crew's unfounded belief in them: "I'm saying let's remove the superstition and get down to physics and chemistry" (DiVono's 1999: 353). But "physics and chemistry" become an inadequate defence against the mounting horror of inexplicable deaths, bizarre behaviour, and strange technological malfunctions. As one of the characters, a believing Mormon, explains the dilemma the crew faces in relation to the base's only survivor:

> Did insanity cause Faden to seek out and experience the powers of darkness through a Ouija board, or did seeking out and experiencing the powers of darkness result in insanity? The result is the same in both cases; however, the first scenario does not depend on faith in the existence of beings whose plane of existence is the spiritual realm, and the other does. (DiVono's 1999: 403)

Presented in this way, the novel seems to be poised on the cusp of what Tzvetan Todorov called "the fantastic": hesitation between a natural and supernatural explanation of the events (Todorov 1975). But at the end, the hesitation is resolved in favour of the supernatural as the Moon turns out to be haunted not just by the spirits of the dead astronauts but by numberless ghosts trapped in its magnetic field. Tseng's crew solves the mystery not by ratiocination but by resorting to a Ouija board communication with the dead, catching "glimpses of a myriad of horribly disfigured corpses" infesting the Far Side (DiVono's 1999: 420). The Gothic imagery of the first half of the book where Tseng's crew investigates the blood-splattered and abandoned moonbase is literalised in the second half where the phantoms of their fear become real.

Blood Moon reverberates with echoes of the moon landing (e.g. the shuttle is called the *Aldritch*). The echoes are even stronger in Johan Harstadt's *172 Hours on the Moon* (2012), a popular YA novel by a Norwegian writer. To kickstart a new space race, NASA engages in a publicity stunt, with three randomly chosen teenagers staying in a hitherto classified moonbase built in the 1970s with an escort of professional astronauts. The base, called DARLAH-2, is the future of the past: a sterile techno environment, "old and futuristic at the same time" (Harstadt 2012: 180). Lunar Gothic warps temporality—a point I will return to below.

As communication and life support systems begin to fail and the adults are dying, flashbacks to the Apollo Program reveal that the programme encountered the same danger that is plaguing DARLAH-2: doppelgängers. Mia, one of the teens and the "Final Girl" of this techno-horror script, encounters her double as she is trying to escape to DARLAH-1. Eventually, she makes it back to Earth alive, but of course, the Mia who comes back is not the same Mia who left. Even though the focalisation through Mia seems to indicate that she escapes the Moon, the last chapter reveals that she in fact dies in space and the creature who comes back unleashes a plague of doppelgängers. "Four identical copies of Mia moved from room to room with such ruthless efficiency that before long there were legions of copies sweeping through the hotel", killing everybody in sight (Harstadt 2012: 350).

The novel ends right there, with no explanation of what these creatures are. Aliens? Selenites? We do not know. The abrupt ending serves a similar purpose to the sudden shift at the end of *Blood Moon*: undermining the rationalistic ethos of SF without providing any coherent alternative explanation. Lunar Gothic derives its power from confounding the reader's generic expectations rather than from embracing the full supernatural modality of traditional Gothic and horror.

Even in novels where the seemingly supernatural events on the Moon are explained away by some familiar SF trope, the sense of horror and dislocation persists. In Peter Clines *Dead Moon* (2019), the idea of the Moon as the abode of the dead is purged of its Gothic connotations: the Moon is used as a giant cemetery for the overcrowded Earth. But then the Gothic comes back through the tritest of all horror tropes: a zombie invasion. Eventually it turns out that the zombies are created by an alien, a conventionally tentacled creature straight out of H. G. Wells *War of the Worlds*. But the visuals of the zombie horde in the lifeless moonscape evoke the aesthetics of a horror movie, not SF: "The frozen bodies lumbered forward on stiff legs. A few still had their arms crossed over their chests.... They kicked up dust as they stumbled and dragged their feet. Clouds billowed behind them, hiding their full numbers" (Clines 2019, 61).

In Rick Chesler's *Luna* (2015), the Moon is infested by giant worms, unaccountably surviving in the airless space. But just as in Wells and Żuławski, the depiction of the lunar fauna is cast in the unmistakable idiom of monstrosity: "A glistening, slimy cavern, sort of like a raspy tongue with rows upon rows of tooth-like structures. Moving, like a swallowing throat..." (Chesler 2015: 88). And the horror of lifelessness which plagues the characters of Clines is flipped over into the horror of teeming, uncontrollably proliferating life: "...that they had mistaken the very walls and floors and ceilings of the tunnel network for rock, when much of it was living flesh..." (Chesler 2015: 114).

One may, of course, argue that these are just run-of-the-mill SF/horror generic hybrids. But the fact that this generic hybridisation so persistently attaches itself to the Moon testifies to the lingering ambiguity in the representations of our satellite: the ambiguity that is exacerbated, rather than resolved, by the legacy of the moon landing.

Howling at the Moon

But not all interactions between humanity and the Moon involve the clanking technology of lunar rovers and suited astronauts. The Moon has had a significant presence in folklore and pagan religions for millennia. It is also involved in modern paganism, such as Wicca (Hutton 2001). But my focus is not on the history of lunar superstitions but rather on the ways in which this history is refracted through the narrative conventions of contemporary Lunar Gothic. It is significant that the fertility aspects of ancient lunar cults are not particularly prominent in modern horror fiction. Rather, Lunar Gothic is more interested in the two Moon-related folkloric traditions that resonate with our fears of uncontrollable violence and loss of control: lycanthropy and lunacy.

Lycanthropy is the ancient belief that when the Moon is full some people shapeshift into werewolves. It is referred to in John Webester's Jacobean tragedy *The Duchess of Malfi* (16) when Ferdinand, driven mad by his guilt over the murder of his sister, descends into lycanthropy:

> One met the duke 'bout midnight in a lane
> Behind Saint Mark's church, with the leg of a man
> Upon his shoulder; and he howl'd fearfully;
> Said he was a wolf, only the difference
> Was, a wolf's skin was hairy on the outside,
> His on the inside. (Act 5, Scene 2)

Even in this quote the ambiguity of lycanthropy and its progenitor, the Moon, is obvious. Is Ferdinand mad or possessed? Does he only imagine himself to be a wolf "on the inside" or does he really become one? In modern popular fiction, this ambiguity becomes even more pronounced as Lunar Gothic emerges on the seam between science and superstition, implausible and impossible.

In Al Sarrantonio's 1989 novel *Moonbane*, a massive outbreak of lycanthropy kills millions on a single night and transforms the narrator's son into "something inhuman and monstrous" (Sarrantonio 1989: 4). Almost like a preview of *The Walking Dead* but with werewolves instead of zombies, the novel's first part follows the narrator's increasingly bloody battles with werewolves and attempts to rescue his son. However, the ending offers an unexpected twist. When the narrator joins a scientific expedition to the Moon to eradicate the source of the werewolf contagion, the members of the expedition are infected with lycanthropy instead. But the narrator continues his story uninterrupted; his voice remains the same. It is only in retrospect that the wrenching shift in the narrator's ontological status becomes obvious. He used to delight in the killing of "monsters", but now he looks forward to killing humans instead: "With the unwitting help of Mission Control, we will open the base to attack, and the Sacred Song of Blood—for blood gives life, even in death, and in this way death is life—will fill the air" (Sarrantonio 1989: 192).

The manipulation of language is significant, as the narrator is a poet, and the novel begins and ends with one of his verses. Poetic language, poised between literal and metaphorical, parallels the ambiguity of the novel's fictional world, poised between the rationalistic ethos of science (lycanthropy is a contagion) and the supernatural ethos of folklore (lycanthropy is a curse). Similarly, the emotional affect of the novel is poised between beauty and dread, curiosity and revulsion: "I went out and looked at the Man in the Moon on many other nights after that, and always I had the same feeling of uneasiness, that he knew something we on Earth, with all our smug technology and Moon landers, didn't" (Sarrantonio 1989: 4).

At the end of the novel, however, it is precisely this "smug technology" that facilitates the lycanthropic plague that will turn Earth into "the new Moon" (Sarrantonio 1989: 193). Like poetry, the Moon lander is the bridge not just between Earth and the Moon but between science and superstition, human and nonhuman, the future and the past.

Lunacy, an old word for madness, indicates the belief that the Moon rules our brains, much like the related belief that the Moon rules women's menstrual cycles.

In Paul Kane's *Lunar* (2016), the ancient influence of the Moon creates an apocalypse of "lunatics" or "loons". The narrator Nick wakes up to find himself attacked by his girlfriend whose eyes have gone silver-white. Chased through the darkened landscape of rural England by maddened crowds, Nick is waiting for the sunrise when the full Moon, which he instantly blames for the epidemic of madness, will be defeated by the sun: "I looked at the moon, still visible in the sky (it seemed to be wherever you went, looking fown, mocking, a completely different character to the one the previous evening when we'd walked down by the river). You just wait. Wait till this sun comes up, pal, You're a goner" (Kane 2016: Chap. 2).

But the sun never comes up. The full Moon, breeding hordes of predatory lunatics or "loons", never sets. The night is endless. Time is frozen, "at one second past the hour" (Kane 2016: Chap. 2). It turns out that mass lunacy is literally the result of the death of time, brought about by too many people (including Nick himself) wishing that a perfect night would just go on forever. And it does, under the watchful eye of the eternal Moon, whipping the "loons" into frenzy.

It seems that the novel is pure supernatural Gothic, hinging on the literalisation of a stale metaphor, as many Gothic texts do. Nick finds out in his library research that "many prehistoric and ancient cultures believed that the Moon was either a deity…or some kind of supernatural phenomenon, with the power to work magic" and accepts moon magic as the explanation for the catastrophe (Kane 2016: Chap. 6).

But just as Lunar SF is haunted by ancient ghosts, Lunar horror is haunted by science. Nick is never quite sure that magic is the right answer, going back to the library again and again to find some physical explanation. And "time is fighting back. There's a war waging between that big, old Moon up there and time. The world is trying to move forward again.... Can't beat physics" (Kane 2016: Chap. 14).

No matter how far into the supernatural territory Lunar Gothic moves, it never abandons its tie to the rationalistic ethos of SF. Its generic terrain is the battlefield where ancient magic fights against modern science, neither winning but neither willing to surrender.

Moontime

The plot device of stopping time in *Lunar* brings to the surface what is only implicit in other texts of Lunar Gothic: the connection between the Moon and temporality. Lunar calendars are among the oldest in history; and phases of the Moon are often used to measure the passage of time even in solar-oriented cultures. But in Lunar Gothic, the Moon is seen not as a neutral time-measuring astronomical body but rather as a cause of temporal disturbances, warping time and history. The endless night of Lunar is one way in which what might be called "moontime" is manifested. Other ways include time loops, as in the movie *Moon*, time dilation, as in *The Lunar Trilogy*, and perhaps most significantly, the historical acceleration of revolutionary time.

Two of the best-known hard SF novels set on the Moon are Robert Heinlein's *The Moon Is a Harsh Mistress* (1966) and Kim Stanley Robinson's *Red Moon* (2018). In both, the Moon becomes the stage for a violent social upheaval, modelled either on the American Revolution (Heinlein) or the October Revolution in Russia (Robinson). Revolutionary time is a break in linear temporality that undermines the traditional modalities of historical continuity. Fanny Soderback suggests a model of revolutionary time which is, paradoxically, both circular and broken, constituting a sort of quantum leap into the future: "Revolutionary time is modeled on a perpetual movement of return that is meant to retrieve the very body that was repressed in order to construct the linear-cyclical dichotomy and paradigm" (Soderback 2012: 303).

But revolutionary time can also be envisioned as a strange time loop, in which the present is haunted by the future, as in the opening of Marx's *Communist Manifesto*, or as infinite duration, as in the "time golem" of

China Mieville's fantasy novel *Iron Council* (2004). Especially in the aftermath of the collapse of the USSR, revolutionary time acquires a tinge of nostalgia, looking backward from the vantage point of what Francis Fukuyama called "the end of history". The peculiar connection between revolution and the Moon can be framed within a larger concept of "moon-time" that collapses the distinctions between past and present, chronology and duration, objective measurement and subjective experience.

In Lunar Gothic, the Moon becomes a monstrous space, embracing science and superstition, ancient fears and modern anxieties, spirituality and technology. Like any monster, the Moon is a cultural oxymoron, in which ideologically constructed binaries are interrogated, inverted, and collapsed. Our satellite, no matter how well mapped and explored, will never lose the aura of mystery and dread. And Lunar Gothic is the genre in which this duality comes to light.

References

Aldiss, Brian. 1973. *Billion Year Spree: The True History of Science Fiction*. London: Doubleday.

Botting, Fred. 2014. *Gothic*. New York: Routledge.

Brunner, Bernd. 2010. *Moon: A Brief History*. New Haven: Yale University Press.

Chesler, Rick. 2015. *Luna*. Hobart: Severed Press.

Clines, Peter. 2019. Dead Moon. Amazon Self-Publishing.

DiVono, Sharman. 1999. *Blood Moon*. New York: DAW Books.

Harstad, Johan. 2012. *172 Hours on the Moon* [Norwegian original in 2008]. London: Hachette.

Hutton, Ronald. 2001. *The Triumph of the Moon: A History of Modern Pagan Witchcraft*. Oxford: Oxford University Press.

Kane, Paul. 2016. *Lunar*. London: Macabre Ink Press.

Marshall, Helen. 2017. *Weird Fiction Review*. https://weirdfictionreview.com/2017/11/the-state-of-weird/. Accessed 28 October 2024.

Milette, Holly-Gale. 2020. Post-Human Interstellar Gothic. In *The Gothic Handbook, Vol. III: Modern Gothic, 1900–2019; Part II. Gothic Reborn,* edited by Clive Bloom. Basingstoke: Palgrave-Macmillan, 1191–1208.

Punter, David. 1996. *The Literature of Terror: A History of Gothic Fictions from 1765 to the Present Day*, The Gothic Tradition. Vol. 1. London: Routledge.

Robinson, Kim Stanley. 2018. Red Moon. Orbit

Sarrantonio, Al. 1989. *Moonbane*. Spectra Books.

Soderback, Fanny. 2012. Revolutionary Time: Revolt as Temporal Return. *Signs* 37 (2): 301–324, Unfinished Revolutions.

Suvin, Darko. 2016. *Metamorphoses of Science Fiction: On the Poetics and History of a Literary Genre*. London: Peter Lang.

Taunton, Matthew. 2016. Moon Voyaging, Selenography, and the Scientific Romance. In *Oxford Handbooks Online: Late Victorian into Modern*, ed. Laura Marcus, Michèle Mendelssohn, and Kirsten E. Shepherd-Barr, 1–17. Oxford: Oxford University Press.

Todorov, Tzvetan. 1975. *The Fantastic: A Structural Approach to a Literary Genre*. Ithaca: Cornell University Press.

Vieira, Mark E. 2003. *Hollywood Horror: From Gothic to Cosmic*. New York: Harry N. Abrams.

Webster, John. 1623. *The Duchess of Malfi*. https://www.gutenberg.org/files/2232/2232-h/2232-h.htm. Accessed 28 October 2024.

Wells, Herbert George. 1901. *The First Men in the Moon*. https://www.gutenberg.org/files/52501/52501-h/52501-h.htm. Accessed 28 October 2024.

Żuławski, Jerzy. 2020. *The Moon Trilogy*. Point Pleasant: Zmok Books.

CHAPTER 17

Sterility Across Chasms: Dead Worlds and Technological Imaginations in Meredith Ann Pierce's *Darkangel* Series

Octavia Cade

Constructing Ecological History on a Dead World

The first pages of *The Darkangel* are indicative, to careful readers, of the lunar setting of the series. The nouns "Solstar" and "Oceanus"—the latter a blue-green, clouded planet that is by far the largest object in the sky—are clear references to the sun and Earth respectively, and this heavily implies that the world the characters are inhabiting, and the place from which they are observing both sun and planet, is the moon. That is where the similarity to the current lunar environment ends. Consider the following passage, where the protagonist of the series, Aeriel, is searching a mountainside for a particular flower:

> She listened to the bell-thorn, silvery thin briars that tinkled like glass in the rare mountain wind. She watched the small, rose-coloured lizards sunning themselves in the last hours of Solstar before crawling into their crags again to sleep for another long nightshade. She looked at the petrified bones in

O. Cade (✉)
University of Otago, Dunedin, New Zealand

E. Gomel, S. Bacon (eds.), *Lunar Gothic*, Palgrave Gothic,
https://doi.org/10.1007/978-3-031-92621-1_17

> the rocks, bones of fishes, eels, and water plants left over from the time when the steeps had been nothing but flat mud bottom, and all the world a sea. (Pierce 1998: 8)

It should be noted here that Aeriel, along with her companion Eoduin, is searching the lunar landscape without the benefit of breathing apparatus or spacesuit. Both girls are wandering the moon's surface in much the same way as readers of the series wander the surface of Earth: naturally, and as a matter of course. In this they are unexceptional: all the lunar inhabitants of the series, including plants and animals, are perfectly adapted to their environment.

That environment is fully realised. As the above excerpt illustrates, the moon is home not only to intelligent beings who present as fully human, but to plants and animals as well. This implies the presence of both a breathable atmosphere and easily available water; while some science fiction narratives posit life forms that can survive in the absence of one or both, that does not appear to be the case here. Furthermore, the presence of briars and lizards indicates a wider ecosystem. While theoretically, the briar may be a primary producer, the lizard may eat the briar, and the human characters may eat the lizards, this is a thin, extremely unconvincing ecological relationship. The survival of all three species must be dependent on the existence of other lunar life forms, including soil bacteria and other micro-organisms.

While the presence of these species may be ascribed, in another narrative, to colonisation and terraforming, the presence of fossils in the lunar rocks—of fish and water plants, which may potentially be algae—indicates that life has evolved in this lunar environment, regardless of how that life was introduced there. Through the presence of these fossils, readers are encouraged to see this lunar environment as one that not only supports life, but has supported life for a significant period of time. The previous existence of a substantial, if perhaps not global, sea alongside the evidence of fossilisation is another indication of the time period involved.

This early example within the text of widespread lunar life and established ecology is continually supported throughout the series. That life often takes on fantastical and legendary forms, lending the books the tone of a dark, even a Gothic, fairy tale. As the story develops and Aeriel travels through diverse landscapes, she experiences a number of different habitats, as well as the different life forms that have adapted to those environments. This is, clearly, a very different lunar environment than might be expected in a more realistic speculative narrative. That difference encourages two questions: How has the moon developed in this way, when compared to the lifeless sterility that readers are primed by reality to expect, and how has this difference impacted the relationship between the moon and the Earth?

The answer to the first question is hinted at a short time later. The Unknown-Nameless Ones, as they are referred to—Aeriel prays to them as if they are divinities—are said to have "fallen from the sky in fire to quicken this, a then-dead world, the moon of Oceanus, into life" (Pierce 1998: 32). This establishes two things: that the moon was once lifeless, effectively sterile, and that life was introduced there from an outside source. No origin is given for that source, and no motivation is stated either. The explanation for lunar life appears to be couched in almost mythological terms, and this fits with the apparent development of the lunar populations. Such technology as appears is extremely simple, and the lifestyles of the lunar peoples seem more suited to a (historical) fantasy rather than to the science fiction genre, especially when the latter involves space travel and colonisation of other worlds.

This mythological understanding of the origin of lunar life is one that is understandable for someone with Aeriel's life experience. As a young adult and a slave, she lacks both the experience and the education to recognise or devise a more rational explanation. Her understanding of the mythological, however, transforms into an understanding of the technological when she meets Talb, a character who is much older and who is educated in the sciences. He explains that lunar life developed when the inhabitants of Oceanus "grafted life onto the land" (Pierce 1998: 62). They created an atmosphere, brought the water out of the ground, and engineered suitable forms of life, including intelligent ones, that would be capable of living freely in the new lunar landscape. The colonising humans, incapable of living that way on the moon themselves, resided in lunar domes, protected from the thin atmosphere and other environmental variables until they nearly all died out.

Crucially, he notes that it was not only the human inhabitants of the moon who died. "Great wars on their homeland destroyed them" (Pierce 1998: 63), he says of the inhabitants of Earth, and if any survived on that planet, their capacity to travel between terrestrial and lunar environments was lost. It is confirmed, in *The Pearl of the Soul of the World*, that no second wave of lunar colonisation is forthcoming. Ravenna, the last colonist from Oceanus to survive in the lunar domes, states that "Oceanus destroyed itself. That is why it glows in heaven with such a cold and spectral light: quick with the poison that never ends. Nothing is left alive there. *This* is the only world that remains" (Pierce 1999: 116).

By transforming the previously lifeless lunar environment into a thriving ecosystem, therefore, the human colonisers from Oceanus utilised a technological capacity that, when applied in more destructive ways, rendered their home planet lifeless in its turn. This transformative relationship is repeated within the text, albeit on a smaller scale, with regard to the darkangel and his wives.

Vampirism and the Lunar Undead

The titular antagonist of the first novel, the darkangel, is referred to in the text as a "vampyre" and is a typical, if somewhat romanticised, representation of the undead. Capable of flight, he possesses enormous black wings but otherwise presents as a beautiful young man. He is exceptionally pale in skin tone and eye colour, and when Aeriel is pressed against him, she finds that his body is "colder than shadow, so cold she felt the warmth of her own body running away into his while his own cold invaded her" (Pierce 1998: 38). Despite this corpse-like characteristic, however, what really marks his vampiric nature is his feeding habits. The darkangel preys on young women who are as beautiful as he is—this does not include Aeriel, who is abducted by him to act as a servant to his partially consumed wives—and his character is marked by cruelty.

This cruelty is primarily illustrated in the treatment of the darkangel's wives, who are essentially undead themselves. The darkangel has drunk their blood, torn out their hearts, and stolen their souls. The last have not yet been consumed, which explains the wives' liminal status: they cannot truly die while their souls remain undevoured, but in the absence of blood and a heart they cannot be said to be alive either. As the victimised undead, the wives are hideous: they are starved, emaciated, with "the skin of their faces pulled so tight Aeriel could see the imprint of their teeth through their lips" (Pierce 1998: 45). They can barely stand and must sometimes resort to crawling due to their physical frailty. They are also barely sane, and their long-term memories are so compromised that the wives are unaware of their former identities and cannot tell themselves apart. Aeriel is horrified at the sight of them: "These are wraiths and not women, Aeriel though suddenly—the soulless and undying dead" (Pierce 1998: 46).

The transformation of each wife from beautiful young woman into the undead occurs on her wedding night. The darkangel abducts a victim, forces them into marriage, and then consumes them. Given their subsequent undead state and physical incapacity, it is no surprise that each marriage is childless. The wives as well as the darkangel are sterile, and in this they act as subverted mirrors of the lunar landscape. If the moon, originally lifeless, is transformed into a place of rich and fertile biology, then the undead that live within that ecosystem are previously healthy bodies made barren by their own oppositional transformation. Furthermore, that transformation reflects, again, the relationship between the lunar environment and Oceanus. The latter, as the darkangel and his wives, was transformed from a healthy system into a site of sterility, continuing the paired relationships of fertility and sterility that permeate the text.

Notably, the wedding nights of the darkangel and his brides contain, in their bloody and violent consummation, an act of life-giving that is bleakly parodic. When the darkangel steals the souls of his brides, he seals them away in little vials which he wears in the form of a necklace. The darkangel must acquire fourteen souls from fourteen brides, and upon the accumulation of this number he is to give them, along with his own soul, to his adopted mother, the water witch. Once she consumes them, the darkangel's own transformation will be complete. As a child, he was abducted by the witch so that she could make him into a vampyre, and the completion of his transformation into the undead is contingent upon his stealing the lives of others. While a typical wedding night would normally include a sexual consummation, with the potential—at least in heterosexual couples—to create *new* life, the darkangel requires a different sort of consummation in order to achieve *eternal* life.

The contradiction between simultaneously being undead and possessed of eternal life is one that has been routinely present in vampiric narratives. The vampiric experience of immortality is often one that is characterised, in fiction, by stasis and an inability to undergo meaningful change. Living apart from society, both as an outsider and to avoid detection and confrontation, can isolate the vampiric figure from social and scientific revolutions. Butler notes, for instance, that the title character of Bram Stoker's *Dracula* (1897) is "stuck in the past" (2002: 28)—not only is he detached from the technological developments of the time, but those developments are actively used against him, with the modernised world effectively weaponised by the human characters in order to successfully counter the vampiric threat.

The Isolation of Constructed Bodies

If the relationship between Oceanus and the lunar setting of *The Darkangel* is one of opposing—and transforming—fertility and sterility, then this is a relationship that is primarily mirrored in the central pairing of the text. The darkangel himself is a sterile figure, and one who can forcibly create sterile figures of his wives. Arguably, this transformation from living to undead can be said to be procreative in nature, in that the act of vampirism can reproduce new generations of the undead. An alternate reading of the text, however, can interpret the increasing numbers of the undead, within *The Darkangel*, as a form of contagion. Vampirism has frequently been associated with the language and imagery of infection, giving "physical form both to the contagion itself as well as the associated anxieties around the perceived causes and spread of the disease" (Bacon 2023: 2); in this, its diseased presentation is a social as well as a biological experience (Piatti-Farnell 2018: 41). Vampirism has especially been associated with sexually transmitted infections such as syphilis (Chou 2008). The close contact required for such an infection—for example, that experienced by the darkangel's brides on their respective wedding nights—may emphasise this particular reading.

Infection is a multifaceted metaphor when it comes to vampirism, and much of its metaphorical power comes from its flexible application to vampiric texts; *Dracula* is again a typical example here. Useful examples of metaphor that can be applied to Pierce's series come from Forman and Mighall: Forman (2016: 928) considers vampirism in *Dracula* as having parasitic qualities, where "the parasitic trope functions as a way to drain women of their sexuality". He was specifically referring to Lucy, but the darkangel's wives—drained of all vitality, and transformed into ghoulish, undead husks—provide another illustration of the trope. Mighall, on the other hand, interprets vampirism through the Victorian lens of socially contagious masturbation—with so-called victims being "initiated into this practice by another" (1999: 111)—which leads to a wasting effect in its practitioners. Admittedly, there is no obvious metaphorical masturbation in *The Darkangel*, but the perversion of the wedding nights between the darkangel and his newly skeletal brides can also be interpreted as a deliberate waste of reproductive capacity, and a choice for sterility over fertility.

Exposure to the darkangel's unhealthy, undermined biology spreads contagion. Each fully transformed vampyre within the series infects a minimum of fourteen people, fourteen transformed, undead brides being necessary to ensure that the turn to vampirism is permanent. Crucially, however, the transformation of the brides from living to undead does not endow them with eternal life themselves; the vampiric parody of marriage and reproduction that takes place between the vampire and his wives is one that ultimately ensures isolation for the darkangel instead of companionship.

When the darkangel chooses to make Aeriel his fourteenth wife, however, the marriage between them results in a different sort of transformation, one that eschews the sterility of the undead. Previously, the two of them—the central almost-romance of the series—exist as opposites. With one of them living and the other the sterile undead, they represent in their own bodies the fundamental relationship between the Earth and the moon. That relationship began with the planet a place of blooming life and the satellite a wasteland where life had never developed. The inhabitants of the planet colonise the satellite, transforming it into a site of established ecology, complete with fantastical life forms. After doing so, that life-giving planet becomes poisoned and sterile: the two bodies have in a sense taken on the other's primary characteristic, with one a place of life and the other of death.

When the darkangel takes a wife, it is with the intent to effectively infect and colonise her body, transforming her into an image that is reflective of himself. When the darkangel takes *Aeriel* as a wife, however, it is he who is both infected and colonised. Aeriel provides him with a drink with which to toast their wedding; the potion makes her feel "stronger, more awake, and more alive" (Pierce 1998: 243), but when the darkangel ingests it he is poisoned by it. The potion is harmless to living things, and only acts as a toxin to those who are already compromised by their status as the vampiric undead. Once the darkangel is rendered unconscious, Aeriel is meant to kill him (to end his un-life), but instead she essentially transforms his wasteland of a body with her own. This is terraforming as much as transformation, as the embodied wasteland of the darkangel's undead form is returned to a healthy, living system. Aeriel's compassionate tears for the darkangel are transformed into blood—into her blood, implicitly, derived as it is from her body—which she then pours over the darkangel. His body absorbs her blood "like rain into a thirsty earth" (Pierce 1998: 263). Aeriel also takes the darkangel's compromised heart and replaces it with her own, essentially inserting one of her own organs into his body and completing her own colonisation of a sterile biological landscape. Instead of a bride losing her blood and her heart, a bridegroom receives a new heart and a liquid substitute for his own tainted plasma. This reversal of the vampiric transformation of the darkangel and the wedding ceremony between the two characters restores humanity to the undead figure. In effect, it returns the prospect of fertility to a previously sterile system, and health to a wasteland.

Salazar (2017) comments on the ability of blood transfusions to mitigate the effects of vampirism, and Raza Kolb (2022: 301) notes in her study of the colonial Gothic, as it is influenced by vampirism, that diseased people may be "revitalized" by infusions from healthy bodies and their associated goods and beliefs, which is an interesting twist on what Burns describes as the "reverse colonialism" of vampiric narratives (2017: n.p.). Furthermore, blood is, as Stephanou points out, both a scientific and a symbolic substance, and blood transfusion is "a gift, creating and reasserting the bonds of a community" (2013: 54). The notion of community is paramount here, in that it recalls the concept of an ecosystem. Vampiric communities, compared to society outside those communities, is often limited and isolated; such is the case with the darkangel, who has minimal meaningful bonds and exists as largely a sterile figure, representative of an increasing wasteland that is itself suffering from a degenerating ecosystem. By introducing her blood into the darkangel's body, Aeriel is reintroducing—reinforcing—his ties to a living community.

Aeriel's decision to attempt to restore the darkangel to life—rather than to ensure, from undeath, his actual death—is true to her nature. She has agency, and she is certainly representative of the trend in which, over the last century or so, the female vampiric victim has come to be represented as an avenger (Amador 2003). Yet her intended vengeance, against the creature who transformed her living friend into an undead bride, is subverted. She succeeds in rendering the darkangel unconscious and immediately vulnerable, but her final choice is one of life: "I cannot kill him" (Pierce 1998: 258). Faced with an undead body—a body which is itself representative of a wasteland—her instinct lies in restoration. This is a choice that not only reflects the choice of the Ancients of Oceanus who, when faced with a lunar wasteland, chose to enliven it, but also one which prefigures Aeriel's role at the end of the series: she becomes, essentially, the transformed guardian of the lunar ecosystem, preventing its return to a dead and sterile landscape.

There is a sense of dark romance to the relationship between the darkangel and Aeriel, even as the narrative acknowledges that he is a deeply problematic and unashamedly evil figure. The darkangel's physical attractiveness and almost mesmeric compulsion, combined with his motivation and his choices, make him a solid and threatening antagonist. He is strongly situated in the fairy tale Gothic, and the first book ends with his restoration and the prospect of romance between the two main characters. Given that the planetary system of the series, however, is one of deeply entrenched opposites, the romantic bodies of the protagonists are primed to represent the same. When Aeriel is paired with the darkangel, they present an image of life and death, of fertility and sterility, of biology and nightmare imagination. With the darkangel transformed into Irrylath, the person he was before his own vampiric infection and bodily corruption began, their relationship comes to be defined by imbalance; Aeriel and Irrylath are, by nature, too much alike, and are thus no longer representative of the orbital relationship that so defines the series' setting.

Without that compulsive draw between them (the attraction of opposites, an attraction that is gravitational as well as romantic, given that they are both bodies of mass as well as narrative), their relationship is inevitably subject to its own transformation. Aeriel may be in love with Irrylath, but the feeling is not truly returned. He is grateful to her, but the fairy tale ending where the reward for a successful quest is the hand of a prince (or princess) is continually subverted. Recall here the presence of the lunar fossils that Aeriel notes near the beginning of *The Darkangel*. The moon may have been colonised with life forms that were initially devised and constructed on Earth, but evolution further adapted those organisms to lunar life. That some of those constructed organisms were inspired by story does not negate the evolutionary process; stories evolve as well as organisms do, and those that best fit one environment (or culture) may not necessarily flourish in another. Indeed this is the case, for if Aeriel and Irrylath had chosen to maintain an ordinary marriage for their time and culture—a typical fairy tale ending, for instance—the series outcome would be quite different.

Pierce, who has so carefully constructed a narrative of opposites and of a continued balance between consistently transforming elements, does not abandon this basic theme once the darkangel is restored to Irrylath. The unsettled relationship between him and Aeriel is indicative of a further transformation. As he, like the lunar environment around him, has been changed from a dead (or an undead) system into a living one, Aeriel undergoes a similar change, but in reverse. The witch that created the darkangels in the first place has also inflicted a form of sterility on the landscape, being responsible for a drought that is slowly taking over the lunar environment, a process which will slowly but surely return the moon to its original state. Aeriel is able to stop the witch and thereby return the land to a more fruitful state—"'This will never be a Wasteland again,' she murmured full of wonder, 'but a fertile marsh'" (Pierce 1999: 270)—but in doing so she loses her own life.

That life, however, is restored to her, albeit in an unusual way. Ravenna, the last of the Ancient Ones, the colonisers from Oceanus who brought life to the moon, reconstitutes Aeriel's body using the technology locked away in the domed cities, technology which has kept the lunar ecosystem functional. Aeriel is horrified to discover her new identity, believing herself a mechanical construct, essentially a golem—a monstrous creature of old technology, no longer human. She is assured that she retains her status as a "biological construct" (Pierce 1999: 260) and that some of her old body remains to her: she retains her eyes and her mind, and is able to retrieve her heart. Aeriel, however, considers her body to be "a new engine" (Pierce 1999: 260), and that new engine comes with new powers.

She is now functionally immortal, incapable of dying as once the darkangel was. She has sharper vision. She casts no shadow. This is reminiscent of the *cast no reflection* ability so often given to vampires in literature; it is even said of Dracula that he "throws no shadow" (Stoker 1998: 239) and neither do his three monstrous handmaidens (Stoker 1998: 37). If shadows '"symbolize a person's soul" (Alexander 2015: 107), then both Dracula and Aeriel are soulless. It is notable that in the first book of the series even the darkangel casts a shadow (Pierce 1998: 95), and this indicates that Aeriel's newly constructed body is even more non-natural than his ever was—the darkangel, remember, kept possession of his own soul until he obtained the souls of his fourteen wives, and as Aeriel restores him to life before this occurs, he is undead but never truly soulless. Furthermore, given that her new nature is explicitly said to render her ineligible for marriage—"Irrylath deserves a bride who will age with him" (Pierce 1999: 263)—and thus, perhaps, for reproduction, Aeriel has become a new version of the sterile undead. Certainly a more positive version, as her remit is to nurture rather than to murder, and to take the place of the Ancient Ones in rebuilding and maintaining the lunar world, but the sterile undead nonetheless.

She does not consider this a positive outcome. Being transformed, and forcibly transformed at that, into the undying (or the undead) permanently isolates Aeriel from her chosen husband, her family, and most of her friends. She will spend the rest of her very long life largely separate from loved ones. Her experience of other people from this time forth will primarily consist of their deaths, and she will continue to outlive anyone who might get close to her. The series ends with the central pairing having largely swapped their identities, either by undergoing transformation from the undead to the living or by the reverse. In this, they are a mirror of the relationship between Oceanus and the moon.

Vermeir comments that "In the early modern period, people believed that the imagination could generate diseases and particular illnesses, such as madness and hypochondria, but also the plague" (2012: 365). He includes vampirism in this list of imaginative maladies, and indeed the history of vampirism as perceived disease underlines the connection between epidemiology and horror here. It is a link that is particularly relevant to the orbital and individual relationships within the *Darkangel* series, as while perceptions of the vampire came, from the nineteenth century, to focus on more "rational explanations of the phenomenon" (Senf 1988: 22), the horrific imaginative potential of the vampire remained strongly influential in popular culture and fiction. As part of this the vampire has often been linked with the moon, and the moon itself is associated with darkness, madness, and loneliness (Alexander 2015: 113).

The technological developments of the people of Oceanus allowed them to transform the lunar environment into a thriving ecosystem. They engineered the moon to be a "pleasure garden" (Pierce 1999: 110)—a place of leisure and imagination and exploitation of the created lunar inhabitants. The technology that supported this construction, however, was eventually also used to create the darkangels: creatures that had previously only existed, in one vampiric form or another, in the imagination. As the darkangels flourished, the landscapes that they represented, in embodied form, became similarly sterile and undead as drought and technological degeneration made the landscape less sustainable. Ravenna describes how the last of the colonists from Oceanus decided to let the moon "decline gradually and see if we could find a balance-point", a new ecological equilibrium that would let some parts of the lunar environment endure (Pierce 1999: 114). It is worth noting that Yang and Healey state that "Disordered landscapes in the Gothic represent the chaos of a culture in transition" (2016: 5), but also that the deliberately constructed, architectural elements of that landscape symbolise the "inadequate protection of rationality" (2016: 6). Given that every living element on the moon is, within the series, a deliberately constructed element of a Gothic landscape that is in a stage of overall transition, it is certainly believable that rationality is not, by itself, an adequate protector of the lunar landscape of *The Darkangel*.

With the technological construction of an imaginary disease, in the form of darkangels, this lunar vampirism infected, in physical and metaphorical form, both body and landscape. It does so on orbital as well as lunar scales. Technological imbalance on Oceanus led to the destruction of the planet; imaginative imbalance on the moon may well lead to the same. Only by restoring balance can the lunar system be preserved. Aeriel, who begins the series attempting vengeance against the sterile undead, becomes representative of that state herself, and the darkangel, in return, is restored to life. Aeriel, cognisant of both balance and necessity, is then able to assume the role of guardian to a world that requires both a technological and imaginative approach to maintain a balanced and sustainable ecosystem.

Conclusion: Fertile Dreams and Orbital Relationships

The depiction of the Lunar Gothic, in the *Darkangel* series, is one of change and mirrored, determined imbalance. This is initially illustrated through setting: the relationship between the moon and Oceanus, a relationship which is itself reflected in that between Aeriel and the darkangel. If vampirism within Pierce's text is in some ways metaphorically representative of a changing Gothic landscape, specifically of the transformation of dead to living systems and back again, then the geographic wasteland that has already been established on Oceanus is itself beginning to manifest in the lunar environment. Instead of an excess of toxins, however, the increasing lunar wasteland is developing due to an absence of water.

Unleavened by the imaginative and metaphorical creativity that the people of Oceanus have literally outsourced to another world, Oceanus is eventually destroyed by its technology. Without that technology, the people of the moon can no longer maintain their own environment, and are literally consumed by figures of sterility and superstition. Only by integrating both the horror of unrestrained metaphor and the horror of unrestrained technology into her own body can the protagonist confine sterility to herself, and ensure that the moon continues to exist as a place of vast and blooming life.

References

Alexander, Rachel. 2015. *Myths, Symbols and Legends of Solar System Bodies.* New York: Springer.

Amador, Victoria. 2003. The Post-feminist Vampire: A Heroine for the Twenty-first Century. *Journal of Dracula Studies* 5 (1): 3. https://doi.org/10.70013/29p7q8r9.

Bacon, Simon. 2023. *Contagion and the Vampire: The Vampiric Body as Locus of Disease and Global Epidemics in the 21st Century.* London: Palgrave Macmillan.

Burns, Stu. 2017. Vampire and Empire: Dracula and the Imperial Gaze. *ETropic: Electronic Journal of Studies in the Tropics* 16 (1): 10.25120/etropic.16.1.2017.3563.

Butler, Erik. 2002. Writing and Vampiric Contagion in *Dracula. Iowa Journal of Cultural Studies* 2:13–32.

Chou, C. Jennifer. 2008. "Syphilis and the Vampire Literature." *The Proceedings of the 17th Annual History of Medicine Days* 36–42.

Forman, Ross G. 2016. A Parasite for Sore Eyes: Rereading Infection Metaphors in Bram Stoker's *Dracula. Victorian Literature and Culture* 44 (4): 925–947.

Mighall, R. 1999. 'A Pestilence Which Walketh in Darkness': Diagnosing the Victorian Vampire. In *Spectral Readings*, ed. G. Byron and D. Punter. London: Palgrave Macmillan.

Piatti-Farnell, Lorna. 2018. *The Vampire in Contemporary Popular Literature.* London: Routledge.

Pierce, Meredith Ann. 1998. *The Darkangel.* San Diego: Magic Carpet Books.

Pierce, Meredith Ann. 1999. *The Pearl of the Soul of the World.* San Diego: Magic Carpet Books.

Raza Kolb, Anjuli Fatima. 2022. Meta-Dracula: Contagion and the Colonial Gothic. *Journal of Victorian Culture* 27 (2): 292–301.

Salazar, Anthony. 2017. Curing the Vampire Disease with Transfusion: The Narrative Structure of Bram Stoker's *Dracula. English Language and Literature Studies* 7 (3): 1–7.

Senf, Carol A. 1988. *The Vampire in Nineteenth-Century English Literature.* Bowling Green: Bowling Green State University Popular Press.

Stephanou, Aspasia. 2013. A 'Ghastly Operation': Transfusing Blood, Science and the Supernatural in Vampire Texts. *Gothic Studies* 15 (2): 53–65.

Stoker, Bram. 1998. *Dracula.* Oxford: Oxford University Press.

Vermeir, Koen. 2012. Vampires as Creatures of the Imagination: Theories of Body, Soul, and Imagination in Early Modern Vampire Tracts (1659–1755). In *Diseases of the Imagination and Imaginary Disease in the Early Modern Period*, ed. Yasmin Haskell, 341–373. Turnhout: Brepols Publishers.

Yang, Sharon Rose, and Kathleen Healey. 2016. Introduction: Haunted Landscapes and Fearful Spaces—Expanding Views on the Geography of the Gothic. In *Gothic Landscapes: Changing Eras, Changing Cultures, Changing Anxieties*, ed. Sharon Rose Yang and Kathleen Healey, 1–18. London: Palgrave Macmillan.

Index[1]

[1] Note: Page numbers followed by 'n' refer to notes.

E. Gomel, S. Bacon (eds.), *Lunar Gothic*, Palgrave Gothic, https://doi.org/10.1007/978-3-031-92621-1

www.ingramcontent.com/pod-product-compliance
Ingram Content Group UK Ltd.
Pitfield, Milton Keynes, MK11 3LW, UK
UKHW020818131025
463706UK00030B/11
* 9 7 8 3 0 3 1 9 2 6 2 0 4 *